I0818217

Tales of Vagary

By Virgil Thornton II

For Big Red and RisyMae

PUBLISHED BY **WEIRD DISCIPLE PUBLISHING**
EDITED BY **MARRISA THORNTON, ARTICULATE**

ISBN (E-BOOK): 978-1-7326548-1-5
ISBN (PAPERBACK): 978-1-7326548-6-0
ISBN (HARDBACK): 978-1-7326548-8-4

TRIAL OF SHENSHIMU

THE TALE OF DAIKI

Earth has been restored by Matthew and his friends, but a little mishap throws a new, unsuspecting hero into the mix.

TABLE OF CONTENTS

PRELUDE

~ ~ ~

My mind is empty as I walk my bike up the hill. The cold air feels good against my face, and I want to take off my winter uniform coat, but I do not. The air makes my hands sting less. I look down and see that the pink marks from slip ups at kendo practice are fading. I let one of the new guys wear the last pair of fighting gloves. Maybe by next practice they will have more.

The sky is calm and grey. It is snowing but not very much; just enough to put a little powder on roofs and branches. I keep my head down so snowflakes will not land on my glasses. Aside from the call of birds, my clicking bike, and the whir of an AC unit every once and a while, it is silent. Everyone is indoors, preparing for a comfortable winter night.

When I reach the top of the hill, I notice the familiar policeman on the bicycle at the bottom. He looks up from his phone and waves at me. That is my dad. Why did he ride out in the cold to meet me? I hop on my bike and coast down the hill to find out.

I get to the bottom and he greets me, "Did I surprise you?"

"Yes! How was your day?" I reply.

"Very busy," he sighs, tucking away his phone, "How about yours? Today was the last day of the semester, right?"

“It was. No more school for us until next year.” I report, putting up two fingers.

My dad notices my hands and frowns in that stern policeman way, “Is that from kendo? They need to go easier next time…”

I smile and wave my hand, “Oh, I am fine. There were some new people who wanted to give kendo a try before the break, so there were not enough gloves.”

My dad nods, but for some reason, he is still concerned, “Are you cold or tired? If not, how about we bike to City Park?”

“Let’s do it.” I say.

We both mount our bikes and ride into the neighborhood. The two of us coast past houses and cars in silence. When we go under the bridge and the only sounds are our bikes, I realize how odd this is. My dad would have said something by now; maybe talking more about his day at the station or giving me random life advice. He must be worried.

We pass our normal turn and take the next, turning from the narrow street to the narrow footpath. Overhead, the canopy of telephone wires is replaced with bare branches. Soon, the trees break and a red gazebo by a lake comes into view.

There is a young couple reading some placards near the forest. Three older women are gazing out into the lake and talking. Father and I get off of our bikes and walk them up to the stone bridge by the lake.

As I look at the red reflection in the grey water, I realize that the snow stopped. The two of us do like the older women and stare out at the calming lake. Father says nothing, so I just look at the gazebo and the bluffs and the distant radio towers.

"Daiki." My father says, still looking at the water.

"Yes Father?" I reply, gentle and a little afraid.

For a moment I am bracing myself, and then he says, "I love you very much."

I almost let out a laugh, "I know, I love you too, Dad."

But the seriousness of my father does not go away.

He sighs, then continues, "Ojiisan and his lab have finally finished the project."

I am both stunned and confused. Sofu (another name for Ojiisan) has been working with an engineering lab for his entire life. He has worked up from an intern to a project lead, and his project was to change transportation forever. He decided to try to make a portal that could take things from one side of the country to another in seconds.

He had a lot of smart-sounding theories, but everyone was sure it would fail. He worked on this for decades, but for the last two years, he has often spent busy nights at his lab, working into the morning. I suppose this is why I am happy for Sofu and very surprised the portal works, but why did my father bring me out here to tell me this?

“So,” I start, thinking through it all, “Ojiisan built a portal? So we can teleport things now?”

“Exactly,” my father replies, “very historic, is it not?”

“Yes! This… he has changed everything now!” I say, looking up at the sky and trying to understand all the new possibilities this portal makes.

My father hums a short agreement.

“Do you think that odd event a few months ago was due to him?” I ask.

There used to be a story on the news for a while about everything turning blue and becoming sand. It was said to happen about three hours past midnight in Japan, so many people were asleep during it. There was very little information outside of that and not much sense could be made from it, so I thought it was some sort of worldwide rumor. Now I am starting to feel open-minded.

“I do not know, son…”, my father pauses, then continues, “Ojiisan insists that… that you be the first person to travel through the portal.”

At first, the words of my father have no meaning. Then, I realize what he is saying and I look at him to see if he is joking. He seems like he is about to cry. Then, he wraps me in a hug. Stunned, I hug him back.

“Will you honor your grandfather’s wish?” He asks, almost shaking with sadness.

I am still taking time to understand, so I do not answer right away. Sofu and I were never close. He is a quiet, busy man who does not like small talk. Not to be mean, but I do not think he is close with anyone in my family. My sister Ume has a better relationship with him than I do.

That does not matter, though. He is my grandfather, the head of the family, and I must respect his wishes. If he wants me, out of everyone, to do this historic thing, I will. I trust his invention; he is a smart and careful man so I know it is safe.

"I will," I say, putting aside my wishes for this break, "When will he need me?"

My father pulls back and pats my shoulder, "Tomorrow."

CHAPTER 1

THE PORTAL

~ PRESENTATION ~

Today is the winter solstice. I remembered because that is the only thing my father has said during this car ride. Mother wrings her hands in the passenger's seat. Father is statue still; only his arms move to drive the car. I sit in the back seat, staring at nothing. To the right, I notice another driver, a boy around my age, singing to the radio with his coat on.

I wear a Shajiku Sun (the lab of my grandfather) t-shirt and heavy jeans. My coat sits in the seat beside me. Across my legs is Amanokaze, the family katana. It was made by my great grandfather and has rested on the mantel above the bed of my grandfather since before I can remember.

It is cloudy outside, but the navy-blue scabbard is still shiny. Flowers are painted along the side. The guard is bronze, and the hilt still has dust on it. It is hard to believe I am really holding the family sword. It is hard to believe a lot of things that are happening right now.

We arrive at the facility and the parking lot is full. A security car guides us to our parking spot. As we follow it, I notice some of the cars out here. Many are news vans. One small green sedan belongs to my sister Ume. She is in college so she no longer lives with us; she said she would meet us here.

As we pull into the spot security led us to, I get an odd feeling. This moment is like my very first kendo tournament. The seat placement of my parents and I are the same. I have a weapon that I am surprised I am allowed to hold, just like before the match. Ume arrived before us, like she did back then.

But my parents are silent this time, and I am much more scared than I was then.

Mother, Father, and I follow the security guards out of the parking garage and into the lab. The first room we enter is a great warehouse space. In the very center is a 3-meter-wide circle made of white plastic and smooth metal. It sits upright with a small staircase and platform in front of it. Thick, colorful wires pour out of it from all sides, hooking up to machines and computers. That must be the portal.

There are a lot more people here than I imagined. Dozens of engineers busy themselves with the computers. News crews are setting up equipment. Government officials are having small conversations with one another. I even spot a few other family members.

"Daiki. It is good to see you." Sofu says, appearing from a cloud of reporters.

I give him a nod-bow and he returns one. A few people in white coats walk up behind him and bow in our direction. We return the greeting, and then Sofu starts talking again.

"Masanori, Erina, please join the others at the viewing area. Daiki, follow me."

My parents give me a proud look before heading over to the crowd. I lock eyes with Sofu, and then he begins walking towards the other side of the warehouse. The people in white follow him, and I do the same.

We walk for a long time, past the reporters, the portal, and the rest of the equipment. We enter a doorway, walk through a hall, and then go through three more rooms. The next room we enter has a glass wall, where a group of people are in hooded hazmat suits, cleaning clothes.

Sofu stops, and so do the rest of the people around him.

"Alright Daiki, the portal has been tested many times and is thought to be safe to be inside. However, we still need to be careful. Go and take a hot shower, and when you are finished, we can get you a suit and an air tank. We will also sterilize your clothes. Did you bring Amanokaze?"

I raise the sword a little, though I am sure Sofu already noticed it. Either way, he smiles.

"Good. I am sure you are confused about why I wanted you to bring it. I will tell you after you get suited up. These researchers will take you to the showers."

The people in white coats lead me to a small side room. In front of me is the shower, and on one of the shower walls is another door. They tell me to go through that door when I am finished, then they exit through the open doorway.

I undress fast and get in the shower before anyone walks by. The water is very warm, and with all of my thoughts, it is hard to keep the shower short. I clean myself with the toiletries in the shower, then will myself to turn off the water.

Instead of a towel, there is just a button marked “dry” on the wall. I press it, and after three mysterious beeps, I am blasted from every direction with powerful wind. After a moment of panic, I figure out that this is the dryer, so I stretch out my limbs and spin around to make sure I am dried off everywhere. The wind is much less pleasant than the water.

After a while, the dryers shut off. By then, the shower and I are all the way dry. Still naked, I open the next door, trying to cover myself in case someone is on the other side. There is only a small white room with a sliding door. My clothes and glasses lay folded on a bench, along with Amanokaze, a headset, and a hazmat suit with air tanks on it.

I can hear people moving around and muffled talking behind the door, so I hurry and get dressed. To my surprise and delight, many of the marks on my glasses have disappeared. I have a bit of difficulty with the suit, but then I realize there is an instruction paper on the wall, so I read it and figure it out.

Once I am dressed, covered, and have the family sword in hand, I press the "open" button next to the door. There is a buzzing noise, and then the sliding door pops, hisses, and rolls away. In front of me is the clean room I saw through the window. I spot my grandfather out of the dozens of people, and he walks over to me along with another man.

"Daiki, this is Nakamura Ryusei. He is a researcher from the lab that will be recording your journey."

I bow to the middle-aged man, and he returns the bow.

"We will begin the presentation when the Princess arrives. The Emperor would be joining her, but he got a cold and could not make it. Do not be nervous." Sofu adds that last sentence after looking at my face.

He and Mr. Nakamura share a laugh, and then he continues, "The presentation will be simple. The president of Shajiku Sun will speak, I will introduce the project, and if either of you want to speak, I will let you. Then, we will start the portal. Your destination will be our main off-site lab in Osaka. This portal has a 94% accuracy, so I can assure that you will arrive where you need to. You should be back in time for school tomorrow."

I do not have school tomorrow, but I choose not to correct him. My fingers are cold and tingling, but I nod anyway. Mr. Nakamura does the same, but he seems much more confident.

"Good. So Daiki, about Amanokaze. Did you know that the sword is magic?"

Sofu said that so serious and calm that I am surprised, "Magic?"

"Yes, magic," my grandfather, a scientist and engineer, says, "The sword can entrance people if it is in the sun. It even entranced me once!"

I do not know how to reply. Is Sofu going senile? Maybe he is loopy under the stress? Perhaps that was a joke to lighten the mood? It should be best if I play along.

"Okay. Will I need to use it in Osaka?" I ask, trying to make it sound like I am joking.

"Oh not at all," Sofu laughs, "I just thought you would like to know because you are carrying it. Whether you use it or not, it is a good luck charm. We had many more swords, like Gon Yami the spirit lantern or Sutomusuza the storm-splitter, but all of those have been destroyed through experiments."

He pats me on the shoulder, which makes a crinkling noise, "Magic or not, that sword represents our family, and I am proud that you will be bearing it in front of the world today."

I get nervous again when he mentions what is about to happen. With a smile and a nod, he goes toward what must be the exit to this room. Mr. Nakamura follows him, as well as everyone else, and so I do too.

We enter a long hallway where everyone stops and takes off their suits. For a moment I am confused, but then someone lets me know that Mr. Nakamura and I are to keep ours on. Once everyone else is undressed, many leave through a side exit while my grandfather and a few others stay behind.

We stand for a while, and then one of the researchers looks down at his watch. He bows to my grandfather, which everyone else in the room does too, then opens the door at the end of the hallway.

I follow everyone else out into the warehouse, which is now a bit fancier. Behind the row of reporters, there are new carpets and more guards. I soon spot the Princess, dressed in a suit and seated like many others. Everyone is quiet. We all stop and bow very low, then continue.

We approach the portal fast, going around the crowd and stopping next to the podium space. The portal stands at the end of its platform just a few meters to my left. It is as quiet as the crowd. The president of Shajiku Sun gives a speech, but I am too nervous to pay attention. My grandfather goes next, talking about the history and mechanics of the portal. I can see and hear his nervousness, but he speaks well and the audience claps.

Someone comes up and fits a professional camcorder on the shoulder of Mr. Nakamura. They also strap a much smaller camera around my chest. The entire time, photo flashes go off behind us and reporters zoom in from every angle.

More time passes, then Mr. Nakamura and I go up the small staircase and stand at either side of the portal platform, facing one another. We stand and wait for a while, and I notice engineers over to the left running programs and checking graphs.

For some reason, Mr. Nakamura raises his right hand. I stare back at him, unsure of what is going on. I can feel the air growing heavy with expectancy, so I shift Amanokaze to my left and raise my hand too.

He puts his hand down and I do so a second later. Right after that, he goes and turns on his shoulder camcorder. I follow his lead, pressing the small button on my body camera. He raises his hand again, and I raise mine. They must have shared some instructions earlier that I missed.

The lights dim. I become even more nervous than before. Is this portal going to work? As if to answer my question, lights on the edges of the portal click to life. There are a few red flickers at the left corner of my vision, and then a hot blue flash. Flickering, swirling light washes over the warehouse as clapping erupts from the audience.

Oh my goodness! I am going to be in history books! My grandfather has really made a portal! We are really doing this?! What is it going to feel like inside of the portal? Will this hurt? How long will I be in there?

Mr. Nakamura takes a step forward, which means I must take a step forward, and I almost faint because of this. But then I remember that the whole world is watching and that my family sword is in my hands, so I will myself to step forward and meet Mr. Nakamura.

We stop and turn to face the portal. It is a flashing, swaying mess of color and light. It is something from beyond this world. The platform below us hums with energy from all the wires, but the portal does nothing. It does not suck or blow wind. It is not cold or hot. It does not make any noise. It is just a silent oval stretched in front of us, smooth and still.

Mr. Nakamura looks at me. I must be the first to step in.

And so I am.

CHAPTER 2

OUR DESTINATION

~ POST-PRESENTATION ~

I **open my eyes to a room full of scientists.** The last thing I remember was falling, or maybe floating. Amanokaze was tight in my hands. Everything was pink, black, neon, and swirling. It was very interesting but I do not ever want to do that again.

I look at the faces of the scientists, but none of them are happy. In fact, they look worried. I sit up in my chair and bow to them. They all give very short bows back. The pale, middle-aged man in the middle must be the lead scientist. I notice my family sword is gone. It must be with one of the scientists.

"Was the presentation a success?" I ask him, even though I know the answer.

"No." He replies.

I give a small grin at what must be an ill-timed joke, but none of the scientists smile back, so I get concerned.

"I do not understand." I reply.

"We will explain everything very shortly, Oshiro. Please wake your companion." The lead scientist says.

I hear a big snore on my left. Mr. Nakamura is slumped in the seat beside me, mouth open and twisted in sleep. I nudge him and he sits up.

“Hmmm. Hm? Hm! Good afternoon, Osaka Branch!”

“We are not associated with Shajiku Sun, Nakamura. We are not in Osaka, or in Japan, or even on Earth,” the lead scientist pauses, then continues, “The information I will give you will be quite shocking. Let me know when you are prepared for it.”

Mr. Nakamura looks at me, but I shake my head. His face becomes serious. I do not know much about the company my grandfather works for, but I know they are very professional and would not joke for this long. Mr. Nakamura must have realized this too.

“Tell us.”

“I am Otoroto Saino, president of Tanken Corp. When you ran your tests back on Earth, we happened to be running ours as well. Instead of going to Osaka, you came here; a country called Shenshimu in a continent called the Adataka Islands on a planet called Iesias.”

Nakamura and I stare at the man, shocked. This has to be a poor joke. It is impossible for this man to be telling the truth!

“We believe it was the faulty signal in Oshiro’s headset that caused the tracking to get offset. They made the signal strong to keep in contact, but a little too strong. Because of this, the Osaka Branch did not open their portal in enough time, and so you were taken to the next open space; here. Such a drastic displacement has rendered both of your headsets useless."

"Faulty signal?" Nakamura asks, disbelief in his voice, "That is not possible. Oshiro's headset was working just fine! Isn't that right, Oshiro?"

"I suppose so. No one ever said anything through it, but it did not look damaged when I put it on."

Mr. Nakamura recoils a bit, looking embarrassed and surprised, "But then how did you know to put your hand up for the audio signal test?"

I feel my face turning red from embarrassment and surprise too, "Oh… I was just copying you."

"Oshiro!" Mr. Nakamura cries, "Oh no… this is not good."

"No it is not," Mr. Otoroto adds, "In more ways than one."

"Oh really?" Mr. Nakamura replies, anger and panic in his voice, "What else is there, then?"

"Your planet's governments have not shown IPSHA to the public yet, so everything you are experiencing now is forbidden information. Most of it has already been captured with your cameras, so there is not much we can do."

"IPSHA? It sounds like you are making this up." Mr. Nakamura challenges.

"I have never heard of anything like this." I add.

"It was a matter of time," Mr. Otoroto says, "the governments here regulate information about IPSHA and the existence of other planets, so it is not necessarily a secret as it is with your planet, nor is it common knowledge. The only things we know about Earth, outside of it being very far away, is that it has one moon, large oceans, seven continents instead of two, and is very polluted. Everything else we learned from your personal identification cards, the tracking signatures on your equipment, and deduction."

Mr. Nakamura and I cannot find the air to speak, so Mr. Otoroto continues, "In terms of equipment, some members of the team decided to make modifications so that the signal reaches Earth. Oshiro, your chest camera is still live as we speak, but the shoulder camera can only store footage because it also records audio."

"If you are aliens like you said and all of this is a big secret, then why are you giving us such 'advanced' equipment?" Mr. Nakamura asks.

Mr. Otoroto pauses for a moment, then says, "First, many members of our staff like retrofitting. But mainly because… you will most likely never return to Earth."

My whole body becomes cold. My stomach begins to tingle and I can feel panic coming. This all has to be some trick. There is no way this is real. It is just a very bad joke. That must be it!

"That is… that cannot be true! How can we come here but not go back?" I ask, hoping to end this prank.

"You two got here by pure luck. We just began this project three months ago, and we were simply doing a power test when you showed up. Only our electricity sensors were running; no real systems have even been made yet. It would take us at least 60 years to actually create a working portal."

"So you have great camera equipment but no teleportation?!" Mr. Nakamura asks, angry.

Some of the scientists chuckle, and Mr. Otoroto smiles, "Yes Nakamura. Just because we are advanced in one place does not mean we are everywhere. It seems as though Earth has beaten us in the teleportation field."

"Well," I think hard, "if my grandfather can see us through the cameras, why can he not just… bring us back?"

"Teleportation does not work that way, Oshiro," Mr. Nakamura says, "Imagine teleportation as a hallway and your grandfather's machines as doors. To get from one room to another, you must open a door, go through the hallway, and exit through the next door. If you want to return to the first room, you must go through the hallway once more. But to get to the hallway, you need a door. There is no way for you to skip these elements and just be 'brought back' to the first room."

The faces of the scientists become serious again as some of them write down notes, and my heart sinks. 60 years before they can create this 'door'… I will be 75 by then. Sofu, Mother, and Father will be long gone. My sister and all of my friends from school will be grandparents. Everything will be changed forever. It would be worthless to go back then.

I feel myself about to cry. The world is pushing in on me. Everything is too fast, too final. I cannot breathe! I feel like at any moment I might pass out!

"Please Mr. Otoroto," I gasp, fighting for composure, "is there any other way we can get back at all? I cannot leave my family behind forever like this!"

Mr. Otoroto looks back at the other scientists, and a few of them shake their heads while others begin to talk with each other. It is hard to hear what they are saying because they are very quiet; they seem to speak about my fitness and Amanokaze, which I still have not seen yet.

Then, Mr. Otoroto raises his hand. Everyone stops talking, and then he speaks, "There are two other ways in which you can get home. Do you want to hear them?"

Mr. Nakamura and I nod.

"The first is by going through IPSHA. I am not certain if they can get you home, but I imagine they could. Even still, it would take months, if not years, to be approved for access to their equipment. On top of that, the main continent, Uykic, is over 10,000 kilometers from here, and there are many sea monsters. Getting to IPSHA to begin with will not be easy, safe, or cheap.

"The second is purely theoretical. You could possibly complete this in as little as one to seven weeks. There are seven local enchanted spirits which live in shrines around the island. If you summon and defeat all seven of them, they will give you what you want. This is known as the Trial of Shenshimu."

"Can we not fly to the mainland instead?" Mr. Nakamura asks.

"Only government officials and cargo can fly here on Iesias."

"Why is this second option only theoretical?" I ask.

"The spirits are deadly and will try to kill you. The fourth spirit in particular is so deadly that all who make it that far are killed by it. No one has ever even seen the last three spirits."

Mr. Nakamura is as quiet as I am, and then he says, "So we are choosing between death and death?"

"Unfortunately." Mr. Otoroto says.

I look at Mr. Nakamura and he looks back at me. His face is confused, defeated, and disbelieving all at once. I feel the same way. What do we say? What do we do? Is this real life?

"It seems as though the two of you need time to think," Mr. Otoroto says, "Luckily for you, we are a short walk away from Sihi Beach, which is where the first shrine is. There are also ports nearby, where you might find a ship brave enough to try and take you to Uykic.

"If you want to try the Trial, I suggest you do so today. It is the exact middle of the year, which is the only time the first spirit will respond. If you want to keep going after the first one, you have to get the next one to respond in a week."

"Respond?" I ask, "What does that mean?"

"Go up to the shrine and tap it three times with your weapon. If you are using your fists for some reason, just knock on the shrine three times. Then, get on your knees and sit on your ankles. Present your weapon to the shrine with open hands, or just open your hands if you are using fists. Make sure your back is straight and stare directly at the shrine. This will provoke the spirit."

****

The warm sea breeze blows in my hair. I can smell salt and sand. Our hazmat pants swish as Mr. Nakamura and I make our way to Sihi Beach. We left our air tanks and wrapped the top parts of our suits around our waists because the air is safe to breathe. We have pants under these pants, but I just decided to keep them on and so did he.

Amanokaze is tied to my belt, and the camcorder is with Mr. Nakamura. The scientists gave us back all of our belongings before sending us off. We are going to check out the first spirit, and then see what we should do from there. If we both fight it at the same time, we should win.

We walk through grass fields. The sounds of people and sea birds grow. Everything looks very normal aside from the hovering cars and the strange, blue-feathered sea birds. People laugh and play. There are carts selling food. The sky is smooth and full of big, puffy clouds.

I wish the scenery would calm me down, but it does not. What are we going to do? Am I ever going to see my parents again?! Am I really going to die?! My fear only grows stronger when Mr. Nakamura and I get to the beach.

Mr. Otoroto said we would not be able to miss the shrine, and he was right. On the left side of the beach, there are hundreds of people, enjoying the sun and the waves. On the right is the same. In the middle, it is empty. All that is there is a small stone shrine and dozens of short, obsidian pillars.

Nervous, Mr. Nakamura and I make our way over to it. It feels awkward stepping onto the sand with my boots, knowing we should not be here. There is a long, pale stick washed up on the beach, and Mr. Nakamura runs off to get it. As I get a closer look, I can see names etched into the black pillars. Are… are these graves?!

"I do not think we should do this." Mr. Nakamura says as he comes back and sees the graves.

I turn and look at him. A few meters away, I notice people staring at us and talking with one another. Many of them begin to head to the grassy field, where they set up their chairs and blankets. Are they planning on watching us?

"I agree, but we must give it a try. I hope it is all fake." I say, turning back to the shrine.

Mr. Nakamura grunts and walks up next to me. I unsheathe Amanokaze for the first time ever, and it flickers in the sunlight. Nervous, I extend it to the shrine. Am I really about to do this?

Tap tap tap.

Chapter 3

The Scorpion Woman

~ First Spirit ~

The red and black shrine stands out against the dark blue horizon. I can feel the warmth of the sand a little through my two layers of pants. Mr. Nakamura taps the shrine and kneels beside me. We wait, staring at the small wooden box with pagoda roofs.

神一つ目

火 - 石 - 剣

("First Spirit" : its name : "fire – rock – sword")

Below the shrine is a small sign coming up from the sand. I think it is something from the local government warning people. I cannot read it though because I am supposed to stare at the shrine. Seconds pass, wind blows, waves roll. In the corner of my vision, I can see the beach is empty. I can hear everyone on the grass.

A cloud passes above, covering everything in a cool shadow.

“How about we give it a full minute and then try the ports?” Mr. Nakamura asks from beside me.

“Let’s do it.” I say.

As soon as I say that, I hear soft thunder. The cloud that passed must be a storm cloud. Then, the entire sky flickers, and with a whoosh, a huge blast of lightning explodes behind the shrine. I fall back from the force, heat, and surprise. The shadow of the shrine is burned into my vision.

I blink a lot as I get up. From behind the shrine stands a strong, brown woman with long, black hair. She wears a bright red kimono with pictures of mountains and flames around the edges. Her eyes are big and brown. She looks about 20 years old but seems ancient somehow.

“I am Seinasaiwa, Spirit of the Volcano, the first in the Trial of Shenshimu…”

She stops and looks at the two of us, surprised. I look over to see if maybe Mr. Nakamura is doing something weird. He is standing and trembling, eyes wide, just like me.

“Is this it? No one else will be joining you?” The spirit asks.

Mr. Nakamura and I are too afraid to speak, so we just shake our heads. What is going on?! Is this real?

“Strange; people usually like to bring big groups for this. Very well. What are your names?”

“N-Nakamura Ryusei.” Mr. Nakamura says.

“Oshiro Daiki.” I say.

"Since you summoned me, you can call me Seina from now on. No matter though. I will only need your names so I can etch them onto your graves, and you will only need my name so you can beg for mercy!"

In a loud burst, bright fire shoots up from all around her. I shield my face from the painful heat and light. When it is all blown away by the wind, Seina is wearing different clothes. She has on a pair of red hakama trousers. Armor made of black rocks covers her chest and shoulders. Her hair is tied back in a ponytail.

I take a few steps back as I notice what is behind her. A large black snake made of rocks stretches up like a tail. On the end of it is a blade as long and wide as my leg. It glows orange with heat. Mr. Nakamura and I take a stunned look at one another, and then the spirit begins to trudge through the sand towards us.

"Look, we do not want any trouble, Great Lord Seina, we just want to go home–"

In a spray of sand, Seina jumps and spins, whipping her tail towards us. It comes faster than either of us can move, slicing the stick Mr. Nakamura holds in two. As soon as she lands, her hands burst into flames. She looks at us, not hurt, an excitement for battle in her eyes.

"In that case, hold still so I can send you to the afterlife!"

She punches with both fists and the fire leaps from her arms into the air. I duck and the arrow of fire flies over me. Mr. Nakamura also dodged, and he is backing away to the right. Seina is already trudging towards us again.

Although I am scared, I will myself to think. I know this is crazy but I must win if I want to go home. Oh my goodness, I am too scared! No, I must control myself. I see the bladed tail rise, and then I dive to the left as it comes down. It makes a splash and a thud in the sand.

I stand fast. Seina looks at me, then Mr. Nakamura. He is closer, so she begins to trudge towards him. He lets out a terrified cry and stumbles backwards, tripping over a grave. As he is scrambling to his feet, waving his sticks at the spirit, I try to calm myself.

For a moment, I empty my mind. I focus on the clouds rolling away in the sky, the ocean breeze, and the waves on the shore. Then, a worrying cry comes from Mr. Nakamura. I look back over, and Seina has him grabbed by the waistband.

To my surprise, she lifts him into the air with one hand. In a violent swing, she throws his entire body right at me. Before I can overcome my surprise and react, the back of Mr. Nakamura slams into my chest. His elbow hits my head and the two of us fall hard on the sand.

Pain pounds in my face. My chest is aching, and I cannot breathe. I roll a bit in the sand, hurting everywhere, trying to get my breath back. Mr. Nakamura is grabbing at his back, rolling around like me. I am surprised my glasses are not broken.

I go onto my side and get my breath back. Even then, I cannot get up. I watch Seina trudge closer and closer. It hurts too much to even try to escape. Soon, she is standing over me, and I try to curl onto my stomach. She pushes me onto my back with her bare foot, then plants it hard and heavy on my aching chest. Her eyes are terrifying and excited.

"Goodbye." Says the spirit as she raises her arms.

When she brings them down, fire comes out of her palms and pours down onto me. Unbearable pain fills my face, arms, and chest. I scream and swing my arms, trying to knock away her hands, but then the fire stops. Moving fast, I roll onto the sand to put out the fires on my shirt.

My face still hurts very much, and the only reason I can see is because of my glasses. I notice that I hear clapping from the onlookers in the field. I look to see Mr. Nakamura on top of Seina, trying to stab her in the stomach with the sharp end of his stick.

I struggle to my knees and get ready to stand. At the same time, Seina starts to overpower Mr. Nakamura. She is already grabbing the stick to keep from being stabbed, and with a jerk, she snaps it.

Mr. Nakamura falls to the side, but then she grabs him by the collar and waistband. She stands up and lifts him high above her head, then throws him with violence straight into the ground. He hits the sand very hard and does not move anymore.

The spirit turns to me, her rock tail coiling behind her. I stumble back, horrified, as she begins to smile and trudge towards me. I notice the family sword lying on the ground and pick it up fast. Seina continues toward me, and I back away, pointing my trembling sword at her to try and scare her.

I have a weapon; what am I doing? I know she is scary but I must defend myself. This is my family sword! I know kendo! Even if I do not win, I will fight her with what I have and die with honor!

I hold the sword with two hands and squat down. I ignore my screaming face, the grit on the sword hilt, my aching chest, my pounding heart. This will be my greatest kendo match, and perhaps my final. With that thought, I stand.

Nervous, I watch her approach. One step, another, another, now she is in striking distance! I do not hesitate and let out a kakegoe – battle cry – before lunging forward as hard as I can. Just like practice, the katana goes in a high arc above me.

"HELMET!" I scream as I swing my blade down where a helmet would be.

The sword sinks deep; I have struck her! But my lunge was too forceful, so I skip through the sand, carrying my sword and my battle cry with me. As I quiet down, I notice the onlookers are clapping. I am facing her, but she is still facing away from me. Did I win?

She turns around and I brace myself for a bloody mess. Instead, I see excited eyes and a very faint scar where I hit her. Oh no.

"Did you really think I'd be beaten that easily?" Seina asks as she begins to come towards me, faster now.

I am frozen in surprise, and then she is right in front of me. She stops, and I notice her rock tail bending backwards. As fast as I can, I raise my sword to block, and she brings her blade down a second later. The impact is very heavy and I almost drop my sword.

There is a screech from where the blades meet, and then smoke starts to rise. I look up and see that the sword of Seina is beginning to sink into mine. What?! I have got to do something before she cuts my sword in half!

Thinking fast, I dig my boot into the sand and kick some of it in her face. Her hands fly up as she turns away. The tail continues to press its blade into mine. It did not work! The spirit brushes her face clean. Her smile gets bigger; I guess I missed her eyes, too.

Her blade has sunk about halfway through mine now. Any moment, my family sword will snap in half, leaving me to be cut open by this giant heat blade. What a bizarre way to die. I decide to look out at the beach instead of at Seina for my last sight.

Onlookers stare back at me, sad. Parents cover the eyes of their children. The sky is blue and promising. The ocean sparkles and the beach looks nice. All the clouds have passed, and the sun is glaring. Wait… the sun…

All at once I get an idea. Sun glaring, eye attack, my family sword … grandfather! His story about the sword being magic! He said it entrances people whenever it is in the sun… but it is in the sun right now! Then I guess… what if that means I must shine the sun off my sword and into the eyes of Seina to entrance her?

Testing, I tilt my sword up more. The sword hisses more and lets out a scary amount of smoke, but I see a line of light run up the body of the spirit. I stop it right at her eyes.

She notices and squints up at the sword, almost raising her arms to block the light, but then stops and laughs, "If shining this in my face will make you feel any better about your death, go ahead."

As soon as she finishes saying that, her eyes lose their life. Her shoulders and face relax, and the tail grows limp. Because of this, her heavy blade falls over to the side, snapping my family sword in half as it hits the sand.

I shuffle back, sad over my family sword and terrified of another attack from Seina. But she just stands there, looking at the half of my sword still in my hands. Did it work? Is she entranced or playing a trick? Testing, I move the sword around. Her head follows it.

I do not know if this is a trick or how long this trance might last, so I rush Seina with another kakegoe. Instead of one strike to the head, I do as many as I can, hitting her over and over with the half sword.

After the first hit, she seems to be released from the trance, but I am striking too fast and too many times for her to block. She tries to pull back out of my attacks, and I notice her tail raising behind her. No, I am too close to winning! Why are none of my attacks doing anything?!

"THRUST!" I scream, pushing the cut end of my blade into the soft middle where her throat meets her chest.

There is a large spray of sparks as the sword pushes all the way through. She falls to the ground and I fall with her. She tries to grab the sword and pull it out, but I am putting all my weight on it.

Seina struggles with me for a moment before melting into golden beads.

CHAPTER 4

MANY GIFTS

~ BLESSING ~

Beeping from my alarm clock wakes me. I sit up and my vision begins to clear. Though the room is dark, fluorescent light comes through the window on the door. My bed is weird and angled upwards. The sheets are soft and feel like wool. This is not my bedroom.

The last thing I remember was killing Seina. Once she disappeared, everyone clapped and cheered. I went over to Mr. Nakamura to check on him, but my face started to hurt more and more until I could not see. There were people saying things and hands grabbing me, but I could not understand anything over the pain. Then there was a punch in my arm… and swirling lights?

The quiet beeping from the hospital machine keeps going. There is some type of tube or medicine stuck in my arm. I am not a very knowing person with medicines, but I still do not think I have seen anything like this before.

There is a man wearing dark green, reading a glowing tablet in the chair beside my bed. A city sparkles in the window behind him; black towers, bright screens, and many lights rise in the distance. Rain makes it all blurry, hushing against the outside of the wall.

The man notices me as I clear my throat.

"Ah, Oshiro, it is good to see you are awake. I am Doctor Utsaka Yotu. Looks like you were one of the lucky ones during today's fight?"

"I think so." I reply, feeling a little dizzy. It must be something in this medicine.

"Huh, I guess it does not feel like it, does it? Do not worry, the dizziness will wear off soon. We spent all day on that nasty burn. There are no scars either, so count yourself lucky."

I smile in thanks and he returns a smile.

"Do not worry about the medical costs. As you know, the government covers it since one of the spirits injured you."

I feel relief I did not know I had. Dr. Utsaka reaches in his pocket and pulls out two slips of paper. It is hard to tell in the dim light, but one is dark red and the other is light blue.

"Since the government is paying for your healing, they want you to work for them. Of course, once you are old enough. Oh, and after you finish getting your blessings from the spirits."

"Blessings?" I ask, reaching out and taking the papers.

"Yes, Lord Seinasaiwa didn't bless you after your battle?"

I think hard… "No, I do not think so."

"Make sure to return to Sihi Beach tonight! Blessings are the most important part of the entire event!" Dr. Utsaka urges.

I smile and nod, though I do not plan to go to the beach; I do not want to see that spirit ever again! Still, I am happy about what I have been told, so I look down at my papers to learn more. The dark red one has more details about joining the government.

I remember what Mr. Otoroto said about government officials being able to use planes. Though that seems nice, I must also remember that I am only 15. I still have some years before I can join, and then I would need more years to build tenure.

The light blue paper says something about a hospital meal for patients. It has a lot of numbers and symbols on it, so I am not quite sure what it is. Confused, I look at Dr. Utsaka.

"That is a pass for a free meal at the cafeteria. You should certainly eat soon, that will help the effects of the medicine wear off faster."

The doctor takes the tubes out of my arms and leg, then helps me to stand. Everything feels fuzzy. He guides me to the bathroom, where I change out of this dress and back into my normal clothes. Once everything is on, including my body camera and hazmat suit, I realize that only the scabbard is left. My family sword is still at the beach.

Dr. Utsaka then helps me into the very bright hallway, walking me all the way to the cafeteria before leaving.

There are two people with bandages around their heads drinking from steaming cups near the window. All the tables and chairs are empty and wiped clean. A woman sits behind a counter, reading a glowing tablet. Above her is a big menu, and on either side of her is bagged food.

I go over to her and order fried fish with salad and tea. I think it is odd that a different planet has the same food, but I am not complaining! I wait for my meal to cook in silence, surprised that they have normal food here, and then I hand over the blue paper once it is done. As I am turning to pick a seat, a man limps up next to me: Mr. Nakamura!

He orders noodles with sea chips (neither of us know what this is) and tea, then the two of us pick a table near a window and begin to eat. It is still raining very hard outside, and the parking lot is quiet and full. The two of us eat, silent for a while, just glad that the other is alive.

"Did your doctor tell you about the blessings?" Mr. Nakamura asks.

"Yes, we would need to go back to the beach for them." I reply.

"Are you going?" He asks.

The empty scabbard tied to my hip makes me say yes.

"What are you going to do after? Continue with the spirits, or join me working for the government?"

"I do not know," I admit, "It would take me a few years to be able to work, then even more to build tenure. But these spirits are very dangerous. I guess I will decide after the blessing tonight."

Mr. Nakamura does not reply for a long time. We just keep eating and looking at the rain. Then, he reaches into his pocket and pulls out a brown oval coin.

"Here," he says, putting it next to my food, "take this."

“What is it?” I ask, picking it up.

“A tempo tsuho, passed down through my family for a long time as a good luck coin.”

“Why are you giving this to me? You should hold on to it.” I say, but he stops me before I can return it to him.

“I do not think there is much hope left for me, Oshiro.”

I put down the coin, surprised, “What?! Why do you say that?”

“Think about it. I am 59; even if it took me only ten years, I would be almost 70 by the time I built tenure to be an official.”

“Then we can do the spirit fights! If we stay together, we have a better chance of winning!” I try.

Mr. Nakamura laughs, which then turns into painful coughing, “Look at me, Oshiro. I am old! The doctor said it is going to take me almost three weeks to recover from that fight. My body does not come back like yours does.”

I can see what he is talking about. The wrinkles from past smiles are still in his face. His black hair is full of white-grey rows. Unlike earlier this morning (how bizarre!) his eyes have no energy. He does not look like he is near death, but I can see he is older. I do not care; we got here together so we leave together. He sees that I feel this way and smiles.

“Do not be sad, Oshiro. I am just talking bluntly; there is always a chance that I could make it back. Plus, I am almost certain you will make it back, too. You are a good, determined, strong kid, and definitely the grandson of Oshiro Tadashi. Keep your chin up,

Oshiro. The best things happen when you work hard and stay consistent."

I nod, trying not to be upset, and he struggles to stand. I just now noticed that he finished his meal. We trade a bow, and Mr. Nakamura hobbles away.

This was the last time I would ever see him.

****

The summer night is warm. After an hour of walking and following road signs, I have made it to Sihi Beach. The moon, much larger than what I am used to, shines off the black ocean water. Puddles glisten on the sidewalks, filling the air with the smell of rain. There are too many city lights behind me to see all the stars.

The beach is empty. No night creatures, no people staying after close. Just the shrine and even more graves, all wet with rain. I walk towards the shrine, becoming more and more afraid as I get closer to it.

"Oshiro!" Echoes a familiar, heavy voice.

I look over to my left. The beach rises into a rocky bluff. Standing at the top is the figure of a person. As I make my way over, I realize it is a woman… wearing red… a red kimono. Seina greets me with a smile as I reach the top of the bluff.

I am very scared right now, and the fact that I am alone without a weapon makes me want to run. But Seina does not attack. Instead, she sits down on the rocks, patting one next to her as to invite me to sit there. I do as she asks.

We sit next to one another, watching the black waves and the big moon. Seina shifts. There is a scraping noise, and I am filled with fear. A long, gleaming blade comes from her other side, but before I can scream, she offers it to me. With the bright moon, I realize it is Amanokaze, my family sword. It is in one piece, too!

"Thank you for the fight earlier. I thought you might want this back. Also, I went ahead and made sure that it won't break, bend, stain, or grow dull ever again."

Impressed but still a little uneasy, I sheathe the sword. Now I feel a little better.

"Is Nakamura coming?" She asks.

"No." I reply, trying not to be sad like he wished. His coin is deep in my pocket.

"What a shame; you two made a great team. I decided to turn that camera of his into a head guard, so you can have that too."

With another shift and scrape, she puts a kabuto – samurai helmet – on my lap.

"This will stop any attack that touches it, no matter the type. It won't break or bend, either."

Oh, that is really useful! Excited, I wrap my arms around the helmet and pull it close. It feels like the best thing to come from this whole day, plus my better sword. We stare at the water, and then Seina scoots closer to me. Now our arms are touching.

I do not know what to do. Does she want me to move? Stay put? Confused and a little scared, I stay where I am. She then hugs me and puts her head on my shoulder. Is… is she sad? Feeling alone? What does she want me to do?

Just as I am about to rest my head on hers, she says, "Close your eyes and focus on breathing."

Surprised at the silence being spoken into, I do as she says. The moonlight on the ocean is blocked out, and I focus on my lungs. In, out, iiiiiiiiiiiiin, oooooooooout. My shoulders are not tense anymore. The breeze and the sea fade away. All I feel is the warm hug from Seina.

"Good," the spirit says as she pulls back, "You can open your eyes now."

I do so. The night looks a little brighter, but nothing else has changed. I look at Seina for guidance.

"Put out your hands." She commands.

I do, and she grabs them. With a loud pop, fire begins to flicker inside of our hands. I let out a scream of horror, but then I realize something: this does not hurt. No? …no! This is okay! I am on fire and I am fine!

"What is this?!" I ask Seina, watching as the fire starts to flick out from between our fingers.

"I made it so that fire does not harm you. Now, if you were to fight me again, I might not be a big threat!"

She lets go of my hands and the fire goes away. I look at my hands, still stunned at what happened. Everything is fine! This is magic! I bow and thank Seina very much, and she gives a little bow back and a smile.

"Thank you for visiting and putting up a good fight. I know most people just take the blessing and give up here, but I hope you go on to win it all. Until we meet again, Oshiro. May the Goddess give you strength."

I nod, stand, and walk back down the bluff. Is someone looking at me? When I get to the shrine on the beach, I stop. It feels like someone is staring at me. I look back at the bluff to see if it is Seina.

It is.

CHAPTER 5

GREATEST BATTLE EVER

~ SECOND SPIRIT ~

The sea goes out of view and green mountains take their place. My kabuto and katana lay across my lap. Calm flute music plays from the car radio. Memate, the old woman driving, still has the happy look she had when we met last night. She was going for a walk while I was searching for a place to stay. She let me sleep at her house, and this morning she gave me a big breakfast before agreeing to take me to the next shrine.

"This next spirit is really sweet; always playing with the kiddies around her shrine and offering fruit to anyone who's hungry. Heck, there is a good chance she might not even fight you." Memate says, driving the car around the spiral road.

"Really? That makes me feel better!" I tell her, and it is true.

For most of last night I could not sleep, fearing that I made the wrong choice in leaving Mr. Nakamura. I knew for sure that without his help, I would die. Even with the blessings from Seina, fighting another person like her would be too much for me. I was so confused and scared, I almost cried.

Memate made me some tea and a bath. Seeing the joy the old lady had in helping me out made me feel better. Even now, I cannot help but smile at her friendliness.

"She even has a little hotel that she watches over, Edeka Park Inn, and she lets the homeless or people who win her challenge sleep there. Rumors say that the beds are magic… oh, if I weren't so old, I'd join you out there!"

"If you come along with me, she certainly will not harm us!" I joke, smiling.

She turns from the spiral road to a gravel path, smiling too, "Oh no, that's alright. You showing up and being such a sweetheart is enough fun to last me the whole year!"

Soon, we reach a small parking lot full of different types of cars. Memate turns our car around, then stops.

"You stay safe now, Oshiro! She should probably feed you and give you a bed for the night, so I'll pick you up tomorrow morning and take you where you want to go next."

"Thank you very much, Ms. Memate." I say as I open the door and pull my things out behind me.

"Oh, just Memate is fine! See you tomorrow!" The old woman reassures.

I nod and close the door, and then the two of us wave as she drives off. Still smiling, I turn and head towards the big clearing in front of the parking lot.

Gravel crunches under my boots. The warm wind blows through the trees. Sunlight pours many dots of white into the shaded forest. In the clearing, it is easy to see the next wooden shrine. On both sides of it, there are what look like cherry blossom trees, large and pink.

Behind it is a sliding door which leads into a long wooden house. There are sliding doors all along the sides, and what look like apple trees shade its back porch. That must be the hotel. Beyond it, there is a play area for children. I can hear laughter coming from there.

People are having lunch in the clearing, and a few of them notice me as I come out of the woods. Once I have tied on Amanokaze and the new kabuto helmet Seina gave me (it is very comfortable), I walk up to the shrine and read it.

神二つ目

花 - 木 - 拳

("Second Spirit": its name : "flower – wood – fist")

With a nervous sigh, I unsheathe my sword. Before I can start the ritual, the sliding door behind the shrine opens and the head of a young woman peeks out. She has short, dark brown hair and pretty, green eyes.

"Hi there." She says.

"Hello." I reply, lowering my sword.

"What are you doing?" The woman asks in a nice way.

“Oh, I am doing the Trial of Shenshimu…” I explain, worrying that I may have done something wrong.

The woman slides the door all the way open. She is wearing a green kimono with pictures of flowers all over it. Barefoot, she walks out of the hotel, comes around the shrine, and stands really close to me. I have to turn my body to make sure my sword is not facing her.

“No need to summon anything, I’m right here!” The woman says with a smile.

I am full of surprise and fear at once, “Y-you are the next spirit?!”

I do not have time or space to bring up my sword, because as soon as I stumble backward, she steps forward and is really close to me again.

“Yep! I’m taking it you are a challenger?” She asks.

“Y-yes.” I reply.

She raises an eyebrow and smiles, looking cute, “Very well! Sheathe your sword and put it at the base of that blossom tree, then knock on the shrine three times.”

I remember what Mr. Otoroto said about knocking on the shrine; it means I am fighting with my fists.

“I am sorry, but I fight with my sword.” I tell the spirit, raising it a little to show her.

“I know, but we might not even have a fight!” She replies.

I nod, sheathing Amanokaze and untying it from my belt. I lay it down on the roots of one of the trees. Then, I think about whether or not to take off my kabuto helmet too. After a moment, I choose not to. What if her friendliness is a trap?

Knock, knock, knock.

I turn to the spirit, scared as to what will happen next. She looks back at me, still smiling, then raises her arms. Wind blows hard from our left, picking cherry blossom pedals off of the ground and trees. They swirl around her body, making a pink wall, and then the wind stops and all the pedals flutter to the ground.

The spirit now wears different clothes; a pair of green hakama trousers with a light green tube top.

"I am Yokosorana, Spirit of the Meadow and the second in the Trial of Shenshimu. Since you summoned me, you can call me Yoko from now on. What can I call you?"

"Oshiro Daiki." I say, stepping back and raising a guard. This will be tough; I do not know any weaponless martial arts. My dad taught my sister and me some self-defense moves when we were younger, so I hope those will be good enough.

"Oshiro Daiki?" she repeats, sounding interested, "What an odd name! And that blinking light on your chest must be from a camera? Are you from the mainland?"

"Um… no I am not." I reply, still trying to ready myself for the fist fight.

"Is that so? Where are you from, then?"

Why has she not put up her guard? Is she going to fight me?

"I am from… I am from a very distant planet."

It sounds so foolish to me, but she looks very excited, "Really?! An alien?! By the Goddess, how cool! What planet are you from?"

She has still not prepared. Perhaps I will talk my way out of this one! My shoulders relax as I say, "Earth."

I expect her to continue to be excited, but her entire mood becomes like ice.

"Earth?" She repeats, looking surprised and almost… angry?

"Um, yes." I reply, a little scared.

"Oh, so then you are used to things like this, aren't you?" Yoko asks, sounding bitter.

"Things like what?" I ask, trying to take a step back but bumping into the shrine.

"Things like trampling all over nature. Things like tearing the land to shreds and having your way with the resources! Tossing me around should be normal for you, huh?" She asks, making fists.

"Wait, what?" I ask, raising my hands.

"All you Earthlings are the same; you think you can take whatever you want and give nothing but filth in return! You'll pay for what your kind has done!"

"N-no! I am not like that!", but Yoko is not listening.

Her face is red with anger, and she runs right at me. I dive to the side, expecting her to do some crazy attack, but she skids to a stop, turning towards me. I crawl towards my sword and try it pick it up, but it does not move. Roots have grown over it! Then, the hands of Yoko grab my leg and pull me hard.

I tried to ready myself to be thrown across the field, but unlike Seina, Yoko seems to have the opposite of super strength. It felt as though I had been tugged by a child. Surprised and confused, I look back. Yoko is trying her very best to pull me, I can see the real anger in her eyes, but she is much too weak.

Testing, I stand, and she stands very fast along with me.

"Die, Earthling scum!"

I shield myself from a storm of punches, but her little fists hit me as if they were small pillows. Peering over my arm, I can see that she is still red-faced, hitting me with what must really be her strongest attacks. It is rather cute.

"Die! Die!" she screams, "I will kill you a thousand times over! I will scatter your limbs across this world like you would trash in yours! Suffer, Oshiro! Feel my wrath!"

Her fists beat into me as though I am getting a mild massage. It takes all that I have not to burst into laughter. She is quite serious, though, and I do not want to make her any angrier.

"Stand down, Lord Yoko," I say, "I do not wish to harm you."

"*Harm me?!*" she screams, trying to shove me but ending up pushing herself backwards, "You're a coward, Oshiro! A coward! Fight me and lose with honor, you halfwit! You spawn of garbage!"

She begins to claw at me, but her nails are trimmed very short and her fingers are little, so it is more like a forceful stroking than a painful attack. I just keep my body turned away from her, holding my laughter as much as possible, letting her numb my arm with her 'attacks'.

Soon, she begins to slow down, growing tired. Her punches rest on my arm for longer and longer, until she is just leaning against me with her fists balled, panting insults.

"You… are a weak… ling and… you will… never defeat me… give up you… pathetic… Earth… p-person…"

Yoko marked her last three words with fruitless pounds against me, then she bows her head and gasps. My smile has left. I am now a little angry from her insults and worried that she has some sort of second form.

"Will you give up now?" I ask.

"No!" She shouts, whipping her head up, "I won't stop until you fight me! Try your best! Hurt me like you hurt your planet all the time! It shouldn't be anything new for you, you disgrace!"

My small anger grows larger. She notices this.

"Yeah, I said it! *A disgrace!* To your family and your country and your planet! You filthy, good-for-nothing Earth leech!"

Something about her sharp voice, maybe the tone, fills me with too much anger. She will really call me a disgrace? Though she knows nothing of my family, nothing of my history?!

"You want to be hurt?" I ask, my body swelling with fire.

"Just try!" She says, standing back and raising a guard.

"Very well… you are the true disgrace to this Trial!" I shout, "You are by far the weakest thing I have ever seen. A child can fight better than you. If I hit you with any amount of power, I am quite sure I would break that ugly face of yours!"

The face of Yoko (I admit, to call her ugly is a grave lie) fills with shock. Her arms lower, as does her jaw. I keep going, pushed by anger.

"With a nature spirit such as yourself, I am surprised this planet is not riddled with pollution! You call me a polluter, yet you know nothing of my life? Of the values of my family? I am proud of my planet, but I am very sure no one here can say the same with *you* as the Spirit of the Meadow."

The eyes of Yoko begin to glisten, "Wait, I meant–"

"Perhaps if you took a moment to stop your yelling and instead learned how to fight, I would throw a fist at you! But you are not worth the effort, or even half the effort. You are..."

Yoko is crying. At first this means nothing to me, as the fire inside is still burning hot, eager to insult. But as she continues to cry, shoulders bouncing, head bowing, face twisted and pink, I start to feel as though I have acted without manners.

"I... I am sorry for my disrespect. I only wanted you to sur–"

"Fine!" she cries, "You want me to surrender? Fine! You win!"

She continues crying as I stand there, awkward. I do not know what to say. I have never made anyone cry before. This is also the first time I have ever really insulted someone. While I am not sorry for hurting her feelings, I do believe that perhaps I could have gone about it a different way.

“I… do not think you are ugly.”

Yoko sucks in her crying to give me an unhappy look. I look at the ground. That was a dumb thing to say.

She then pulls a powder from her trouser pockets, blows it at me, and I crumple to the ground with sleep.

Chapter 6

Spirit of Affection

~ Blessing ~

There is softness and warmth around me when I wake. Everything is white; the puffy sheets, the walls, even the sunlight coming through the window. A large painting of flowers is above the door. I can hear trees and birds outside. Soon, I realize I am very hungry. The bed is so soft that when I go to sit up, I sink in it.

As soon as I am sitting up, the sliding door to this room opens. Standing there is a familiar woman… Yoko! I say nothing, feeling neither good nor bad about insulting her earlier, and then the spirit crosses her arms.

"Finally, you're awake. Get up so we can get this over with."

I do as she says, trying to prepare myself for an attack. We never really fought… did I win for real? My boots, sword, and helmet are all laid in a neat way by my bed. Yoko is still staring at me, silent, so I put them on as fast as I can.

"Alright, take out your sword." Yoko says with a sigh.

I unsheathe Amanokaze. She makes a motion for me to hand it to her, and I do so. She holds it with two hands, pulls it close, and then closes her eyes. After a few moments of slow breathing, she gives the sword back.

"Squeeze the handle." She says.

I do. Nothing happens, and then I start to notice that there is a second blade coming out of the back of my sword like a ghost. I loosen my grip and the second blade goes away.

"Harder!" She says.

I grab the handle harder. The ghost blade rises until I realize that it is, in fact, blue fire. For a moment I am scared, but then I remember that fire does not hurt me because of Seina, so I squeeze the handle even more. The fire begins to roll and flicker. Then, I feel awake and strong.

"Squeezing the handle will help you get your energy back. That's your blessing." Yoko says, her voice flat.

I smile and go to bow in gratitude, but Yoko interrupts me, "Enough with the acting."

Confused, I look up at her. She has her face turned, looking off into the hallway.

"No amount of flattering will change my mind about you. You aren't getting plant powers or photosynthesis like other winners. You better be glad you even got what you did."

For a moment, I can feel my anger returning, but then I realize that perhaps anger is not the best solution now. She seems to be fastened with her thought about Earthlings, and I do not think arguing will change that. I will just be nice and change her thoughts that way.

I shrug with a happy face, "I still really like it, thank you."

Yoko rolls her eyes and says, "I can't stand you."

She turns and walks into the hallway, waving for me to follow her. I sheathe my sword and follow. The hallway has a wooden floor with what looks like bamboo walls and blue blossoms covering the ceiling.

There are many rooms to our left and right. Some of them are closed off with sliding doors. Others are open, showing empty, green futons and white tatami mats. Each room also has nice wooden vases with tall flowers in them. Nice, but nothing like the giant bed I was in.

"Lord Yoko… whose bed was I in?" I ask.

"*Just* Yoko," she says, mean, "and it was mine. All the rooms were full and I couldn't have you sleep outside because that would be too Earthling of me."

I raise an eyebrow. That was… very kind of her. Does she really hate me… or is she not being honest?

"Thank you for your kindness." I say.

It looks as though she is about to turn to me, but then she stops.

"Whatever, idiot." She says as she starts walking faster.

Even though she cannot see me, I shrug and smile again. I really think she is not being honest.

We reach the main door. Next to it is a basket filled with… shapes? I am not sure what those are. There are yellow heart-shaped things and blue things with spikes. There are triple nuts and pickle-like rods and many other odd, colorful items in the basket. Perhaps this is… fruit?

Yoko stops at the last room door. I think she wants me to leave, so I go to the main door. Before I can slide it open, she scoffs.

“So you aren’t even going to take your breakfast? You Earthlings really are dumb.”

I turn to her, surprised.

“That is for me?”

“Who else would it be for?” She replies, looking away.

I try not to smile as I pick up the very full basket. I am almost certain she is not being honest.

“Why did you do this?” I ask, though I know why.

Her face turns red and she looks down, “B-because I don’t want you to use hunger as an excuse for when you get beat next time.”

“Oh really?” I ask, not fooled.

“Yes really! I don’t like you or anything, I just don’t want you blaming me for when you lose!”

Fighting back a laugh is very hard now.

“If you say so, Yoko.”

“Shut up! Let me get the door so you don’t spill that, stupid.”

She runs around me and slides open the door, hiding her face by looking off… at the wall?

“Thanks a lot, Yoko.” I tease as I step outside.

I hear her let out an annoyed sigh, then she slams the door shut behind me and stomps back to her room.

Laughing to myself, I turn and look at the field. The bright sun shines off the dew on the grass. The trees sway in the wind. The air is warm and smells like dirt and flowers. From across the field I can see Memate, the old woman, sitting in the shade next to a basket of food.

She waves at me and I raise my basket of what may be fruit in reply. After a few steps, I hear Yoko call out, "Oshiro."

I turn to her, letting the basket hang in my arms.

"You like living, right?"

I nod, awaiting a joke.

She pauses, serious, then says, "You should give up."

My stomach drops and my happy mood goes away, "Why?"

"The next spirit is a very hard fight, one that I honestly don't think you can handle. And after her, well… no one has ever beaten the fourth spirit."

We are both silent, so she continues, "If you died, I probably wouldn't care, but that old woman will. She must really believe in you, so don't ruin it for her."

Yoko then slides the door closed.

****

The salty, roasted eel from lunch earlier becomes a stone in my stomach. Outside of the window, houses and trees pass by. There is a distant river that we have been driving towards, and as all the buildings begin to fade away, I can see it better.

Memate sees that I am worried. She saw it back when I last talked to Yoko. After spending the entire day with her yesterday, gardening, shopping, cooking, and cleaning, I felt better. She even got me new glasses, so everything is clearer than before. As the river and the next spirit comes closer, that calmness is fading.

With one last turn, we reach a parking lot. To our right, downstream, are small buildings that mark the edge of the town we just went through. To our left, upstream, is a trail with low hanging trees. The river is very big, maybe a hundred meters wide.

In front of us, the blue waters look very clean and very deep. If I walk upstream a little, the river becomes shallow and rocky. Standing on top of a big, smooth, black rock is the next shrine. The red stands out in the middle of the blue and white water.

"Thank you very much for the ride." I say as I open my door.

"Of course sweetie." She replies as she… opens her door?

I stop moving and she does the same.

"Are you getting out for some reason?" I ask, assuming that maybe she is going for another walk or visiting a market.

"Yes, so that I can help you with this next fight!" She says.

I smile, "That is very nice of you but I do not think–"

"Oh come on Oshiro, let's go! I've been cooped up in that little beach house for too long. It's time to give these old bones a good stretch! Zimu River is where I used to always take my kids."

This is cute but I am also very concerned.

“Memate, what weapon will you use? What if you get hurt?”

“I may look old but I’ve got a mean throwing arm! And don’t worry about me getting hurt, if anything, I should be worrying about you!”

Before I can speak again, she gets out of the car and closes her door. For a moment I am scared. The warning from Yoko was serious; what if I *do* die in front of Memate? What if Memate really *does* get hurt?

I look out the window at the old woman waiting by the trail. Well, I suppose I have no choice. I would dishonor all that has happened if I gave up now, and Memate is my elder, so I will respect her. We will do this together.

I get out of the car and walk over to Memate, then the two of us go down the forest trail. The noises of the town behind us fade as the sound of the river in the rocks grows. It is a short walk to the rocky area.

“I’ll collect rocks, and you go make sure that spirit doesn’t suspect a thing.” Memate says as she finds a stump to sit on.

I nod, then turn to the river. Steeling my mind, I put one boot out onto the rocks. They are slippery and shifty, but I can still walk. I take another step, then another, and make my way to the shrine.

Soon, I am there, with the shrine in front of me and the shifty rocks under my feet. The sounds of the river are in my ears. I unsheathe my sword, but before I tap the shrine, I squeeze the handle hard. The blue flames come just as Yoko had promised.

I squeeze a few more times, just to make sure. The blue flames come and go with each squeeze. After each squeeze, I get a little push of strength and reassurance. Okay, it really works! I then look down and read the shrine.

神三つ目

素敵澄川

水 - 潮 - 浮

("Third Spirit" : its name : "water – tide – float")

There is no use in delay. Gathering my courage, I raise Amanokaze and tap the shrine three times. Then, like with Seina, I get down on my knees and hold the sword out in front of me. I can feel the emptiness where Mr. Nakamura would be.

Like before, nothing happens for a while. The sounds of the river cover everything, and sometimes I can hear the rocks clattering where Memate is. I am surprised when I notice clouds rolling in, quick and silent, from my right.

They get closer and darker, and before I can steel my mind, the river behind the shrine explodes as a lightning bolt hits it. I feel small pricks of electricity from the water, even through my boots and two layers of pants. Water shoots into the air and rains down on the shrine and me.

I stand, and another figure does behind the shrine. She is very tall and pretty, with long, silver hair and weird blue eyes. Waves and fish-like creatures dance on her blue kimono. She looks older than the other two spirits, still youthful but something about her just feels more mature. Perhaps her eyes!

"I am Suturi'akawa, Spirit of the River and the third in the Trial of Shenshimu. Since you summoned me, you can call me Suturi from now on. What can I call you?"

The 'tu' will be difficult to pronounce. The way she talks is slow and gentle, and she sounds amused.

"I am Oshiro Daiki."

"Oh! With a name like that and a weird camera on your chest, I'd say you aren't from around here." She says, her words smooth.

"I… I am not." I confirm. I was about to go into detail, but I do not want a repeat of last time.

"My my, Oshiro… I'm not sure if the other two told you, but you are quite handsome."

I smile.

"It would be a shame if you died here." She adds.

I stop smiling.

At first, I thought she was standing on the rocks like me, but as she is moving, no, sliding, I realize she cannot be. Confused, I look at her feet as she comes around the left side of the shrine. No, she is not walking. She is floating!

"You are fighting me with a sword?" She asks.

I back away as she floats closer. Amanokaze is raised.

"Yes."

"That's it? No friends? Nothing more powerful?"

I grunt in reply, deepening my stance. This is going to be a hard fight. She is very tall and can fly, and she may be able to control water too. I cannot lie and say that I am not afraid.

"Has the fight started yet? You want me to start throwing?" The voice of an old woman shouts from behind Suturi.

We both look and see Memate, sleeves rolled up, with her left arm hugging a lot of dripping pebbles. Her frail right arm is ready to throw. I had forgotten she was here! Suturi looks at me, then Memate, then begins to giggle. My stomach falls.

"It looks like you do have an ally… and she seems pretty dangerous at that! I don't know if I'll be able to beat the two of you alone!" Suturi taunts.

"Please do not hurt her!" I say, lowering my sword.

"Don't hurt her? If I don't want to go down in one hit, I'm going to need an ally of my own!" She mocks.

Suturi points at an area on the right side of the shrine. The rocks there begin to move as something underneath, a person, stands up. The rocks and water fall away. I know who it is at once.

Seina.

CHAPTER 7

DOUBLE TROUBLE

~ THIRD SPIRIT ~

"**Come on, Suturi!** You think you could summon me out of the sky next time? First some teenagers summon me and run away, now this?" Seina asks, picking rocks out of the folds of her wet kimono.

I am having trouble staying on my feet. Everything is cold and I feel dizzy. This… this must be a joke. Mr. Nakamura and I almost did not survive fighting Seina the first time. Well, I can see that she no longer has her scorpion tail. Either way, must I face both her and Suturi by myself? I hope this is a joke!

"Huh, I guess all this water is annoying with those clothes, right?" Suturi asks, "How's this?"

The spirit snaps, then she and Seina are now in… matching swimsuits?! Suturi is in blue while Seina is in red. I can feel warm air on my chest. My socks turn to ice. A breeze runs through my hair and my vision gets a little blurry. I look down… what?! Where are my clothes?! Where is my helmet?! The only thing I have on are white swim trunks and thin river shoes!

Even the scabbard of Amanokaze is gone, but the sword is still in my hands. I back away. Seina stretches her sides and Suturi winks at me. This is not good. Not only are there two of them, but now the small amount of armor I had is gone. From where they are standing, they can press in on me from both sides with ease. This cannot be happening.

"Surely this is a joke." I say, lowering my sword.

"We're as serious as the Goddess!" Suturi says, smiling.

"You and your ally versus Suturi and me! This time no one will get overwhelmed, unlike last time." Seina pretends to pout.

I turn to Memate. She is a few steps into the river. Her shoes are by the tree stump. She took off her hair cloth and holds the wet rocks in them. Her right hand now holds a bigger rock, and she looks at me, ready for my lead.

"Memate, run!" I scream.

The old woman shakes her fist, "Listen to me, young man! You'd better start swinging that sword so I can start throwing these rocks! They're getting heavy!"

I am surprised at her willingness. Perhaps she does not know what these spirits are capable of! But I cannot talk back, for she is my superior, and to do so would dishonor her generosity.

Ready to die, I shift my kendo stance until I have found solid rocks. I then raise Amanokaze. I will try my best to keep both Memate and myself alive.

"Oh, handsome *and* brave? He's going to stay and fight even though we can clearly dominate him!" Suturi mocks.

I get cold again with the fear of death, but I am already in my kendo stance. I have already committed to this.

"Maybe he's just not too bright." Seina says.

"Why don't we test that out?" Suturi asks.

She bends over and picks up a rock. Since she's wearing a swimsuit, I want to look away to be respectful, but Suturi is my opponent, so I do not.

After she stands, she offers me the rock. I lean forward and take it. It looks and feels normal.

"Think hard about someone and skip that rock across the water. Wherever it sinks, that person you thought of will come out of the water and help you."

I am filled with hope. This is wonderful! I can summon my kendo master! No, the strongest man in the world! Wait, I could summon my father! With his police training and pistol, we are sure to win!

"Just as long as you know their entire name and they live on these islands, they are yours for the summoning." Suturi adds with a mean smile.

My stomach drops again. Oh. I… this stone is useless then. I do not know anyone here outside of Memate. Perhaps Mr. Nakamura? No, I do not think he would like that very much. I also do not believe he would be of much help since he should not have recovered yet.

Who else have I met on this planet? My doctor? He seemed youthful and strong. But I do not remember his first name! The woman I got my first meal from? I do not even know her surname!

This is hopeless.

I stare at the smiling spirits, sadness in my stomach, realizing how bad this will end for me. I look at Memate. She gives me a fierce nod, still holding her rocks. She believes so much in me. Too bad we will die here.

Wait! *Memate believes in me!* I know who to summon!

Excited, I think of the name and throw the stone at the surface of the water. It bounces once and then sinks. Nothing happens. Was this a joke? Did I remember the right name? Will this person even count?

The rocks around the sunken one begin to move.

A third woman in a green bathing suit stands up from the rocks, spitting and wiping water from her face.

"Good morning Suturi! Why did you–" she then notices me.

For a moment, her face is blank, and then I see the anger and surprise growing. Perhaps this was a mistake.

"OSHIRO!" Yoko yells, "WHAT ARE YOU DOING HERE?!"

"I… I need help with–"

"YOU PERVERT! YOU JUST WANT TO SEE ME IN A BATHING SUIT, DON'T YOU?"

I am overcome with surprise.

"W-what?! No! I just need an ally to fight these two spirits and you were the only one I could think of!"

She is still crossing her arms, looking at me with anger. I then remember that she is very weak and I am filled with fear again.

Perhaps Memate really *was* the better option.

"Likely story. Why would I ever help scum like you?" She asks.

Before I can say anything, Memate yells from the shore, "That girl better be there to help you Oshiro, or I'll throw rocks at her too!"

Yoko looks shocked, then her eyes get even angrier for a moment before she turns to Memate. When she starts talking, she sounds very sweet and nice, like she was when we first met.

"No worries, miss. I'll make sure he is just fine! Why don't you take a seat on that stump and rest for a bit?"

Memate gives me a look to see if I agree. I nod, so she thanks Yoko and walks back to her stump. Yoko bows to Memate with a kind smile, then turns to me and goes back to frowning.

"Are you sure this is a fight, or are we all just going to stand here and let Oshiro ogle us?" Yoko asks.

"Good point." Suturi says.

She begins floating towards me, and I back away, raising my sword to fight. There are openings everywhere. She has no armor and no weapons. She may have magical water, but if I can strike fast enough, I may be able to end this first.

There is movement in the corner of my vision, but before I can act, a pair of brown arms wrap across my chest. Seina! She pulls hard, squeezing my arms and ribs. She is squeezing me so tight that I cannot move. I cannot even grunt in pain.

Suturi brings her arm up, then the water underneath me begins shooting up like a geyser. Hard, very fast water rushes against the front of my body. My eyes, ears, and nose are all filled with ice water. I cannot breathe! I cannot move!

Everything is burning and pressing and rushing. Seina then lets go and I try to take a gulp of air, but the water is still in my face. Some of the water goes in instead, and I am filled with pain. I fall over onto my hands and knees, numb, coughing and vomiting water.

To my right, Yoko is trying to pull Seina back in a head lock, but Seina overpowers her with ease. She reaches around and pulls the arm of the other spirit away. Then, she throws her by the arm onto some of the rocks further away.

Yoko recovers well, but then the hands of Seina catch on fire and Yoko begins to back away. I can see the worry in her eyes. I will myself to stand, but I still feel weak and lightheaded. The two of them are a little too far away for me to do a surprise attack.

I go to yell for attention from Seina, but instead, water and burning coughs come up from my lungs. It hurts so much that I fall over again. I cannot do this! A pair of soft hands push on my back, but not very hard. Is that… Suturi? Is she trying to drown me? If so, why is she so gentle?

I push back, but it is much harder than I thought. It is like her arms are steel, and the cold water around my legs is sucking me down towards the rocks. The surface of the water gets closer. I need more strength!

Remembering the Blessing of Yoko, I hold my sword in both hands and grip hard. Even though there is water on it, the blue flames still rush up. A moment later, I am filled with power.

I move a leg until my foot is secure, then push up against Suturi. Her strength challenges me for a moment, then gives away. I shrug her off of me and rush towards Seina, who is throwing streams of fire at Yoko.

The spirit hears me running in the water, so she turns to me and pulls both arms back. At first, I am afraid, but then I remember that I am fireproof. Wait, *she* gave me that power! It looks as though she has forgotten!

She pushes, and a huge cloud of fire rushes to kill me. It looks very scary, but I know I will be fine, so I hold my sword in the thrusting manner and scream forward.

The fire hits me, covering me in hot air, but nothing else happens. After her attack ends, I am still running, still fine, with flames flapping on my trunks. Seina looks very surprised, and I almost want to laugh.

"THRU–" but before I can finish my battle cry, the rocks become very slippery and I fall over.

There is a loud hiss as I am smacked with cold and my flaming trunks are put out. I am more surprised than in pain. Why did that happen? Over the sounds of the river, I hear Suturi and Seina laughing. Embarrassed, I roll over and try to get up, but then Seina pins my back onto the smooth rocks with her foot. That one hurt.

Suturi hovers into my vision and then the two spirits smile down at me. I try looking for an opening to strike, but this is not a very good place to attack from. Then, a foot hits Seina in the side of her head. Though it bounces off as if it were made of paper, Seina stumbles to the side anyway, then Yoko takes her place.

"Get up, idiot!" She yells before turning to fight more.

I do as she says. I am surprised to see that Suturi just watches me. Once I am on my feet again, I grip Amanokaze with two hands and start to back away. Suturi hovers towards me, slow and smiling, with her arms still lowered.

"You know, the further you are from me, the more of an advantage *I* have, right?" Suturi asks.

I think about her words. For a moment, I think she is trying to trick me, but then I realize that she is right. She can control the water from anywhere, but my sword has a smaller range. I stop backing up at once and begin coming towards her. She stops hovering after me and… lets me?

What is she doing? Why has she not attacked me?! I cannot tell if this is a trick or a test of sorts… her calmness is scaring me! Perhaps she thinks I am too slow to hit her. If this is the case, then let me prove her wrong!

I recover my kendo stance and walk closer. She does not move. I want to rush her, but I have a feeling she would be able to react quicker. I pretend to still be confused, then, with all the speed I have, I take a silent downward strike for her head.

She just turns her body and I miss. How is she so graceful?! I have no defense! I am quick to raise the sword again and bring it down at an angle, this time with a kakegoe scream. She watches the blade go up, then ducks in a very smooth way. I miss again.

She is still hovering right in front of me! I raise Amanokaze in defense. A splash of water knocks it to the side. Before I can raise my sword again, another cold splash hits me in my face, and then a kick hits me in the stomach.

I stumble back, wiping my face and trying to get my stance back. My knees feel weak from that kick. As soon as I can see again, both hands grip my sword and I go for a sideways strike. She is just out of range. I have no defense again. Afraid, I take another quick swing, shouting a weak kakegoe, but she has not moved from before, so I miss again.

“Come on, handsome! Don’t be shy, hit me!” She taunts, and another fast kick hits the side of my head.

As I turn to raise my guard again, a third graceful kick hits me hard in the nose. Water begins to run down my lip from it. I can taste metal. This is not water; it is blood.

I lunge and strike at an angle, but I can feel that I was too slow, and she moves out of range with ease. How am I supposed to hit her? She dodges everything I throw! This is impossible!

Hopeless, I start to circle her, looking for an opening. She just hovers there, turning so she is always facing me. The view shifts behind her. First it is Memate asleep by her stump, then it is the river and the town downstream, then it is Yoko and Seina wrestling with the sun shining above them.

The sun! I can entrance her! I tilt and angle my sword until I can find the reflection in the water, then I move it until it is in her eyes. Seina seems to notice the flash of light in the background. Suturi squints and goes to block her eyes, but then stops.

"No Suturi!" Seina yells, "Cover your eyes!"

The water spirit looks away and raises her arm. No! That was my only hope! Wait… she is unprepared! Wordless, I lunge forward and strike. She hears the water splashing under my feet and leans back. I would have hit her if I were a second faster! Instead, I cut one of the straps on her bathing suit.

For a moment, neither of us understand what this means, but when I start to see the cloth fall down, I look away. I am filled with embarrassment.

"Lord Suturi! I am deeply –" before I can say sorry, the spirit lets out a surprised gasp.

"Oshiro! That was a wonderful display of control!" She says.

I go to look at her, confused, but the hanging strap makes me embarrassed again, so I look off to the sky behind her. For a second, I am about to ask for clarity, but then I get the feeling that I should play along.

"You think so?"

"Yes! If you leaned forward a little more or angled the blade like I'm sure you wanted to, you could have taken me out right then and there. But you chose not to hit me, missing by such an impressively small window, too!"

"R-right. Yes, thank you." I nod.

"My, my," she continues, her voice a little lower, "You're a very good boy. It's only natural that I give you a reward."

I swallow, uncomfortable.

"How about we… skip the fight and get right to it, then?"

"Okay."

CHAPTER 8

GOODBYE

~ BLESSING ~

"L**ooks like he's more skilled than we thought.**" Suturi says to the other spirits.

Everyone is in their normal clothes now. One of the other spirits says something, maybe Seina, but I am not listening. That kick to the stomach, the time when I was squeezed, my bleeding nose, the water in my lungs. Everything hurts! Now that the rush of battle is gone, I realize just how weak and in pain I am.

"Hey stupid, you aren't going to pass out, are you?" Yoko asks.

"No, I should be okay," I reply, "that was just a very painful fight. I will need some time to recover."

Suturi giggles, "How about this: I give you a blessing and then you take a swim in the river with us? The water is magical; I promise you'll feel much better once you're done."

I just want the pain to stop, so I nod.

"Great! You might want to tell your grandma to leave, though. This next blessing I'm going to give you… let's just say she's definitely not going to want to see it." Suturi says.

My pain is blocked by nervousness for a moment.

Obeying Suturi, I walk through the water to the shore. Memate is still sleeping. Rocks are spilled all around her. As I approach, I begin to worry. Why did she fall asleep? She *is* just sleeping, yes?

Now scared, I trudge faster through the water. When I get to the shore my clothes come back, but I am too worried to care. I run up, kneel down, and shake Memate. Nothing. What? No!

"Memate!" I shout, shaking her arm harder.

She jumps, "Huh? Did we die?"

I laugh with relief, "Thankfully not!"

"But how?" she asks, confused, "I saw you get swallowed in a big cloud of fire… and then I fainted. And old ladies fainting usually doesn't end well."

I smile at her, "Well, it looks like we both have a happy ending! I was made fireproof by Lord Seina in a former battle, and you are stronger than you think!"

She smiles back at me, "That's very sweet of you. Now, could you please help me up?"

I am gentle as I pick up the old woman, and she gives me a hug. Then, she sits down on the stump and starts to put on her shoes.

"So, that's the last one, right?" She asks with a big grin, "I'll make a huge batch of dumplings tonight to celebrate!"

"Um, Memate, there are actually four more spirits left." I say.

She waves a hand, "Well, yes, but obviously we aren't going to fight those!"

I do not say anything. I realize all at once what must be done.

Memate looks up at me, laughing, "Oh surely you aren't thinking of continuing on, right?"

I nod.

She stops smiling, "Oshiro… you know that no one gets past the fourth spirit, right?"

I nod.

"Why are you continuing on then? You've already got your blessings…" She asks.

"It is the only way I can return to my home." I say.

We are both quiet. Although I never told her about Earth, I know she knows about the wish reward at the end of the journey.

"So this is it? You don't want to spend one more night together?" She asks, and I can hear in her voice that she may cry.

"I do… but I cannot." I lie.

I know that if I spent another night with her, neither of us would want me to leave tomorrow.

She nods and looks at her shoes, "I understand. Well Oshiro, it was fun spending time with you. Just know that, wherever you go, I'm rooting for you. It'll be… different without you around."

I bow low, then reach into my pockets to offer a final gift. All that I have are folded hospital papers, my wallet, and the coin of Mr. Nakamura. Right, Mr. Nakamura! Memate finishes putting on her shoes, then stands and bows back to me.

"Memate, please do not be sad. I have a friend down at the hospital, and he will gladly spend time with you."

She nods, still sad, "Okay. What is his name?"

"Nakamura Ryusei."

"I will make sure to tell him all about our adventures."

I feel tears of my own coming. We trade one final bow, and then she shuffles off towards her car. I watch her get in and drive away. Her car shrinks, going further and further, until it disappears into the town.

Saddened, I return to the spirits.

"That seemed a lot more emotional than I thought it would be." Suturi says, "What did you two talk about?"

"Nothing." I lie. I do not want to think about it.

The three spirits look at one another, then Suturi starts talking again, "Well, okay. Let's give you your blessing."

The three of them walk out to the deeper part of the river, and I follow. My clothes are gone and I am in swim trunks again, so I do not mind the cool water. My body is still sore and tired, and now my heart is, too. Once we all get to where only our necks are out of the water, Suturi turns to me. The water is no longer cold but feels nice.

"Now, this is going to be very unpleasant if you don't follow my instructions, okay?"

"Wait," I say as I wade in the water, "it seems like Amanokaze went away with my clothes. May I get it back?"

"No, the little spell I put on you switches everything for right now. Anyway, listen close. Hold your breath until my hands are on your chest, then breathe only through your mouth, okay?"

I nod, unsure, then think of a question, "When do I start holding my breath?"

Suturi looks at Seina and Yoko, frowns, and then nods to Seina. Then, the arms of Seina wrap around mine in a tight hug. Before I can ask what is happening, I feel her skin… turn to stone! We dip under the water and sink fast.

The sun is covered with a layer of water and starts to shine less and less. I have to squint as blue comes in from everywhere. I want to scream and thrash! What is Seina doing? She is going to drown me!

I notice two figures swimming down after us. One swims for real, Yoko, and the other glides through the water like an eel, Suturi. Seina and I touch the river bottom, and my lungs are starting to burn. I did not take a deep breath before this. I cannot hold this for much longer.

Suturi slows in front of me, then puts both her hands on my chest, right above the arms of Seina. I squint at her, and she has her eyes closed. I am about to die! What is she doing?! Yoko swims down beside her and starts pointing to her mouth. Is she going to give me air?

I look at her, but she just keeps pointing to her mouth. Everything is fuzzy. My lungs are hot and empty. I have maybe one more second until I breathe in a bunch of water. Why are they killing me now? Did I not win? Was their kindness false? I cannot believe this is how I die, not to a fight but to a trick. All alone. Drowned by three spirits in the middle of an alien river.

I gasp, trying to ready myself for the burning water to stuff my lungs and kill me, but my bracing does not work. Because no water enters my lungs. It rushes into my mouth and then stops at the top of my throat.

The only way I can explain this feeling is like having broth and small noodles in one of those pots with the holes in the bottom, and having the noodles blocked while the broth runs free. For me, the water is like the noodles and the air is like the broth. It is a squeezed, tickling feeling. I feel very strange.

I breathe out in a cloud of bubbles, and when I breathe in again, the water stops at the top of my throat and splits into air. Yoko nods and swims back up to the surface. Suturi opens her eyes and smiles at me.

We look at one another as I continue to breathe this air-water. It is so weird! It is so impossible! This is amazing! I laugh, Suturi laughs, and then Seina turns back to normal. The three of us swim back to the surface to meet Yoko.

"Why did you wait for so long, stupid?!" Yoko yells, "You had me worried! I thought you were going to die the way you were looking!"

"I thought I was going to die too, that is why I held my breath!"

After a moment of thought, I add, "You were worried? That is very sweet of you, Yoko."

Her face turns red and she splashes me with water.

“Shut up! I was just worried that Suturi might ruin her–”

But I cannot hold it any longer. I am so happy to be alive, so happy to have this new ability, and the bad lying from Yoko is so funny that I end up splashing her back before she can finish her sentence.

She tries to turn away but she is too slow and gets a face full of water. Her face goes from shock to anger, but then Seina splashes her… and me! I splash Seina back, and all four of us begin laughing and splashing one another.

****

Everyone is breathing hard with smiles still on their faces. Splashing takes a lot of energy! As I breathe, I notice that my lungs feel better. My stomach does not hurt any longer, and I wipe my nose to see there is no blood. I guess this water *is* magic!

“Feel any better?” Suturi asks, and I nod.

“Good,” she adds, “so what’s next?”

My smile goes away as I remember Memate leaving and the rest of my journey.

“I feel very refreshed, like I just had a good night of sleep, so I want to go and face the next spirit.”

“Idiot! You make it this far and you decide to kill yourself?!” Yoko yells.

“I have no other choice. I must complete this journey so I can return home." I say.

"Why do you want to go back?! Why can't you just stay here? I can let you stay in a room in my inn if you aren't going to live with that old lady anymore!"

I smile at the fact that my options for housing are growing.

"Thank you, Yoko, but no. It is my duty to make it back to my family. I have started this journey with that goal, and I will end it the same way." I say.

"You're so stupid!" Yoko says, then she turns into a bunch of flower pedals that float away in the wind.

The three of us left are silent for a moment, and then Seina speaks, "Are you sure you are ready? Maybe you should take the week for training."

I consider her words, then say, "That is a good idea, but to be honest, I am unsure that I can bring myself to do this fight if I do not do it now."

Seina nods, "That might be for the best. Think about it: you've had the easy way on all of your fights. Against me, you had Nakamura. Against Yoko, she surrendered. Against Suturi, you impressed her into forfeiting. But no one is going to hold your hand in this next fight."

After that, she turns into a stack of black rocks that splash down into the river. I look at Suturi. I feel so unsure that I laugh.

"Are you going to try and scare me too?" I ask.

Suturi smiles and shakes her head, "I won't. As with everyone, I think you can be the first to beat her. If you made it this far, you can win."

I return the smile, but I do not feel happy. I feel scared.

"While you are in the river, I'll be with you. But I can only guide you to the swamp and, if you make it out, I can guide you to the fifth spirit. As long as you're in the water, you'll have your trunks, but when you get out, you'll be dry and in your normal clothes. Are you ready?"

I nod even though I no longer feel ready. The advice from Seina has cut deep. The offer from Yoko seems very good. Perhaps I am being foolish. Perhaps returning home will lead me into death. Perhaps staying here is what I am really supposed to do.

Suturi ducks below the surface of the river and I follow her.

The cool water stops flowing. Then, the current pushes us forward, very hard. We are flowing upstream! Shadows of trees flicker overhead. Suturi floats nearby, looking at me as if trying to solve a puzzle.

She starts to ask me questions about my powers and abilities. I tell her about kendo, the entrancing sun beam, my fireproof ability, the Blessing of Yoko, and of course she knows I can now breathe water. She is silent, then begins to ask me what I would do in different moments.

We talk about plans for an hour, and then at once, the water gets dark and cold. Suturi stops in the middle of her sentence.

"This is as far as I can take you. Remember your plans, your powers, and your goals. I want to see you on the other side of this swamp." She says.

I start to get afraid. What was she going to say before she stopped? Does she really have to leave right now?

She becomes a cloud of bubbles, and then a moment later, the current stops pushing me forward. Now the water is still. Even though it should still be the afternoon, the water is almost grey. Dark shadows float near where the shore should be. There are only small beams of sunlight every now and then.

Afraid and still only in my trunks, I take a deep, cold breath, then swim forward.

CHAPTER 9

BLACK BUNRAKU

~ DEATH SPIRIT ~

The pointy object I just bumped into is a human skeleton. Shocked and disgusted, I swim back, noticing all the other skeletons floating around it. Some are human, some are animals. Some still have skin hanging on them; it looks green and old!

I rise fast to the surface and spit out all the water. What is going on here?! Why are there so many skeletons? I kick my feet to stay up and wipe water from my eyes. When I can see better, I shiver. It is not from the cold water.

Black trees twist up above, blocking the sky. Mud and tree roots make the ground. There are skeletons everywhere. Some hang in the trees. Some float in the water. Some look like they have been swallowed by the mud halfway. All of them have different amounts of skin and clothes still on them.

All I can do is swim in one spot and panic. My natural feeling says that an animal did this, but I know that is not true. Everything here is dead. The trees lean above me with brown leaves, even though it is summer. Animal bones of all kinds are scattered on the shore. Despite all of this, there is no smell. This must be the work of the spirit.

I swim over to a part of shore that has a small amount of bones. As soon as all of me is out of the water, I am dry and all my clothes are back. I tighten my kabuto helmet and unsheathe Amanokaze.

I look around again. The big grey lake I was in is one of many. They are everywhere, circled by dead trees, mud, and bones. There are much less bones in every direction, so where I am now must be close to the shrine.

I walk forward. The only sound is my breath and my boots in the mud. No birds, no bugs. No running water, no wind in the trees. Other than my squishing footsteps, it is silent.

A very loud beep comes from right below me. I jump back and swing Amanokaze downward, but nothing is there. For a few seconds I look around the swamp, trying to see what that noise was, but then I realize it was my camera.

I look down at it. The red light no longer blinks, and there are no numbers in the small screen next to the lens. It is dead. The video feed to Earth is over. Now I am really alone.

I look up from my camera and see it. The shrine is in the distance, standing in a clearing of mud and roots. The skeletons around it have more and more skin until they can be called bodies. But the clearing around the shrine has nothing in it but a white lump. I ready myself and walk forward.

The silence is scaring me. It feels as though something will attack me at any second. Yet I know, in my heart, that I am the only living creature around. As I get closer, I have a dark thought. I hope one of these people is still alive, so that maybe I can have someone to help or talk to.

All of the faces are filled with deep holes. They are very dead.

I approach the shrine and read it.

神四つ目

舞夜未亡人

影 - 米 - 槍

("Fourth Spirit" : its name : "shadows – rice – spear")

Even though the white lump is right in front of me, I still cannot tell what it is. Perhaps a silk-like cloth? It is in a lump covering something. It is dirty and yellowish but still white, while everything else is brown and gray and black.

I go to kick it but stop myself. At first, I thought it would be best to see what this is before I tap the shrine and bow next to it. But I will instead tap the shrine and bow as far away as I can.

I reach out with Amanokaze, tap the red roof three times, and then back up until I am at a nice striking range of the white cloth pile. Then I sink my knees into the mud and hold my sword out. Nothing happens, and the silence feels like it is pressing on me.

The white cloth pile starts to move. Not towards me, but towards the shrine. It does not look like it is moving on its own, but rather, it looks like someone is pulling it. My heart is pounding and my knees shake as I stand. There was no lightning… that must mean the spirit is already here, like with Yoko. Is this it?!

The cloth pile gets to the shrine, then gets pulled up into the air. It hangs there for a bit, and then something slips out of the cloth. Pitch black hair. The other side of the cloth gets pulled up, and I start to realize what this is. The hair hangs down between the two pulled ends of cloth; this is a girl.

The hanging hair clumps together like someone gathered it, and then it is thrown back to show… ! The face of a little girl stares into mine. Her face is as white as paper with purple veins underneath. One of her eyes is filled with black fuzz. The other eye is still and shines like glass.

It looks like her lips are pried open, then instead of saying something, everything is pulled out of the air and into her. It was silent, but now there is true silence. It is as if the very planet I am standing on has died. The air has lost its lightness.

Bright spots begin to appear in my vision as the air presses in on me. Everything gets darker, but as it does, I start to see what is behind her: a bunch of arms holding spears made of smoke, raised and pointed at me.

The girl in the dress is pulled behind the shrine. Her dress covers it for a moment, but when it is out of the way, there is a bowl of rice sitting on top of the shrine. A pair of chopsticks stick straight up from the bowl.

Eat it. Eat the rice. I know what will happen when I do. Eating the rice is accepting my death. The spears will kill me. But the air beckons. The girl beckons. The arms beckon. I must eat. I feel so weak, and it would be rude and foolish not to.

I take a step forward, then stop. Something is in my hand. My sword. It is so heavy! How have I been carrying this when I feel so weak? I look at it. My sword. My family sword. I feel weak holding it. I was talking to someone earlier today and we said I should do something if I feel weak holding this sword.

That is not important. I must eat the rice. I must accept my death. It is my destiny. I take another step forward. It is so hard to see. The air is so heavy. Why have I not dropped this sword yet? What was the thing that person said I should do?

Let go of the sword. Reach out and grab the bowl. The rice is so close. It smells so good. Black fills my vision everywhere outside of the bowl. My head is stuck bending, looking at my meal. I can feel my grip loosen on the sword.

Join the rest of the world. Every living thing on this planet will face the same fate. This sleep… this rice. I am too tired and weak to resist. I let the sword fall from my hands and into nothing. I reach out from the darkness and take the bowl.

The side feels warm in my h– ouch! With a jump, I let go of the bowl. It falls into the mud and the rice turns into black fuzz. The air becomes air again, and in one big gasp, the shadows leave my vision.

That bowl was hotter than any dish I have ever touched! I look down at my hand to see that it is pink. It burned me! Wait, what am I doing? The spirit is right in front of me! I back away as the girl stares forward, hanging in the air. The way she pauses makes me think she is confused.

I look around for my sword but I cannot find it. It must have sunk into the mud. Perhaps I can use a branch to fight? No time! Even though I cannot see the many arms, I see the smoke spears rising, getting ready to launch. In defense, I lower my head to block with my kabuto.

The spears shoot at me a second later. Some of them hit my helmet, some of them miss, and two of them hit me. Pain screams from my arm and hip, where the spears struck. I can feel the energy pouring out of me.

The other spears begin to float again, preparing for another attack. If I do not do something, I will die. I stumble towards the girl as she hangs in the air, staring at me. My stomach and groin hurt every time I take a step. Stupid spear!

With a scream, I pull the spear out of my hip. Blood and much pain comes with it. The smoke feels solid and cold in my hands. I swing the spear like a long sword and almost faint with pain. She is not fast enough to dodge, so I cut through her stomach.

Black blood pours out onto her dress but she keeps hovering. Her lips are drawn back in a smile, and she begins to dance like a puppet in the air. I stare at her, stunned that she does not seem hurt, and then my back and legs are filled with burning pain.

All of the spears have struck me deep. I stumble forward and plant my weapon in the mud, quick to bear my weight on it so that I do not fall all the way. This hurts so much that I am almost unable to move. I cannot even scream.

I am going to die here. I have been damaged too much to survive. There is no one around to help. But I will die with honor. Even though it hurts more than anything has ever hurt before, I remove the spear from the ground and swing it again. I am too dizzy to aim but the spearhead hits her neck.

In a splash of black, her head falls back and snaps off, splatting in the mud. I feel a rush of happiness, but it turns into confusion as her body continues to float and dance. A giggle comes from her neck. The swamp dims and swirls around me. The pain is starting to fade. I… I must keep… fighting.

Perhaps I lifted my spear, I am not sure. The cool, smoky weapon is in front of me, pointing at the puppet girl, but I have no strength to swing. Knowing that I have lost, I stumble toward her… for one last attack.

My legs seem to fade away, and I fall forward. The spear slips into her bleeding stomach with my weight, pushing through the rot and into the dark air behind her. There is a second thing it hits, more solid, and a spray of sparks lights up the swamp.

Then I am lying in the mud, spears rising from my back.

Chapter 10

Odd Spirit

~ Blessing ~

I **pull my pillow closer, and it... purrs at me?** My eyes open fast. I am in a field with many fruit trees. The sky is cool and dark, as if the sun is about to rise. The grass under me feels nice and warm. And my pillow has pink hair with cat ears sticking up from it?

This is not a pillow; this is a human girl with a cat ear hair band. As soon as I realize this, I get up and back away. I do not know who she is. Confused and uncomfortable, I take a look around this field I am in.

My sword is in the grass next to the shrine. I walk over, pick it up, and sheathe it. The shrine is no longer just red and black; now it has many colors painted on it as if a child had done so. The field goes out in every direction for a few meters, and then it becomes swamp again.

I am standing in a circle of life? What is happening? All I remember is the darkness and the spears in my back, and then I thought I was winning… but then I died, right? This place does not look like the afterlife nor normal life.

The grass behind me rustles. I turn and see that the little girl wearing the cat ears has stood. She rubs her eyes and grabs in the air at me, as if asking me to come back to sleep.

"Who are you?" I ask, putting my hand on my sheath.

My voice seems to scare her awake. She jumps back, and the ears on her head straighten. What?

"Oh! I'm so sowwy, I shouwd pwobabwy intwoduce mysewf." She says.

"Yes you should, and please talk normally so I can understand you. How old are you? Where are your parents?" I ask, taking my hand off of Amanokaze.

"I'm as old as this planet, silly, and I guess my only parent is the Grand Goddess!"

I laugh, but she pouts as if she wants me to be serious.

"I am Hapa'ineko, Spirit of the Wildlife and number three-and-a-half in the Trial of Shenthingy! But since you beat Danyoruojin, you can call me Hapa!"

Another spirit! I pull out Amanokaze as fast as I can and leap back, ready to attack.

"Gah! Please don't hurt me!" She says, backing away with her arms raised, "I'm not going to fight you! I want to help!"

I look at her, nervous; she seems too nice. I notice a pink snake standing straight up in the air behind her. Hapa is wearing a yellow kimono, and it looks like there is a little hole in it where the snake comes out.

"There is a snake coming out of you?" I ask.

"No silly! Have you never seen a tail before?" She taunts.

"Never on a… where am I?!" I repeat, gripping my sword hard enough for the blue fire to come up from it.

She jumps back again and covers her head with her arms.

"Eek! Please don't hurt me Mr. Alien you're in Kaeyo Swamp just like before and after you beat Danyo it looked like you were going to die and I was confused so I healed you and then you just looked so cuddly so I took a nap next to you I'm so sorry!"

Hapa is shivering with fear and it looks like she might start crying. I cannot bring myself to strike her in this state. I sheathe Amanokaze and get on one knee.

"Hey, it is alright. I have put the sword away." I say.

She sniffs and squints her eyes open, "Really?"

"Really."

She lowers her arms all the way and smiles, "Thanks for not hurting me, Mr. Alien! If you attacked me, I don't know what I would do!"

"How do you know I am an alien?" I ask her.

"Well, the bowl hurt you, and it's not supposed to do that, so you're obviously not from this planet." Hapa says.

"I am sorry, but I do not understand. Can you tell me more?"

She thinks for a moment, then smiles like a prankster, "Only if you do two things first!"

"What are they?"

"Promise you won't hurt me and… give me a hug!"

I frown. The first is easy but the second is odd.

"Um, do I really have to hug–"

"Yep! Either those two things or no deal!"

I sigh, walk over to her, then I get on my knee again.

"I will not hurt you." I tell her.

I open my arms and lean in. She jumps on me with a hug. She then lets me go and I stand.

"Thanks so much! Follow me and I'll tell you everything you want!" Hapa says.

She then turns and begins to walk deeper in the swamp. The circle of green grass and living trees around us… follows her? She stays in the exact center. The area in front of the circle becomes alive again as she approaches, and the area behind it returns to dead swamp.

I quicken my pace to catch up and stay in the middle.

"So the rice you saw was Danyo's Sleepy Trap. She says that nobody can turn away from the trap. The bowl is made from the planet's core, so if you are from here, it feels really really good to hold. And then once the people eat the rice, they start screaming and crying because they're so happy that they can finally see Danyo! Some people start running around too!"

I shiver. I know she does not know the truth.

"And then she pokes them with her Sleepy Sticks to calm them down, though I guess since you're an alien it hurts you for some reason. But most of the time they just go to sleep and do their disappearing trick."

"Disappearing trick?" I ask, feeling even more scared.

"Yeah! I guess people from where you are don't have it, but people here do! Whenever someone falls asleep for a really long time, they start to disappear and reappear back in their beds at home. It looks kind of funny at times, but it's really cool!"

Oh my goodness. I try to swallow my fear, walking a bit closer to the spirit. I want to be as far away from the swamp as possible. I look around outside of this field. The grey and black trees look darker since the sun has not risen.

"Uwu!" Hapa shouts, and before I can turn to her, she has jumped on my back.

I panic at first, thinking this is some sort of attack, but then she laughs, "Now you have to give me a shoulder ride!"

She continues to climb up my back, pulling at my clothes and helmet, until her legs are around my neck.

"Come on! Carry me!" She says.

"What are you–"

"Hurry up, slowpoke! Don't you want to get your blessing? Onward!"

I walk forward and the circle of life follows me. I am silent for a moment, feeling uncomfortable. Hapa is happy and purring, curled on my helmet. Her tail brushes my back, and I can feel fur in some places, so there must be holes in my shirt.

She starts talking again, "So Danyo really likes putting on puppet shows for me. Sometimes they're tea parties, sometimes they're plays, and a lot of the time they're really funny! She uses the sleeping humans as puppets, and she's really good at making them do funny stuff!"

I try not to shiver again. This Danyo spirit seems scarier by the moment. Perhaps I will use this time to get more information.

"So… how do you know Lord Danyo?" I ask.

"We're friends! Way way back when we first started doing this Shengymabob with the humans, we played a game to get to pick who would fight the humans and who would give them the blessings. The fighter would have the whole forest to themselves to decorate and impress the humans. Can you guess who won the fighter spot?"

"Lord Danyo." I say.

"Right. But she cheated! So we decided that we would both be the fighter and the blessing person."

"So the two of you fought me at the same time? How?" I ask.

"Well, Danyo is really shy, but if you got to see her normally, she's sooo tall and pretty with long hair and pointy teeth and lots and lots of really long arms. That's how she does the puppets!"

I shiver.

"She uses her arms to hold all her Sleepy Sticks… oh, and me as the distraction."

I think about what Hapa said, then ask, "You? Does that mean… you were the girl in white?"

"Yep! That was my scary face! Danyo says it's really good, what do you think?"

"You did well."

Hapa gives a happy purr. I think more about what she said, then realize something. Hapa said she both fights and gives the blessing *with* Danyo, so…

"Where is Lord Danyo now?" I ask, and I can feel my heart speed up.

"She's my kimono! She's also the circle around us that keeps all her decorations out and my decorations in!"

I am quiet. This is all too scary. I walk faster, then realize that I am not sure where I am going.

"Where are we going?" I ask.

"Straight ahead. After the curtain of flowers is my favorite decoration! I think you'll love it!"

The field inside the circle is just grass. Ahead of us are more trees and mud, but all the water is gone. The only curtain I see is a wall of dried, sharp branches. It is hard to see them in the dark of the morning.

As the branches touch the edge of the circle, they turn green, and colorful flowers begin to grow on them. When I get up close, I can smell them. They smell nice! Hapa reaches out and pulls a part of the curtain back for me to walk through.

I duck us under and see the edge of the swamp. The trees and mud circle around one big, grey lake, and then the water leads to the river again. Empty fields go out to distant mountains. The sky above the mountains is turning light purple.

There is a big tree over to the right. It is a great brown skeleton with black roots sticking out of the mud.

"Walk over to that tree and then you'll get your blessing."

I do as Hapa says. When the circle first touches the tree, nothing happens. I keep walking closer until the entire tree is in the circle, then the magic starts. All of the wood on the tree turns white. The branches fill with bright fruit and green leaves. Birds and insects that look like colored origami fly around its branches and sing to the sky.

I am surprised to see life for once! Now that we are where she wanted, I put her down. It seems like she does not want to get off. She walks in front of me and bows with an odd amount of formality.

"Okay Mr. Alien, please kneel." She says.

I do so, trying not to smile. Although Mr. Alien is not my name, I will not correct her. We both look at each other, waiting for the other to do something.

"Oh, right. Put out your hands and close your eyes." She says.

I do that as well. Then, I feel small hands wrap around mine. For a moment, there is just the sounds of birds chirping.

"There! All done!" She says with a big smile.

"Thank you," I say, standing, "What did I get?"

Hapa shrugs, "I don't know. But I do know you're going to love my blessing!"

I look at her, confused, "Did you not just give me your blessing?"

"No, that was part of Danyo's blessing. Surprise, we swapped! Now she's going to give you mine! Well, *ours*; she helped me a lot with this one… anyway, good luck Mr. Alien, and I hope you like it!"

Before I can stop her, she becomes a cute, pink cat that runs off into the swamp. The kimono Hapa wore falls to the ground. It is soon silent again. I stare at the yellow silk, afraid. The birds and insects on the tree have flown off after Hapa.

The circle of life around me starts to get smaller. The branches on the tree darken and grow weak. I back away and end up stepping in mud. I put my hand on my sheath as the circle closes in on the kimono.

Then, the kimono becomes a large box wrapped in a black blanket. A white note is on top. I do not approach it. Instead, I look around the swamp. Nothing but black wood and heavy mud. I look back, and the box has moved closer to me. For a moment, I stare, trying to figure out if it is my mind playing tricks or not. I look away and look back.

It is even closer.

I turn and run as fast as I can to the river. Whispers float in the wind. A coldness and silence unlike anything I have felt comes closer from behind me. I cannot look back! Mud flies past me as I run around the shore of the lake.

The river is right in front of me! I look back just before I jump in the river. The box is right behind me and it looks like there is the face of a woman in one of the trees. I trip over something and slam into the river.

Bubbles and water rise all around me. My clothes and glasses melt away, leaving only white swim trunks. I look up at the surface. It is very dark, but I can see a large, darker shadow looking down at me. I turn and try to swim away, but then I run into a body. Arms go to wrap around me!

I scream and flail, trying to see through the water and the dark with no glasses. Amanokaze and all my armor is gone. I cannot hold what little breath I have left for much longer.

"Oshiro!" Says a familiar voice, muffled in the water, "Calm down and breathe. It's me, Suturi!"

I am confused for a few more moments until I remember who Suturi is and that I can, in fact, breathe water because of her. Testing, I let water into my mouth. It stops at the top of my throat and turns to air.

"See? Nothing to worry about. Why are you so worked up, anyway? You won, right?"

I look back up at the surface. The large shadow is gone. Or perhaps it is not?

"I… just want to get to the next spirit." I lie.

"Alright then," Suturi says, knowing I am lying, "let's go."

****

Suturi and I sit on the river shore, watching the sunrise with our feet in the water. We just spent the last few hours with the current pushing us upstream. I was surprised to see that we would reach the surface and find desert.

Suturi finishes telling me how what I am doing is historic for perhaps the ninth time, and then she gets quiet. I look at her, and she is looking at me.

"Is everything alright?" I ask.

Her eyes begin to water, then she leans forward and kisses me on the mouth!

"L-Lord Suturi!" I say, feeling my face turn red, "Did you mean to do that?"

"I'm so happy, Daiki," she looks like she is about to cry, "for once in the thousands of years I've been doing this, someone has finally met me on the other side of the swamp. I always used to hope so deeply. But after a while it just turned to empty flirting and encouragement. I just wanted to get a taste of those personalities before they left forever."

Suturi puts a hand on the side of my face.

"But you actually made it. I don't know what Danyo's been doing, but you figured it out. You won. And now your beautiful life doesn't have to end panicking and alone in a dark swamp."

She kisses me on the mouth again! I do not resist out of surprise and curiosity.

"I wish I could stay with you and protect you. I want to see you win, to live, to have many more adventures and enjoy life. I want to stay by your side, but I have to return to my shrine. Another challenger is approaching."

She takes her hand off of my face. She turns and I turn too. The desert reaches out into the dark side of the sky. A small tower sits on the horizon.

"There, Izuchi Desert Tower, is where the next spirit will be. Please stay safe, Daiki. I truly wish you the best."

I prepare for a third kiss, but instead, she gives a short bow before sliding into the river and turning into bubbles.

For a moment I watch the sunrise, stunned that a girl kissed me *and* used my given name, then I take my feet out of the water. At once, my clothes, glasses, kabuto helmet, and sword appear. I get up and brush sand off of my hands, then turn.

A box wrapped in black cloth sits on the ground in front of me.

I look around for anyone, but there is only sand, plants, cliffs, and the tower in the distance. Scared, I walk forward and read the letter on top of the box.

おしろだいきさんへ。

僕に大勝した君におめでとうと言うよ。君の渾身の努力と決心に感動させられたよ。その感動を一番好きな文楽に費やすとするさ。

あなたは今、あなたの影を使って無生物のオブジェクトと対話できることに気付くだろう。お前の通常の強さはお前の影の強さに変換されるのだ。この贈物を賢く使って楽しむが良い。

私も用意したこの食事を楽しんでくれたまえ。それは次の神への道のりは長い、私はお前が空腹になるだろうと思っていた。心配するな、ご飯は本物だ。ハパインコが容器を作った。だから保管しておけ。

お前の時間が終わりに近づくにつれ、お前が決意を示し続けることを私は願っている。それはお前にとって多くの恩恵をもたらすだろう。健闘を祈る。またお前に会うのが待ちきれない…ああ、すぐにな。

舞夜未亡人、シェンシムの試練の四目。

Dear Oshiro Daiki,

Congratulations on your impressive victory over me. Seeing the amount of effort and determination you put into winning has filled me with joy. I only felt it best to return that joy through my favorite hobby, puppetry.

You will find that you can now interact with inanimate objects using your shadow. Your normal strength translates to your shadow's strength. Use this gift wisely and have fun.

Please enjoy this meal I have prepared as well. It is a long walk to the next spirit, so I thought you would get hungry. Do not worry, the rice is real. Hapa'ineko(?) made the containers so please keep them.

As your time draws to a close, I ask that you continue to show determination. It will do a lot for you. Best of luck, and I cannot wait to see you again... very soon.

Your affectionate admirer,

Danyoruojin(?), Spirit of the Dead, Fourth in the Trial of Shenshimu

CHAPTER 11

BLOOD AND LIGHTNING

~ PENULTIMATE SPIRIT ~

I screw the drink container closed, satisfied with my meal. My stomach is full and I am happy. I had to take a break because I was so hungry. A part of me wanted to never open the box, but the long walk and not having eaten since lunch yesterday have changed that.

Danyo packed me a large meal of meat, rice, cold tea, and water. The meats were all cooked and seasoned very well. The rice was sticky and tasty, and the tea and water felt good to drink. I hope Danyo was kind and did not poison this, because if she did, I ate every bit of the poison.

The sun has gotten higher in the sky. The desert is dry and very hot. I have never been in a desert before and I knew they were hot. This, however, I was not expecting. Since I am the only one out here, I take off my kabuto, outer pants, camera, and shirt.

Both my shirt and pants are full of holes in the back from where the spears were. It is odd what I have been through so far. But there is no time to think! I must get to the tower and get out of the sun! I pack my clothes and the colorful containers from Hapa in the large box, then wrap it up again. I put my helmet on my hip, pick up the box, and use the lid as a hat.

****

Lucky for me the red door to the tower is unlocked. I pull it open with ease, step inside, and close it behind me. The cool of the room hits me and I lay face first on the wooden floor, tired and happy that I made it. For a long while I lay there, resting, and then I get up and take off my shoes. I would take off everything if I could!

I unwrap the box and drink the rest of the water and tea, looking around the room while I drink. It looks like an old library, with faded books in shelves on the wall. A big, square staircase is in the middle of the room, leading up to the ceiling way above me. There are small windows in the wall along the staircase.

There is a bed in the corner that I go sit on, and then I see a doorway. It looks like there is a bathroom behind it. I get up and take a closer look. Yes? Yes! A Western toilet, a sink, a mirror, a trash can, soap, and even a paper towel machine? I try the light switch and it works. This is odd!

The water smells and looks safe. For the next few minutes, I wash sand and sweat off of me. In the windows, I can see some clouds rolling in. They will cool off everything even more. After my sink bath, I sit back on the bed and let my feet rest some more.

Once I feel rested, I put on my outer pants, boots, shirt, camera, and helmet again. The camera is still dead and the clothes smell like sweat and feel cold. I do not wish to wear these, but I will need the armor for the battle. I search around the library, but I cannot find the shrine. Perhaps it is at the top of the stairs.

The stairs are longer and more difficult to climb than I had thought they would be. At the top, I see a ladder that leads to a door on the ceiling. The door has a puzzle lock on the handle.

I regain my strength by squeezing Amanokaze, then sheathe my sword, climb the ladder, and look at the puzzle. It looks like it is made of gold and has a few things to twist and push. The puzzle is rather easy to figure out after thinking about it for a moment.

With a click, the door unlocks, and I push it up as I climb the rest of the ladder. Outside, the gentle wind blows. Below, I can see clouds of sand spinning across the ground. Above, grey and white clouds block the sun.

There are four pillars supporting a roof above me, and short railing is the only shield from a long drop to the ground. The shrine sits right in front of me. I climb all the way onto this floor, then close the door and read the shrine.

神五つ目

天風打

風 - 雷 - 速

("Fifth Spirit" : its name : "wind – lightning – speed")

This does not seem like it will be an easy fight. I am the first person to ever do this as well. Nervous, I try the staircase door. It is locked. Afraid, I turn back to the shrine. I am going to have to fight this wind, lightning, and speed spirit on this small floor up in the air.

I have a feeling this is not going to go well at all.

A look down the side of the tower shows me I cannot climb down it. Perhaps this fight will be like all the others, which end with pain and difficulty yet on a light note. But I am alone, and the last time I was alone I only survived by a few seconds and a lot of luck.

When I tap the shrine this time, I am more scared than ever.

I try to use my kendo training to calm me as I kneel and wait. I just need to focus. I have many supernatural powers as is. The kabuto helmet, the reflecting sun trick, fireproof skin, the Blessing of Yoko, breathing water, and controlling shadows.

I cannot see how most of those will be useful here.

Thunder begins to roll. The sky darkens with a nearing storm. The wind, however, is still very gentle and flowing. I am happy for that, as my current height and the seeable weakness of the rails are making me uncomfortable.

There is a flash and a very loud clap of thunder. The wood floor under me shakes. I almost scream with fear. When I can see again, there is a woman about my size staring back at me. She has surprised, black eyes and medium black hair done in a double bun.

At the edges of her gray kimono are clouds and strings of lightning. She is floating in the air without wings. She looks at me as if I were on fire, eyes wide and still. Then, faster than I can see, she flies up very close to me.

The wind from her flying slams into me and I am taken up in the air. Before I can go flying over the rail, I am hit by another burst of wind from behind, sending me stumbling forward. I realize I do not see her in front of me.

I turn around and there she is, looking me up and down with confusion and awe. Unsure, I raise my sword and back away in defense. She does not seem to care, moving it out of the way with her finger and walking much too close for comfort.

I have run out of room to back up, so I raise my hand and turn my face to prevent a kissing mistake. She grabs my hand hard, stares at it with tears in her eyes, and then begins… rubbing it all over her face? I want to pull my hand away as this is very odd, but I feel as though that would be disrespectful.

In a moment, she stops and looks up at me, confused.

"Am I still a giant bird?" She asks, and her voice sounds heavier and more casual than I would have thought, from her face.

"N-no. You are a woman in a kimono?" I tell her.

"So then why are you looking at me like that?" She asks, and she sounds confused.

"Um… because there are a different set of greeting rules that most others follow." I say as nice as I can.

“Really?” she drops my hand, “I’m sorry, this is my first time ever seeing a human before. I didn’t know you all were this… I don’t know. Either way, I’m glad to see you. Um, congratulations on actually surviving this far.”

“Thank you.” I say.

I am waiting for her to look away so I can wipe her tears and spit off of my hand, but she continues to stare at me.

“I’m sorry, what were we doing?” She asks.

“Greeting one another.” I reply, confused that she could forget this so fast.

“Oh, right! I am Tengokazuma, Spirit of the Tempest, the fifth in the Trial of… S-Word…”

“Shenshimu?” I offer.

“Yeah, that’s it! But since you are the first to summon me, you can call me whatever you want. Do… do humans have names?”

“Yes,” I say, trying not to let my confusion show, “and I am Oshiro Daiki.”

“You have two names?” Tengo asks, “Which is your favorite?”

I pause and think. This is not a question I have ever gotten before.

“I am unsure. Oshiro is my family name and Daiki is my given name. It would be best if you called me Oshiro.”

“Oshiro it is then!” Tengo says.

She continues to look at me. I wipe my hand on my pants but try to make it look like I am brushing off dust. Her silent stare is making me uncomfortable.

"So," I start, careful and thinking, "how do I get the blessing?"

Her face looks even more surprised for a moment, as if she had never even thought of that, then she smiles.

"I guess… I guess you have to fight me!"

She continues to smile wider but does not back up. My confusion becomes fear.

"That's right! I've never fought a human before! I've never even been this close to one, especially a not-girl one! Oh, I'm so excited! I hope I get to…"

She then stops and looks away.

"Yes?" I ask, curious but sword still ready.

"To taste your… ah… oh this is embarrassing."

I lower my sword, "T-taste my what?"

"Are you sure you want to know?" Tengo asks, blushing.

"Please tell me!" I say, "This is getting weird!"

Her head is bowed and her hair hangs above her eyes.

"I want to taste your… your… *blood*."

It takes me a moment to understand her.

"What?"

"You heard me. For centuries, the other four have been able to have their fun with you humans. Now, after all this waiting, it's finally my turn."

She raises her head. Her eyes are much too wide and excited.

"I've wanted this for so long, Oshiro. To know the feeling of giving a human the deepest pain and suffering it's ever felt. To listen to the screams. To taste the blood. So many stories, years of fantasies. And now, you're all mine!"

What?! Before I can raise my sword, her hand is around my throat. Her grip is not very strong, but she has my legs against the railing and I cannot reach any pillars, so one push could be the end of my life.

"Okay okay," I say, afraid, "perhaps–"

But she pushes up around my throat and I cannot talk.

"Shhhh. I've already made up my mind!" Her wide eyes stare into mine as she keeps talking, "We're going to have so much fun! And when we're done, I'll drink all your blood until there's none left and you're inside me forever!"

I spin to the side and throw her off me. She stumbles back, and I almost fall off of the tower. I swing my sword but she dodges to the side and blows air at me. Her breath is now speeding wind, and before I can understand what happened, I am thrown off the floor and… land in the air just outside of the railing.

I am… not falling?

I just stay there in that one place. I can feel gravity pulling me but I am not falling? There is no floor under me or strings holding me. I cannot feel how I am staying in the air. I do not dare move as I look at Tengo. My fear has become relief and confusion.

"Don't think I'd kill you like that; the fun is in watching your suffering~! Go on, try flying around a bit. I thought it would be fun to give this power to you for a little while… it'll be like a hunt!"

She said 'hunt' as if it were 'date' or 'sleepover'.

I am still frozen, floating in air, scared that I will fall if I breathe. I do not want to lean forward and grab the rail. I wish I could just fly from here and be on the tower already! Like that, I slide in the air, still in my falling pose. Once I am over the tower platform, I put my feet back down and breathe again.

She watches me, smiling as I catch my breath. What in the world is happening right now? I am unsure of whether to raise Amanokaze or thank Tengo. Before I can choose, hard wind blows in on me from every direction.

I duck my head and raise my arms to block my face, but it is over. When I look back up, Tengo is wearing black hakama trousers with a grey karate gi top.

Her hand becomes a blur, then I am thrown into the air again. I look around, panicking, but then a blast of wind hits me and my face is filled with stinging pain. My glasses fly off and spin down to the now somewhat fuzzy ground. I cannot block before there is another blast and sting, and another, and another. She is so fast that I cannot even see her!

I duck my sore face and take wild swings with Amanokaze. Tengo stops at once, right out of range. With a thought, I slide forward in the air and swing. She dodges, but in a way I have never seen before. Instead of moving out of the way, she stays in the path of the sword but moves to the side as fast as the swing.

I turn to her, then try a diagonal strike in the other direction, this time with a kakegoe scream. She moves to the outside of my sword and follows its path a centimeter behind, all in the moment of one swing. I can do nothing but stare at her, surprised and afraid.

"Wow! Humans are really slow!" She says with a thinking face.

Tengo palm strikes me before I even see her arm move, then slaps me in the face with the back of her hand. I make myself slide back in the air. This is impossible! She is much too fast!

"Aw, Oshiro, are you trying to leave me?" She asks, her eyes widening, "Come back! I haven't gotten a taste yet!"

She raises her arms. The clouds above begin to swirl and wind pulls me hard towards her. I am thinking as hard as I can about sliding backwards, but the wind is so strong that I stay in place. Light starts to pop in her hands. This is a lightning attack!

This is not good. There is no way I can dodge this attack, I cannot fly in and hit her, and my kabuto helmet is only but so large. Perhaps my fireproof skin will be enough! Tengo screams with laughter as the wind pulls harder and more lightning begins to pop and flash. Perhaps my fireproof skin will not be enough.

At once, I get a risky idea. What if I let go of my sword? The wind is pulling so fast that it will stab her before she sees it. Even though it is giving up my weapon, the only other choice is death. I must act fast, for I do not know when the wind will stop.

Afraid, I make myself let go of the sword. It is gone, and a moment later, all the wind and lightning stops. The clouds smooth in the sky. Tengo is floating with her back turned to me, shivering.

Did it work?

She turns around, smiling and holding Amanokaze.

It pops and sparks a little, then stops. Hot, glowing lines of electricity fade on the side of the blade. My heart almost stops in my chest. This is the worst result possible.

"AHAHAHAHA! NOW IT'S BLOOD TIME!!"

She disappears toward me and I only have a single second to lower my head as a block. Everything is noise and light. I feel Amanokaze bounce off of my helmet. Now is my chance! I look up and throw a punch.

It hits her in the face with a good amount of force. I must keep attacking! I come around with another punch, but she is now just out of range. Before I can pull my arm back, she has grabbed it. Then Tengo raises Amanokaze in her other hand. I am fast to stop her hand with my foot.

"OH EHEEHEEHEE! SO MANY CHOICES~! YOUR ARM, YOUR LEG, YOUR BACK, SO MUCH BLOOD! MAYBE I CAN TASTE YOUR TEARS TOO! AND THEN I'LL –"

Enough! I come up with my other foot and kick her in the face. I wish I could grab Amanokaze, but I am not flexible enough. I know what I must do. I swing my foot and kick the sword out of her hand. It falls, very close to cutting me, and then bounces on the ground far below.

The only way to defeat her now is with my hands. I twist the arm she is grabbing and catch her wrist. Then I pull her towards me and put my right arm in front of her neck. This is a terrible hold and her face is almost in my armpit, but I keep pulling her arm anyway. This hold cannot kill. This hold does not even seem to be hurting her very much. But it is all I have.

Perhaps my lock would have worked if we were standing on the ground. But we are in the air. She just flips backwards around my arm and she is behind me in a moment. Before I can try and flip over her arm, she hugs me.

Sharp, buzzing pain shoots through my body. There is a nice sounding chime that comes from my chest, followed by a beep. Was that my camera turning back on?!

“Oh! I didn’t know humans made funny noises when I lightning them. I’ll keep that in mind for later!” She sings the last part.

I want to fight, but it feels like I have been exercising for many hours. My arms and legs burn and feel too heavy to keep using. Tengo slips her arm out of my hand and puts me into her own, better hold.

In a moment, she has my arms pinned, her legs around mine, and still another free hand. With that hand, she pulls my head and helmet to the side. I cannot see what she is doing from this angle.

“Oh yesss…” she whispers, “I can barely see straight I’m so excited. Finally, I get to taste blood! I think I’ll blow your skin off and lick it up that way.”

She takes a deep breath and I brace myself, but then she stops.

“Actually, I don’t think that would be deep enough… maybe I’ll just bite you instead!"

I feel her smile against my neck. At once, I realize I must surrender. She was too fast and too powerful. There is no one for kilometers that can save me. Another challenger is not coming, since one would have to be an alien to defeat Danyo. I must give up now with hopes that I can return next year and try again. Perhaps I will live with Memate or Yoko.

"I…" I swallow the rest of my honor, "I surrender."

The mouth of Tengo is further away, "What? Really?"

"Yes." I say.

The spirit is quiet for a little, then, "Oh, okay. I don't care."

"What?! What do you mean?!" I try to slip free but she is wrapped around me too tight and everything still burns.

She giggles on my neck and says, "I *mean* I'm not letting you go! I've been waiting for this for eons. There is nothing in the universe even the Goddess could offer me to spare you."

My stomach sinks, "No, please! Great Lord Tengo, I-I promise I surrender, I really do! That means you must spare me!"

She is not listening, "Don't worry, Oshiro. I'll try not to make it too deep. I want to keep you alive for at least a week! We'll have so much fun together. But now I've waited long enough for this blood. Just let me get a little taste…"

"No, wait! Lord Tengo, I– AAAAAH!" I cannot help but scream as she bites down on my neck.

It hurts so much! I want to fight but she is much too strong now.

She stops biting, surprised by something, and then bites harder. The pain is bursting. She is really going to make me bleed! I can feel her jaw closing, her teeth pushing deeper and deeper, trying to cut into my skin.

Then, she is gone and I am free.

I turn my sore body and look around for her. She is back in front of the shrine at the top of the tower. Her body is wrapped around nothing, and I hear a click as she bites down on air. She opens her eyes, confused and angry.

There is someone kneeling before the shrine?!

A young woman with brown hair holds a strange staff. Moving fast, she draws a star inside of a circle with her finger, painting yellow light in the air. From here I cannot understand what she said, but I know it was in English and a very advanced word.

The air around her then fills with… balls of fire?! They spin up from the floor and fly at Tengo, shooting all over the place like wild fireworks. Tengo shields her face and lets out a scream, sliding away from the woman.

What is going on?! I stay still in the air, my arms and legs buzzing, staring at the brown-haired woman. Tengo shoots upward and stops above where all the fireballs are shooting. With a deep breath, she blows hard at the top of the tower.

The roof, pillars, and rails are all torn away with the wind. The shrine, the tower, and the woman are still there. She points her staff at Tengo, says some more advanced English, and a blast of lightning comes out of the end of the staff. It misses Tengo by a lot, though.

"OH, WE'RE DOING LIGHTNING?" Tengo asks, raising her arms to the sky, "THEN HOW ABOUT ENOUGH LIGHTNING TO TURN THIS ENTIRE DESERT INTO GLASS?"

The flickering light and thunder grows quicker now. The clouds spin faster. The lightning attack Tengo was going to use against me was the size of a normal ball. This one is perhaps ten meters across, giving off a loud cracking noise and shining like the sun. Everything around her gets dark.

I need to get out of here! I make myself slide down to the ground and, arms burning, grab Amanokaze. My broken glasses are useless. A look at Tengo tells me running is also useless.

At once, the ball of lightning is a ball of ice.

It falls on Tengo. Very surprised, she tries to hold it, but it is much too heavy. She uses her flight to keep it from crushing her. Her angry eyes stare at the brown-haired woman, who is staring back, not attacking.

Perhaps she was using a weapon and it is empty? She does not look tired, just very nervous. I feel as though turning the lightning to ice was the last trick she was able to perform. Tengo smiles and begins grunting, trying to tilt her body and make the ice slide off of her.

I must act! What can I do? I have Amanokaze back and the ability of flight… and she is pinned by the ice so she cannot dodge! I think of myself flying towards her and I start to pick up speed, sliding through the air faster and faster. My grip tightens around my sword, starting the Blessing of Yoko and filling me with strength.

I turn the sword to cut sideways. Its blue fire flaps in the wind. Tengo notices me shooting straight for her. The next moment, my sword is almost ripped from my hands as sparks and golden beads fly. Then I am floating high in the air, blade still and in front of me. I have cut through her.

The ice ball shatters to the ground as I sheathe my sword.

CHAPTER 12

HOUSE ON DESERT SHORE

~ BLESSING ~

Tengo is sitting on the bed and the brown-haired woman stands by the staircase. Outside, the sun is back, lighting up the library room. It smells of paper and hot sand. The witch gives me a smile and a thumbs up, but then Tengo starts to talk.

"I don't really want to give you your gifts. Oshiro, you surrendered, and you, whatever your name is, interrupted very important business *and* didn't even let me introduce myself."

The brown-haired woman shrugs with a smile. I scratch the back of my neck. A smile comes to Tengo as the one on the brown-haired woman goes away. I feel nervous.

"Since both of you played unfair, both of you have to do something special in order to get your blessings."

"Something special like what?" I ask, taking a step back.

"You," she looks at the witch, "what's your name?"

"Allecia Rose." She replies, and it sounds like she has a Spanish accent.

Ms. Rose looks like an adult but still very young. She has big, grey eyes and is wearing jeans with a purple blouse and green boots. Her face and nose make her look like a Westerner.

“Well then, Allecia, Oshiro, you both have to receive your blessings… alone. The other must wait outside until I’m done.”

I look at Ms. Rose and she looks back at me. I do not know how she got here or how she did all that magic, but she is the only reason I am alive. I do not want her out of my sight for the rest of this journey.

“Allecia, you’re up first. Go wait outside until I tap on the window, Oshiro.” Tengo says.

For some reason I am both relieved and surprised to not be picked first. I walk out the door and wait outside. A few meters away, the giant pieces of the ice ball melt in the sun. In about 10 seconds, I realize just how hot it is out here. In a minute, I can begin to feel sweat. Three minutes and I begin pacing. Five minutes and I am both angry and worried.

Allecia comes out after the five-minute mark, squinting, then nods at me without smiling. I walk into the doorframe and the wind slams the door shut behind me. Tengo is sitting on the bed in her kimono smiling at me.

“Hmm… how about… you take off your sword and helmet and leave them by the door?” She asks.

I will not! I stare at her, afraid, but she does not move.

“Allecia is probably going to get very hot in that sun out there. We wouldn’t want to keep her waiting, would we?” She adds.

I frown. She is right. Even though I do not want to, I take off Amanokaze and the helmet and put them next to the door. Tengo then pats the area on the bed next to her. Oh, I am *certain* I will not!

I shake my head and cross my arms. She just shrugs and looks at me. I look into her eyes, knowing that every second I pause is another of Ms. Rose in the sun, and soon I sigh and do as the spirit asks. Her smile widens as I sit next to her.

I must breathe and stay calm.

"Uh… it's too hot for that shirt. Give it to me."

I have accepted that I will be harmed at some time in this ritual and am preparing my mind for it. Taking off my shirt has no effect on me. She folds it in her lap, then gets up and stores it away above some books. I know she will never give it back to me.

"Let's see… why don't you… lay down and close your eyes?" She asks as she turns from the bookshelf.

She is going to harm me. I know it. She is being too gentle and kind. I lie down as calm as I can, bracing myself for pain. I will my eyes closed and then hear her footsteps cross the room. She walks up to the bed, gets on her knees, then stops.

"What was I doing? Oh, right!"

A moment later, I feel her blow wind across my body. She starts from my feet and goes all the way up to my head in one go. It is silent for a moment, and I can feel her shaky breath on my neck next. She is going to bite me, I know it.

"You can open your eyes now." She sighs.

I do. She did not hurt me? What did she do?

"What was the blessing?" I ask.

She stands with a frown and knocks on the window, inviting Ms. Rose back inside.

"You now have the favor of the wind. Whenever you throw something or fall or run or jump, the wind will blow in the direction you need it to. To remind you that I am always watching."

I am nodding and smiling until that last part. Ms. Rose comes in, looking surprised to see me without a shirt.

"Why don't you two stay for a while? I can see you're tired and it's super hot out. You could clean up in the bathroom, I could make you a meal, and then you could take a nap." Tengo says as she sits next to me again, sounding happier the more she talks.

"*No gracias*," Ms. Rose says as she sees my discomfort, "Daiki, *coges tus cosas y vamos…*" she looks confused at my discomfort.

"Mmm… how about English? Do you understand me now?" She asks in English.

"Yes." I reply, also in English

"You did not understand me before?"

I shake my head, "Sorry, but I did not."

"Really? The spirit was speaking in Spanish and you looked like you understood."

I look at Tengo, confused. The spirit nods, very happy.

"See? There are so many things about me and the others I could teach you that you don't know about! We don't speak any language; we just talk and you understand us! Cool, right? I can tell you more cool facts if you stick around."

I get up from the bed, "Thank you very much but we must go to the next spirit."

"Nonsense!" Tengo says as she gets up too, "You don't even know where she is!"

I look at Ms. Rose. She frowns and shrugs. Tengo is right.

"Please tell us." I say.

"She… huh." It seems as though Tengo has forgotten.

"Did you… forget?" Ms. Rose asks.

"Uh, well no it was simple it was just," Tengo thinks, "She's just where the moon rises, right? Ukizima Beach? And the moon always rises opposite of the sun… I think… so just go opposite of the sun?"

I look out the windows. It seems as if the sun is almost in the middle of the sky. I cannot tell if it is a little after morning or a little before afternoon.

"Thank you for the information. I know where the sun was when I left the river… we will go the other way." Ms. Rose says with a bow that looks like it does not feel normal.

She takes a pair of sunglasses out of her shirt and puts them on. In her hand is her strange staff as well as Amanokaze, in its sheath. The straps of my helmet are around her wrist. She must have gathered my items while we were talking.

I see the black-wrapped box that Danyo and Hapa gifted me. I remember in her letter, Danyo told me to keep it. I would not want to disobey her, so I walk over and grab it. Tengo follows me, and as soon as I grab the box, she grabs my wrist.

Ms. Rose, who had already opened the door, closes it, confused.

"Oshiro, you should really stay for a bit. Let Allecia go ahead of you and scout the way. You're obviously more tired than she is."

Her grip is strong but I could slip out if I tried very hard.

"I am fine, thank you. We must leave now." I say, trying to stay calm. I can still feel where she tried to bite me.

"What for? It's the hottest part of the day! The next spirit can't even be summoned until nightfall… I think. Allecia, go on ahead. Oshiro is obviously a bit woozy from fatigue and isn't thinking straight. I'll make sure to take good care of him!"

Allecia is silent, looking from me to Tengo and back to me. I want to scream for her to help but Tengo is still holding me. I cannot mouth anything because the spirit is looking at me.

"Well you see," Allecia starts, "I have a fear of the desert. I don't want to be out there alone!"

"You would rather see your friend hurt than go into the desert alone?" Tengo asks.

"He looks healthy. I can *heel?* (I have not learned this English word) him too if he needs it." Allecia says with a smile.

Tengo then pulls me close and begins talking just under her breath, fast and low so that only I can hear, "*If it wasn't for that stupid wench I would have sucked you dry by now don't think you've escaped we will surely meet again and next time it'll be the two of us alone and I'll make sure you're a shriveled husk after I'm finished playing with you.*"

She lets go of me.

"Safe travels~!" She says with a smile, then she becomes smoke and fades away.

I look at Ms. Rose. She nods and opens the door again.

****

The sun is still hot but much lower in the sky. Ms. Rose and I have red faces from heat and embarrassment. Neither of us have deodorant, and I have no shirt, so we begin to smell very bad in the sun. The only reason we have not passed out is because Ms. Rose cools us with magic every now and then. She also repaired my glasses, so everything is clearer.

For a long time we did not talk, but now that we have gotten over a large hill and see a coast with a very distant house, she seems happier.

"Are you okay?" she asks, "I cannot really *heel*, so we will take a break if you need that."

"No, I am fine. Thank you." I say.

There is silence. It smells like sand and sea water. I have many questions to ask, but I need to plan how to ask them.

"So Ms. Rose," I start, "How did you get here?"

"Please, call me Allecia. And… hmm. I remember a dark room

and a floating *dee~d~m?*. There were candles and my hands were bleeding. And there was a man in a suit with a *lokit?*… then I fell, and I woke up on the beach."

Some of her English is beyond what I have learned, but from what I can understand, that was much different than I had expected.

"I do not understand… how did this happen?"

"I'm not sure, Daiki. It must have been magic, but I don't know who did it or why I came here."

I am silent for another moment. This is odd, but by the calmness in her voice, perhaps it is normal for her? I can hear the waves on the shore. Sand, rocks, and desert plants spill down the hill as we walk towards the far house.

I just now realize how much English I am speaking. Outside of me going through the portal, learning extra English was the only other thing my grandfather insisted that I do. I have him to thank… and perhaps *not* thank.

"I want to ask you about magic, but first, how do you know my given name?" I ask. Every time she has said it, I have winced inside.

She laughs, "Everyone knows your name, Daiki! Your camera sends video to hundreds of news stations. The *kwa~~tee?* is very bad and there is no sound, but it has made for interesting days on Earth."

She gives a smile and a thumbs up to me, then puts up two fingers to the camera. The ocean wind blows her hair. Even though she seems happy, I feel odd. This seems like it is bad. All the things I have seen on this planet have felt like a dream. To know that this is real and that the whole world was with me… and is with me now… I can only imagine what is going on in Japan.

"Oh, and about magic. Yes, I'm a *w~ch?*. I can do *sp~ls?* and *sum~n?* helpers out of air."

This is all too odd and new. But something about Allecia makes me not want to look like a fool in front of her, so I pretend I understand all of the advanced English she is using.

"Good. Can you tell me more about you? Where are you from, what do you do, how was your time here, perhaps your favorite food or magic?"

Ms. Rose lets out a laugh, "Sure, I can talk about myself more! Well, I live in Granada so I am a Spaniard, I am 21, and I am an accountant for a technology *outso~~sing?* company. My family…"

I look over from the closer beach house to Ms. Rose. She frowns.

"I don't think about them often."

"I see." I say. I will avoid that topic from now on.

"Let's see… my favorite food is plato alpujarreño sin morcilla, which is a dish with lots of potatoes and eggs and pork. My favorite *spehl?* is Fusillade, the fireballs you saw, and my favorite *sumun?* is Orion, a *bo?* and *aro?* made of stars."

I give an empty head nod, hoping she cannot see my confusion, and the mention of pork makes my stomach grumble. This walk has made me thirsty and hungry. We are close enough to the house to see it in good detail. It is very nice.

It is made of light blue wood with windows large enough to see through clearly. Inside there are black cloth zaisu – chairs without legs – and comfortable looking tatami mats. The tables are low and made of smooth wood and shiny steel bars. The kitchen is black with marble. The stairs, smooth wood, lead up from the front door, which is glass with a tatami blind rolled up above it.

In front of the entrance to the house is a shrine. It sticks up from the sand but does not look worn.

神六つ目

綺麗月陶工

月 - 試 - 化

("Sixth Spirit" : its name : "moon – test – change")

Ms. Rose and I look at the shrine, then at each other.

"Didn't the other spirit say this one only comes at night?"

"Yes. Perhaps we can wait inside?" I say.

"I'll open the door in case anyone is inside." Ms. Rose says.

I know there is no one who lives in this house. Even though it looks clean and new, there is no driveway, no garage, no cars, and no road. All the lights are off as well. But Ms. Rose is an adult and has magic powers, so I let her go first.

As soon as the door opens, we both freeze.

"*Santo cielo!* Do you smell that?" Ms. Rose asks.

"Yes. It smells like pork." I say.

We follow the smell and get to the table. It is the same table I saw from the large side window, but this time it has food on it. It is a long table, but the dishes are placed across from each other in the middle.

On one side is my favorite dish: gyoza – pork and cabbage dumplings – with rice, cucumber salad, and yakisoba – stir fry noodles. On the other side is a plate filled with fried potatoes, onions, peppers, ham, fried eggs, and sausage. Two cups sit by either dish, one with water and one with a dark liquid.

I look at Ms. Rose. Her eyes are wide. Our stomachs grumble almost at the same time.

"It could be a…" I cannot think of the word in English.

Ms. Rose takes a few steps forward, "Trap? Well, let's think about that for a moment."

She looks at me, then the food, then back at me, "Let me sit so I can think better."

She and I both rush over to the table. She sits on the floor cushion with her legs crossed and rests her elbows on the table. I want to sit too but I must stand. If I sit, I will give in to the tasty smells. Ms. Rose closes her eyes and tries to think. I can hear her stomach grumble a little once again. She opens her eyes and she looks as if she may cry.

"Let's eat this. W-we want to be strong enough to win against the next spirit, and it is either this or nothing."

"Right," I say, sitting on my heels, "we will need our strength."

As such, we begin eating. The food is amazing, better than any I have tasted for quite some time now. We eat in happy silence for a while, and once we start to get a little full, we begin to laugh at how hungry we were.

"Have you drank the darker drink yet, Ms. Rose?" I ask.

"Ah, what did I say? Don't be so formal, you can call me Allecia! I won't speak again until you do." Ms. Rose says, crossing her arms and smiling.

It feels disrespectful and is difficult to pronounce, but I do it anyway, "Allecia."

"Good! No, I haven't tried it yet. Do you want to drink it together?"

"Sure." I say, picking up the cold cup.

She picks up hers and raises it, "To getting back home."

I nod, and we both take a sip. It is sparkling and cold and tastes like my favorite dark soda.

We drink and eat in more silence. Soon, we are finished with our meals. Allecia goes off to find the shower while I explore the house. It has a lot of space but looks like it is only made for one person. The upstairs is just one large bedroom with a very big futon and closets making up the wall. I hear Allecia start her shower as I approach the closets.

I slide back the door to see… clothes! At first, I am worried that someone does, in fact, live here, but then I realize that the clothes are all my size. They are also all just the clothes I have on now but with different colors.

I slide through the rows of Shajiku Sun shirts, heavy jeans, and hazmat suit pants. Many pairs of tall, dark boots are tucked under the clothes, and along the top are pairs of underwear. The closet beside this one has clothes that must be for Allecia. All the other closets are empty.

Downstairs, the refrigerator is full of food. One side is all brands I remember from home, and the other side is in what looks like Spanish. The pantry is the same way. Pots, pans, cutlery, plates, bowls, cups, and chopsticks fill cabinets and drawers, all very clean and neat. How odd!

Allecia is soon done with her shower and dressed like she was when we first met. I go take a shower next. It is one of the most pleasant experiences of my life. The soap smells very nice, and the water is not too hot or cold. After a long while, all of the sand, sweat, spit, and fear from the day are washed off. I dry off and put on my clothes after, feeling warm.

I feel through my old pockets before I gather the clothes and take them to the laundry room. I find old hospital papers that I leave, my wallet that I take, and… the coin of Mr. Nakamura. I hold the coin between my fingers and lift it to the orange sky in the roof window. I wonder what he and Memate are doing now. I wonder what the rest of his life will be like.

What would my life have been like if I decided to stay with him?

****

The phone of Allecia has a soft alarm that wakes the two of us. We were resting in the tatami area of the main room since the meal and shower felt so nice. This area has zaisu chairs and faces the ocean from behind glass walls. When we got here, the sun was red and setting. Now the sky is black and the big moon makes the water look very nice.

Allecia stands and so do I. I put on my body camera. We gather our weapons and go outside. It is much cooler now. We come around the side of the shrine. Allecia taps it first. For a moment, I fear this spirit will be like Tengo, but since Allecia is here, I feel safer. Once I tap the shrine, we both kneel. I expect to see clouds roll, but, without warning, lightning flashes down right in front of us. Allecia covers her eyes.

It does not make any noise or explosion. It does not fade either. It just sits there, like a tree of light. Then, it melts together and becomes a person. She is tall and thin with pale skin and very long, white hair. Her kimono is purple, with a half moon and snowflakes around the edges of it. Her eyes are orange, lined with red makeup. There is a small silver crown on her head.

“Welcome travelers. It is very exciting to see that you have made it this far."

The spirit does not smile and her voice sounds formal. I sigh in relief. Her excitement seems as though it will be sane!

"I am Kireitsutoko, Spirit of the Moon, the sixth in the Trial of Shenshimu. You may call me Kirei. If you can answer at least two of my three questions correctly, I will give you your blessing and send you on to your last challenge, the Grand Goddess. If you get more than one wrong, we shall fight…"

She pauses and points up to the moon. It is big; if the moon on Earth is the size of a coin, this moon is the size of one's fist.

"On my home, the moon. Unlike some other spirits, I will not help you during my fight, so you will have to find your own way to protect yourself from the rest of outer space. I will give you another day to make preparations. The house will provide you food and water. I will see you tomorrow night."

With that, the spirit turns into a cloud of snowflakes.

I turn to Allecia, "Do you know any magic that can help us up on the moon?"

She shakes her head, "We should rest. Tomorrow we will search the house for clues and test each other on what we know."

I nod, and we both go back into the house for the night.

Chapter 13

Final Choice

~ Puzzle Spirit ~

The moon is rising and full again. After a good day of cooking, bathing, and reviewing, Allecia and I feel ready. We tap the shrine again and kneel. Kirei comes down at once, melting out of another silent lightning tree.

"So you returned. Are you prepared?"

I look at Allecia, who nods. I nod as well. Kirei bows low, then raises a hand. The stars and the moon in the sky fade into black. I fight the urge to unsheathe Amanokaze.

A very large, very close moon fades from out of the darkness. If the moon near Earth is the size of a coin, and the normal moon here is the size of a fist, this new moon is the size of a torso. Kirei lowers her hand and slides her arms into her sleeves. Allecia throws on her sunglasses.

"Each question is timed. Either of you can answer. Only one answer attempt is allowed. You can answer before the time is up, but if the time runs out, I will move on to the next question. Any questions unanswered after time for the last question runs out will be counted incorrect. I will give you five seconds to prepare before I give you the first question."

A large shadow of a 5 appears on the moon. It turns into a 4 after a second. I am afraid. Allecia sees this, turns to me, and gives me a smile.

"We'll win. The two of us can answer whatever she asks us!"

I nod, then look back up at the moon. The 1 shadow melts away.

The mouth of Kirei moves, but her voice sounds like it comes from the sky itself, "First question: What are the names of three places in which the shrines along your journey rest? You have 60 seconds before the next question."

A 60 shadow appears on the moon. My stomach drops. I cannot seem to remember any of the names of where the shrines were. Was I even told them?

"I know this place is called Ukizima Beach because I was listening hard during the last spirit's talk. I know there was another beach… do you know what it was called?" Allecia asks.

I remember Mr. Otoroto saying its name. Perhaps my doctor mentioned it too. I went to it twice, and each time I passed the road sign, it said…

"Sihi Beach!" I say.

"Yes, that was it! Do you know any other names?" Allecia asks.

We both look at the clock. It is on 34. It seems like there are too many places to try and remember!

"W-what was the name of the…" I do not know the word for 'swamp' in English. My memories from there are the sharpest.

I begin trying my best to recreate the swamp with my hands,

grabbing like the branches and hanging my arms like the skeletons. It is obvious that Allecia does not understand what I am doing, so I begin speaking to myself.

"It was… K-k… it begins with a K…"

I remember the darkness and fear. I remember the soft, high voice of Hapa. I remember my ears listening well as she told me who she was and where we were. K… I know the name!

"It is Kaeyo…!" I say.

"Sure, that's it! Say it!" Allecia says.

I look up at Kirei and the moon. The shadow is at 13.

"Ukizima Beach, Sihi Beach, and Kaeyo Swamp!" I yell.

"Correct," Kirei says without smiling, and I am filled with happiness, "Second question: Three of the spirits have true forms that are animals. What are those animals? You have 30 seconds before the next question."

Allecia and I turn to each other again.

"Lord Hapa was a cat." I say at once.

"The *tayl?* on the first spirit looked like a *sk~pee~n?*," Allecia says, "what about the third?"

For a moment I try and figure out what Allecia is saying, but then I decide that it can wait. The moon is at 21. I must slow down and think. Yoko could not be an animal. Perhaps Suturi was an eel by the way she swam? Perhaps Danyo was a centipede because of her many arms?

Who is left? Tengo… everything about her was normal… outside of her craziness and when we first met. Wait… she asked me an odd question after she rubbed her face on my hand! She asked me if she still looked like a…

"Bird!" I say to Allecia, "Lord Tengo was a bird!"

"Alright, I'll say this one." She tells me as we turn to Kirei.

The moon is at 5! We must hurry!

"*Gato, escorpión, y pajaro!*" Allecia yells.

There is a pause in which we both hold our breath, and then… "Correct. You will have 1 second to answer this final question."

I look at Allecia, smiling. No matter what, we have won. She also has a big smile on her face and pulls me into a hug. We celebrate so much that we almost miss the third question.

"What is the name of the person you are hugging?" Kirei asks.

"Allecia Rose!" I laugh.

"Daiki Oshiro!" Allecia calls out at the same time.

There is silence as we stop hugging. Allecia then slaps her forehead, almost knocking off her sunglasses.

"Did I say your name the wrong way?!" She asks me.

She said it backwards.

I shrug, "Surely that is–"

"Incorrect." The serious voice of Kirei comes from the entire sky.

My stomach fills with stone as she says that. We both look at Kirei, confused and a little scared. She said it as if we failed… but I am very sure she told us we could get up to one answer wrong. Then, her hand whips from her sleeve and puts up two fingers. A quiet smile replaces her scary staring.

"Congratulations. You won." She says without much excitement.

Allecia and I turn to one another.

"That was scary!" She says, and we both laugh.

The sky fades to normal, with countless stars and a lower, smaller moon. Allecia takes off her sunglasses, then she and Kirei share an odd glance. I am not sure how to explain it, but it is over as soon as it starts. Perhaps it was nothing, as Allecia looks at me next, confused and blushing.

"Oshiro, please untie Amanokaze and hand it to me. Rose, please do the same with your staff. I will bless them." The spirit says.

She walks over and puts out her hands. We do as she says. Once she has our weapons, she takes a few steps back and closes her eyes for a moment. Then there is a flash, and our weapons look different.

Allecia's staff now has a small, silver fan at one end and a silver ball at the other. There are two silver beads that hang down on either side of the fan. Black diamonds circle the top and bottom of the staff, ending right before the silver pieces.

My sheath and hilt are now white instead of navy-blue. The guard is silver instead of bronze. The flowers painted along the sides look brighter and more detailed, and now there are silver dragons flying among the flowers.

We take our weapons back and look at them, impressed.

"Oshiro, whenever it is nighttime, your sword will be twice as long, twice as sharp, and half as heavy. It will also cast light so that you can see better."

I look down at the new Amanokaze. The sword looks different but is still the same length. I unsheathe it like normal, but as soon as I have it in front of me, it begins glowing white and grows much longer. Surprised, I give it a swing. It is very light!

"Rose, whenever it is nighttime, your staff will amplify your magic ten times over. This includes the magic that has already been strengthened by the other spirits' blessings."

Allecia raises her staff to the sky. She says something low in perhaps English, and a moment later, a firework shoots into the sky. It flies very high, then lets out a great explosion. It is so loud I can feel the sand shake, and it is so bright that both Allecia and I must look away.

When the sparkles end, we look at each other and laugh.

Kirei gives a very small smile, then starts talking.

"I am glad you made it this far. Beyond me, there is one more challenge. Look at the horizon."

Allecia and I both look out at the ocean. Everything is black except a very small, silver dot where the water meets the sky.

"That is Oshiya Palace, the mystic island temple of the final challenge in the Trial. Please be warned that this battle will not be against a spirit but against the Grand Goddess, Mother of the Universe, Creator of All of Existence. There is no chance that you will survive. Would you like to turn back?"

I look at Allecia. She looks very surprised but shakes her head.

We must get back home, whatever it takes.

"I see. As with me, the Goddess can only be approached at night. The entirety of the island and temple will disappear when the sun rises, so please defeat her before that happens. I am the only person who can get you to the island. If you attempt to fly, swim, sail, or go by any other means, you will be lost at sea forever. Once I have gotten you to the island, I cannot bring you back. Would you like another day to reconsider?"

I look at Allecia. She still looks worried.

"How do you feel, Daiki?" She asks.

I pause and think, then say, "Very scared."

"Me too. How will you feel after another day of rest?" She asks.

"Better…" I say, even though there is more I want to add.

"But then you will not want to go." Allecia says.

I nod, silent. She is right.

"I feel the same. If we will go, we need to tonight. One more day of rest will not make us any stronger. And if I am honest…"

She sighs, "I won't be able to put together the *keraj?* (maybe this means 'strength') to do this again."

I nod, agreeing.

"I will try my best to keep us safe. Are you ready?" She asks.

I wait for a moment, afraid, but then nod.

Allecia turns to Kirei, who also nods. Beams of moonlight in the form of a glowing, air-like, silver ribbons form around us, and then Allecia and I start floating. We turn from Kirei to the island on the night horizon. The gentle waves and soft wind seem to come from it. Everything in my body is cold with fear. It is as if I did not even receive a blessing.

Kirei comes around our side and looks at us.

"Remember, you are headed to face the Author of Everything. She created you, me, and anything we have ever seen, touched, heard, or interacted with in our entire lives. You, humans with finite limitations, are going to face your Infinite Creator."

There is uncomfortable silence. Kirei keeps talking.

"Alternatively, you could stay with any one of us spirits. My house, with all its resources, could be yours. You could return to Yoko and live with her. You have the option to stay on this planet and live lives filled with fun and adventure. If you decline, this option is gone. Are you completely sure you want to proceed?"

I look at Allecia. She is crying a little and shaking her head.

"What will we do, Daiki?"

"A-Allecia, you are the elder. You must say." I say.

"Yes, I know what I will do. I will… I have to stay with you. So what will you do?" Allecia asks.

I think of all the interesting things that have happened on this planet. Allecia and I could live here. We could. I feel in my pocket and am reminded of Mr. Nakamura. Memate or Yoko could offer us a place to stay if we do not want to live at this house for some reason. We have so many cool powers and stories. This is enough.

I look into the odd eyes of Kirei and prepare to tell her that we have changed our minds. Her eyes look very sad. I feel like even if I told her we were staying, she would give a small smile but still look sad. Though Kirei looks very different, I imagine her as my mother. As my sister. As my father. As the unchanging sadness they would feel if I did not return.

"Let's do it." I say.

Allecia lets out a sigh. Kirei closes her eyes and shakes her head.

"Very well. Goodbye."

CHAPTER FINALE

FUMETSOSHIEGAMI

~ GRAND GODDESS ~

The silver sand is under my boots at once. The black-wrapped box from Danyo and Hapa is on my right. Allecia is on my left. In front of us is a very tall staircase with black steps, leading up a grassy hill to a red castle. The pagoda roofs are black and gold, lined with lanterns around the edges. Lit torches line the staircase, leading to a big, open gateway.

The sky is deep and clear. I can see stars millions of kilometers out. The moon is big and bright, still just above the horizon. I turn back to face where we came from.

There is no land, only darkness and ocean.

"Those are a lot of stairs." Allecia says.

I can hear that she is nervous.

"Yes, they are. Do you have magic we can use to get up them?" I ask. My own voice is shaking too.

"Sure." She says, and with a magic English word, the left side of the stairs start moving like an escalator.

"Cool!" I say as we get on.

The stairs take us up through the night sky, fast and smooth. Each torch we pass is a bubble of heat.

“I learned that *spehl?* (maybe this is another word for ‘magic’) in my down time. University *towmz?* are very fun to read.”

“I see.”

Silence

“Too bad English is the most *de~l~pd?* magic language for Standards. I would have learned it in Spanish if it were as *ad~a~sd?*.” Allecia says, trying to sound casual.

This annoys me a bit, but I do not show it. I just want to focus and be silent, as I always do before a serious kendo match. This coming battle will be the greatest of my lifetime, and there is a high chance I will die for real. Allecia talking is distracting… but if it helps her calm down then I will entertain her.

“Really? How does the magic work, anyway?”

“Oh Daiki,” Allecia says, waving her hand “I need a very big staircase to explain all of that! Is there anything smaller you want to know?”

To be honest, everything or nothing. But that would be rude, so I make myself pick something. What knowledge would help me most in this battle?

“After the fight with Lord Tengo, you did the ice magic and then stopped. Why is that?”

“Oh, right. That was magic fatigue. The more someone uses magic, the harder it is to *aym?*. Don’t worry, I had enough rest and food to where I can use more magic. The only reason I got fatigue with Tengo is because I fought all night.”

I pause for a moment to understand what she said.

"Wait… you did all of the Trial of Shenshimu in one night?"

"Most of it," Allecia says, trying not to look proud, "It wasn't too hard. All I had to do was wait until they introduce themselves and then hit them with my strongest magic. The one with the rice almost got me, but the bowl *ber~d?* (this might be another word for 'hurt') me so I won."

"That is very cool, Allecia. Your strength is giving me… *keraj*."

She blushes and then there is silence. We are almost at the top.

"What a *j~r~ee?*. I start off fighting a *sko~pee~n* woman on the beach and finish off fighting the 'creator of everything'. A big jump in *d~f~k~tee?* (maybe this means 'hardness'), no?"

"Lord Seina was the very first thing you saw?" I ask.

"Yes. She told me that some kids *sumund?* her a few days before, then left, so she had to wait on the beach for a fighter. Lucky me!"

"I agree. It is lucky for me also, for now I get to fight this one with you." I say, trying to sound grateful instead of scared.

We are at the top at last. We step off of the escalator and onto the stone walkway. The stairs are now still and normal again. In front of us is the great gateway; through it is a golden hall. Calligraphy covers the walls with characters so difficult I could never hope to write them myself.

At the end of the hallway is a tall set of white doors. I can hear plucking from a shamisen – three-stringed guitar – coming from behind it. Allecia and I walk into the hallway in silence. I am relieved but nervous that she does not want to talk.

We get to the middle of the hallway when she stops.

"Allecia?" I ask.

"This is…" she pauses and laughs, "I am scared."

"I am also. But we cannot go back so we need to fight."

She holds her staff with two hands and nods. We walk a bit more towards the white doors, and then freeze as they begin to open. I unsheathe Amanokaze and Allecia readies her staff, but nothing comes running at us. There is just a small room covered in gold and jewels. A shrine, like the other spirits except made of gold, sits in the middle. A normal shamisen floats above it, playing itself.

Allecia and I enter the room and the doors close behind us. The shamisen slows to a stop. I look down at the shrine in front of me and read what it says.

無限星女神

"What does it say?" Allecia asks.

"I do not know. I believe it is a name."

It is quite a divine name at that. She sniffs, cracks her neck, then reaches out and taps the shrine with her staff three times. I tap it with Amanokaze, and then we both kneel together.

A voice comes out of everything at the same time. I can hear it from the walls, from the air, even from my very skin.

"I am Fumetsoshiegami, Mother of the Universe, Creator of All, the Grand Goddess of Existence. I am the final in the Trial of Shenshimu, yet I stretch beyond it further than what can be comprehended. Travelers, kiss my shrine in a display of your fear and worship. By doing so, you will surrender to me, and I will bless you fully before returning you to Kireitsutoko."

I look at Allecia. She looks back at me, frowning. That cannot happen. We must return home. Neither of us kiss the shrine.

"You dare defy me?!" The voice blasts from everywhere at once, "Then merely grovel before me. I will no longer bless you, but I will send you back to Kireitsutoko unharmed."

Neither of us lie down. I really want to, but I do not.

"I see," the room says with a cold and sharp voice, "you wish to die at my hands. I have been merciful, yet you do not accept it?"

Silence. I feel as though this is disrespectful, but I cannot think of anything to say. I think Allecia is too afraid to speak.

"Very well, arrogant fools! Allow me to show you the power of your creator! I shall deconstruct you in a thousand ways!"

The room begins to rumble as Allecia and I stand. What happens next is difficult to say. The world *moves* around Allecia and I. We stay in place, but the palace room rushes away from us. The doors and hallway and stairs fly around us, and then we are back on the silver sand outside.

I look at the witch, surprised. She is also surprised. The castle before us begins to spin. The grass, torches, lanterns, and sand around it begin spinning as well, rising into a big pillar of wind. Allecia says a magic English word, and now there is a dome of hard air protecting us.

I notice that the sand underneath us is glowing with symbols and rose petals. I also notice the black-wrapped box from Danyo next to me. The castle whirlwind starts to grow solid, then it is a great woman.

She is perhaps 35 meters tall, and her skin is made out of mirrors. It is as if her kimono is made from the night sky itself. Stars and galaxies spin and sparkle on it, drifting with space clouds. She wears a big, golden crown and a necklace of planets.

Gold armor sits on her shoulders. Two wooden wheels spin at either side of her head, burning with bright red fire. A big, solid gold katana floats in front of her with many ribbons flowing from its hilt. I am frozen with awe.

She opens her eyes and bright light pours out. It is like her eyes are flashlights, or perhaps her eyeballs are small suns. I raise my arm, but Allecia lets out a scream and falls to the ground, grabbing her face and crying out in Spanish.

I start to panic.

"Are you okay? Can you still do magic?"

"Gah! Yes, but I'll need both hands to do strong magic."

I remember the black-wrapped box. I kneel down, unwrap it, stand in front of Allecia and lower her hands, then wrap it around her eyes. The Goddess watches us, waiting until we are prepared.

Perhaps she wants to tear us down at our full strength. I do not think she will have a hard time doing so.

"Are you okay now?" I ask.

"Yes. Thank you." She says.

"Good," says the Goddess, "now that you are ready, I will show you the difference in our power!"

The gold katana makes a heavy noise as it raises to strike. I unsheathe Amanokaze, ready to die armed.

"It's time! Come up, Daughters of Zelophehad, and help us!" Allecia screams, raising both arms.

A great sword, almost as big as the gold katana, shoots out of the sand and blocks us from the coming slash. It is still for a moment, then it splits into five swords. The swords begin floating, staying between the gold katana and us.

The Goddess looks surprised, and I am as well. She then waves a hand and the katana begins striking again. The five swords block and strike back. The clashing noises are so loud I can feel them in my chest.

"What now, Daiki? I can't see; where do we hit?" Allecia asks.

I look at the Goddess through the great, dancing blades. Her layers of kimono look strong, and her mirror skin looks slippery but in a magic way. The only thing that is not armored and looks weak is…

"Her eyes!" I suggest.

"Good idea," Allecia says with a laugh, "but when we hit one, she will block the other. How about you get the first, yell, and I can find the second from that?"

"Okay!" I say, then realize something, "But she is very tall. Is there a... *spehl* that can push her down?"

Allecia smiles, "Yes there is. Start running."

At that moment, the katana takes a heavy swing and knocks the smaller swords up into the air. It rises to chase them. The danger is gone! As such, I run forward in the sand, pointing my blade towards the ground on my left. Allecia is running on my right, using my footsteps as a guide.

White fire spins up around Allecia, and then she grows to become a great blue tiger, almost half the size of the goddess. I jump back in surprise, and a moment later, Allecia pounces on the Goddess, slamming her down and splashing silver sand into the air.

Seeming blind, Allecia begins clawing at the face of the Goddess. Her eyes are closed from the pain of the light and her fangs flash. Now is my chance! I run as fast as I can, almost slipping on sand, trying to get to the head of the Goddess.

There is a hard force that comes out of the chest of the Goddess and shoots out in every direction. I duck down as it hits me and knocks me onto my hands. Allecia is thrown onto her back. The Goddess shifts to stand. No! I have only made it to her shoulder!

As fast as I can, I get up and try to grab onto her upper sleeve. I do, and at once, I am many meters in the air, dangling above the ground. My left hand is filled with pain and I drop Amanokaze so

I can hold on with two hands. I am overcome with disappointment and fear.

I know now that this is not good at all. The gold shoulder armor is only an arm's length away, but I know that if I reach for it, I will slip and fall. Above all, I have no sword.

Then, there is a hard blast of wind that pushes me upward. If I were braver, I would use it to climb up, but I instead use it to better my grip. There is a whipping noise, and then my sword spins up from underneath me, arcs, and lands point-first into the shoulder of the Goddess. For a moment I am confused, but then I remember the Blessing of Tengo: helpful wind.

The Goddess walks over to Allecia as she gets off her back. With every swing of her arm, my grip loosens. I cannot hold this for much longer! Lucky for me, the Goddess stops just short of Allecia. The great tiger shows her fangs, taking swipes at the air.

A glowing pole made of rainbows forms above the Goddess, and she raises her arm to grab it. In this motion, I go from dangling meters above the ground to upside-down and right over the shoulder armor. My grip fails, but I land on the armor!

I can see the black horizon from here. It stretches out in every direction with no land in sight. The stars are so bright and feel very close. I look over and watch the big mirror hand of the Goddess grab the spear out of the air.

Then she brings it down and stabs Allecia in the back.

My stomach drops. The great tiger lets out a bone-shaking roar.

I almost fall off as the Goddess turns and slams her foot on the neck of Allecia. Ice pours out of her foot, freezing the fur and the sand below. Then, the Goddess pulls the spear out and goes to stab Allecia again.

I start running down her shoulder armor and towards her face, pulling out my sword from the kimono as I pass it. I will not let her hurt my partner again!

I want to say something, anything, to get her attention. But the only thing that comes up is the loudest kakegoe scream I have ever done. The Goddess turns her head to me. I can see my angry reflection running towards me. Her eye is so close! It is like a circle of white light!

Before she can blow me off of her shoulder, I dive into her eye hole and land in a spherical mirror cave.

Floating in the middle of the cave is the sun, much smaller and less hot but almost just as bright. To my right, there is the opening that leads to the night sky and the face of the Goddess. A thin line of gold light runs from the small sun to the part of the sphere wall on the left side.

I unsheathe Amanokaze at once and swing down on the cord of light. My blade bounces off. This cord is like a bowstring!

"Ah! You will pay!" Says the Goddess, and then the opening to my right closes.

The small sphere I am in fills with swirling, cold water. I cannot even take another breath before the entire sphere is full. For a moment I panic, but then I remember I can breathe water. I try it… and it still works!

Sword in hand, I push through the water to the sun. It is so bright! Testing, I put an arm over it. It does not burn. I tuck it tight under my arm and begin sawing at the cord with Amanokaze. A very loud scream comes from everywhere, and the water begins swirling faster. My glasses fly off. I hold on as tight as I can, still sawing.

Then, the water goes away. Before I can prepare, I am thrown hard into one of the walls. Gravity switches and I am at the top of the sphere, and then I slam onto the bottom. I try to sheathe Amanokaze, but the walls are moving too fast. I am pressed on the left, then slam hard on the right. It is such a tight space and I am moving so fast that I start getting dizzy.

Gravity keeps slamming me left and right, up and down. I try to grab the walls but they are too far away to bare weight across. I go up, then rush down. I put out a hand to brace myself, but the wall hits it too hard and my wrist snaps in a blast of pain. I let go of my sword and grab my wrist, screaming.

Gravity comes around again and my sword sinks into my calf.

My entire leg is alive with pain. I start to remember the spears from the swamp. The fear of death. The loneliness and silence. Blood is leaking from my leg. I grab onto the cord of light before gravity can switch again, but then gravity stops all the way and I am stuck floating in midair.

Then, the walls turn orange and fire sprays out from everywhere at once, engulfing me in hot air. I have fireproof skin, so I am almost all the way fine. My sword begins to heat up in my leg. Pain unlike anything I have ever felt before runs up my leg. I reach back and rip the sword out. Bright spots flicker in my vision, and I am glad there is no gravity or I would have fallen like a puppet.

My blood is floating in the air, sizzling as the fire cooks it. I bring my sword around and start sawing again. There is another loud scream which might be from pain or anger, and then the fire stops.

"Fine! You will not yield?! You seek to know my defeat?! How about I show you *everything* instead?!" The Goddess screams.

The walls fall away. The fire still on my clothes hisses out. Nothing but space and stars are around me for… forever! I keep looking but there is no end! Just rushing stars and spinning galaxies and floating suns and twisting planets going out in every direction, pulling my mind into endless darkness. All of the planets then swell at once and I am rushed through them, feeling every rock and piece of ice, smelling every crystal.

The empty planets melt away and I am met with people. Countless generations. Every single detail of their lives, from their birth to their death, I live through both in normal time yet also in a single moment.

Emotions, memories, pain, pleasure, scenery, they all crash into my mind in a big rush of senses. Farmers, soldiers, office workers, politicians, adventurers. Crashing and swirling into me like a violent river into a small cup. Each life is so much, yet so small, so meaningless…

I will my eyes closed. My mind returns to me at once, ringing with a billion memories. They fly away like scared birds as the unbearable pain in my wrist and leg awakens again. I bring my sword around, shaking from the pain and mind rush, and continue to saw at the cord.

"LOOK OSHIRO!" screams the Goddess in my ears, sending more of the memories flying away, "LOOK AT ALL I HAVE CREATED! MARVEL AT THE INFINITE SPAN OF MY UNIVERSE! YOU WILL NEVER GET THIS CHANCE AGAIN! OPEN YOUR EYES AND CONSUME THE KNOWLEDGE OF YOUR CREATOR!"

I keep my eyes shut and keep sawing. Then the memories and the noise all melt away and there is silence.

"Oshiro," says a soft, smooth voice, right next to me, "open your eyes. Look at me."

Though I have never heard this voice before, I know who it is. Danyo. This is what I always imagined her voice to be like, the quiet, formal voice of death itself.

"Look at my face. I know you want to. Don't be afraid. Everyone must do it at some point."

I keep sawing. Gentle fingers start trying to separate my eyelids. Cold hands pull my arms, trying to take them away from the cord. I swing my good leg to kick them away.

"You are losing so much blood, Oshiro. You are pretty much

dead. Didn't I say we would meet again soon? Open your eyes," the hands pull harder, "Open them. Open them! Oshiro! OSHIRO!"

Then… it is quiet.

"Daiki?" Asks my father, my real father.

I stop sawing, "Father?!"

"Daiki! Oh my goodness, you are okay! We were so worried about you! Are you bleeding?! Hurry, give me your hand so I can pull you out before the portal closes!"

"I cannot, Father! I must defeat the Goddess and save Allecia!"

"What are you talking about? Open your eyes and look around; you are back in Japan. Well, you will be if you let go and grab my hand!"

I grow suspicious, though I cannot be too sure since it sounds just like my father, even down to the gentle forcefulness of his tone when he is worried.

"If you are truly my father, what is my favorite anime?" I ask.

"What? Daiki, enough games! Grab on to me, now!"

His voice is stern and the disrespect I am showing is killing me. But I must be sure.

"Please just do it, Father!"

"Fine! It's Miss Dorayaki Stewardess! Now grab on to me!"

A rush of cold fear runs over my burning pain.

"You are no father of mine! No one in my family knows that!"

I keep my eyes closed and begin sawing harder on the cord.

"Daiki, stop that!" My father commands, but I know it is not him.

"Daiki!" Allecia shouts, "Stop! You're hitting me!"

It is not her. I keep sawing, feeling weaker.

"Ouch! Oshiro, what are you doing?! Stop!" screams Memate.

Her voice sounds so real but I keep going with the last bit of strength I have. I almost cannot move my arm.

The voice of Memate mixes together with Danyo, Allecia, Father, and the Goddess.

"LET GO! STOP! OSHIRO, STOP! STOOOOOOP!!"

Their voices are too loud and I want to cover my ears but I must-

With a snap, the sun comes loose from the cord. I open my eyes, surprised, but it is true. There is a loud cry and I go flying backwards. Gravity spills me out of the eye and into a big hand.

With everything I have left in me, I scream as loud as I can. I feel my throat go sore. My head is spinning from loss of blood. I cannot move. I want to cry because I am almost sure Allecia is dead and I am next. But I scream anyway, if not for the signal, then for myself.

I hear Allecia scream from further below, and the cry of pain turns into a word. A big line of blue light shoots up from behind me and hits the Goddess in her other eye.

Her head explodes into a cloud of star glass and diamonds.

The spinning wheels next to her lose their fire and fall. Her crown spins off into the night sky. Still holding me in her hand, the Goddess falls to her knees. Slow, almost gentle, she falls forward, and I roll out of her hands when we hit the ground.

****

I wake up and am surprised that I am alive. I am lying in the silver sand. Allecia is sleeping next to me. Is she really sleeping? It is still dark, so I have to watch her for a moment. Yes, she is breathing. I go to get up, but my wrist and leg sting with pain. I am more careful and manage to lean up on my good knee, then get up using my good arm.

A much smaller version of the Goddess sits with her back facing me. She is holding a shamisen. Her crown and flaming wheels are gone. She looks out at the night ocean and her playing is soft. Her katana is also a normal size, planted straight down in the sand. Its ribbons dance in the ocean wind.

Does she think we are dead? Is this her final form? I am unsure of both, so, slow and quiet, I unsheathe Amanokaze. It becomes lighter and longer, and the blade starts to glow. I limp across the silver sand at the speed of a tortoise, trying to be as stealthy as possible. The plucking from her shamisen gets louder as I get closer.

I almost have her in striking range, but I feel like she can hear me. I raise Amanokaze and prepare to strike sideways. If she moves a centimeter, I will lunge forward and take her head off again.

"There is no use in that," she says, still facing forward, "you have won. We are no longer opponents."

Her voice, which now comes from her mouth instead of the world itself, sounds sad and mild. I do not know if this is a trick, so I keep my sword out and stop moving. She stops playing the shamisen.

"You still do not trust me? How is this: if I wanted to destroy you, I could do so in an instant. I have my head back, yet your wounds are only partially healed. Sheathe your weapon and sit next to me. I will not harm you."

She has a strong argument. I sheathe Amanokaze and struggle to sit next to her, allowing for some space. I would sit on my heels but my calf still hurts, so I sit on the side of my good leg instead. The face of the Goddess is blank. Her eyes are still bright lights. The shamisen disappears, then she digs into her kimono and pulls out my glasses, giving them to me.

"Oshiro… I have kept a secret for eons. Since you and Allecia have defeated me, I will tell it to you."

She pauses, then says, "Yes Allecia, I know you are awake. Come and join us."

I look back to see the witch getting up. A moment later, she sits in the space between the Goddess and I, her staff firm in her hand. She squints and looks toward the ground, though. The light must still be hurting her eyes.

"Both of you can refer to me as Fume from now on. Because…"

She lets out a sigh.

"I am not the creator of the universe. There is someone else, far greater and more infinite than I could ever hope to be. He is the true creator. I am no goddess. I am simply another spirit, just much more powerful than the others."

Allecia says nothing. I do not either. Fume is silent as well.

"Uh," Allecia starts, "okay. Well, why did you lie?"

"I thought that I could get away with it. I looked at the true creator and wanted to be just as strong and powerful. It seemed so blissful to have such might, such authority. So I lied and said I did have it. No one confronted me, so I never told the truth. Until now."

The soft ocean breeze blows. My wounds tingle with faint pain. The three of us are silent as we sit there.

"I shall send you home now," Fume says, standing, "And on top of that, I will give both of you an extra wish since you put up such an outstanding fight. Are you ready?"

I look to Allecia, surprised. She looks at me in the same way. I get to go home?! Really?! At last?! There are no more spirits; that was all? I mean, that was the most difficult trial I have ever faced, but receiving the reward still feels unreal!

Allecia and I get up as fast as we can.

"Allecia, give me your staff." Fume says.

The witch obeys. The spirit takes the staff and closes her eyes. It shines bright, making Allecia and I shield our eyes. When it is done, there is the golden head of a dragon in front of the silver fan at one end.

"Now, with this staff in hand, your magic will aim true at all times, no matter how much or little you use."

The face Allecia makes looks as if she was offered a billion dollars.

"*Imposible! Magic stamina infinita?!*"

"Yes. Do you like it?" Fume asks with a smile.

"*Si me gusta?! Por supuesto! Soy invencible!*" Allecia cheers, jumping with joy before remembering her back wound.

Fume smiles and nods, then looks at me, "Oshiro, please take off your glasses and look straight up at the sky."

I obey. A hand with mirror skin comes up and covers one of my eyes. For a moment, I can only see out of one. Then, the hand moves back, but only enough so that I can see the reflections of my eyes. Instead of both of them being black, one of them is golden!

"What happened?" I ask.

Fume moves her hand and I notice a bright star far above lined with blurry rainbows. I close one eye and the rainbows shift into sharp focus, floating in an odd way in the black sky. When I try just the other eye, the rainbows are not there.

"Now, no matter where you are or what you are heading towards, you can always look to the stars and find your way." Fume says.

"Why is the guiding star above me?" I ask.

"Because this is where you need to be! Now, before I send the two of you home, I will let each of you choose a reasonable wish for yourselves. Choose wisely." Fume then closes her stance and stops smiling, staring straight forward.

I know what I will wish for. It seems as though Allecia knows what she wants too.

“*Deseo por la paz mun–*” but the spirit interrupts Allecia.

“Allow me to clarify ‘reasonable’. Your wish can only directly affect you. It cannot be something that directly affects the life of anyone else, such as world peace. It also cannot be anything greater than I, such as turning you into the true creator. You may not wish for more or infinite wishes, either.” Fume then goes silent and blank again.

My first try for everyone to treat one another with kindness and my second try for Mr. Nakamura to come with us both sink into my stomach.

“And we are going home too?” Allecia asks.

“Yes. After you choose your wishes and I grant them, I will send you home.” Fume says.

Allecia and I are quiet and think for a long time. Minutes pass, wind blows, waves roll. The gold ribbons from the sword of Fume dance. I decide to speak to Allecia.

“I am so happy we get to go home that I cannot think of anything. Have you any luck?”

“I am stuck… pay off all my debts? Get rid of the weakness in my eyes? Or maybe a few hundred grams more here? A few kilograms less there…” She thinks as she looks around at herself.

Oh. Those sound like very thought-out wishes. Perhaps I will wish for a large amount of money. Or a good job. Or free schooling! Or I could go for something odd, like superpowers or magic. In a moment I have gone from no options to too many!

"Aha! I know, Daiki!" Allecia says, "You need to think everything through. Use big words."

She then turns to Fume and says a large string of Spanish too fast for me to follow.

Fume nods, "All your curses, outside of death, and debts have been lifted forever."

Allecia stops squinting and smiles.

"Yes! This is much better!" She says.

Fume nods, then turns to me.

I wish I had my father here to advise me on what to wish for. I cannot seem to choose between great wealth and amazing magic powers. Well, I can always earn money through a good job, so no need to waste my wish on that. Perhaps I will even be able to make money with magic. But what if magic money has no value? Would making money with magic be illegal?

But I could fly and become a tiger and shoot fireballs from my hands. Yes, that sounds interesting! But what would I use all that for? Would I become a professional witch? Maybe not. I think I should be an engineer or businessman instead. The magic would be nice, but too odd.

If I could have magic, it would be something low. A little private trick for bored nights or difficult emergencies. All at once, I think of the perfect wish. I hope it will work.

"I wish that I had the power to call up any spirit from the Trial of Shenshimu and have them come to my aid, like Allecia and her swords." I say, hoping that was said well enough.

Fume is silent for a long time. It is like she has become a statue.

"Very well," she says at last, "I will give you the power to summon one spirit from the eight of us at any time you like, though Danyoruojin and Hapa'ineko will appear together."

She steps forward, lifts my body camera, and places her hand in the center of my chest. There is a sharp, warm, pleasing feeling, and then it fades away. I look into my shirt. There is a purple tattoo in the middle of my chest! I can read it with ease:

英雄

("Champion")

"Put your hand to your chest and call for one of us when you need us. If we are not busy, we will come. But you must figure out how to attract us to you first." Fume says the last part with a smile.

I bow in gratitude. What an amazing blessing!

"So," Fume says, putting her hands together, "it is time for you to go home. Make sure you have everything you want, for you have no way to return."

I check my pockets. My wallet and the coin of Mr. Nakamura are both there. Amanokaze is sheathed at my hip. My kabuto is firm on my head, and the glasses Memate got me are back on my nose. My only other possession was the note from Danyo and the box from Hapa.

Before I can turn to go look for them, Fume pulls them out of thin air and hands them to me with a smile. Surprised, I take them and begin to think of going to get Mr. Nakamura. But Fume does not pull him out of thin air.

"Can… can I *en~~oy?* your sword?" Allecia asks.

"For more summoning magic? Sure." Fume says, stepping back.

"Thank you. O, Sword of Fume… what was your name again?"

"Fumetsoshiegami."

"O, Sword of Fume…t-soshhhi…e-egami? Um, I call you to my *sr~is?*! *Rez~~t?* with my magic and be one with me in *batul?*!"

A little spark springs up from the hilt of the sword and the head of Allecia at the same time. She does a small celebration dance, then remembers her wound again.

"Alright," Fume says, "ready?"

I look at Allecia. She nods. At last, we have made it to the end. After all this, I can return back home. I will be leaving Mr. Nakamura and Memate behind. I hope they have fun here together. With one last breath, I nod too.

"May your paths be filled with success. Farewell, Champions of Shenshimu."

The ground opens up under us, and Allecia and I fall into a spinning, flipping world of bright lights and pink dots.

Ashtoreth's Kiss

The Tales of Matthew & Griffin

After Daiki's adventure, these two must go on their own journeys, dealing with the ripples of his actions along the way.

TABLE OF CONTENTS

CHAPTER 1

SOUMYA AND THE CARD

~ MATTHEW ~

I jolt awake in a sweaty panic, knowing for sure that I've missed the bus, but then I remember that it's summer break. Pleased, I ease back into my bed and stare up at the sun-soaked ceiling. Wow… it's really over with! After this summer, I'll be headed off to high school! Time is so weird; it's so slow but so fast.

A glance at my clock tells me that it's way too early to be up on a summer break day, but there is something urging me to stay awake. Something important happens today… but I can't seem to remember. I sit up in my bed a bit more, groggy but trying to think. Hmm… no dice. Maybe some breakfast will help.

I slide my legs out of bed, glad that I can take my time, put on my house shoes, and pull on a shirt. Even though the maid has told me countless times not to, I make up my bed anyway. The rest of my room is unnaturally tidy because of her, so this is the least I can do.

Before I leave, I go to swipe my phone off the nightstand. For some reason, I hesitate. I usually keep it on me just because, even though I only have like 10 people's numbers. For some reason I feel like I need to use it for something today. It's making me a little anxious, too.

Unsettled, I put the phone in my pocket, hoping things don't turn out as badly as I'm feeling. When I walk out into the hallway, it's filled with the usual sounds of a weekend morning; Mom watching TV and Soumya cooking something.

It's so jarring to experience this on a Monday. I make my way past Sam's closed bedroom door and freshen up in the bathroom, then head down the stairs towards the kitchen. The clacking of my slippers alerts both my mom and the maid, and they each greet me in classic fashion.

"Morning, Mootie!"

"Good morning, Sir."

"Morning, Mom. Hey Soumya." I give a nod to the maid and she returns one.

Back when she'd first arrived, she was pretty uncanny to be around. She talked like a robot, moved like she'd never been in a human body before, and constantly breathed through her mouth. Her milky gray eyes and short, super dark purple hair wasn't helping her case either.

According to Mom, Soumya Dhumne moved here from India and was looking for an all-American experience to get her ready for college, both culture- and money-wise. Sam and I were a bit skeptical though. While the physical features match up, her accent-less English and the fact that she looks only a year or two older than me made us suspicious. But we haven't been able to come up with a better story, so we've accepted Mom's.

Over the months, she's changed a lot and has become much cooler to be around. Granted, she still talks like a robot, doesn't remember much about her home, and continues to call us 'Miss and Sir' even though we've told her she can use our first names. But her movements are super precise now, her cooking is amazing, she skateboards sometimes, and she can do a mock country accent that's hilarious.

"Are you hungry? I can put on some bratwursts and eggs for you." The maid offers.

"Yes, please do. Thanks!" I reply, heading into the living room to sit with Mom. Before I do, I remember that something is bugging me.

"Hey Soumya…"

"Yes?"

"Was there anything important I'm supposed to do today?"

The maid thinks for a moment, "Not that I can recall. Make sure to check your calendar or phone for any reminders."

I nod in gratitude, trying not to think about how she sounds like a video game tutorial, "Thanks."

While Soumya goes off to cook, I join my mother in the living room. She's doing what she's always been doing for the past few months; typing away at her laptop with the TV on in the background. Ever since the weird thing with the Japanese TV show ending up on the news, she's been neck-high in reports. Today is easy; the week of the weird military display in Egypt, she was pretty much locked in her office.

She finishes a sentence and closes her laptop without rereading it, heaving a sigh and smiling over at me.

“How did you rest?” She asks.

“Pretty well, you?”

A guilty smile spreads on her face as she looks away, “Didn’t get a lot of hours in, just wrapping up some work stuff.”

“When’s the last time you’ve taken a real break?”

Her smile goes from guilty to amused.

“Awww, I’ll get to it honey, don’t worry about me! Things are starting to quiet down… in a week it’ll be back to normal.”

I nod, hoping she’s right. Suddenly, I hear a door open upstairs and footsteps against the hardwood. Sounds like Sam is up.

“You and your sister have anything planned for today?” Mom asks, totally ignoring whatever gameshow this is.

I shrug, “Not really.”

I hear the sizzling of food on a pan.

“Wanna catch a movie later on today?” Mom asks.

I try to recall that thing I’m forgetting, but I still can’t, so, “Sure, that sounds great.”

“What movie do you want to watch?”

I shrug. All the blockbusters are coming out a bit later in the month, so right now there isn’t anything I’m excited about.

“I’ll have to look at what’s showing.” Mom says.

“S’up.” Sam says from above as she descends the stairs.

“Morning Sam-Sam.”

“Hey Sam.”

“Good morning, Miss.”

Sam pauses on the stairs, “Whatcha cookin’?”

“Bratwursts, eggs, and blueberry pancakes as a surprise.”

Goosebumps tingle at the words ‘blueberry pancakes’. It’s scary how good Soumya makes them.

“You got enough for two?”

“More than enough.” The maid replies as she retrieves a large mixing bowl from the fridge.

Sam practically dances down the rest of the stairs, making Mom and I laugh. She pads over to us and sits next to me, mashing me in the face for no good reason.

“What’s up, dork?” She asks, cheerful.

“Thinking about a movie later today. Any thoughts?”

“Whatever movie you guys want.” Mom adds.

There is a muffled sizzle implying that Soumya is pouring down the pancakes. The room smells amazing.

“Isn’t *Paul Bunyan: Blood Forest* out now?” Sam tries.

I grin as I remember the trailers: Paul Bunyan, machine gun on his back, surfing on a large blue ox, dual wielding chainsaw katanas and deflecting throwing stars from ninja elves. That movie is going to be hilariously awful.

“Ah,” Mom starts, “you can pick any movie *except* that one.”

“But don’t you want to see,” Sam lowers her voice, trying to mimic the movie trailer guy, “*the number one movie in America?*”

“No,” Mom laughs, “and before you say it, I’m not watching any horror movies either.”

Sam and I let out an ‘awww’ in unison.

“Didn’t you say whatever movie we wanted?” Sam asks, pretending to be hurt.

“Well, if I’m paying for it, it better be worth my time,” Mom says, and the way she takes a quick breath lets Sam and I know that she’s about to get into her nagging mode, “And Sam, why don’t you wear any of those tank tops I got you? It’s summertime after all, I know it’s got to be hot sleeping with your rock band shirts on.”

Before my sister can reply, Soumya calls from the kitchen, “Your breakfasts await you on the table.”

“That’s my cue.” Sam says, pointing finger guns at Mom and rolling up off of the couch. I follow her as Mom watches us leave.

The two of us excitedly make our way into the kitchen, passing Soumya, who is smiling as she washes the dishes. Sam and I sit at the table, say grace in a flash, and dig in. It all tastes amazing.

“She’s gotta be putting something illegal in these pancakes.” Sam remarks, cutting off another piece of syrup-covered blueberry goodness.

“Yeah,” I say through a mouthful of egg and sausage, “hey Soumya, you gonna join us?”

"No thank you," says the maid, pausing her dishes to look over at me, "Madam Blue and I ate together earlier."

"Gotcha." I reply, returning to my meal.

****

Sam and I relax at the empty kitchen table, stuffed with breakfast. Mom is enthralled in some soap opera, and Soumya has taken to vacuuming.

"What are you gonna do until the movies?" I ask.

The three of us settled on *Eighth Lantern*, a foreign film that's got really good reviews. Soumya, as always, opted out of joining us. It starts at 2:30 and it's 10AM now, so we have time. Since I have my phone on me, I consider texting our neighbor Aaron and seeing if he wants to hang out.

"I dunno, Yoseph left yesterday for his college tours so…" she taunts, "I'll probably go out and explore the delectable freedoms of a driver's license. Lemme guess, you'll probably travel via bicycle like a *commoner*."

I roll my eyes, amused and honestly a little jealous, "I think I'll probably just play video games or maybe go to the pool with Aaron… I feel like there is something I was supposed to do today, but I can't remember what it is."

"Confess to Soumya?" Sam teases.

"Quit it with that!" I hiss, shooting a nervous glance upstairs. My face is warm in an instant.

"I know you like her." Sam smirks.

"Do not!"

"Do too~!"

"Will you shut up already! That's not it."

"I dunno then," Sam says, shrugging. There is a little pause.

"Is it…" she points to her upper chest.

That's the insider signal between Sam, Yoseph, and I for something to do with Arret. When Sam decided to keep her hair blond instead of dying it black again (she also wears it shorter and it's shaved on one side, which I think looks pretty cool), it was a chest-pointing thing. Sam wearing long shirts to bed so that she can cover her Queen of the Undead tattoo is a chest-pointing thing. We were even convinced Soumya was a chest-pointing thing.

I think about that for a moment… and then it hits me all at once. The business card! The one that guy… whose last name was Volt, left me. The only evidence we had to confirm that Arret actually happened and wasn't just a shared hallucination.

On the back of the card, he'd written me a note, but on the front of the card was contact info. An email address… a street address… a phone number! That's right, I wanted to call him today! I figured the summer break before high school would be the perfect time to start looking into this stuff, especially since I have more time!

"You're right, thanks." I say quickly, getting out of my chair and speed walking toward the stairs.

"Hey wait," Sam calls, sitting up, "what is it?"

I pause and smirk, "Oh, just *commoner* things."

"Why you little…" she gets out of her chair and I take that as a warning to bolt up the stairs.

She comes thundering up after me, with Mom yelling at the two of us to stop horsing around, but luckily, I reach the landing and my bedroom first, laughing and panting as I shut and lock the door. Sam, a little too slow, bumps the door with her shoulder, tries the handle for a bit, then pounds it once with a defeated fist.

"You better be glad we just finished breakfast!"

With that, she thumps away.

I grin and giggle to myself for a moment, then remember the card and straighten up. One look at my room dampens my mood. It's freakishly neat, as spotless as a hotel room in a magazine ad. I have a sinking feeling I won't find it.

After a solid ten minutes of rechecking drawers, filing papers, and sorting clothes, I've come to accept the sad truth that Soumya probably threw the card away months ago. For a moment, I get a little angry at the maid for tampering with my things. Of course she threw *this* one thing away. This is the only thing not in the trash can that she's thrown away; even trash that misses the bin, she neatly folds and places on my desk.

As if on cue, someone tries the handle, then there are three soft knocks at the door. I go to open it but then get suspicious. What if it's just Sam pretending so she can rush in and give me a noogie?

“Sam?” I ask.

“No sir. This is Soumya Dhumne.” Replies a light, monotone voice. Definitely her.

I open it, and sure enough, there she stands, vacuum cleaner resting in front of her. I see Sam leaving her room in street clothes (punk rocky of course), car keys jingling on a lanyard. She spots Soumya and I and, since the maid has her back turned, makes a kissy face before descending the stairs. If only I could throw something at her…

“Sir, would you like for me to vacuum?” Soumya asks.

All of my annoyance from earlier has melted into shyness. Sam’s taunting is making me anxious.

“Sure sure,” I say, still remembering the card, “but could I ask you something?”

“Anything.” Replies the maid.

Do YoU lIkE mE? I can imagine Sam’s voice mocking.

“Do you ever remember throwing away a business card from a guy whose last name was Volt?”

I doubt she even realizes she did it. It was probably months ago. I’m starting to feel dumb for asking.

“Griffin A. Voltaire?” She asks plainly.

My heart almost leaps in my throat. How did she remember?!

“Oh! Uh, yes, that’s him.”

“Surely. If you will follow me, I would like to ask you of a favor.” The maid moves the vacuum to the side, turns, and heads down the hallway.

Clueless, I follow. We go down the hall, down the stairs, past Mom in the living room, and then left of the kitchen to Soumya's room. I start to slow with apprehension as the maid opens her door, but curiosity gets the best of me and I go forward to enter.

I follow the maid into her room for the first time. Inside is as I'd expected. Picture perfect bed, museum-like desk, a dresser that might as well have come straight from the furniture store, and a carpet floor that looks like it hasn't been touched.

The maid opens the top drawer on her dresser and pulls out a small, folded slip of paper from among the neatly stacked documents. I instantly notice that the crease is… glowing purple?

"I let this business card sit on the back of your desk for a while, but once it seemed as though you had forgotten about it, I was interested in giving it a look. I have not made any attempt to contact Mr. Voltaire as of yet, since I do not have your permission, but I did begin to fold the card over and over, curious about the 'tear for appointment' instruction. Eventually, the glowing began."

She hands the card to me and I take it, holding it by the corner as to not touch the glowing part. This is definitely a chest-pointing thing. I'm now starting to wish Sam had stuck around.

"For the sake of catharsis, I was wondering if we could tear this together," the maid asks, "the glowing purple crease is harmless, the tear would not affect the legibility of the contact information nor the note on the back, and even if there were to be some sort of combustion from this, there isn't enough material for it to cause an inextinguishable fire."

I look at the glowing purple crease for a little longer. This is magic. This is Arret stuff. Thoughts of my highest adventures and lowest terrors, of Yatniv, that psychotic dictator, begin to creep into my head. It feels like so long ago. Do I really want to go back to those days? The fear? The awesomeness? Both yes and no… but mostly no…

"Is everything alright, Sir?" Soumya asks.

I realize that I've been staring at the card for longer than I thought.

"Yes, I'm fine. You said you wanted to rip the card together?"

"Correct. It would give me a great sense of completion."

I shake off another wave of uneasiness, "Sure."

"Thank you, Sir." Soumya smiles.

I grab one end and she grabs the other. For a split second, I pause. What if something *does* happen? Sam and Yoseph aren't here. I still haven't found that magic necklace I used to have. Heck, I'm still in my house slippers. A glance at Soumya's mildly eager face makes me feel silly. Obviously, nothing is going to happen.

We rip the card, there is a purple spark, and then we both fall through the floor.

CHAPTER 2

STORIES IN THE FIELD

~ GRIFFIN ~

Welcome to the "Stories in the Field" section of your very own IPSHA-mandated Non-Human Adversary (NHA) Confrontation Handbook. If you are reading this, you have either come across an excerpt, need to study for an upcoming Demonic Behavioral Strategist or Spectral Specialist Licensure, or are completing your required reading for the IPSHA New Recruit Program. Regardless of the reason, I will try my best to make this an entertaining and informative read.

Before we begin, I will introduce my team and set the context for the NHA encounter:

<u>Team Spiral Thunder</u>

1) Voltaire, Griffin Apollos – present
2) Voltaire, Ross Tyrell - incoming
3) Pierson, Paige Kay – incoming
4) Kim, Eunseo – incoming
5) Ferrufino, Homero Manuel Hernandez – absent
6) Isa, Alia – absent
7) St. Paul, Marie Teresa – absent

In this account, names and locations will be protected.

It was a sunny summer day in [city / NORTH AMERICA]. I stood in an unkempt parking lot in the [location] off of [location], preparing myself to enter the abandoned office building.

At this time, the only weapons at my disposal were my two special abilities: electricity generation and super legs. (For those that are unaware, super legs allow the user greatly enhanced speed, jumping height, and kicking power, along with virtual invulnerability in the spine and from the waist down. This is why I showed up to the site well before everyone else.)

Once I gathered my bearings, I entered the abandoned building. Instead of being met with destroyed furniture and graffiti, a skinny, young attendant stood at the entrance of what appeared to be a love hotel.

Eugene "Darklar" Milton, amateur warlock and the main subject of why my team was called in, was lying in a large, circular mattress in only his glasses, polka dot boxers, and a single sock. Six women were lying on the bed alongside Darklar, giggling with one another.

As the attendant addressed me, I observed the room. Intricate wooden designs covered the polished, mahogany walls. Large, oriental lanterns hung from above, filling the room with a dim glow. Incense smoke drifted in the air. I noticed the concerningly large amount of women lying on mats along the edges and corners of the room.

Due to the unnatural ornateness of the room and the sheer amount of women cuddling with Darklar (he is not necessarily the most attractive guy in the world), it was easy to deduce that these women were, in fact, succubi. As is well known, succubi are some of the most dangerous NHAs to encounter, and more than one is generally a tough fight for a single person.

There were about 30 present in this room.

"Hiya," the attendant said, "I see you've got a PASTIM (Personal Automatic Spirit-Tangibility Ignition Material) tied around your wrist there! Wanna grab a seat* and chat for a bit?"

**important: never sit or lie down near a succubus*

I inspected the attendant. She was of East Asian descent, like many of the visible succubi in here, bony and bright-eyed, short, with a black bunny outfit on. Though she was pretty, I was not attracted to her at that time.

I declined her offer and continued to inspect the room* as I requested to speak with Darklar.

**important: avoid prolonged eye contact with a succubus*

"Oh," she grinned, "he's a little busy at the moment. But while you wait, I could keep you company!"

I noticed the bed bump, and then another succubus appeared from behind it, greeting her friends with excessive affection.

I asked the attendant for her name*.

**remembering names and characteristics helps centralize the threat*

"Tasi Phan at you're serv–"

I interrupted her and asked for her true name.

Phan was silent, then, "You know it's not nice to interrupt people…"

I assured her that she was correct.

"Onan, and I'm taking it you won't tell me yours*." She answered in a harsher tone, glaring.

**having your name said in a certain way can be jeopardizing*

The unsmiling look of mischief and confidence in her eyes sent a shiver up my spine.

"You've had a few run-ins with us before, haven't you?" she concluded, walking around me, "I'm surprised; you're pretty calm about this, especially for someone your age."

Now standing between me and the exit, she began to approach. I took a few steps back. The longer I looked at her, the more attractive she seemed. Though I still felt in control, I did not want to risk her touching me.

"I'm sure there are many curiosities you have. Don't feel bad, it's completely natural. Tell me, what do you want to learn about first?" She turned her body and the lighting highlighted her feminine features.

I maintained composure and inquired as to why there were so many succubi present. I made sure to use her true name.

She winced at the utterance of her name, then frowned, then smiled, "It's quite simple; Master Milton opened a portal and summoned us here."

I asked if Darklar closed the portal. Another observation of the bed revealed that one or two more succubi had appeared.

“Nope,” Onan replied, “I guess he’s just super silly like that.”

I wanted to inspect Darklar again, but I was afraid that if I turned around, Onan would run up and hug me. Instead, I theorized aloud that Darklar may have lost the portal key. As I spoke with Onan, I kept my gaze on her bunny ears headband*.

**A safe, neutral place to look is a headdress or hairline*

“Correct, good guess!” she giggled, “Do you want us to give it to you?”

I paused. That was far too simple. Uneasy, I gave the affirmative.

“Okay, but you have to do two things first.” She paused, waiting for me to show some hint of anxiety. I managed to mask it.

“One, my eyes are down here.”

I looked down at her.

“Two, you’ve got to follow me upstairs. Someone whom I think you’d love to meet is up there with it.” She said, holding my gaze the entire time.

I instructed her to lead the way. She nodded and walked around me again. For a split second, my eyes fell to her lips. I quickly scolded myself. I was starting to lose composure and I was aware of this.

However, I decided to continue on. My job was to arrive early and scout, and I believed that leaving now would jeopardize that. Of course, I was simply tricking myself.

If you are ever interacting with succubi or NHAs of any type and are concerned that you are falling under their influence, ask yourself the following:

- *Do I feel any embarrassment or defensiveness? Why?*
- *How would I react if a teammate were to make the same choices? Or a family member?*
- *If this were an actual human, a friend perhaps, how would I go about the situation differently? Why?*
- *What are the logical benefits and consequences of continuing or discontinuing my actions? Which is more beneficial?*

From this moment on I will no longer interject with asterisks, as my actions will all be examples of what *not* to do.

Let's continue. As Onan led me through the room, I looked around to gather more information. The group of succubi curled around Darklar were the only ones not looking at me. The rest, which were all staring me down, were also far more of what I would consider overtly attractive. I am not allowed to share personal preferences within this module, so I will not delve into specific physical features at this time.

Anxious, I walked along as Onan led me to a staircase in the back of the room. I realized at once that the front entrance was also the only exit. Though windows were visible from the outside, they were not from the inside. The only escape was now several meters away and obscured by incense.

Fingers tapped me on the shoulder. I whirled around to see Onan at the base of the staircase, holding the railing. The door was outlined with sunlight, implying that there was a window in the room behind it.

I hesitated a moment longer. My teammates still had not arrived. There may have been a window on the second floor to use as an emergency exit, but there was equal opportunity for trickery or an ambush.

Despite these factors, I followed Onan up the stairs. This marks the point in my story where I hope none of you all pass. Beyond this point, my base nature will lead me to make increasingly poorer decisions until I end up dealing with the consequences.

Regardless, we climbed the staircase. All the while I stared at my feet. Onan opened the door at the top and I followed her inside. Immediately, I noticed the person sitting on the edge of the large bed at the back of the room.

It was an attractive Middle Eastern woman with long, black hair, holding what I presumed to be Darklar's other sock. She wore casual summer wear – a shoulder-less green shirt and pale jean shorts – instead of a bunny outfit. A surprised smile widened below her small, pointy nose.

This was Delilah, a succubus general my team and I had faced once or twice before. The events that happened next confirmed that coming up these stairs was a mistake. Onan shut the door behind me and Delilah squealed with glee.

“Griffin!” Delilah shouted, “I haven’t seen you in forever! You look amazing!”

She threw the sock she was holding on the bed and rushed up for a hug. Before I could stop her, her arms were wrapped tight around me. It felt very nice.

“Ah!” she released me, “How have you been? What brings you here? Have you gotten a chance to meet Onan?”

Onan nodded, “He has! I’m quite happy that he has, too!”

“Fantastic! Have a seat, let’s talk!” Delilah encouraged.

I began to get flustered. *Appendix C2* in the back of this NHA Combat Handbook shows you a graph detailing the effectivity that succubi have on the average person given how many of them there are. For those of you without this chart: two succubi are the strongest. While a single succubus has the highest capacity for intimacy, two succubi can manage roughly the equivalent but with double the persuasiveness. The further you are beyond two, the easier it is to detach yourself from their human pretense.

I weakly attempted to decline the offer, but Delilah was already pulling me by the hand across the hardwood floor. Onan followed closely behind.

It was difficult to concentrate at the moment, but as the bed grew closer, I realized I needed to do something or I would end up on it. As such, I firmly stopped and informed them that I had not intended on staying for long.

Delilah looked crestfallen, “Is that so?”

"Yeah," Onan answered in an accusatory tone, "he just wanted to get his hands on the portal key."

"Oh, that thing?" Delilah asked, pointing to Darklar's sock, "Sure, take it."

I hesitated. That was certainly too easy. The succubi began smiling at my leeriness. I inquired as to whether or not there were any additional stipulations.

"You've gotta sit with me and catch up!" Delilah said.

I looked at her, then Onan, then the sock, then the window. The sock was only a meter away, and the window a few more. I could have just grabbed it, ran, and jumped through the window. In hindsight, this was the optimal option, and if I were to have done this, my risky story would have had a positive ending.

Instead, I asked if such actions were entirely necessary in order to–

"Yes!" Delilah laughed, tugging me playfully towards the bed, "Come sit with meeeee!"

"Come on Griffin," Onan added, pressing herself against my other arm, "it'll just be for a little bit…"

I could feel my heartbeat quickening and my willpower melting. I could not bring myself to say no, nor was I at the point where I would allow them to get me on the bed. I was stuck.

There was a sound, and as it got louder all of my conflicted feelings were replaced with horror.

Thud thud thud THUD THUD THUD

Dozens of footsteps were trotting up the stairs, and I knew for a fact that they were not from my teammates. I tore myself from the two succubi's grasps and shot across the room. A second later, my back rammed into the door, which began giggling and jolting against me in that same instant. Countless succubi were behind it, trying to come inside.

I pushed with all my might to keep the door closed. If I could have gotten traction with my feet, I would have used my super legs and forced the door shut easily. But the floor was hardwood, so my special sneakers shrieked and slid.

"Oh come on Griffin, stop being such a scaredy cat. They aren't going to hurt you~!" Delilah assured as she and Onan began to approach me.

"Yeah," Onan agreed, "don't be so nervous! Just relax…"

To my horror, she hugged my left arm, and Delilah hugged my right. They were going to try and pull me off the door. I braced myself as they pulled. For a split second, I was somehow able to hold off both of the succubi pulling me and the huge group of them pushing the door. But then the pulling pair heaved again and I stumbled forward.

The door swung open and dozens of succubi spilled in, laughing as they tumbled over one another. I scrambled to my feet, they did the same, and I found myself, in that moment, empty-handed, without teammates, and staring down at least twenty lust demons.

If you are ever confronted with fighting multiple NHAs at once, there are many factors to consider:

- *NHAs are not people/animals, so you are encouraged to use deadly force*
- *Positioning yourself in narrow or hard-to-reach areas can give you an environmental advantage*
- *There may be a method of escape you can strategize towards*
- *Using energy efficient movements is crucial; consider even trying to redirect attacks to hit others*
- *You can remove your PASTIM at any time and the NHAs will no longer be able to physically interact with you*

Let's continue. The succubi had fanned out so they were covering the exits. They were all quite attractive, and they were all dressed in bunny outfits with the exception of Delilah, ears crooked and hair messy. A taller, curvaceous one in the back was armed with a large whip.

"Come on ladies! You know what to do!" Delilah shouted, and then the small army of succubi ran towards me.

It did not occur to me to take my PASTIM off. I instead turned and dashed over to the corner farthest away from the lot of them. When I wheeled back around, I was met with Onan. I put out my hands and tightened my core. A sugary, buzzing energy rushed up from the base of my stomach and shot from my hands as lightning. The two blinding bolts hit Onan and another succubus, blasting them off of their feet.

The others around them were barely fazed, coming in from all sides. I leaned against the corner, raised my leg, and used my super legs ability to launch into a widespread barrage of side kicks.

I was kicking about a half dozen times a second, sending succubi flying across the room left and right. One crashed into a group of her friends. Another was sent into a violent backflip. A third flew up and slid across the ceiling.

Still they kept coming, recovering from my super-powered kicks as if they were medium punches. I had only managed to kill one (of course, NHAs don't die, they just dissolve and return to the Underworld for a period of time proportional to the time they spent here), and the rest were either winded or mildly injured.

Many of my kicks were no longer connecting, so I stopped to assess the damage. Immediately, two succubi rushed in from each side and grabbed my kicking leg, pulling hard and causing me to stumble. With a thrust of my other leg and a swing of my arms, I threw myself into a butterfly twist. The succubi were flung from my leg, tumbling into the crowd that had recovered around them.

I landed poorly, on my hands and knees rather than my feet. As I was getting up, I heard a yell come from among the shuffling and staggering mob.

"Everyone stand back!"

Standing a few meters away was an olive-skinned succubus with short, curly hair. She began to draw a magic circle in the air as if to launch a spell at me. I pushed up another mass of lightning and blasted her back into the far wall.

The end of a whip came out of nowhere, cracking me across the face. I spiraled back down to the floor, my cheek screaming with pain, but then after a second, an unnatural rush of euphoria came from the wound. I paused, surprised, and looked up to see the taller succubus raise the magic weapon again.

I hesitated, and then the whip lashed me in the arm, burning as though I had been ripped open. I let out a cry from the pain, but it was cut short as another burst of delight filled the wound.

Two succubi charged in and grabbed me by the shoulders, dragging me across the floor faster than I could gather my bearings. My back slammed into the side of the bed, then they pinned my arms back.

"Not so tough now, are you?" The whip succubus jeered, lumbering closer.

I turned away, and a moment later, she ground the ball of her foot into the side of my face. The other succubi giggled and mocked me, making excessively inappropriate comments which I have decided to exclude from this account.

I grabbed onto both of the succubi pinning me and channeled a large amount of electricity into them. They began flailing and dissolved into death flames before they could escape.

Using the element of surprise, I swung my foot around, knocking the whip succubus' leg from under her and crumpling her to the floor. From there, I kicked off of the nearby wall, glided on my back past all the succubi, and rolled over my shoulder back to a standing position.

They turned around and rushed me, acting with so much haste that I did not have a chance to go for the window. The door was wide open behind me, but I decided to stay due to the fact that I had not yet retrieved the portal key sock.

At this point, I decided that it was best to start using crowd control. A while back, I learned breakdancing as a way to creatively use my super legs, and since this was hardwood flooring, it was the rare opportunity for me to use the dance in combat, as I had practiced but only done once or twice before.

I reared back, readied myself, then swung my leg around and entered into a flare, my most complicated move.

(For those of you unaware, the move involves the individual swinging their entire body in a circular motion while using their arms and hands as pivot points. The individual generally swings with their legs split, alternating hands to allow their body to pass through underneath.)

I felt my heel crack against the side of a succubus' head, but then the mad rush died down and they all began to crowd around me, standing at a safe enough distance as to not get hit by my swinging legs. I attempted to travel over to one of them while still performing the flares, but at this point I had spent too much energy, so I collapsed down and spun on my back instead.

I caught my breath, spinning until I had enough bearings to pass over my shoulder and spring back to standing. Though I tried my hardest to conceal it, I could tell the succubi could see my heavy breathing.

"Very impressive, Griffin!" One of the succubi admitted.

"Yeah," said the whip succubus, still somewhat recovering from my kick, "that was actually really cool."

They all continued to stand in a circle around me, huffing and waiting for me to make a move. My eyes flicked to the window. The only one guarding it was Onan, who was by far the scrawniest of the bunch. She returned an inquisitive grin.

I looked toward the large bed. The whip succubus loomed intimidatingly, waiting for me to make a dash for the sock that rested behind her. The window was the best option, but I could not bring myself to leave without the portal key because of its risk to the surrounding populous.

As casually as I could, I crouched down into a squat, then rocketed forward with all of my might, shoulder tackling the whip succubus and sending us both onto the bed. She flopped onto it, eyes wide with surprise, and everyone else in the room was momentarily stunned.

I snatched up the sock just as the whip succubus realized what was happening. She went to wrap her arms and legs around me, but I ducked away, slipping down off of her. Immediately, several hands and arms latched onto me, yanking me backwards. The sock flew out of my hand as I lost my balance.

All of the succubi seemed to envelop me as I fell. First my back hit the floor, then my eyes bulged as they all piled on top of me. I tried to retaliate but too many of them were falling on me.

Many gathered on my legs, becoming a weight that I was too tired to lift, even with my super ability. Some sat on my arms, a few were pressing near my gut, and one rolled forward, pushing the side of my face against the hardwood floor with some part of her body.

I turned and bit whatever it was as hard as I could. The succubus yelped indecently. In that same moment, I realized I was biting the upper region of her leg. I discontinued my actions.

The mass of bunny girls settled down once they realized I was fully pinned. For a moment, there was just heavy breathing as the succubi brushed hair out of their faces and looked around to see what part of my body they were holding down.

"Wow…" Onan chuckled, "you put up a *fight*!"

The other succubi began giggling and agreeing, until the whole room was alive with jubilant laughter. At this point, I began excepting my fate. I had expelled too much energy to try and use lightning, and my super legs were no good either. They were going to take my soul. I just knew it.

As if by an unspoken command, the bunny girls crawled back so that I was still thoroughly restrained but could now see down my body. A pair of legs slid under my head like a pillow, so now I had no choice but to look at the others.

Delilah sauntered into view with a smug look on her face.

“So, Griffin, what do you think is about to happen now that you’re pinned down and can’t fight back?”

Succubi leered down from all sides. I swallowed, sheepish, and suggested that they let me go with a warning.

They giggled but did not let me go with a warning.

“Our friend here is a bit inexperienced, so let’s help him out,” Delilah sat down in the space between my legs, “What should we do, girls?”

“More whipping?” The whip succubus suggested, making my skin turn cold.

“Not yet… something a bit more subtle first.”

“Suck out his soul?” One of the succubi asked.

“I said subtle, Shechem! We’ll get to that a little later...”

I was obviously rather distressed at this statement and began attempting an escape. I tried to wriggle my PASTIM arm from under a bunch of them to no avail. The collective ten succubi sitting on my legs were also still too heavy to move.

“Whip cream him?” Onan suggested.

“Good start!” Delilah squealed, ogling me, “Let’s keep going.”

“Suck out–”

Delilah glared at one of the succubi on my left arm, “Yes, *Shechem*, I already *said* we’re going to suck out his soul!”

Shechem shrunk back, muttering apologetically.

"Chocolate syrup on his chest?" Suggested the curly haired succubus whose lap I was laying on.

Delilah suddenly looked inspired, "Oh, I've got it! Let's take the syrup *and* the whip cream and–"

"Perhaps we should just put this convo on *ice*." One of my teammates suggested from the doorway.

In the next moment, there was a flurry of chaos as ice shards swirled around the room, succubi screamed and scattered, and death flames began spiraling up. Then, when many had fled or died, Paige Pierson pulled me to my feet. The portal key sock was in her other hand.

I apologized.

"No, *I'm* sorry," Pierson replied, in her normal, soft voice, "that one-liner was bad. I'll work on it."

Although I thought it was clever, she continued, "Anyway, here's the portal key. There is a Pentecostal and a Methodist church down the street, or you could go to St. [name]'s but that's a little further."

I took the sock from her. It would need to be taken to a holy place to be nullified, which is the only way a non-warlock can close a demon portal. While the other two worked, I preferred the third. The extra travel time did not seem too detrimental.

Pierson and I traded a nod, and a moment later, I drop kicked out of the window. It shattered, I fell into a tuck roll, and after rising to my feet, I shot off towards the church.

CHAPTER 3

CRYPTIC CALL

~ MATTHEW ~

Instead of tapping the waiting bell like a normal person, I crash into it foot-first and it breaks under my weight. The rest of my body crumples atop some hard, wooden surface. Soumya slams into the posh chair to my left, causing it to flip over and clatter loudly.

The two of us writhe in this small, white conference room for a little longer before the door opens. A stout girl wearing a hijab and a lean Hispanic guy with a nose ring rush in, looking surprised.

"Are you guys okay?" The boy asks, brushing me off.

"Oh, you went in two at a time!" The girl realizes, helping Soumya off the floor, "This always happens when more than one person goes through a business card."

Soumya and the girl put the chair back in the right position, then the girl offers that seat to her. There is another chair tucked behind the desk, this one netted and on wheels, and the guy brings it around for me.

Soumya and I sit. I don't know about her, but I'm trying my best to look as not hurt as I really am.

"Well," the guy says after an unsure pause, "eh, welcome to our base! We are Team Spiral Thunder. I am Homero…"

The girl waves, "and I'm Alia."

"You guys here to see Griffin?" Homero asks.

I nod. Alia purses her lips together disapprovingly while Homero smiles with amusement.

"Goodness, he's just handing those out like candy." Alia fumes.

"We can always get more," Homero shrugs, "Anyway, where did you two meet Griffin?"

I look at Soumya for some reason, but of course she is just listening in, a look of slight surprise on her usually deadpan face.

"Um… we never really met him. I just kind of…" I look over at my maid, who is waiting for my explanation.

The thought of unveiling the whole Arret thing in front of her feels very wrong. I've hid it from her for so long… how will she react? Is she going to think I'm crazy? Oh man, I wish I didn't have to do the talking. I wish Sam were here!

"… had it." I conclude.

"*Had it*? Just… abruptly?" Alia presses, confused.

"Well I," I swallow my pride and try my best not to look at Soumya, "I woke up… in the forest… this past fall and it was–"

I stop my explanation as Alia and Homero react with surprise.

"You're Matthew Blue?" Homero asks, stunned.

"Y-yes." I reply, a little apprehensive now.

The pair look at one another, shocked.

"Oh…" Alia starts, "well… that's pretty cool."

"Yeah!" Homero says with a lot more enthusiasm, "he saved the entire planet!"

"True, but I was expecting someone a bit…" Alia pauses, "older?"

"You mean 6 foot 4, muscular, and movie star handsome?" Homero taunts.

"Well…" Alia trails off with a shrug.

My self-esteem dips a little as I notice my lack of muscles, impressive height, and facial hair.

"Hey, don't worry about her, man. We're glad to have you here anyway!" Homero assures, "Why'd you take so long?"

"School." I reply.

The two nod, understanding.

"Well, Griffin and most of the team are out on a… job, so they'll be back in like an hour. Eh… so… you want us to show you around?" Homero offers.

Alia gives him a slap on the arm, "Look at the poor kid! He just fell through the ground wherever he was and ended up here! Give him a chance to ask questions!"

"You're right, you're right. Got any questions, Matthew?"

My face grows warm with embarrassment. I turn to Soumya again, hoping she will speak for me, but of course, she is just as silent as I am and probably even more confused. Okay, I'm on my own on this one. Questions… well first is the obvious one.

"Where am I?"

"The Team Spiral Thunder base in–" Homero pauses, "oh no that's right, you're from the States..."

Alia and Homero grit at one another, making my stomach drop.

"You're – and please don't freak out – in Toronto. In Ontario. In Canada." Homero admits.

I pause to let all this sink in. Instead of panic rushing in like I'd feared, it's just self-loathing. I knew it. I *knew* this was going to be some weird magicky Arret business. Ah, why did I do it? Why didn't I just tell Soumya no?!

"Um," I start, trying to think of a question an adult would ask, "okay, so, how can we get back home?"

Alia and Homero frown at one another again, causing more stomach acrobatics.

"Well," Alia starts, "you live in the States… and they aren't really part of IPSHA so we can't 'business card' you down…"

"Maybe there is a base closer to his home that could take him?" Homero offers.

"Good idea!" Alia cheers, pulling out her phone, "Just give us a second, Matt. We'll figure this out."

She pecks around on the screen for a bit, then turns the phone to me. I see some green and black world map with faint text scrolling along the top and bottom. There is a blank space in the middle with a blinking cursor.

"Can you put in your address and hit submit for me?" Alia asks, "Then we'll see the closest base and we can go from there."

"The bases are usually in the capital cities of providences," Homero adds as I put in my address, "if it's the capital of the country, it's probably some type of headquarters."

I finish and hit the submit button. After a second of loading, a list of sites pop up.

The first one is *Spiral Thunder – Toronto, CAN, 1179 km*.

"It…" I turn the phone to them, "it looks like this one is the closest."

Alia's smile falls into a concerned frown as she takes the phone from my hands. She and Homero scan it in disbelief.

"Don't you live in the south part?" Homero said, "Shouldn't you be closer to a base in Mexico?"

I shrug, "I dunno… maybe since I live at the top of the state?"

Alia scrolls a little on her phone, still frowning, "It looks like the next closest ones are all in Cuba."

"That's not gonna work," Homero says, "Don't they have a political thing going on?"

"Homero, it's the States, they have a political thing with every country." Alia comments, still scrolling.

"Well… we could always have him stay the night and fly him there with the flying car tomorrow." Homero says.

I expect Alia to laugh or something, but apparently that wasn't a joke, because she instead does a little sideways nod as if considering it, "We could do that first part but if we flew the car their military would probably shoot us down."

Homero nods and looks off, bested.

Suddenly, Alia jumps and hands the phone to the boy, "Aha! Here we go! Team Speed Star Gracie in the Bahamas! Homero, you give them a call, and I'll go see if we have any of their business cards."

"Hey uh," I half-stand, worried, "the business cards aren't going to be like that last one, right?"

Alia pauses in the doorway, "Oh, my bad. It won't be a business card since the place you'd go to would be the headquarters. No worries, I'll be right back."

Homero also gets out of his chair, "I'm going to give them a quick call. Sit tight."

The two of them exit the room, leaving nothing but Soumya and silence. I watch the door close, wait a couple of moments, then glance over at Soumya. She is staring back at me. I am filled with a rush of embarrassment and look off again.

I know I should say something but I don't know what I would say. *Crazy, huh?* No, that answer is obvious. I definitely need something cooler. Not that I'm trying to impress her or anything but like she's my maid and so… ah, this silence is way too socially awkward! I gotta say something!

"So… Bahamas!" comes out of my stupid, stupid mouth.

Soumya nods, expressionless.

"Bahamas." She reports.

I look away, sweating bullets. What I wouldn't give for a phone call for myself right now. To my surprise, my phone starts buzzing in my pocket! Startled and relieved, I pull it out to answer.

Oh no… it's Mom.

I share a look with Soumya, who glances at my phone and, for the first time ever, looks genuinely worried. Before the call can go to voicemail and make things worse, I force myself to answer.

"Hey Mom, how's it go–"

"Where are you?" She interrupts.

"I-I'm…" I freeze, not knowing what to say… oh goodness, am I really going to tell my mom I'm in freaking Canada?

"Matthew Clement Blue. Tell me where you are. Right. Now."

"I…" I push my stunned brain to act, "I'm outside."

"Outside?" My mother asks, sounding dangerous.

"Y-yes ma'am," I lie, my heart and stomach sinking lower into my body as Soumya covers her face, "Soumya and I went outside for a bit."

"Through the window, I'm taking it? Because there's no exit on that side of the house… not that I know of."

I would much rather face Yatniv again than continue this time bomb of a conversation.

"We–" she cuts me off before I can continue.

"If you're outside, shout. Yell out to let me know where you are. Knock on the window. Do *something*."

There is a pause as I realize, with horror and reluctance, that I have no choice but to tell the truth.

"I can't." I admit.

My mother is quiet for a very long time. Soumya and I shy away from the phone, ready for it to figuratively or literally explode.

"Then where did you go?" She asks.

"I'm in…" there is no use in holding back, "I'm in Canada."

Another long pause. Homero opens the door and goes to say something, but then he sees the phone and our expressions and closes it without entering.

"How did you get there?" Mom questions, sounding… tired?

I bring the phone to my ear, confused, "I… there was a business card that Soumya and I had found, and it made the ground open up, and…" I trail off, knowing this sounds too crazy and Mom is about to make my ears bleed.

"And?" She presses.

"And then we fell through and ended up in an office room with… these people called Team Thunder Spiral?"

Soumya looks like she's about to say something but then she shakes her head.

"Okay. How did the business card take you to Canada?" My mom asks in a tone I haven't heard since my father passed: exhausted acceptance.

Oh no… does she think I'm crazy?

"Soumya and I tore it open. I swear I'm telling the truth, Soumya's right here!"

I shove the phone towards the maid and she flinches before

saying, "Your son is telling the truth, Madam."

Mom pauses, then, "Okay… well, don't worry Matt. I'm not mad at you and you aren't in trouble." She says.

I pause for a moment, trying to think of something to say despite my wild confusion, "S-seriously?"

"Seriously. Well, not unless you *want* to be in trouble…"

"No please!"

My mom giggles to herself, "Okay sweetie. Do you have a place to stay? I can send you some food and travel money."

I'm beginning to grow worried at how oddly well my mother is taking all of this information, "They said they could get me back by… maybe tomorrow. And I think they're letting me stay the night, too."

"Very good," Mom says peacefully, as if she was putting me to bed with a lullaby, "I'll send you some money, and you let me know when you and Soumya get here."

I don't know what to say. Why is she so calm? Why is she believing me? This sounds nothing like what my normal mom would… oh my goodness… what if this isn't really Mom?! It seems silly, but honestly, I can't be sure.

"Mom," I say, firm, "what is my favorite color?"

"Red," she answers, amused, "you also hate peas, your favorite book is *Patchwork of Heartwarming Tales* by Carolyn Guernsey, which you had me read to you at least fifty times, your favorite video game is *Swords and Shanties: Twenty Seas War*, your elementary school crush was Junette Jones, and you used to pee in the bed all the way up until you were–"

"Okay okay you win!" I stop her as she starts laughing. This is definitely my mom.

"Don't worry about me, Mootie. You just stay safe and call me if you need me, okay?"

I am definitely worried about her.

"Okay Mom, thanks again so much for… understanding."

"Of course, sweetie. Love you!"

"Love you too."

Boop.

CHAPTER 4

STORIES IN THE FIELD II

~ GRIFFIN ~

Welcome back to the "Stories in the Field" section of your very own IPSHA-mandated NHA Confrontation Handbook. If you have completed the section review quiz and reflection activity on the back of the last excerpt, please continue below.

Deciding on the furthest church out of the three was a start to the string of bad decisions that would lead me to my ultimate consequence. If I had not just completed a lengthy sprint from the base to the site, fought twenty succubi at once, and done the most complicated breakdancing move I know, it would have been a harmless choice.

I trotted down the sidewalk while trying to catch my breath. When I turned the corner and saw the long driveway leading to the church parking lot, I began to walk, putting my hands on my head and attempting to catch my breath.

By the time I made it to the back door, I felt somewhat refreshed. The silence of the parking lot dismayed me. At that moment I realized that the back door could very well be locked, seeing that it was a Saturday.

The portal key simply had to enter a holy place, so if the door was locked, I planned to cram the sock under the door. To my relief, the handle turned and the door swung in my grip. Then something slammed the door shut.

Her kick slid off the door, she spun, and then a hand reached out to grab me. I stumbled backwards, tripping over my tired feet and landing on my butt. To my surprise, Delilah was standing between me and the church door, smirking.

I went to shoot lightning at her, but she reacted faster, throwing out her hand and sending ropes spiraling towards me. They wrapped around my arm several times in mere seconds, sealing it in what felt like a tight cast.

In her second hand appeared a large razor. Before she could act, I shot a kick into her stomach. She folded over in manageable pain, whereas normally she would have been in the highway in front of the church.

With the last bit of my stamina, I wrapped a majority of my free hand around the rope (pinching the sock to hold it), then pushed up a mass of lightning. The rope burned my hand, and when I jerked away, only a few strands remained uncharred and intact.

Quickly, I grabbed her hand holding the razor and sawed the burnt part. The remaining strands snapped, but then Delilah wrenched from my grasp. Before I could escape, she came around with the razor and pressed the blade hard against my leg.

Due to the sharpness of the razor, a normal person would have been cut should they have decided to move. As mentioned previously, I have super legs, so I escaped without consequence. Though the succubus had fought me before and should have remembered that, she still seemed surprised. My arm was free, so I did not care.

With the portal key sock in my left hand and a rope cocoon around the other, I set off for the street. I began panicking, as all of my exertions had reduced me to a heavy jog, and any other option (the other two churches or the front door of this one) seemed unreasonably far. I did not think to take off my PASTIM, but it was trapped under the ropes either way.

Something sticky and wiry wrapped around my leg with a stinging amount of speed. I tried to pull my leg forward, but it was then yanked out from under me and I slammed into the asphalt. Dazed and now growing truly worried, I turned over to see Delilah approaching me.

I tucked the sock under my cocoon arm and outstretched my left hand, straining to draw up some electricity. It rushed up, Delilah cowered back, and then my hand flashed. There were popping noises, but the bolt never left my palm.

The succubus grinned, and then it was her turn to outstretch a hand. I prepared to dodge whatever attack it was, but it came from the ground. Bronze chains leapt up and slung across my torso and legs, sinking back into the ground and tightening until I was pinned lying down.

I watched, subdued, as Delilah strutted up to me with the razor.

Struggling with the chains was useless; my legs were too tired to break them and they were much too tight to try and worm out of. For a moment I feared that my life was about to end, but then the succubus dropped the blade.

She continued to walk, her grin becoming more and more smug until she was looming over me with a malicious smile. From there, she crouched down and brushed my hair out of my face.

I screamed for assistance from teammates Paige Pierson, Eunseo Kim, and Ross Voltaire.

"Ah ah ah~!" Delilah said, pressing her hand over my mouth, "That razor I dropped back there is a lot closer than your friends. If you keep screaming, you might just figure that out firsthand."

I stopped screaming. She was likely bluffing, but I did not want to find out. Once she saw that I had given up, she removed her hand, paused, and smiled as I remained silent.

"Now then," she said, lying on top of me, "what were you planning to do after you ran off like that, Griffin?"

I did not reply, trying my hardest not to look her in the eyes or acknowledge how nice she smelled.

Her fingers tickled me for a second, making me spasm under the chains, and then she plucked the portal key from my armpit. Smiling, she leaned over and placed the sock a few centimeters away from my cocoon hand.

"Naughty! You were trying to lock us all away, weren't you?"

I did not reply again. My attention continuously returned to her attractive eyes and lips. The warm weight of her lying on me coupled with her obvious intentions were making it difficult to keep composure.

She spoke again, lowering her voice, "Well, I think–"

A car engine coming up the road interrupted her. For a brief moment, I was filled with relief that my teammates had come to rescue me, but then my heart sank as I realized I had never seen that blue pick-up truck before.

The driver eased to a confused stop at the mouth of the parking lot. While I was magically chained to the pavement, arm and leg cocooned with a lust demon lying on top of me, since he was not in possession of a PASTIM, he only saw a boy sprawled on the ground and a sock next to him.

The window rolled down and a middle-aged male voice called out, concerned, "You alright there, buddy?"

I lied and stated that I was alright. Delilah grinned.

"You just… hanging out in a parking lot, eh?" The guy asked.

I lied once more, affirming with a story about taking a rest from a jog. My helplessness annoyed me.

There was a long pause as the civilian digested the lie, then, "You think you're dehydrated? Need some water?"

For a brief moment, I got the brilliant idea to ask him to come take off my PASTIM for me, but Delilah recognized the flicker of inspiration in my eyes and wagged her finger.

I lied a third time, assuring the civilian I was alright and thanking him for his concern.

“No problem.” The driver said as he rolled up his window and eased into a U-turn.

Delilah burst into a fit of laughter.

“That was priceless! The look on your face!”

I sulked, trying not to think about how she was still pressed against me. The succubus composed herself, then brushed some grit out of my hair. In that moment, I realized that I was far too enthralled to be able to use internal succubus fighting techniques.

“Hmm…” she purred, keeping her hand atop my head, “what should I do with you, Griffin?”

My heart was pounding. She propped herself up on her elbows so our faces were even. Her long, black hair made a curtain down around her mesmerizing face. In that moment, I came to terms with the fact that I had lost.

“Let’s see,” she whispered, blushing and staring deep into my eyes, “ah. Here’s one idea…”

Her face, soft and relaxed, lowered towards mine. It felt as though, outside of my hammering heart, everything else in my body had frozen. Her hair folded against the ground, tickling the sides of my face. Her nose brushed mine. Her lips… touched my lips. A powerful rush of delight filled my chest as I indulged in the deep, passionate kiss.

There are a number of reasons why my inaction was literally the stupidest thing I could have done, so I believe it is best to break down some alternative options for a situation like this:

- *Actively avoid the kiss by turning your face*
- *Begin prayer or meditation – the succubus may even disappear due to this*
- *Do not be in this situation in the first place: there were many times I could have escaped this with wiser choices*
- *If you have the ability to, remove your PASTIM*
- *Verbally object in a firm manner; succubi will take further action if you invite them to OR if you do not oppose prior action*

Let's continue. Pleasure fluttered in my face and chest as the kiss continued on, long enough for either of us to have objected. Slowly, Delilah pulled away, and I kept my eyes closed, feeling instant shame.

"Open your eyes, Griffin." Her voice said.

I kept them shut. I felt too much guilt.

"Come on," the voice jested, no longer sounding like Delilah's, "I want to see your reaction."

Confused, my eyes flicked open. Staring down at me was still an attractive woman wearing what Delilah had worn with black hair pouring down, but now she was pale, with plump lips, upturned eyes, and soft, high cheekbones. Her eyes were hot black instead of warm brown.

She grinned, “How do I look?”

I was at a loss for words. As detailed in *Appendix C1* of this handbook, succubi have a standard list of powers. For many of the lesser succubi, they can simply summon things like whips and chocolate syrup and the like. One step above are succubus generals, like Delilah, who have special abilities, such as fire or flight or these magic chains.

But no regular succubus should be able to shapeshift. That is not an ability lesser demons or even demon generals possess. Logically, that would mean she was a demon queen, (the actual result, as you will soon see, is much worse), but I did not want to consider that.

I stammered for an explanation as to how she could–

“Shapeshift? Well… ‘cause I can! Tell me, Griffin, what sort of demons have the ability to shapeshift?”

I swallowed hard. Even though she wore a teasing smile, I recognized how incredibly serious this was. I answered her question, saying that only very strong demons can.

“That’s right – oh come on Griffin, don’t look so pale – and what rank would you give a demon this powerful?”

I proposed a demon of this caliber would be of king/queen rank.

“Rational response,” she taunted, “and now for the big question… what is my name?”

My mind was racing to grasp at my succubus knowledge. As you will see in *Appendix B*, there are only a handful of demon queens in the succubus category since many of the lesser and general succubi are already strong enough. There were the Sisters of Doom, but outside of them, I could not think of many.

I suggested Athaliah.

The succubus chuckled, “Good guess, but Athaliah isn’t a succubus. I’ll give you two more tries.”

I suggested Jezebel.

“Jezebel is a general. One more go.”

I suggested the most infamous succubus in existence, Asherah.

The mystery woman paused and my skin turned cold, then she sat up on my legs and laughed, “Very *very* close. But that’s my sister. I’m Ashtoreth.”

There was no relief at these words, only shifted panic.

Allow me to explain. If you turn to *Appendix A* of this handbook, you will see Ashtoreth as the weakest of the three Supreme Demons, making her the fourth strongest evil entity of all time behind Molek, Chemosh, and of course Satan.

The thing that made her slightly less terrifying than her sister is that Asherah is said to be *irresistible*, meaning that if one were to see her, one’s soul would be as good as gone. Ashtoreth is a very powerful seductress as well, but her incredible strength comes from her combat abilities. She is said to be *unbeatable*, meaning that even at peak strength, anyone to face her would be as good as dead.

I laid there, frozen, my lips buzzing. I knew kissing a demon was bad but was unsure of what would happen to someone who kissed a Supreme Demon. Perhaps I would melt or go insane, or maybe even become a demon myself. I was unsure if I even still had my soul. These thoughts greatly distressed me.

I am unsure of what I looked like, but Ashtoreth seemed to find my expression amusing, "Wow, you're really scared, aren't you?"

Her voice got lower as she began circling her finger on my chest, "Well, you should be. Because you've been a real thorn in our side in the past… and for such an infamous hero you were surprisingly easy to trick."

She leaned in and I turned away, shutting my eyes. Instead of kissing me again, she giggled. I asked why she decided to go after me specifically and if there weren't other, greater heroes to target.

"There are," she whispered, "and we've been getting to them. But since you were on the list and seemed like a quick snack, I thought I'd check the box a bit soon–"

There was a sprinkle of what I thought was rain on my arm, and Ashtoreth jumped off of me like she saw a spider. As soon as she moved, I saw a moon-faced priest towering above the two of us, expression grim and vial of holy water gripped in his hands.

"Impure spirit, you aren't welcome here," he explained, "let this boy alone and leave at once."

"Father [surname]," Ashtoreth started as the priest began to sprinkle water on my shackles, melting them, "how heroic of you to show up. But you're a little too late to sp–"

"I order you out in the name of the Trinity. Depart, conspirer of darkness!"

Ashtoreth was picked up by a rush of light and thrown back a bit, then hit the ground, paused, and got to her feet, much to the collective surprise of the priest and me.

"As I was *saying*, you're a little too late to spare Griffin from what he's earned."

"As servant of the Lord, I am more than content to die here if it means saving this boy's soul." The priest replied without hesitation, flinging more water at her.

It splattered on her and began to hiss, but since she is a Supreme Demon, she brushed it off with little more than a wince. At this, the priest's eyes widened, and he helped me up before backing us away towards the church. Ashtoreth picked up the portal key and began to walk towards us.

"Griffin," she said, amused, "perhaps Father [surname] wasn't the best one to save you. He may be strong, but he's not invincible."

The priest did not reply, continuing to back away with an arm in front of me.

"This is why I love humans so much," Ashtoreth muttered to herself, then, "alright boys, here's the deal. Father… no, [first name], I think it's best that you know I'm *Supreme Demon Ashtoreth*, so if you want to get off scot-free, you should leave now."

The priest's eyes widened and threw an incredulous look at me. Instead of running away like any normal civilian, he turned back to Ashtoreth and continued to escort me to the church.

Ashtoreth smirked, "I guess that's that then. Well, Griffin, the little smooch we shared had a bit more than just love in it," she stopped smiling and said formally, "With this curse, from this very day until the moment you leave this earthly realm, you will suffer attacks from the seven deadly sins, each sin for each day, each attack stronger than the last."

There was a heavy silence as the words lingered in the air. I felt many emotions; dread, betrayal, and somewhere in the back of my mind was the feeble thought that surely this was all just a ruse or a bad dream.

My back bumped into the door, and the priest took a quick glance to figure out why I had stopped moving. For a moment, I feared Ashtoreth would rush us, but she stopped walking, too.

"Going inside? Okay then, see ya!"

She tossed me the sock and I reached out to catch it. The priest shouted, Ashtoreth rushed forward in a stream of darkness, and as soon as I grabbed the sock, I fell unconscious.

This concludes my narrative in the "Stories in the Field" section of your very own IPSHA-mandated NHA Confrontation Handbook. I hope this has been an enlightening experience and a good look into the do's and don'ts of field work. Godspeed, and please remember to make smart decisions.

CHAPTER 5

A FREAKING FLYING CAR

~ MATTHEW ~

Both of their ideas backfired so we have to go with the flying car option. Alia couldn't find whatever she needed to teleport us to the base in the Bahamas. Even still, Homero said that their best wizard took the week off due to food poisoning and wouldn't be able to teleport me home.

We've been sitting in the living room of this base (which feels more like one of those weird house-office places) waiting on the rest of the team to arrive. Alia has been reading for the past two hours. Homero has been on his phone, Soumya has just been sitting there, and I've been thinking about Mom.

Is she really going to be okay? That was so weird for her. I mean, I've never been in a situation anywhere near this one before, but still, I didn't expect her to react with so much acceptance. I remember when I stayed for an after-school club instead of heading straight home one day and I thought she was going to take my head off. Now I'm magically in Canada and she's just fine?

Homero suddenly jumps as if he too got a call from his mother.

"It's the others…" he says, rushing off towards what I assume to be the front door.

Out of the window, there is a very stylish, very expensive looking blue-gray sports car in the driveway. Two teenagers hurry out of it. One of them is big and muscular, and the other one is dressed like a ninja. Homero approaches them, but then the biggest one begins shouting and charges past.

"… his phone at the church, and now Kay is gone too, and–"

The buff, light-skinned Black guy stops booming as he notices Soumya and I in the living room. The guy in the full ninja outfit files in behind him, stopping abruptly.

"Perfect time to have guests," he breathes, striding over to us, "Hey, I'm Ross."

"Matt," I say, shaking his hand, "Oh, and this is Soumya."

My maid trades a nod with the guy, hers much more formal than his. I'm glad he spared her his crushing grip.

"So Matt, Soumya," he says, throwing car keys on the kitchen counter, "you probably know Homero and Alia by now. Again, I'm Ross, and this is Eunseo."

My maid and I trade nods and short waves with the ninja. The only thing I can see is his eyes, and there is a large Japanese symbol tattooed over his right one, like an eyepatch.

"I'm going to take a wild guess," Ross pauses, "you're Matt as in Matthew Blue?"

"Yes." I reply.

Ross sighs in relief, "Awesome, we need a world saver right now," I begin to grow nervous, but then he turns his attention to the others, "apparently, Griffin is headed to Vancouver and Kay is just… gone."

"What do you mean?" Alia asks, sitting up.

"We finished fighting the succubi, then Kay went to go looking for Griffin and she never came back. So then we go out to find the two of them and finally find a church with some 'Father Roy' guy that knows some answers…"

Ross grumbles, "But old dude was all like *no, I must keep confessions private so I can only tell you the boy is headed to Vancouver*. To make matters worse, he said he didn't even see Kay–"

The muscular guy's hands start smoking and he annoyedly waves them until they're extinguished. No one else seems to be startled by that, so I pretend not to be either.

"Can we call them?" Homero asks.

Ross digs into his pocket and produces a smart phone, shaking it angrily, "well here's *Griffin's* phone and Kay has hers turned off."

Homero and Alia look like they are at a loss for words. Eunseo is silent, studying me. I'm not going to say anything, and I don't think Soumya will either. Ross realizes all of this and shakes his head, gathering himself.

"Alright, I'm gonna set up the car to fly and we're gonna get Griff back. I'm not taking the heat from our mom on this one. Does anyone know where Marie is?"

I recoil as I realize that this flying car thing really isn't a joke.

"She's at home," Alia barely breathes before, "you know, Matt and Soumya need to get home too, and the only other base that can do that has a wizard on sick leave."

"Well, where is their home? We can use a business card to…" he sees Alia and Homero's faces, "Oh, he lives in the States?"

"Yeah," the pair respond.

Ross is silent, visibly frustrated.

"Well," he starts, looking at me, "we'll just take you with us. You won't be getting home today but we'll try to make it by the end of the week."

I feel my insides curl up. I'm going to have to call my mom again. Alia and Homero look at me with pity.

Ross speaks out again, "Someone call Marie because I want her to come with us. When we catch up to Griffin, he better explain everything, and she'll be there if he's lying. Also Eunseo," the ninja nods, "I want you to come with us too. You've got the super vision and tracking skills; you might be able to spot Griff or Kay from above."

"Do I change clothes now?" The ninja asks, a Korean accent making his words curl and chop.

"Yeah, and you can relax, too. The fight is over, remember?"

The ninja nods and practically glides over to a back hallway, his feet hardly making any noise.

"Homero, Alia, you two stay and keep holding down the fort." Ross says, rushing off to go grab something.

Homero nods and ducks out with his phone in hand, probably to call whoever Marie is.

"You're supposed to be the engineer," Alia calls, "How are you going to fit yourself, Eunseo, the nun, and our two guests into a four-seater car? That's not to include Kay and Griffin once you get them."

"Good point. We'll take the glider, too." Ross concludes before ducking into a side hallway.

"Who's going to fly it, smarty?" Alia asks.

Ross reappears in the room, looking annoyed but bested.

"I don't know," he says, "Eunseo?"

Both Alia and Ross cringe in unison.

"Right, never mind," Ross corrects, "she's horrible with tech. Well then… Marie is blind so…" he glances at me, "Matt, how old are you?"

"Uh, thirteen." I reply, momentarily forgetting my age.

"What about you, Soumya?" Ross tries after a wince.

"According to my readings, in Western culture, a woman is never supposed to reveal her age or weight." Soumya reports.

The room falls into uncomfortable silence. Alia looks like she wants to object but Ross starts speaking before she can.

"Oookay then… Matt, do you know how to fly a car?"

I swallow hard, "N-no?"

The muscular guy smirks, "Don't worry, it'll be easy."

Alia calls after him again but he disappears down the hallway, opening and shutting a door a moment later.

"He can't seriously be thinking of letting you fly the car! That's outrageous!" Alia complains, adjusting her hijab.

My self-esteem dips once again, but Alia is right. The only formal driving education I've had is sitting in the back seat while Mom was helping Sam with her learner's permit. That felt about as scary as flying, if that counts.

"Okay," Homero suddenly announces from behind me, "Marie should be here in a little. Alia, I guess I'll be staying at the base for a couple more days. You?"

"I'm certainly not spending the night but I'll hang out for a good while." Alia states, dipping back into her book.

Homero shrugs as he enters the kitchen, opening the fridge and grabbing a soda.

A girl abruptly emerges from the hallway Eunseo went down, wearing a long hoodie, leggings, very stylish basketball shoes, and headphones around her neck, backwards. Her short hair is tied up in a fountain ponytail. She has the same across-the-eye tattoo as the ninja. Wait… I'm starting to feel like she *is* the ninja. Yeah… yeah, definitely. Whoops.

"Where is Ross?" Eunseo asks, looking around.

"He's outside, getting the car ready. It'll probably take him an hour or two." Alia answers, gesturing for her to redo her headphones.

"Okay. Can we play Spades now?" Eunseo offers, rounding the

couch with an eerie amount of noiselessness.

Homero perks up at the word ‘Spades’. Alia thuds her large book closed with a sigh.

“I am surprised, everyone seems to like watching me win.” She taunts.

“As if,” Homero says, then he looks at me, “I’m going to grab the cards. You and Soumya want to play?”

The maid looks at me. I’m not feeling like the biggest social butterfly at the moment, and I don’t even know how to play Spades, *and* I still need to call Mom and update her. Oh man, I should probably get to that now.

“No thanks,” I shake my head, “I need to call my mom. But Soumya, you go ahead.”

Homero and my maid nod, and then Soumya turns to the room, announcing, “Please go slowly as I am not familiar with Spades.”

The rest of the room bursts into excited jeers and jumbled explanations, but I’ve already ducked into a hallway. Using what little knowledge I have of the place, I open the second door on the right and… yep, that’s the blank, white meeting room from before. Concerned and curious as to what’s going to happen, I pull out my phone to redial my mom.

Sam’s face suddenly pops up on the screen. What?! I answer the call, nervous yet intrigued.

“Hey Matt, are you okay?” She rushes.

“Yeah, I’m good, why?” I respond.

"Because you're magically in *Canada* for some reason and Mom is acting like you're just over at Yoseph's house." Sam says this in sort of a hard whisper.

My already neutral spirits drop. What is going on with my mother? Why isn't she freaking out? Have I… broken her?

"S-Sam," I ask, worried, "do you think Mom is going to be okay?"

I expect my sister to snap back with a snarky comment, but she replies with a thoughtful seriousness that makes my spirits sink even further, "I hope so Matt… she looks okay and she's acting more tired than worried so… when will you be back?"

I wish I could say that I would be back tonight, especially after what Sam told me, but I tell her the truth about it being maybe another week.

"You can't try to make it back any earlier? Like, come back on a commercial airliner or something?" Sam tries, sounding annoyed.

"I… don't think that's an option." I say.

"What do you mean 'I don't think that's…" she stops, and when she starts again, there is a bored knowingness in her voice, "this is a chest-pointing thing, isn't it?"

"I'm pretty sure." I respond.

She sighs, "Should've known. Of course the baby gets all the action while I'm at the bowling alley with Rachel and Nadia. Well, whatever. I'll let Mom know you'll be late. Stay safe and whatnot; don't die or I'll kill you."

"Er… okay."

"Love ya." She jabs. She always says that quickly, as if she doesn't want to be caught saying it.

"Love you too." I reply, finding my sister's affection uplifting.

Boop.

CHAPTER 6

ALMOST KILLED SOMEONE

~ GRIFFIN ~

I duck into the coffee shop as the floodgates open in the afternoon sky above Detroit. Rain batters the window in sheets behind me, but it is faint over the sounds of chatter and coffee machines hissing. The line to the barista is outrageous, and I'm not particularly thirsty anyway, so I start to hunt for a seat.

I find an empty table rather quickly, but a rain-soaked woman and her two toddlers swoop in and claim it before I can. Alright, guess I'm sitting with someone else. I scan the coffee shop a few times before finding a young, lean, Indian guy by himself at a two-seater. Luckily no additional drenched families come in to claim that spot on my walk over there.

He pulls out his earbuds as I approach.

"Mind if I sit here?" I ask, trying my best to sound as hard and American as possible.

"Sure thing bro." He says.

I sit and he goes to put his earbuds back in, then hesitates and places them down with a reluctant sigh.

"I'm pushing myself to be a bit more social on the daily so," he extends his hand, "how's it going? I'm Karthik."

“Karthik,” I reply, shaking, “I’m Griffin.”

“Dope name,” he comments, sitting back, “how’s the weather?”

I laugh, “Abysmal. You came here because of the rain, too?”

“Yeah, and I was just stopping by to use the free wifi for a bit. The lunch traffic looked iffy and the jam doesn’t start for another hour or so.” Karthik explains.

“Jam?” I ask, amazed.

“Yeah, it’s pretty much a competition for people who breakdance.” He explains.

“No way! You’re a breaker?!” I ask, sitting up.

Karthik laughs, “Yeah dawg, don’t tell me you’re one too!”

“I am!” I say, beaming, “what are the odds?”

“I know man, I’m glad I decided to get social for once! When did you start breaking?” Karthik leans forward, sounding fascinated.

“About two years ago. You?”

“Phew… maybe five years at this point?” He grins, still trying to get over the chance of it all, “Are you headed to the jam, too?”

“Nah, I’m…” my mood falters as I realize why I’m here, “I’m headed to Vancouver.”

“Vancouver? Are you from Toronto?” Karthik inquires.

“Is it the way I speak?”

Karthik laughs, “I’m surprised you haven’t said ‘eh?’ yet. Why are you down here in the US, though?”

“It’s faster this way, road-wise and all.” I admit.

“Huh, is that so?” He says, intrigued, “And I’m guessing… the outfit is what Canadians usually wear?"

I chuckle. My superhero gear feels normal to me at this point, but I guess my GPS head's-up display goggles, long sleeve shirt, basketball shorts, and special sneakers aren't very fashionable.

"It's for a convention." I lie.

"Is that what's waiting for you in Vancouver?" Karthik concludes.

"Yep." I lie again, and an odd, bitter feeling flashes once in my heart.

"Dope." Karthik says, going to look out the window.

It's already cleared up outside. Sunlight is shining timidly down through the after-storm haze.

"Huh, would you look at that. Cleared up already!" He begins gathering his belongings, "Must be one of those summer storms."

"Yeah."

There is an awkward pause as he shoulders the second strap of his bag, then, "Hey, did you… wanna come to the jam with me?"

My mood crashes at this and I have to try my hardest to put on a smile, "Oh no thanks, I was going to grab something and hit the road again."

"Gotcha," Karthik says, waving and heading towards the exit, "take it easy, playah!"

"You too." I say with a nod and short wave.

I watch as he delightedly crosses the street and heads off to what I assume to be a parking garage. I would usually be just as delighted as he was at such an awesome conversation. I would usually leap at the offer to go to a jam. But for some reason, in this very moment, I am furious.

Not at Karthik, I am sure he's a great guy. I just… I'm… I'm jealous. I wish I were him. I wish I were anyone else in this shop right now. The chubby guy in the corner, the drenched mom of two, heck, even the overworked barista.

Anger begins building up in my chest. Why? Why did it have to be me? Out of all the people that could have this curse, that could run into freaking *Ashtoreth*, why was it me? What are the odds of that happening? Like a billion to one!

Why couldn't I be like these other people? My biggest concern for the day could've been the inconvenience of a little cloudburst, or the nervousness of battling in a jam, instead of racing across the country before my soul is consumed by darkness. Why did I get the unfair end of the stick for one mistake?

A brown hand taps me on the shoulder. For a second, I think that it's Karthik coming back for something, but then I realize it's just some guy and his wife wanting my table. Before he can even ask, I get up and stride out of the coffee shop, livid.

By the time I'm on the sidewalk, I can feel lightning swelling up. All of those stares as I walked out. How I wish I could just swap bodies with those people. Let them see how it feels to be cursed for life. If it were in my power, I'd –

Envy.

I stop walking. Oh… that's what this is called. Well, I hate it already, and apparently I'm going to go my whole life with it, so that's just fantastic. I keep walking, glaring at the sky. This is really going to suck, isn't it?

I turn the street corner and there Ashtoreth stands – purse tucked under her arm and glancing at me before screaming as my hands begin popping with lightning – and perhaps her face is different and her proportions are different – and my PASTIM is in my pocket so I shouldn't be able to see her anyway – oh *wait that isn't Ashtoreth that's just some random woman* – and she looks at me horrified as I speed walk away.

I round the next corner and plop down on the steps of an oddly placed church. My face immediately goes into my hands. I can't do this. Her face… The memories of what happened after I caught that sock come flooding back. Ashtoreth everywhere, crawling, strutting, taunting, kissing… laughing.

And then the pain. The darkness, and the ripping, bones stabbing through my skin, tendons stretching. It felt like I was in there forever. Searing hot yet biting cold. Never-ending agony. Every part of my body raked with blades for hours, days, years, until I finally awoke to Father Roy exorcising me.

I realize I'm crying. Embarrassed even though no one is looking at me, I wipe my face. For a while I just stare down at the concrete steps, feeling hopeless. What am I doing? Did I really think I could run to the *other side of the country* and have my Godmom fix all this in secret?

I notice the silver cross dangling from my neck. It doesn't register for a bit, then I pick it up and look at it. I was so young when I first got this. Ross had just joined the family. My parents were so proud of the two of us getting recruited to IPSHA. Of course, we were like 5 years old, so we weren't going to do any actual work yet, but they were still overjoyed.

To think; I'd grow up, Ross and I would get this fantastic team, and then I'd end up kissing a Sister of Doom. Oh, my team! They're going to *flip* when they hear about this. Marie's probably going to faint, Alia will no doubt yell at me until my ears fall off, Ross and the others should take it pretty well, Kay…

Now anxious and determined, I stand. My godmother, Eleanor Carden, is a world-renowned curse specialist. If I could just make it to her home in Vancouver, I have no doubt she can help me. No, *when* I make it to her home, she *will* help me! It'll work!

Motivated, I double tap my glasses, bring up her address on my head's up display, and begin trotting down the city sidewalk.

CHAPTER 7

DRIVER'S ED IN THE SKY

~ MATTHEW ~

Everything is coasting in the sky. *Golden clouds roll lazily. Soumya, wearing a festive belly dancer garb, twirls on a passing cloud. Alia and Homero come gliding by, surfing on giant playing cards.*

I look over at Ross, but for some reason his voice sounds all cartoony, and he tells me not to look down or I'll fall. But then, before I can look down, I'm spiraling, and my grandpa is laughing at me, and my mom is sprinkling shredded business cards into her pancake batter, and –

"*Evigilaris!*" Alia's voice slices through my dream, rushing me awake faster than I ever thought possible.

She tucks a thin stick of wood into her belt and leans back onto the couch, a sliver of a triumphant smile on her face. Without a hint of sleep, I look around the room. Homero is eating a sandwich at the kitchen table. Soumya is on the couch next to Alia, sitting at attention.

Ross and Eunseo are standing next to the door, bookbags on their backs. I notice that there are also tattoos in Eunseo's palms. A short lady stands nearby, wearing a modest, green dress, a nun headdress, and a blindfold. She has a backpack slung across her shoulder as well.

I turn back to Alia, disoriented as to how awake I am, and then I hear myself blurt, "How did you do that?"

"Isn't it obvious?" she smirks, opening her book again, "I used magic."

"Well yeah…" I say, "but that wasn't like any magic I've seen before."

All the magic Yatniv did was with skeletons and glowing circles and stuff, and even though I didn't know what he was saying, I know it didn't sound anything like what Alia just said. This magic is like something out of a movie.

Alia raises her eyebrows, continuing to smirk, "You've probably only seen tomic magic, but I use gothic magic."

She peeks over, sees my confused face, and continues in a voice that sounds like she's narrating a documentary, "There are actually three magic styles, Matt. There's runic magic, with the floating symbols and complex geometry, and then tomic magic, mainstream *garbage*–"

I wince at how forcefully she said garbage.

"–with all of its difficult English and magic circles and flashiness and swords," she waves her hand annoyedly, "and of course gothic magic, the only *real* magic, using the language of spells and the skillful swish of a wand."

"Come on, bud," Ross interjects, offering out a hand, "if she were to go through all this stuff we wouldn't fly until this time next week."

Nervous and intimidated, I take Ross' hand and follow the party outside. Homero and Alia wish us good luck as we exit. Waiting for me outside is a blue-gray sports car with two sets of black wings springing out from either side of the roof. Small turbines hang down from the wings, also blue-gray.

"This baddie here is Skylar, named after my first girlfriend," Ross pats the hood of the vehicle, "She runs on a combination of a hybrid engine and hyper-solar. Gets up to about 350 kilos per hour on the road, twice as fast in the sky. For you Matt, I think that's around 220 miles per hour on land, you can calculate the rest in your head."

I quickly reassure myself that that is 440 before he continues.

"I've got it set up so she pretty much guides herself. Fully automated takeoff and midflight options, though the takeoff isn't too pleasant, and semi-automated landing sequence, which is a lot harder than it seems."

My stomach drops, and probably not for the last time today.

"Alright, go on and climb in. Your maid and Maria are riding with you, and Eunseo will be with me."

Soumya, looking a little pale, and Marie, looking blissfully unaware, open their respective doors. I grab the sunbaked driver's door handle and look back at Ross. There is a cable leading from the nose of a sleek, white glider and off into the nearby woods.

Ross and Eunseo climb in casually. I sigh and force myself into the driver's seat.

As soon as I sit down, I cringe. I've been sitting in the back or in the passenger seat my whole life. I've had the luxuries of arm and leg space all this time. Now, my legs feel cramped, my feet feel too close yet too far from the pedals, the door and the gear shift thingy feel unnatural under my arms, and the steering wheel juts out at me with such intimidating pressure that it feels as if Skylar herself is offering me a loaded gun.

"Alright, buckle up, ground rules…" the staticky voice of Ross comes from a walkie talkie in the cupholder, "First things first, don't touch the turn signals, which is that black stick to the left of the steering wheel. Normally that would just cut on one of your signals, but as of right now, that's the quick-lock mechanism for the wings. So, if you hit it, your wings are coming off."

I start panicking trying to recall what a signal is. It's the flashing light thing, right? It isn't helping that there is an identical black stick coming out of the right of the steering wheel, tattooed with similarly confusing symbols.

"Next, don't roll down the windows. They're helping pin some important machinery and wiring together, and you wouldn't want that flying out."

I look around and indeed see wires and cables running from the doors to the roof and through the top of the rolled-up window. How safe is this?

"Alright, enough ground rules. We're already losing daylight, so if you don't have any questions, let's take off."

"Wait!" I say, racking my brain for something, anything to stall this maniac from letting me *fly a car* at *thirteen years old.*

"Make sure to press the button on the side of the walkie talkie before you speak." The nun, Marie, says from the back seat.

I snatch the walkie talkie out of the cupholder, press the button on the side, and begin speaking, lips almost pressed against the face of the thing, "Wait wait Ross!"

"Yep?" He replies patiently, as if expecting me to be freaking out.

"Are you sure this is safe? I don't want to like, crash or anything!" Surely, he doesn't want that either!

"You'll be fine," he reassures, "now, listen up. We can do this two ways: you can take off manually, which would probably be the most comfortable, or you could use the automated take off, which, despite what I'm about to tell you next, is probably the scariest. Ready?"

"Okay." I say, definitely not ready, trying my best to look at all of the numbers and buttons and twisty things at the same time.

"It's pretty easy manually. All you gotta do is drive down the longer part of the driveway until you get to around 280-290 kilos, then pull the gearshift back towards you and *make sure to keep the steering wheel straight.* Sound easy enough?" Ross instructs.

I look at the steering wheel, which seems dangerous to touch, and then look down at the smooth, leather thing to my right. The long driveway stretches beyond the hood, running down a large, open field and making a U turn at the tree line. Okay, all I gotta do is drive until I get to 280 mph… my goodness… then I … pull the wheel… no… turn the blinkers…

"What's the other option?" I ask through the walkie, and I hear my voice crack.

"Well, you see that big red triangle off to your right?"

"Yeah?" It's quite hard to miss.

"Just press it."

I pause, "That's… that's all I have to do? No steering or anything?"

"Right. The wheel will lock and the pedal will control itself. The gear shift will take care of itself too, but then you'll need to even out when you get up in the sky. You'll have to do that regardless of which way you get up there."

I try to control my breathing, if not for myself, then for Soumya, who is pressed into the passenger seat and squeezing the life out of the handle at the top of the door, face pale and grim. I glance back at the nun, who is sitting at attention, smiling kindly and still blindfolded.

"Has Marie started evangelizing to you yet?" Ross jokes.

The nun laughs.

"I… I think I'm ready," I reply, in anything but a joking mood, "Just push the button–"

"You're doing auto?" Ross inquires, "Your call then. If so, all you have to do is hit the triangle button, wait until you get in the sky, and level out with the gear shift by pushing it *away* from you. Then, when you–"

"Wait, away from me?" I ask quickly. I thought he said pull it towards me just a second ago!

"Yes, *away* from you," he repeats, "Away to go down, towards to go up. Got it?"

"Yeah yeah." I respond, chanting *away to go down towards to go up* in my head

"When you get leveled out, press the 'map' button next to the GPS and it's smooth sailing from there. I already put the coordinates of our first hotel in and linked the map button with cruise control, so that will keep you flying at a steady rate."

Press triangle button, pull… no push lever, press map. Triangle, push, map. Triangle, push, map…

"Triangle push map, got it." I report, my voice sounding a hint steadier.

"Are you sure?" Ross taunts, "I only got one pack of boxers in the trunk and we're already going to have to share…"

"100%. Ready for take… off." I say, the first part sounding cool but my voice catching on the last word.

Ross chuckles, "You got the most ladies, you go first."

I nod, goosebumps prickling on my skin. I can't help but recall those two times we fell out of the sky on Arret. If I remember correctly, an angel helped us the second time but the first time was pure dumb luck. Well, Yoseph, Sam, and I tried plenty of times to summon that angel again to no avail, and I'm not feeling particularly lucky at the moment, so I hope this works.

With a deep breath I reach out and, detaching myself as much as possible, press the triangle button. Immediately, there is a click, then my seatbelt tightens and I'm thrusted into the back of my chair. I watch in horror as the digital numbers on the dashboard climb, the engine roars, and wind crashes around us.

The tree line swells with horrific speed, the field around me turning into a rush of light and dark greens. My heart leaps in my throat as I feel our wings catch a mass of wind, the car shudders, then the ground melts away from beneath us.

I grab the door and the center console, bracing, feeling like I'm going to plummet at any second. Soumya is next to me squealing with fear, one hand on the inner roof handle and another pressed against the glove compartment. Marie sings hymns in the back.

The trees and highways and buildings shrink more and more as we continue to rocket upward. Clouds are starting to look a little closer now. My ears begin swelling with pressure.

"Okay, that's a good spot to start leveling out!" Ross' voice shouts from the walkie talkie.

Oh no, what was the mantra? Triangle… push!... map! Okay okay! I grab the stick in the gearshift and push away. The car begins to tilt forward, and everything in my body raises to touch the roof.

Soumya lets out a petrified cry while Marie joins her in a melody of giggles. I level us out and everything dips harshly for a bit, then we're gliding straight. I press 'map' after wiping my eyes and the whole car chimes.

This is an awful yet amazing feeling. The engine purrs, turbines joining them with muffled whines. Afternoon clouds roll by, their reflections stretched and fluid against the car's sleek hood. Forests spread out in a wooly green blanket on the land below. Ant-like cars coast along on the freeway, passing super small buildings.

"S-sir…" Soumya starts, "my ears! They hurt!"

She touches the side of her face as if to search for a wound.

"Try swallowing." I say, clenching the door in case the floor is about to fall out from beneath me.

There is silence, and then, "I can't… my mouth is too dry."

"Yawn?" I suggest.

The maid opens her mouth and takes a sharp inhale, pauses, and then leans back into a full yawn. When she finishes, she looks very happy.

"Thank you very much Sir!"

"You've never flown before?" Marie asks from the back seat.

"I have memories of flying when I was younger, but I don't remember the pain in my ears…" Soumya trails off.

A white glider with long, thin wings, rises up into the sky, lower than we are and further off to the left. I can barely make out Ross and Eunseo inside.

“Nice! Very nice!” Ross calls from the walkie as Eunseo cries a steady ‘aaaaah’ in the background, “You’re a pilot!”

CHAPTER 8

OH CRAP

~ GRIFFIN ~

My body is incredibly sore when I wake up. Getting out of bed burns. Brushing my teeth burns. Somehow even taking a cold shower burns. I pull on the super cheap outfit I bought yesterday, snag the hotel soaps, stuff them in the little backpack I got as well, then put on my cross necklace and head downstairs for the continental breakfast.

Four boiled eggs, five yogurt cups, two bagels and a half liter of orange juice later, I'm back in the woods alongside the freeway, trudging along. I'm a little further back than I'd thought I'd be, since apparently there was a ferry I needed to take on a part of this journey?

I was quite the opposite of excited when I arrived at a giant, random shoreline in the middle of my running path, and even more so when I discovered I had to wait two hours for the next ferry. It was admittedly beautiful, but by the time I got to Milwaukee, it was almost 23:00. I wasn't about to sprint through the woods at night, so I did some light supermarket shopping and got a hotel early.

Minneapolis will be the last big city I'll pass through until

Seattle, so I think I'll do a midday rest there, then see if I might be able to catch a train or hitchhike for a bit of the journey, because if not, this whole thing is going to take a long, *long* time to finish. Feeling refreshed and ready to trek, I continue crunching forward.

****

Minneapolis is much bigger and much further away than I'd expected. Skyscrapers spring up all around. Cars make their way through busy side streets, there are taxis and bikers and countless sidewalk stores. It doesn't feel like Toronto, but I still am getting a 'big city' aura from it.

I marvel at the buildings, covered in shadows and golden sunlight. Maybe I should try to find a city staple or something where I can grab dinner. Relaxed, I mosey along after my GPS, looking around at the shops and banks. The day is pretty much gone, and aside from the soreness this morning, I've felt pretty good.

So good in fact that I'm a bit concerned. This whole day I haven't felt unnatural tugs to darkness or anything like yesterday. What could today's sin possibly be? Did Ashtoreth know what she was talking about, or was it all just a trick?

Before I can continue racking my brain, trying to figure out what I need to prepare for, I automatically stop walking. I can feel someone staring at me. It isn't just the normal "that guy is kind of tall" or "wow he's super amazing and handsome" stare that I get on a pretty regular basis, but rather, this is the stare of someone who doesn't have the friendliest of intentions.

I scan my surroundings as casually as I can, looking out for a sketchy guy in a trench coat or a hunched figure ducking into an alley. Nothing. Stupidly, I try the skyline, but of course there isn't anything up there, either.

I'm about to continue on when I get a curious idea. What if I put my PASTIM on? I've never done it before in the States… I don't think anyone has, really. I pause to think. Many others would consider this a stupid decision for two big reasons.

One, I'm in an urban area, which is recognized in every IPSHA-mandated guidebook as the absolute worst place to fight an NHA due to property damage and public exposure and civilian injuries and the list goes on.

Two, and most importantly, the States aren't a part of IPSHA due to some weird political stuff. I could zap a NHA with lightning in Canada and the police would try to tell locals it was a downed power wire. Here in the States, I'd either get shot, experimented on, or sent to prison. Knowing my luck, probably all three.

For a second, I hesitate, then shrug it off and sling my bag onto the ground. It's probably nothing. I'll just look around, see a handful of really minor demons, then take it off and tuck it away again.

I do just that, taking the green, double-starred bandana out of my backpack and gripping it tightly. There are a handful of jagged fire snakes zipping about from car to car on the highway. Those are piques, wrath demons. That seems about right. I scan around one last time before – what in the world is *that* thing?!

It looks like a small, tan hang glider is coasting through the air. That isn't any type of lesser demon I've seen before… it's either a guy in a really fancy wingsuit or some sort of stronger demon, and considering everyone's nonchalance, I'm going to have to go with the second option.

Concerned, I pack up my bag and begin tying my PASTIM on my wrist as I track the thing, trotting down the sidewalk to keep up with it in the sky. After a few steps I realize that I'm the only one who can see it and everyone else is just looking at me funny, so I play it cool by squinting harder, then shaking my head, pretending to have confused it for a cloud or something. Not the smoothest performance, but it will have to suffice.

I turn the corner, trying to keep track of it through reflections and whatnot. It wavers in the air, flapping what seem to be massive wings, then it begins coasting in a circle in one particular area, throwing something down at the people below.

Of course, no one is getting physically injured because no one has a PASTIM, but since it's an attack from a demon, I'm quite sure those people aren't having a fun time either way. Maybe it's a really big gremlin – fear demon? But those don't throw anything…

Curious and still trying to lay low, I begin to walk over to the shattering noises coming from the spot the demon is circling above. As I approach, I notice that the people exiting what appears to be a glass shower all have oddly discouraged looks on their faces. Whatever is going on, I need to put a stop to it.

On its next pass, the flying thing almost caught me with some of its glass. I dance back and wheel around, pretending to have just remembered something. The hovering thing stops throwing glass and starts flapping behind me. *Oh crap oh crap oh crap.*

I dip around a corner, almost bump into someone, then continue speed walking. The flapping grows faint for a moment and then gets loud again, approaching. *Oh goodness it's following me*. What do I do? I can't glance back or it'll notice me! I can't shoot lightning or take off in a super sprint because there are civilians around!

"Hey!" a man's voice calls out, "You can see me, can't you?"

I try to pretend like I can't hear his voice or feel his wings beating as he continues to come closer. Do I duck in a building? He'll just follow me inside! I could have pulled out my phone and pretended I was talking on it as I talked to him, but I left my phone in Canada! And for a big city, I can't seem to find any alleys anywhere!

"You a psychic? You don't look like a priest so… I got nothing better to do, I could follow you all year– wait, is that a PASTIM my dude?!"

Oh fantastic.

“What’s a superhero doing in the US?” the voice taunts, “Last time I checked, this was a hero-free zone!”

I briefly think about taking off my PASTIM, but he seems like a pretty big deal. I’ve got to find a more secluded area to take this guy on. A rooftop might be a bit cramped… parking garage seems a bit dangerous… he can probably enter a church but I wouldn’t want to wreck the place.

“Oh, silent treatment, huh?” the guy tests from behind me, “well buddy, I’ve got all day! You’re the only superhero for miles, and luckily you don’t look like anything to be afraid of, either.”

I stop, cheesed, and wheel around. The demon is tall and lean like me with bronze skin, baggy gray sweatpants, and the head of an eagle. I’m immediately taken aback.

“Yeah,” the guy says, landing and drawing his massive wings up like a feathery cape, “pretty cool haircut, huh?”

“Who are you?” I ask, ignoring the group of businessmen giving me the side-eye.

“Nisroch, demon king, responsible for all sorts of shattered dreams and the ‘delicate temptation of complacency’. I think they put me somewhere in the Pride or Worry category. You?”

I try not to get intimidated. Demon *king*? That’s pretty high up there. Then again, he could be a Pride demon, and all of them are generals and kings anyway.

“Griffin Voltaire, world class demon killer.” I reply.

Instead of smirking (however an eagle would go about doing

that) or saying something snide, his beak opens wide and his gold, beady eyes light up. He excitedly turns his head side to side, getting a good look at me with either eye. It makes me a little uncomfortable.

"*You're* Griffin?" He asks.

"So you've heard about me, eh?" I respond coolly, tilting my head back and raising an eyebrow to look even more cool.

Nisroch caws a tickled, wheezing laugh, which wasn't the reaction I was going for at all.

"Of course! Oh this is rich! *Kaaaa*haha! Torie – you know her as Ashtoreth – told the whole Underworld about you!"

My confidence tanks. Memories of my weakness, of the kiss, of her taunting laughter and the endless suffering, start to bubble up. As does lightning.

"Stop laughing at me." I say, feeling my breathing quicken.

"Kahaha! What are you going to do about it? Cry on me?"

I was crying so much during the torture that I could hardly see when I came to. I can't believe she told everyone that.

"Scream out for your dad?"

I screamed for both my heavenly and earthly fathers to help me in that infinite darkness. She even… that evil, wicked–

"Beg me to stop like you did with Torie?"

"That's enough!" I growl, seething with rage.

"Oh? Oooooh? You want to pick a fight with me, big guy?" he spreads his wings dramatically, his wingspan fanning out about 5 meters, "Do you even know what I can do?"

"I don't care. Leave me alone." I tremble, feeling electricity buzzing in my fingertips.

"Aw, is somebody upset 'cause Torie hurt them? Or is it 'cause Nisroch is teasing them and they can't do anything about–"

Before I can stop myself, lightning bursts from my hand, hitting Nisroch square in the chest. He flies back and falls on his butt, phasing through people who are now running from me, wide-eyed and shouting. I activate the tint on my glasses, turn on my heels, and take off in the other direction.

Pride.

Yeah, yeah I know! Pride's my biggest struggle, I gotta get over myself, today felt natural because today's my pride day and I'm always being prideful. Yes haha very funny very poetic but right now I need to get the *heck* out of here. I can probably take this guy but doing so in the middle of the city isn't the best idea.

I whip around the corner and bolt down the street, growing in speed until I'm suddenly at the next intersection. I don't have time to look both ways, so I leap over the entire street in a single bound, land in a tuck roll on the other side, and keep sprinting past the amazed onlookers. Glass begins zinging and shattering all around me. All of these attacks are spiritual, so they won't hurt anyone else, but they'll definitely cut me up if they hit me.

I slip off my PASTIM and stuff it in the water bottle portion of my backpack. Immediately, the whirling clear projectiles and intimidating flapping vanish. Relieved, I begin to slow down to a normal run, taking the crosswalk as the crossing light comes on.

There is a resounding, deafening crash as all the glass on the skyscraper behind me shatters, sending tons of shards raining down towards me. Luckily, there is only a lone businesswoman on this sidewalk, so I bolt forward, scoop her up, and dive out of the way.

Glass bounces off of my legs and cuts my clothes. Sugary bits and diamond-like pieces gush down on the ground all around us. I look at the lady, who has a few cuts but mostly looks petrified. I notice the glass underneath her beginning to float. *Wait, he can affect the* physical *world too?!*

Hurriedly, I put the lady down and bolt into the middle of the street. Yes, I know it's dangerous, but I have a pretty good feeling that all that glass is going to come flying after me. I weave through a pair of cars, leap onto the back of a semi-truck and look back.

Greenish blue flecks of glass swirl in a horrific spiral towards me, catching the sunlight and slicing the paint off of the vehicles it passes. Oh yeah, that is very real glass. How strong is this Nisroch guy? Why did I think it was a good idea to mess with a demon *king*?

I leap off of the truck as it comes to a surprised halt, doing a flip and landing into a run. I can hear the storm of glass catching up, clinking against one another, pattering and pinging off cars like bladed hail. Guess I gotta lose him, then!

Nervous, I pour on even more speed. Cars whip by and

intersections come like hurdles. The glass keeps getting faster, too. Creeping up as one giant, dangerous, aerial river. I don't know what to do! I'm going too fast to turn and the glass is going too fast for me to slow down!

Thinking quickly, I reach back and grab my PASTIM. Nisroch's shouts and taunts become audible once more.

"– keep running like a –"

On the next intersection jump I spin in the air and fire off a blast of lightning in his general direction. Glass splashes everywhere and, even though the bolt missed, he banks out of surprise, phasing through a building. I turn back and land, almost tripping. The glass surge behind me grows silent.

I slow down as quickly as I can. There is a braking bus in front of me and I'm going at a non-fatal speed, so I brace myself and slam into the back of it. The world goes spinning around me, and then I'm lying on the asphalt, trying to get my wind back.

Nisroch glides out of the side of an office building and the glass begins to swirl and flex around him again. He scans the ground as he flies in a circle, and by the Ashtoreth-related taunts he's shouting, it's obvious he's looking for me.

A couple of people rush over, asking something that I can't understand right now. I wave them off as I stumble to my feet, dizzy, trying to get a clear shot to keep running. A glance in the afternoon sky reveals Nisroch staring down at me, flapping in place with glass swirling like a blizzard around him.

"Too slow!" He yells, and then the glass swarm fans out and rushes down around me.

Soon, the nearby civilians and I are trapped in an open roof snow globe. Most of them are cowering in panic or fruitlessly trying to break the glass. I stare up at Nisroch, who is still surrounded by swarms of see-through blades. A police helicopter banks around in the distance.

"Bow down in worship, Griffin!" Nisroch shouts, "Renounce your superhero title! Beg for mercy! Then maybe, juuuust maybe, I might spare you! Kaaaahahaha!"

Even from here, I can tell he's lying. Regardless of what I do, that demon king is going to kill us all.

CHAPTER 9

BOARDGAMES GALORE

~ MATTHEW ~

The news drones on in the background and the center of the room enters another roll of chuckles. Ross, Eunseo, and Soumya have been playing spades for the past ten minutes while Marie has been 'out and about'. I thought she was blind but she moves around without a cane and everyone acts as though she can see perfectly fine, so I don't bring it up.

"Soumya, you can play this game very good. But, before now, you do not play?" Eunseo asks.

"Yes ma'am. The first time I have ever heard about this game was earlier today." My maid grins.

Ross and I lock eyes for a moment, then he asks, "Hey, why don't you come over here and play?"

"He does not know how." Eunseo explains before I can.

"Well, I guess today's your lucky day!" Ross says, waving me over, "Don't look so down, it's a lot easier than flying a car."

The news hasn't been interesting: random but steady evacuations in Paris, a trade deal with Ecuador, a bank robber got caught, and a carnival coming soon. I get up from my edge of the bed, closest to the TV. The three of them are sitting on the floor in between the beds, backs against the frames. As soon as I stand, Soumya scoots over to make a spot for me. I try to make sure my face isn't red as I sit down crisscross applesauce next to her.

Ross explains the rules of 'cutthroat spades' and deals me in.

I look at my hand. No ace of spades; king of clubs is my highest. We go around, I put down my king, and I end up winning the round. Victoriously, I slide the pile towards myself. Big mistake. The other's play increasingly higher cards as the game goes on, and on the last round, Ross puts down a king of hearts, I dejectedly throw out my three of clubs, Eunseo puts down a king of spades, and then Soumya smirks as she tosses out the ace of spades.

Everyone chuckles at how fruitless the last round was, and then Soumya collects the cards.

"Good job! Everyone want to play again?" Ross asks.

Soumya and Eunseo accept and so do I. This game actually seems pretty fun. Ross starts shuffling, and then the door opens and Marie storms in with a large box tucked under one arm and a bag grasped in her other hand. She bumps into the corner of the desk, tosses the belongings onto it with perfect aim, then flops on the bed, almost missing and giving me a heart attack.

"What's up with you?" Ross asks, continuing to shuffle.

"I don't want to talk about it." Marie replies, voice muffled in the comforter.

"Understandable." Ross says absently, dishing out the cards.

Marie shifts until her face is pointed at Ross and, when she senses that no one is going to press any further, she sighs, “Fiiine I’ll tell yoouuu.”

She sits up rather ceremoniously and sighs again.

“The Prophecy Canvas is today.”

Ross stops dealing cards, eyebrows raised, “Really?”

“Yes, that’s what’s in the package on the desk.”

“How does it come here if all other years it goes to our base?” Eunseo asks.

“The concierge at the front desk said someone dropped it off for me. The person mentioned me by description, apparently.”

I grow a little concerned since that sounds like stalking, but Ross and Eunseo chuckle.

“Looks like they aren’t letting you skip out this time.” Ross jests.

“They *never* let me skip out.” Marie snaps, sounding unhappy.

Ross pauses, then, “… I just got the urge to say something super Griffin-like just now.”

“What is it?” Marie asks, both amused curiosity and annoyed bite in her voice.

“Don’t be such an un-fun nun.” Ross recites, face twisting as if the words tasted like lint.

Eunseo and Soumya don’t react, but I chuckle a bit, mostly at the way Ross said it. Marie fights back a smirk as well.

“One, I’m a *spiritual sister*, not a *nun*. And two, I wanted to just relax and listen to music but now we have to spend the next half-hour interpreting. Anyone want to volunteer?”

Ross looks down at the tally of round winners. Outside of that very first round, I haven't won a thing. I instantly understand what this means.

"Matt can help you." Ross says, then goes back to dealing, this time around me.

****

To my surprise, the hotel closet is big enough to fit both of us and a medium-sized box. The cover is laminated like a boardgame but, instead of fancy colors and energetic font, it's just white with "PROPHECY CANVAS VER. 29.3.7", Marie's name, and the year in black, Arial font.

The nu– *spiritual sister* pops the tape off the sides with her thumb and slides the cover off of the box. The inside looks suspiciously close to Yahtzee, with a shaker, five dice, a pen, and a notepad. Unlike Yahtzee, however, there is also a large, black board with holes, what looks like a wooden doorknob with a spike coming out, a big sheet of paper, a couple vials of clear-ish liquid, what appear to be spices, and a sticky note maybe?

She feels around and grabs the black board. Opening it like a book, she grabs the big sheet, smooths it inside, closes the board, and then grabs the spiked doorknob.

"This is my stylus and slate, pretty much my pen and paper. Alright, so this is what I need you to do. First things first, grab the shaker and put the five dice in."

I do as she says.

"Next, hand me the pink vial."

I do. She puts the stylus in her lap and begins to rub the vial between her hands.

"I always hate doing these," she comments, still rubbing, "they feel borderline pagan."

"Why do you have to do it?" I ask, looking at her blindfold.

"IPSHA sends these out to every team every two years in order to piece together some sort of look at any major future threats or events. Even though not everyone is a psychic, they insist that all teams do it. Probably the more people that do it, the more solid the results."

"Oh. Well, I meant, why do *you* have to do it?" I clarify.

"Right. So, the 'caster' as they call it has to be either a wizard or a 'spiritually active team member' for some reason. Plus, it was about the only Braille reading material they had at the base and Alia never read the manuals – despite all the other reading she does – so I've got to take up the task."

"What exactly are we doing?" I ask.

She stops rubbing the vial, "I am going to roll the dice and you write down the numbers, then I take notes. This would be a lot faster if I could see but…" she points at her blindfold and I feel a pang of sympathy.

"Anyway, hand me the shaker, then sprinkle all of the blue herbs into the casting box." I hand her the shaker and she… pours the contents of the vial into it?

Marie closes the shaker back up and starts shaking the dice-vial mixture, filling the closet with a maraca-like sound.

I pick up the container with the blue herbs and sprinkle them inside the box like I'm seasoning a steak. This is undoubtedly the weirdest thing I've done. I suppose she heard me finish, since a few moments after I finish sprinkling, she tosses the dice in.

They bounce down into the powder, showing no signs of moisture, and then the blue herbs begin to hiss. The dice continue to bounce around like popcorn as the herbs fizzle away into a blue fog, then it all disperses.

"Write down the numbers on the notepad and read them aloud to me when you're ready," she picks up the stylus, "I'll be waiting."

"2, 4, 4, 3, 5."

She mutters the numbers as she pokes at the paper in the free spaces between her slate.

"That was the blue herb so… that sets the context of the setting. Like… a journey or a marriage or a battle… In this case it's a battle which is either going to take place inside a volcano, between friends, or against celestial beings. Probably not the last one because those aren't really a thing."

I silently watch her poke, then she says, "Sprinkle half of the orange powder in there."

I do so and she rolls again. More popcorn bouncing, hissing, and colored fog.

"Three 3s and two 5s."

Her eyebrows raise, "Neat, a Blades of Trinity. The orange powder by itself is to see who the good guys are, and a Blades of Trinity literally just means three people with swords. No specific gender or age, name or heritage, just a sword-wielding trio."

I nod as she pokes those notes down. Next is the rest of the orange powder followed by white flakes. After the bouncing and hissing, the fog clears once more and I read the numbers.

"All 1s."

Marie shrugs, "Okay, so the only constraint on the Blades of Trinity is that they have to be the first at something notable. Maybe the first ever to complete a specific quest or defeat a certain evil, that kind of stuff."

I nod. For a fleeting moment I think about how odd it is that we are predicting the future of three random pioneering swordsmen. I wonder who they are. Will I ever meet any of them? What do they look like? How strong are they?

Instead of tossing in more powders and stuff, Marie asks me for the second vial. She begins rubbing it in her hands like the first. A high-pitched shriek of triumph comes from Eunseo as Ross annoyedly says he let her win. Soumya is chuckling.

I observe Marie as she rubs. The nun… spiritual sister hat is already jarring enough, so the blindfold takes it to the next level. She then abruptly stops, looking worried.

"W-what's wrong?" I ask.

"I sense a presence very close by…" Marie grins, "staring at me."

"Sorry." I say, my face turning red.

"Never seen a blind person before?" She asks, continuing to rub.

"No." I reply, feeling more and more sheepish.

"Yeah, me neither." Marie says.

I'm not sure whether to laugh or apologize.

"Oh lighten up," she jabs, "I don't need to see to get around. I just follow what the Holy Spirit tells me to do and I'm fine."

There is heavy silence as she rubs the vial. After a little while it gets too awkward to stay silent, so I decide to just say something.

"…oh, is that so?"

She stops and smirks.

"Why yes, it's quite pleasant, really. I just relax, clearing my mind and preparing to go wherever I'm led. Then, a comforting feeling comes over me, like being in a cozy room during a storm, and I simply know what to do next. Where to walk, how to move, where to face, I just listen and the feeling guides me."

Yet another weird pause comes and I'm pushed to fill it.

"…interesting."

"Quite. Now, you may be wondering: *if all this is true, why did she bump into that table when she came in?* Well, I was frustrated and just started walking on my own so… I suppose I chose not to listen to Him. He guides me everywhere I go without fail so, well, I guess to not listen to Him was pretty foolish, wasn't it?"

I nod and squirm a little. I've never been the religious talks type; not only do I hate confrontation, but they always make me feel like I'm the dumbest person in the room. Whether someone is for me, against me, or neutral, they seem to constantly know years more information than I do.

"Are you evangelizing again, Marie?" Ross calls, voice muffled and amused, from the main room.

The sister's smile falls into an annoyed frown.

"Hardly, since you keep calling it out like that!" She replies as she goes back to rubbing, trying to pretend she isn't that bothered.

As if to validate what she said earlier, the vial slips from her hand and bounces across the closet floor. She feels around for it, still fuming, then sighs and asks me for help. I pick it up and place it in her hands, feeling awkward. She smiles in thanks.

Soon, it's time to roll again. I apply half of an indigo powder, she rolls, and I read her the numbers after the fog clears.

"Two 1s, three 5s."

The sister grimaces, "Now we're figuring out the bad guy. The two 1s usually means it's something serpentine, and the three 5s means whatever it is, it's very difficult to defeat. Might be a giant snake or…" her face brightens, "or a dragon! That would be neat!"

I nod, then realize with a rush of embarrassment that all of my nodding is a bit insensitive. To make up for it, I mutter a small "agreed" instead, trying to make it sound natural.

Next, I put in the rest of the indigo powder and the red herbs.

"Two 2s, two 4s, and a 6."

She frowns, "Okay… so… I guess there is also a scroll involved? Or papyrus? It generally means something to do with documents, but it's not specific. But I guess that doesn't matter. Now it's time to get to the most important part. Take the petal and put it in the middle of the box."

The last component left is what I thought was a sticky note, so I pick it up. Sure enough, it's silky and delicate like a flower petal. I place it where she instructed. She puts the shaker full of dice on top of it and, as soon as she moves her finger, the shaker snaps open, throwing dice high into the air. They land around the shaker in an unnaturally perfect pentagon and don't roll or clatter.

"All 6s." I report.

"… what?" Marie asks.

"Um… all 6s?" I say, counting again just to make sure.

She presses her lips together, "Odd… and you're certain?"

"Absolutely." I say, panicking and counting a third time.

She pauses, then brings herself to start poking her slate.

"What does all 6s mean?" I ask.

"Well, this is to determine what the stakes are. Generally four 6s means something's fate is on the line, and the success or failure of whatever we predicted before determines the preservation or destruction of something. The last die determines the scale of that something…"

She continues to poke, frowning, "But what you said is literally unquantifiable. 1 is a city, 2 is a country, 3, a continent, 4, a planet… but there has never been a 5 or a 6 before."

I look down into the boardgame box. The five dice stand confidently, still in their perfect pentagon, still with all 6s facing upward. There is a sinking feeling in my stomach.

"It's probably just a fluke," Marie shrugs, "I'll get packed up and mail this in, you head on back and play some more cards. I'll see if Ross wants us all to grab dinner after."

"Sure." I say, crouching to an uncertain stand.

"Oh, and thanks for your help, Matthew," Marie says, still facing forward, "I got you some shoes since it sounds like you've been shuffling around in slippers this whole time."

I can tell in her voice she is trying to hide uneasiness.

"I appreciate that, Marie." I respond, also a little uneasy.

****

That night, I end up having a dream about the prophecy.

My grandfather and I are sitting in rocking chairs inside some giant marble hallway. Rows upon rows of candles line the wall on my right, their flames reflected in the floor. To my left are glowing, stained glass windows that depict events from Arret.

Grandpa rocks in silence for a bit. Behind him is a large glass orb wrapped and suspended by chains. It is empty and also surrounded by candles. I don't question any of this.

"Some prophecy, huh?" Grandpa asks.

"Yeah," I say, "Wonder who those three sword guys are."

"Do you remember that show you saw last year? The one in first-person, with the Japanese boy and those shrine spirits?"

"Yeah, Journey of Shrines."

"I think that kid is probably one of them."

I let out a laugh, "Grandpa, that was a TV show."

He smirks, "Oh, whoops. I could have sworn we'd watched it on the news channel."

"Yeah, but that doesn't mean it really happened."

We rock in our rocking chairs, sending ripples across the hallway. Grandpa tells me some pretty funny jokes I can't remember and I laugh at them. Then it is silent for a little.

"You're probably one, too." He says, observing the candles.

"One of the Blades of Trinity?" I ask, and he nods.

"That would be pretty neat: my own grandson, a legendary hero twice in a row! With a Japanese celebrity as a friend, too!"

I stop rocking, "Grandpa, I have to be the first at something to be in the prophecy. But I'm never the first."

It begins raining in the hallway. I can't feel the wetness of the water. Grandpa and I both stand and hug each other.

"You're the first at being you, Matt."

CHAPTER 10

MY COOL ULTIMATE ATTACK

~ GRIFFIN ~

hat’s it going to be, Griffin? Give up forever, or get turned into human salsa?”

I stare up at Nisroch, stumped. Regardless of whether I give up or refuse, he’s going to kill me. Although the walls of this half-dome are high and thick, I could easily jump out or shatter this whole thing with a single kick. But I don’t think I could do any of that fast enough. At the very least, the civilians would get hurt. Most likely, we’d all die anyway.

“That’s some pretty quiet begging you’re doing there, dude!” Nisroch taunts, “Could you speak up? Or maybe I should just end it now! Kaaaahahaha!”

The walls of the dome sprout glass spikes, making all of the civilians scream and cower towards the center. This is bad. I don’t think there’s any real way out of this.

Wait wait wait… maybe… maybe that’s it!

Summoning up every morsel of confidence I have, I begin a full-blown villainous cackle. This gets the concerned attention of all the citizens around me. As well as Nisroch.

“Hey,” he squawks, “what are you laughing at?”

"You really think you did something special, don't you?" I ask, forcing a smug smirk.

"Well, you're surrounded by my glass and about to die, so I'd say something more special than you." Nisroch insults.

I fight back dread and manage a chuckle, "Then I guess it's finally time for my ultimate attack, eh?"

"Ultimate attack?" Nisroch asks, "What makes you think I'm going to wait around for you to get it ready?"

I swallow hard and try to keep up the act, "B-because you… would be a coward otherwise. You'd be scared. Chicken!"

That was the stupidest, most elementary insult I could've used, but Nisroch flares with genuine anger and yells, "Stop calling me a chicken, I'm obviously an *eagle*!"

That upset him? Oh wait, he's a Pride/Worry Demon, right!

"My apologies, Sir Chicken. I'll be sure to respect you once you prove to me you can survive my ultimate attack."

The civilians, who can't see or hear Nisroch, are eyeing me with confusion.

"Fine!" The demon bellows, "Hit me with your ultimate attack! I'll show you how pathetic you really are!"

"Well I…" *how can I prolong this, think, think,* "I can't do it with so many civilians nearby. Obviously, they'd get hurt too. Man, I really thought you turkeys were smarter than this–"

"I'm *an eagle!* Whatever, just hurry up!" Nisroch waves his hand and the half dome dissolves into glass shards again, swirling back up to join the coiling sphere around him.

The civilians immediately scatter in every direction. I've got a clear shot to just book it full speed down the main street, but I've got a feeling that wouldn't end well for me. The demon descends until he's only a few meters above the ground, the glass floating in a giant, quiet spiral behind him.

I chuckle and get into a cool ninjutsu stance I saw Eunseo do one time, "You just made the biggest mistake of your life."

"What are you gonna do, cry on me?" Nisroch crosses his arms.

"What am I going to do?" I repeat, "Let me explain something to you, Ostrich Face. I could level every building in this city. I could shoot off enough lightning to kick start an Olympic stadium. And now that the civilians are gone… I can go all out."

The police helicopter has disappeared, so I decide to pull off a little theatrics. I try to make a bit of electricity buzz just below my skin. To my delight, my hands start glowing blue, sparks and snaps of light crackling between my outstretched fingers.

Surprisingly, Nisroch cowers back a little, "L-liar! You can't really do all that stuff!"

Granted, while I actually might be able to level one of these buildings with a single kick, it'd take me about a month and a half to do the whole city. The bit about the Olympic stadium is also true, but I'd probably die of exhaustion right after.

I simply chuckle and squat down a little more, "Hold still."

Theatrically, I bring my hands together like an O, then push out enough electricity to make a crackling white triangle, moving it so Nisroch is in the center. Since I don't actually have an ultimate attack, I just pretend to charge something up by reciting an Act of Contrition prayer in a slow, threatening tone.

Luckily for me, Nisroch starts blabbering, "Th-the civilians are out of sight, but still nearby! You could still hurt them!"

The police helicopter banks back into view and I quickly disperse the lightning, pretending to be annoyed.

"Ka*ha*!" Nisroch sounds more confident now, "What are you gonna do?! There's only one of you and a lot of me… not unless those guys are with you."

He points behind me and I turn. Two death metal rock stars are running towards us. One is an Asian guy, college-aged, lugging a portable drum set. The other, a blonde near my age, is holding a double-necked guitar. Both of them have skull make up and black clothing, and they're both wearing PASTIMs too.

I turn back to Nisroch, "Yeah, they're with me! They just got word that I was about to unleash…" *uh-oh what's a cool name uuuuhh*, "my Big Thunder and came to stop me."

"Big Thunder?" Nisroch asks, unimpressed, "*That's* the name of your ultimate move?"

"W-well that's not the full name, it's actually, uh, Big Thunder: Vicar of Divine Justice! I… was just saying the short version because–"

"You've caused enough damage here, demon king. This ends

now." The drummer says, materializing on my left.

"Yeah! Get ready to eat dirt, Bird Brain!" The guitarist threatens from my right, her voice surprisingly familiar.

I look at her, she looks at me, and we both recoil.

"Is that *the* Griffin?!" She shouts.

"Wade?!" I reply.

"Oh my gosh it's so good to seeee yoooouuu!" My friend from middle school squeals, hugging me.

"It's been forever! You joined IPSHA?" I ask, happy.

"Yeah! After we moved to Montreal I got the cha–"

"Eh *hem*," Nisroch interrupts, "last time I checked, you guys were fighting a demon king. Isn't that right, drummer?"

"Ivan," the drummer responds, "and yes."

"Alright," the demon encourages, "then how about a little less of you catching up and a little more of you getting beat up?"

"You're outnumbered! Can't you count, Goose Boy?" I taunt.

"*Eagle, Man!* Still, my glass will destroy you three. Plus, you can't even use your Big Thunder! Don't make me laugh."

"Actually, it's four!" Wade announces, playing an awesome little rift on her electric guitar.

The silhouette of an ancient high priest slides into existence from behind her. He is made of vantablack shadows, his clothes weaved entirely from heatless fire, with two glowing yellow circles for eyes and a bladed metal cross slung over his shoulder.

"Ready, Caiaphas?" Wade asks him.

"BLASHPHEMERS SHALL BE DESTROYED. YOU MUST DIE FOR THE SAKE OF THE PEOPLE." Caiaphas informs, brandishing the cross like an upside-down sword.

Nisroch starts sweating, "O-okay then, maybe four people. But that means nothing! My glass will shred you all to ribbons before you even get the chance to strike! Kahaha!"

The glass behind him flexes into individual strands, speeding through the air in deadly bladed circles. Ivan and Wade shuffle back, as do I.

"When he attacks," Ivan says lowly, "I'll start playing my drums and make a force field. Wade, you send Caiaphas around on the right, then Griffin and I can–"

"Make it five!" A descending voice calls.

We all turn and watch as a silver-haired girl wearing a baseball cap, a blue shirt, and yoga pants falls out of the sky and lands next to Ivan, raising her guard. I immediately recognize her and my heart falls through my feet. It's freaking *Kay*?!

"I'm ready to hurt something." she growls, abnormally angry, "Let's do this, *now*."

"W-wait, five?!" Nisroch stammers.

Ice crystals are forming up and down Kay's arms. Frosted fog billows from her feet, and the air around her is so cold that wind starts to rush in. She's glaring at Nisroch with pure malice.

"Five." She assures.

"Yeah no. When that warlock Capital Black summoned me here,

I was expecting a vacation, not whatever this is. Five heroes? In the *US*? Doesn't that only happen in New York?"

"What's about to happen is your funeral if you don't scram, you stupid seagull!" Wade cheers, eager to send Caiaphas off.

"*Ea*-gle! But before I leave," Nisroch points at Kay, "that landing was cheesy," he points at Ivan, "your make-up sucks," he points at me, "Torie is going to hear about this," he points at Wade, "that little rift was total garbage," he points at Caiaphas, "I don't even know why heroes are using you."

With that, he gives another person-sounding caw before sweeping together his wings and blinking out of existence. All the glass that was floating behind him clatters to the ground. For a moment, there is just the breeze and the distant wail of sirens. Wade jumps and pumps her fist into the air.

"Woohoo, we–" but I guess the sirens weren't as distant as I thought, because dozens of police cars surround us, officers springing from them and raising their guns, screaming for us to get on the ground.

****

Wade nods kindly as the waitress refills her glass. Ivan sips his water. The two of them are still dressed in all black with spikes but they're now missing make-up. Kay is slouching beside me, silent, either tired, angry, hungry, or a horrifying mixture of them. I am also silent because Kay is silent. She's usually silent, but not *this* type of silent.

"So, how did your interrogations go?" Wade asks, glancing at the police station across the street.

"When you said 'road trip through the States' I didn't think 'falling asleep at 2AM in a jail cell'." Ivan mutters.

"Shut up Ivan," Wade says quickly, "what about you guys?"

I know Kay isn't going to say anything, but I still pause before I begin, "Well, the cop kept forcefully saying 'eh' after all his sentences once he found out I was Canadian. And he asked me 'what device I had to cause the electricity' and 'who else was part of the terrorist attack' like sixty times, even after the evidence came back in my favor."

"Yeah, they were super redundant," Wade agrees, "the good cop bad cop routine was only funny for the first two and a half hours. They ate up soooooo much time."

There is a conversational pause to allow Kay to offer input, but she just nods and sips her water. I can't tell her emotion but it certainly isn't pleased.

"So," I start, "how did you join IPSHA?"

Wade starts beaming, "Well, after my family and I moved to Montreal, I did some digging around and figured out more about that one time with Kyle."

I still remember Kyle from my second year in junior high, that big meathead, shoving Wade around in the hallway because she rejected him at lunch. That was the last day Wade came to school (moving to Montreal very soon after) and the day I found out I could do more than just run fast (I may or may not have given Kyle a mild… er, *medium* cardiac arrest).

"As you know, digging around in IPSHA business gets you one of two places."

"In IPSHA or in an asylum." I complete.

She nods.

"Well, I'm glad you joined." I say, beaming with pride.

"Couldn't let you be the only cool one." Wade winks.

My heart flutters at the wink and I quickly look off at the police station, taking a sip from my water. Today is my lust day (no need for dramatics, I figured that out the moment I woke up) and I am determined not to give Ashtoreth any satisfaction, because this is no doubt a day she must've been looking forward to.

Despite my determination, I must admit that Wade is quite pretty. Of course, she was pretty in middle school, but I was still naive about girls around then, so it didn't matter much to me. She's certainly grown since the last time I saw her. Taller, leaner… and something about the blueness in her eyes…

Another pair of blue eyes, these ones sulky and cold, swing over from the window and scrape across my face. Okay, yeah, Kay is definitely not happy. The silence seems dangerously fragile, so I start talking again.

"… your guitar! I never knew you liked death metal..." I start, gesturing to her spikes and skulls and black leather.

"Oh no, it's all just for laughs. I don't have any powers or magic, so I had to become a bearer when I joined IPSHA. During the entrance test I put that I was really good at the guitar, so they suggested a weapon called the Chords of Judgement. Of course that sounded awesome, so I took it."

She pats the double-necked electric guitar, which rests between her and the wall, "All I gotta do is jam out and I can summon one of two helpers, Caiaphas or Pilate. Pilate is purely physical, though, so I couldn't summon him against Nisroch. Oh, and he's pretty lame, too."

She pauses, then, "I guess they're both pretty lame."

There is another dangerous bout of silence and, before I can fill it with something, Kay begins talking. My stomach sinks into my hips.

"What brings you two to Minneapolis?" She asks.

Oh crap I know where this is going.

It takes everything inside of me to restrain myself from jumping out of the window.

"Oh, we're headed to a music fest in Vancouver and just happened to stop through – Ivan get off your phone and be social." Wade nudges her bandmate.

"Shut up Wade, you're not my mom." Ivan mutters, shooting her a displeased look and tucking away his phone.

Oh man, if Wade returns the question like I know she will...

"Vancouver?" I blurt, "That's crazy, I'm headed there too!"

"*We.*" Kay corrects, playfully punching me in the arm.

"Heh heh, right. We." I almost poop myself.

"Would you look at that!" Wade beams, "What for?"

Kay might as well have laser vision added to her list of powers, because I can almost feel the skin melting off the side of my face from her expectant glare.

"Just paying my godmother a visit." I say.

"Oh, that's so sweet. Just saying hi?" Wade asks.

"More or less, yeah."

My my where is our food?

"How did you all get here? Train or something?" Wade questions, taking a sip of water.

I would much rather fight three Nisrochs at the same time than answer that question.

"… ran it." I say dismissively, sipping water too.

My haste didn't take the spotlight off me; in fact, even Ivan looks confused.

"You *ran* it?" The drummer asks, "Did you start last month?"

"Oh no, he's got super speed," Wade turns to me, "I remember you thought that was your only power before the thing with Kyle. But Paige…?"

"I have ice powers and I can fly." The falsely friendly girl beside me replies.

"Pretty neat! That must be tiring, though. Why didn't you just take a flight or something?" Wade asks, seeming confused.

"You know… just looking out for the environment and stuff."

The table is skeptically silent, then the waitress comes back around with a large tray of plated food. Relief blossoms in my heart as my unhealthy breakfast sandwich with shredded potatoes clinks in front of me.

Everyone digs into their food for a moment, quiet and pleased. After a little while, Wade turns to Ivan.

"Hey, how much room do we have in the car?" She asks, skewering some scrambled eggs with her fork.

"Yes they can come." The drummer responds, exasperated, through a mouthful of toast.

"Do you guys wanna ride with us to Vancouver? Seeing as we're all headed that way anyway…" Wade shrugs.

"Heck yeah!" I reply, excited.

Kay nods, smiling.

Wade almost drops her fork, "Woohoo! Road triiiip!"

CHAPTER 11

AZIMUTH THE WANDERING

~ MATTHEW ~

The last bits of green and lavender slip past the horizon, revealing a billion stars and the bright moon. Pinpricks of light twinkle and stretch across the hood of the car. Eunseo and Ross drift through the sky not too far away, their usually white glider now a black silhouette of itself, illuminated only by the red lights on its wings and the occasional flash beneath it. Far below us is complete darkness, a Canadian forest without a soul for miles.

Soumya rests peacefully beside me, her head leaned against the window. Marie is sitting in the back, feet up and arms behind her head. She, Ross, and I have been talking back and forth, joking, theorizing, and telling stories. Now we're having a small debate and it's hilarious.

"Since it is a something put between two other somethings," Ross says firmly, "it is a sandwich."

"No it isn't," Marie replies, "you don't go to a sandwich shop and order a hotdog; therefore a hotdog is not a sandwich."

"But you can't buy an ice cream sandwich at a sandwich shop either. Are you saying *that* isn't a sandwich, even though it has sandwich in the name?"

“Even with this approach, your argument falls flat. A hotdog is not sandwiched between two buns but stuffed into a split, singular bun, therefore making it not a sandwich by your own definition.” Marie replies so quickly and academically that I’m thrown into another fit of silent, side-splitting laughter.

“Outstanding move,” Ross compliments, “but hoagies operate in the same fashion, with meats and other sandwich fillings placed inside of a split, singular bun. Yet you can buy them at a sandwich shop, thus meaning they are sandwiches, thus implying that by correlation–”

He stops talking and I see why. One of the stars is growing.

“Matt, you see that?” He asks.

“Yeah, is it a meteor?” I respond.

“I don’t know, I think a meteor should’ve broken apart by now…”

The two of us watch, concerned, as the star begins to glow brighter, sliding more noticeably through the air. Whatever this is, it’s so brilliant that the sky around it begins to turn a lighter blue as if time sped up and it was suddenly daybreak.

“Is everything alright?” Marie asks.

“I hope so…” I reply, unsure and afraid.

What if this is an actual meteor? Is it going to kill us all?! The falling item becomes a little more recognizable and, to my confused horror, looks like the blinding silhouette of a person.

“Hey, doesn’t that look like a guy to you?” Ross asks, with

Eunseo stirring in the background.

"It does…" I say, watching the person-shaped thing zoom from the sky and into the forest below.

The night erupts in a crackling boom as a huge column of dirt rushes up into the air, spewing trees and giant slabs of rock towards the clouds.

"Alright… let's head down, we gotta give it a look." Ross sighs, then the walkie goes silent and the figure of his glider banks left.

****

Dust still swirls around in the air, turning our phone flashlights into columns of opaque tan. The high beams of the car are now distant white dots, still visible but nearly useless. The five of us creep deeper into the swirling, silent forest, shirts over our noses and eyes squinted.

The thick trees around us abruptly clear. Ross, who is in front, stops. Eunseo, now outfitted with a grappling hook and some hip pouches, tenses up next to him. Soumya and Marie, who are huddled together yet seeming more confused than afraid, scoot a bit closer to me.

"That's a big crater." He comments, shining his light down into a drop off.

I expect him to jump down into the crater next, but he just crouches there, peering down.

“I can look.” Eunseo says.

“From here.” Ross reassures, and the ninja nods.

She closes her eyes and bows her head. Suddenly, the tattoo on her eye begins to glow dark red. She opens her eyes, with the tattoo still glowing, and squints. For a moment it is silent as we all watch her peer beyond the wall of dust, then she tilts her head.

“Computer person. Big. Very strong. Head is… like triangle.”

“I’m not sure I understand.” Ross says.

“It is…” Eunseo pauses, “*robot*, I think. I am… uh, computers… not good at...”

“Don’t worry about that,” Ross chuckles, “it just looks like a robot, right?”

“I do not know. It has flashing lights and metal lizard skin. Very weird.”

Ross stares into the dust, “Huh. Guess we’ll take a closer look.”

The floating column of dust and debris soon clears enough to uncover our noses. Ross was right, this is a big crater, about 50 feet across. Crumbly sod slopes down about 10 feet to a rocky, scorched circle. In the middle of the circle is a spiral of steam. The figure of something human-like lies inside it.

Ross looks back at the rest of us, then reluctantly makes his way down the drop off. We all follow him, climbing down the rough walls until we reach the crater floor. Having the mysterious smoking figure at eye level is even more ominous.

For a moment, the five of us just stare at it, brushing off dirt.

What are we supposed to do in a situation like this? I, for one, would've just called the police, but apparently it's our job to do this… so what now?

"Any suggestions?" Ross asks as he eyes the spire of steam.

"Kunai?" Eunseo offers, pulling a small knife from one of her hip pouches.

"Not yet." Ross replies.

"Is it the robot?" Marie questions.

"Yep. Pretty tall too, and it looks like it has a pyramid for a head…" Ross reports.

The smoke is just hanging there around the figure, refusing to dissipate. Is this something… or someone… from Arret? Like legitimately *from* the planet?

"Medicine?" Eunseo asks, reaching for another hip pouch.

"Well, it's a robot, so I don't think medicine will help," Ross concludes, taking a few steps further, "and it should have hit the ground as a pile of ash, if that. Since it's in one piece, it might actually be okay."

There is a startling series of beeps and whines as patches of the figures body start flashing with colors and lights. Suddenly, its pyramid head swivels until it reveals a large, glowing, blue circle, perhaps its eye. The eye swells with light.

"Duck!" Ross screams.

Eunseo cartwheels to the side. Soumya and Marie hit the floor. I run and dive out of the way. A thick beam of blue light shoots out of the pyramid's eye, hitting the crater wall and exploding in a deafening flash of fire and rock.

I curl against the trembling ground for a moment, covering my head and thoroughly freaking out. A small hand grabs me hard, and I look up to see Soumya, wide-eyed and ducking.

"*Sir I found a hiding spot.*"

Wordlessly, I follow her at a crouch, and soon, we are bunched up behind a large rock with Marie. For a moment there is just beeping and violent synth noises. Ross and Eunseo are nowhere to be seen, but I'm not necessarily looking for them right now.

Then it happens: I start getting flashbacks from Arret. People scream as an explosion rips our plane in half mid-flight… the escalator lurches as a missile blasts a portion of it off… the sky and forest coastline tilts forward, miles of air rushing to engulf me… Yatniv zapping people with fire and lightning and laughing as he chases my sister…

"Matt, is that you?" Marie asks, "Calm down. I know it's scary but panicking is just going to make it worse. We have earthly and heavenly protection. Rest assured; the Lord is with us."

I realize that I am, in fact, hyperventilating. It takes me a bit, but I soon find my bearings and manage to stabilize myself again.

"Huh… AAAAH!" I hear Ross shout from further in the clearing.

A part of me is perfectly content with staying behind this rock and hoping that wasn't a cry of pain, but Soumya's selflessness from earlier is fresh in my mind, so I look anyway. The steam has cleared around the figure so it is fully visible.

It stands around fifteen feet tall, limbs covered in metallic scales, the spaces in between glowing an ominous cyan. Indicators and screens are freckled across its body, and a much larger, slightly scratched screen blankets its stomach, displaying a bunch of flashing, rainbow symbols. Its pyramid head is made of some sort of navy-blue metal.

Ross stands in front of the being with his arms up, bright orange lava spewing out of his palms. The molten rock coats the blinking figure, turning red as it congeals on its body. A series of sirens and unfamiliar chimes come from the being, and then its head begins spinning violently, flinging lava everywhere. Eunseo, who was sneaking up for an attack, zips away with a back handspring.

The pyramid eye glows red, and then a bright, continuous laser shoots out, buzzing as it passes over us again and again. The sound of trees snapping and falling echoes from outside of the crater. The being is much taller than we are, so the laser beam keeps missing us, sweeping well above our heads and beaming out into the forest.

Soumya peers over the rock alongside me, looks hard at the screen on the being's chest, and gasps. Without warning, she leaps over the rock and sprints towards the tall figure.

"Soumya!" I yell, stunned, "What are you doing?!"

"Stop fighting!" my maid screams, urgency in her voice, "Stop! Stop, it doesn't want to fight!"

This is so unlike her that I don't know what to do. Ross and

Eunseo look equally taken aback as Soumya scrambles past them, right up in front of the cooling lava around the killer lighthouse. She looks up at the pyramid head and says something, and then the being lets out a siren noise before stopping its spinning laser.

We all pause, astonished, waiting for something to happen. The being tilts its pyramid head so its eye is trained on Soumya, then a booming series of vocal clicks and guttural hums come from it. Soumya… responds?! I can't hear her well from here, but it sounds like she struggled to return a sentence in the same language.

There is another pause, then a pleasant thrum comes out of the being. The screens and indicators on its body dim in sync with the eye turning from red to what looks like a black light. The main screen on its stomach lights up, showing a series of symbols.

Soumya reads in silence, then shouts, "Everyone, it will no longer attack us. Please come and interact."

I glance at Marie, astonished. Her face is unreadable. I look at Ross and Eunseo next. They seem about as perplexed as I feel.

"Please everyone," Soumya calls again, monotone per usual but a little gentler, "It wants to communicate with us."

Eunseo creeps forward. Ross shoots her a disbelieving look, then glances at me for input. I shrug, feeling more lost that I ever have in my entire life. He shrugs in return, then follows Eunseo.

I simply sit back down.

"What's going on?" Marie asks.

"They…" I fight to keep my mind clear enough to talk, "they've got it to calm down and they are going to speak with it."

"How?" Marie asks, standing to her feet.

"I don't… I guess through Soumya." I reply, getting up as well.

I walk with the blind sister across the crater floor, numb with confusion. Soumya can speak to this thing. Right now in fact, she's pointing to symbols on its stomach and explaining them to Ross and Eunseo. What… what does this mean?

The leftover lava dripping down the being is still hot and smothering. Its body is motionless, not breathing or swaying or anything. It is silent outside of a gentle, very quiet hum.

"Sir, this says, 'we wish you no harm'. Please don't look so scared." My maid says.

"Is it in…" I freeze, momentarily forgetting the name of the language people in India speak. I know it's not Indian.

"Hindi?" Ross fills in, "That's definitely not it."

Ross is right. The characters on the screen look nothing like any human language I've seen… but they do look familiar. Maybe I saw this on Arret before? It all looks more like a weird piece of art than a paragraph. All I see are diagonal rows of squares with a bunch of circles and lines inside them.

"This is where you start reading," Soumya says, getting on her tippy toes to point at the top left corner of the screen, "Then you go to the next line down, read diagonally upwards and to the right, then begin again on the next line down."

"Soumya," I breathe, "how do you know this?"

"I…" her voice catches, "I do not know, Sir."

"Marie?" Ross mutters.

"No, she's definitely telling the truth." The sister replies.

"This is very weird! You know this language? What now?" Eunseo points to the screen as the symbols are replaced with different ones.

"*We apologize for the misunderstanding. Our initial attack was due to a sensor malfunction, and the second attack was to dissuade further conflict. We come in peace, simply to journal this place in our cosmic expedition. What is this planet's name?*"

Ross gives me an uncertain look.

"Earth!" Eunseo responds, sounding mystified.

Soumya turns back to the screen, "*Eerith.*"

The symbols change on the screen again and Soumya begins to translate, "*We have heard krrt-tt-tmmyt* – this roughly translates to 'much in quantity but little in substance' – *about this planet, the Land of the First Race. Many inhabitants will find our presence startling, we assume?*"

"Absolutely." Ross mutters.

"*Tkt-mmm-tkt.*" Soumya says to the screen.

The being lets out something that sounds like a deep-voiced dolphin trying to imitate a revving chainsaw. A laugh, I hope?

"*Very normal for inhabited planets. Even we believed this design was unnerving when we created it. We shall depart and return in the distant future. Thank you again for your understanding. Do you want any information from us before we depart?*" Soumya reads.

"Yeah, who the heck is we?" Ross asks.

Soumya says that in alien-tongue to the screen, and then when the symbols come back around this time, they are much smaller and many, many more of them.

"*We are 15,813 researchers, engineers, scientists, and farmers that inhabited the Greatest Moon of tr-rl-fft* – 'Tillayf' is what this would sound like in English. *Tillayf was destroyed a very long time ago. Due to the last reports we received from our home, we suspect it was due to a group of eco-terrorists tampering with an artifact we only know as 'The Scroll'.*"

I give Marie a horrified look. She seems equally as concerned. She mentioned a scroll during the bad guy portion of her prophecy boardgame…

"*Once our planet was destroyed, we saw no more purpose for our research. We joined together and built this vessel with the purpose of traveling throughout the universe, learning and experiencing all we could. Our defense systems were installed to help us resurface after landing and, if we were to ever find The Scroll, annihilate it.*"

Everyone is quiet, digesting the information. This is all so strange and outlandish that I'm having a hard time believing that it all isn't one big fever dream. Stuff like this is supposed to happen on Arret, not Earth, right?!

"So you all, like, uploaded your consciousnesses into some

central network?" Ross asks.

My maid translates, and the screen changes to a single box with a circle in the top corner and a few vertical lines placed in odd intervals.

"*Correct.*" Soumya reads.

"Do you know where The Scroll is?" Marie tries.

Soumya translates, reads, and replies, "*We do not.*"

"How long have you all been travelling?" Ross asks.

Soumya does her thing, "*What are your time units?*"

"Uh… 60 seconds in a minute, 60 minutes in an hour, 24 hours a day, 365 days a year." Ross lists off.

Soumya repeats it to the screen, then reads the almost instant response, "*1,158 years, 203 days, 19 hours, 46 minutes, and 18 seconds.*"

Ross is silent, stunned, but it seems as though Eunseo is still the excited-mystified as opposed to the concerned-mystified.

"This is cool. What is your name?"

Soumya translates, and the being lets out another dolphin chainsaw noise.

"*We have never considered that. Allow us to run a poll,*" Soumya waits, then more characters appear on the screen and her face twists, "The literal translation is '*those who wander in the direction of suns*' but a more colloquial translation might come out to be '*Azimuth the Wandering*'."

"Very cool name!" Eunseo compliments.

Before Soumya can respond, Azimuth swivels their head to a portion of the forest slightly to our right. A spotlight comes out of their eye, illuminating a very unhappy, very tall girl armed with a very large bow.

It looks like she is wearing burlap coveralls and a cape made of moss. Two black braids stretch down to her waist, shining in the spotlight. There are dark rings under her eyes and her brown lips are twisted into a serious frown.

Ross raises a guard, “And who are you?”

Eunseo pulls two knives from her pouch and gets into a menacing stance, and her, “Yes, tell us!” comes out in the intimidating, low, guy-ish voice that she had when I first met her.

“Azimuth is asking the same thing.” Soumya reports.

“I am the one here to defend this forest and the people nearby from the destruction you’re bringing. Leave now or I will… let me give you an example.”

She pulls a long arrow out of a quiver on her hip and nocks it. Before anyone can object, I notice her twitch, then there is a short brushing sound, like bristles smacking against concrete. The arrow disappears from her bow, then a small black thing darts in front of me and there is a resolute snap.

I leap back, startled, and look down. A large arrow lies sliced in two at my feet, and the end of a throwing knife sticks up from the dirt. That looks like… one of Eunseo’s pouch knives! Did she… throw it fast enough to break an arrow *mid-flight*?!

Stunned, I look over at the ninja. She has one hand on her pouch, and the other is open with the palm tattoo glowing red. She and the archer are glaring at one another. Everyone else, even Azimuth, seems as stunned as I am.

"So you *want* to fight? I'll put one between your eyes!" The archer threatens, nocking an arrow and drawing back with terrifying smoothness and speed.

"There is no fight when I unlock Sihon and beat you! Easy! I can show you *now*!" Eunseo whips her hand out of her pouch, now with three knives, each tucked between her knuckles like claws.

Ross puts up his hands, "Whoa, there's no need for unleashing demons or shooting people, alright?"

Both of the women are frozen in their attack positions, glaring and ready to seriously injure one another.

Ross starts again, "We just saw something fall out of the sky and came to check it out. Now we're talking to… this giant alien man about his space journey. The point is, we aren't looking for trouble, which is why Eunseo is putting away her kunai now."

Eunseo doesn't move.

"…which is why *Eunseo* is putting *away–*"

She begrudgingly slides her knives back in the hip pouch.

The archer is silent for a moment, staring down at us with suspicion, and then says, "I'll come and see for myself, but you'd better leave once I'm done."

She doesn't wait for a reply, returning the arrow to its quiver and starting down the crater wall with longbow in hand.

"Alright, tell big guy to wrap it up. First him, or *them* I guess, now her… I just want to lie down." Ross says.

Soumya speaks quickly to the being, gets a response, and begins reading, "*Very well. Before we depart, allow us to thank you once more. Just through our short interaction tonight, we have already learned a large amount about humans and Earth, as our scanners can gather plenty of data from milliseconds of observation. Would you accept a gift?*"

"…depends. Ask him what it is first." Ross suggests.

Soumya speaks for a long bout with the screen, no doubt giving Ross' response and explaining the situation with the archer. By the time a reply appears, the bow lady has reached us. She approaches Eunseo, who still looks ready to fight, then takes one step closer to her and starts grinding the ball of her foot into the dirt. The archer begins speaking casually, and at first I thought it was English but after a couple of moments I realize it's not.

"*We would like to give you a star core, an item which supplies us power. We have 15, and each of them gives us enough energy to sustain 10,000 years of lightspeed travel. Please, take one and develop it. We will return 300 years from today, visit you all, and marvel at the progress you've made using the core.*"

"Uuuuh, nah," Ross decides, "that's cool and all but just by the name itself I can tell there'd be some radiation poison going on. Tell them we… 'want to preserve their lifespan as much as possible'. Oh, and speaking of lifespans, let them know humans live like 100ish years max, so visitation probably won't be a two-way thing."

Soumya nods and feeds the altered info back to Azimuth. Meanwhile, the defender finishes her mantra with Eunseo and steps back. Blue smoke drifts up from the spot where her foot was. She studies it, closes her eyes for a moment, and then nods at Eunseo before moving on to Marie.

"*Very noble, humans. We will remember that when we return and will honor your graves. Before we depart, a warning; there is a starship fleet very close by that does not seem to be affiliated with your planet. It is heavily armed. We do not wish to engage in conflict, but it is information that may be useful to you.*"

Everyone pauses except the archer, who is now foot grinding near Soumya. That certainly doesn't sound good at all.

"Think it's the Bukanarions again?" Ross asks Marie.

"No doubt," she replies, "after the incident with the Anubis Drill, they more than likely would return to fulfill their threats."

"Would you like for me to translate this?" Soumya asks, completely ignoring the archer's ritual.

"No, we'll come up with a reply in a sec." Ross says, and Soumya nods and says something that probably translates to 'one moment'.

"Bukanarions?" I ask, exhausted, "Is that, like, some sort of nationality or something?"

First the meteor, then Azimuth, then Soumya speaking alien-tongue, then the prophecy gets mentioned, then the archer showing up, and now this talk about Bukanarions… I'm less surprised and more tired at this point.

"We all have a lot of explaining to do tomorrow," Ross informs me, ignoring the archer's ritual in a fashion similar to Soumya, "but for now, this lady is almost done and so am I, so we need to wrap this up. Soumya, ask them how far away this starship is."

They respond, "*If they maintain their speed, they are 20 hours, 57 minutes, and 44 seconds away from reaching the outermost layer of this atmosphere.*"

"Okay, that's actually quite bad," Ross concludes, "Eunseo, can you let Shuvo know once we get back into some cell phone signals?"

"Yes. I must… cell phone use… and signal send… to Shuvo." She nods uncertainly.

Ross frowns, "Actually, never mind, I'll let him know myself."

The archer approaches me. Her hard gaze and sheer height are even more intimidating up close; annoyance radiates from her dark brown eyes, which are about a head and a half above mine.

She begins grinding her foot in the ground in front of me, starting the incantation. From afar I thought she was Hispanic and up close she seems more Asian, but now this language makes me think maybe… Indonesian specifically? I'm not sure what's going on but I know we're running out of time.

"Soumya, quick, ask them where it's headed!" Ross advises.

Soumya rushes her next sentence, adding an urgent bit at the end that probably conveyed our closing time limit. From what I've noticed of the archer performing this ritual four times before, she's nearing the end. The being suddenly raises its left arm.

My maid reads the text as it is popping up across the screen, "*We unfortunately cannot tell you since our units of distance and location are undoubtedly different –* "

"Oh, come on…" Ross sighs.

" *– undoubtedly different, but we can say that, if we are to face this direction,* " Soumya points alongside the being, *"about a quarter of this planet's circumference away seems to be –* "

The archer steps away from me and the rising smoke alerts everyone that we've run out of time.

" *– seemstobetheanticipatedlandingsite*." Soumya rushes.

"Fantastic, tell Azimuth good luck and safe travels. Marie and Eunseo, please tell me you'll remember all that."

"Yes!" Eunseo reports.

"Likewise." Marie adds.

We all look at the archer to see what her reaction to us running out of time will be. She simply stares at the twin wisps of smoke coming from the ground, expressionless.

Outside of Soumya offering an extended and probably cordial goodbye to Azimuth, it is silent. Eunseo has her knives in hand again, her palms glowing once more. The archer looks from the ground to my face. Her hard eyes flick to mine for a moment before looking me up and down.

Then she reaches into her coveralls and produces a large, smooth, wooden pebble. It's a little ovular and has a hole at the top, like half of an avocado pit turned into a keychain.

"Keep this with you, and when you are in the forest of Canada again, plant this in order to summon me. You… I think I ought to speak to you more about something."

I take the pebble from her, uncomfortable from all of the eyes boring into me.

"Place this on your key ring so that you don't lose it." She instructs.

I nod, but when she keeps standing there, I obediently take out my key ring and loop the pebble onto it.

"Okay, your time is up. Leave now or you know what I'm going to do." She growls.

"Cool," Ross says, "nice meeting you Azimuth, you too lady, everyone, let's go."

Just like that, the five of us make our way to the crater wall, brimming with confusion and stiff under the gazes of Azimuth and the archer.

CHAPTER 12

IMMORAL PUDDING RECIPE

~ GRIFFIN ~

I flop on the bed, exhausted, as the others lay down their bags and personals. The trip today was awesome, full of all kinds of jokes, music, weird radio stations, and gas station hijinks. I'm not really that tired, but I want to stay in so I can avoid any slip-ups with lust and my curse. I know the others are going to want to go out for food, though.

Sure enough, Wade slings off her guitar, then, "Whoa there Griff, you aren't throwing in the towel now, are you? We just got here!"

"Yeah, sorry Wade," I do my best old man impression, "my bones ain't as young as they used to be."

Wade laughs, while Kay and Ivan smirk.

"Are you sure? We haven't eaten since," Wade snickers, "*Porkly Johnson's*."

The room goes into a bout of low chuckles as we remember the round, eccentric gas-station-convenience-store-hog-farm-carvery-pay-day-loan-bait-and-tackle-shop owner from four hours ago. I knew more about his second marriage in the first hour of meeting him than nine years of learning my own country's history.

"I'm still working off all of that fryer oil and sugar cakes," I joke, "but if you grab me something while you're out, I'll pay you back."

"Fair enough," Wade says, sounding a little disappointed, "well, Ivan? Paige?"

"Of course." The drummer says.

I look at Kay and she looks at me. Her gaze is still and unreadable, like that of a motionless panther. *Oh dear heavens please go with them.*

"Yeah, sounds fun. You guys head out and I'll catch up in just a second." She says softly.

"No rush, we can–"

"Sure thing, we'll head to the lobby~!" Wade interrupts, hooking her arm through Ivan's.

The drummer looks displeased at being interrupted and even more so at Wade hugging up on him, but he obliges as she whisks him towards the exit. Before closing the door, Wade looks back at me and winks. Oh Wade, if only you knew the horror.

Kay pretends to sort her bag a second longer before stopping and looking up at me. Out of all the evil villains, insane warlocks, and demon generals I've stared down, looking into the rage-filled eyes of Paige Pierson has got to be the most horrifying of them all. It's as if her eyes suck all of the kindness out of the air. I've never seen Kay this angry, or angry at all, really…

"*What were you thinking?*" she hisses sharply, making me jump with surprise, "Running off without your *phone*? Putting on your *PASTIM* and… and using your *powers*? In the *States*?! And trying to fight a demon king *by yourself*?! Do you understand how *much trouble you could have gotTEN IN? YOU COULD HAVE DIED, GRIFFIN!*"

I have never heard anyone shout so loudly in my entire life. Kay is the quietest one on my team; I couldn't have guessed her voice was this strong. It's like all the times my mother told me off combined. All I can do is gape back at her, face cold, goosebumps of fear fresh on my skin.

"Don't just look at me, *explain yourself*!" She snaps.

"I– I– I was just, uh–"

"You were *what*? You were just *what*, Griffin? 'Going to visit your godmother' – don't give me that crap *tell me the truth*!"

Her blue eyes, almost always mild, are wide with anger. Her long, bushy, silver hair is trembling in her fury. Her face, typically a little warmer than pale, is bright pink. Ice crystals are forming on her clenched fists. It feels like I got the wind knocked out of me. Panicking, I gather my breath to try and say a response before she turns me into an icicle.

"I really do have to see my godmom because of a curse." My voice sounds so small.

"A… a what?" Kay asks.

"A curse…" I repeat.

"How did you get a curse?" She prods, concerned.

My heart leaps into my throat. Kay is my biggest crush and one of my oldest friends. After all the screaming she did, it's obvious she cares about me, too. I know that if I tell her the full truth now, she will either legitimately kill me or turn, walk out the door, and I'll never see her again.

"Delilah turned out to be Ashtoreth in disguise," Kay gasps at the name of the Supreme Demon, "and she cornered me at the church and…" tears well up alongside the truth, both of which feel awful and thus get shoved back down, "put a curse on me."

"Just… put a curse on you? Like that?" Kay asks with a wave.

"Yes." I lie, feeling a knife sink into my heart.

"Well… why didn't you tell anyone?" She prods.

I remain silent. The guilt of lying to her just then is too strong.

"Your pride." She concludes, sounding disappointed.

I nod; she is partially correct. Kay doesn't say anything for a while, then hurriedly gathers her belongings. Before she can head out the door, she turns to me, and there is a look of pity in her eyes.

"Griff… I'm sorry for yelling at you. You're a guy, and I know guys have a hard time asking for help. I won't nag you about the curse at all but just know that I'm here for you and," she blushes, not from anger, "I really care about you."

She then zips out the door and it eases closed behind her. I just lie there on the bed and stare at the ceiling. Guilt echoes in my empty chest, way worse than after the kiss with Ashtoreth. I don't think I've ever felt so disappointed in myself before.

Ashtoreth. She's horrible. I can imagine her smug face now. Her pretty… n-no, *very* evil eyes. Those round, soft, I-I mean stupid lips, smirking at me. And that cute, er, *not*-cute laugh…

Wait, didn't she subject me to eons of torture and cause this whole disaster with Kay? I hate her! R-right? Well… well sure but, I'm mean, not gonna lie, she is *quite* hot. I gotta admit, if–

No no no no no. I stand up. *No it's the lust day we aren't going there that's what she wants*. I pace around the room, racking my brain. I hate her, no buts! I can't let her win this one, I just can't. For a moment I consider keeping busy with a phone call, but my cellphone is back in Canada and I don't have anyone's number memorized.

The TV remote is sitting nearby, so I pick it up and press the power button. Might as well deaden the brain a little.

"– to be pepperoni, it can be any topping, just make sure you put about a half cup." The chef says, thumbing slices of meat onto a bed of mozzarella in a pan.

Nice; cooking! The camera zooms out to show the chef putting a lid on the skillet and placing it on the stove. As she cranks the dial, I look hard. She seems familiar… perhaps I've seen her show before? I suppose the States show Canadian cooking sometimes?

"Now we're gonna put the pan over medium heat and let it cook, fully covered, for 10 minutes. After that," she turns to the camera – she looks very familiar and admittedly cute, but I still don't know where I've seen her, "let it cook an additional 5 minutes vented. If you don't have a vented lid, try cooking with the lid slightly ajar."

She presses a few timer buttons on the stove, ducks down below the camera, and emerges a moment later with a witch's hat.

"The pan is full, the food is in it, take us forward 15 minutes!" She chants, shrugging her shoulders and wiggling her fingers.

I laugh as the screen does a ripple transition into the next scene, where the 15 minutes are up. The chef, now with oven mitts and a spatula instead of a witch hat, turns to the pan. Inside is a fully cooked, thin crust pizza.

She uses the spatula to dish the pie onto a cutting board. It then transitions to close ups of her performing actions in slow motion as she narrates them.

"Let it cool for five minutes, sprinkle with basil, cut, and you're ready to serve!"

It shows her fully again, this time holding a plate full of yummy-looking pepperoni pizza slices.

"I am Connie Cubinez, and that," she tilts the plate, "is how to make a thin-crust pizza on the stove. Thanks for watching!"

The screen fades to black as she waves. Huh, that actually sounds pretty neat. Pizza in a pan… I'm going to have to look that one up sometime. Chef Cubinez's voice fills the room again.

"What better way to celebrate the summer than with some refreshing frozen cherry limeade? Turn up the heat with my signature buffalo chicken dip! And finish off the day with a delicious banana pudding! Sound good?"

"Yeah!" I shout to the TV, ready to waste the night away.

"Well, I'm going to show you how! Let's get started!"

Unfortunately, Chef Cubinez uses imperial instead of metric with all her measurements, so she whirls about listing gallons and cups and quarts and whatnot for the limeade. I'm still entertained, though, especially when she does a surprisingly stylish backflip into a pool, in her normal clothes, to illustrate how the limeade would 'make a splash at your next party! Woohoo!'

After a commercial break, she moves on to the buffalo chicken dip, now wearing a different pair of jeans, button-up, and apron. It's actually much easier of a dish than I anticipated, and once that segment is complete, we cut to commercial again.

The second break passes, this one showing the same poorly animated local lawyer's advertisement twice in a row, then we get to the banana pudding. She appears in the kitchen again, this time with a button-up blouse and no apron.

"It's been a long summer day full of sun and fun, and now friends and family are looking forward to a wonderful dessert to finish it off. Let's kick back, get relaxed, and make some show-stopping banana pudding!"

"Alright!" I call back at the screen, excited.

She lays out the bananas, milk, frozen whipped topping, vanilla extract, wafers, and pudding mix, informing me all the while on the ounces and cups we'll be using. Chef Cubinez puts the whipped topping in a bowl and mixes it until it's less like a brick and more like a fluff.

She then adds the milk, pudding mix, and vanilla, going on a tangent about a summer day she spent with friends back when she was a kid. Chef Cubinez then folds in a little more of the whipped topping, thumbs down the wafers similar to how she did with the pepperonis, and heads over to the bananas by the cutting board.

"You know," she peels one of the bananas, "there used to be a joke I always heard that said you could actually sweeten up the bananas by licking them. Of course that's not true. But… we could always try…"

To my surprise, she actually does it. The chef seductively licks the banana, frowns, then licks it a second time while also starting to unbutton her shirt with her free hand.

I raise the remote and switch channels.

"– with vegetables are typically on the menu for dinner at the Fen Sing Temple."

It shows a room full of bald boys in dark green robes eating in some sort of cafeteria.

For a moment I just stare at the screen. The narrator keeps talking, but his words bounce off my ears. My mind is just one loud, confused dial tone as it works to process what I just saw. Then, in a rush, the pieces fall into place.

What in the name of the stars above did they just put on this TV screen for my young impressionable eyes to see?!

I sit back in bed, confused, stunned, and somewhat betrayed. The narrator drones on about clay pots.

The… huh? What did I just watch? Who… how… *why*? Wasn't

that the cooking channel? I check the TV pamphlet, scan a little, and see that it was indeed the cooking channel. But that… I… what kind of insanity do they allow on American television?

For a long while I just stare at the monk documentary, chuckling at the absurdity of what just happened. I haven't watched TV in a while; is this what things have come to? Even the cooking channel?!

Curiosity arises, tempting me towards turning back and seeing how things play out, but I know that's exactly what Ashtoreth wants, so I force myself to tune in to what's happening on the screen. The camera shows a large group of pagoda roofs tucked into a forested mountainside and begins to pan up to the sun.

"… as though we all have a bit to learn from Liao's story. Thanks for watching."

It fades to black for a little; I guess it ended. I check the time. It's been around an hour since the others left. They should be getting back any moment now.

Suddenly, the next show starts, abrupt and loud but quickly fading to a normal volume.

"WELCOME back to Chance a Dance, the only show on air where *I* teach *you* all the latest dance moves! I'm your host, Tasi Phan, and today we're going to be learning all sorts of different routines. Get ready to chance a dance!"

For some reason, I knew Tasi Phan was her name before she said it. Huh, maybe she's some famous dancer or actress or something.

Either way, I sit up in bed, ready to steal some moves for my breakdancing rounds.

"Joining me today is a special guest known all throughout the world for tearing it up, not just on the dance floor, but also in the kitchen. It's Connie Cubinez!"

My stomach drops as the camera zooms out, showing the waving chef on set as well, dressed in workout shorts and a tank top like Tasi. *Oh you gotta be kidding me.*

"Thanks for having me, Tasi," the chef says, "I'm excited! What are we learning first?"

"Nothing." I reply, and switch channels.

"The Wara-Pom-Pom Dance!" Tasi continues, "It's a spicy little routine that's a bit on the feminine side, but our male viewers can certainly still join in."

What? Why didn't the channel change? I inspect the remote, then press the button again.

"Oh, you know I like spicy! Do you think it's hotter than my habanero chili?" Chef Cubinez jokes.

Now I am violently mashing the up and down arrows on the remote. *But nothing is happening what the heck?!*

"It just might be, Connie!" Tasi laughs, then she turns to the camera, "This dance does get quite… suggestive at parts, so please be advised if there are any little ones in the room."

Panicking, I snatch up the TV pamphlet and scan it for literally any music station. Aha! Smooth Jazz – 201! I'm more of a boom bap kind of guy but I punch in the station number anyway.

"Alright, you know the drill!' Tasi cheers, the three white numbers I put in hovering uselessly at the top corner, "we've gotta get stretched before we start dancing. Hamstrings first!"

"No!" I scream, turning away and pressing the power button.

"Oof! I can really feel this one!" Chef Cubinez grunts.

How?! How is literally none of this working?! I press and hold down on the power button, my free hand clasped over my eyes, fighting the temptation to look.

"Oh! I didn't know you were so flexible, Connie!" Tasi remarks.

Fine! I... I'll just leave the room then! With my eyes still covered, I toss the remote in frustration and feel around on the nightstand for the room card. I almost knock over the alarm clock, then I feel up and grab some silk cloth.

The show's background music is replaced by jazz and the laughter of two girls.

I uncover my eyes to see Tasi Phan and Connie Cubinez, here, in my hotel room, holding each other as they double over in tear-filled giggles. My PASTIM is in my hands. There is a sudden wave of realization, and I recognize these two as Onan and the curly-haired magician succubus from back in Toronto.

"You were so..." Onan gasps, "... you were so confused!"

"And then you started screaming..." the curly-haired one doubles over again, raising a hand as if to ward off more humor, "it was so hard not to laugh!"

I sit there, growing more uneasy, as the two of them gather themselves. This is bad. Smooth jazz is playing in the background, I can't find the remote, and I'm in a hotel room at night with just the two of them on my lust curse day.

... no don't panic, it's okay, I can handle this.

"Sorry for laughing." The curly-haired one says, now calmer.

"Why apologize?" Onan teases, "It was pretty funny seeing him be a big prude!"

"Onan!" Peeps the curly-haired one, "That wasn't very nice…"

"He's tough, he can handle it," Onan grins at me and I feel my chest flutter, "Oh, and Griffin, this is Cozbi. She was the one you *bit* back in Toronto."

Both the false chef and I blush as she walks to my bedside and puts out her hand. Feeling awkward, I rise a little and shake it. Her hand is warm and delicate. Ah… that wasn't the smartest move.

"N-nice to meet you again, Griffin."

I nod, not making eye contact, just trying to figure out how the heck I'm supposed to mitigate this. Oh? There is an envelope in Cozbi's other hand!

"So, you… got a parcel?" I ask, forced casual, struggling to tie my PASTIM on my wrist with one hand.

"Here," Onan rushes over to me, "I'll get that, you klutz."

She plants a knee on the bed and leans over me, tying the PASTIM around my wrist with surprising gentleness. My eyes seem to have a mind of their own, and I begin to notice that Onan isn't sickly thin like back with Darklar.

Cozbi clears her throat and I look over to see her pouting.

"Well… *I* was sent here to drop this off, but a certain *meanie* just decided to tag along. Isn't that right, Onan?"

Onan is silent, blushing and looking at the floor. I find myself blushing too. With a happy smirk, Cozbi plops the envelope on the TV dresser and goes to sit down on the bed opposite of me, then hesitates.

"Sorry. Is it okay if I sit here?"

Onan chuckles, "The goody-two shoes wouldn't have the heart to tell you no!"

She tauntingly pokes me in the chest. There is a pause as her mischievous expression softens in amazement, then she reaches out to touch me again with her whole hand.

"Hey!" Cozbi calls, her voice still soft and passive, "have some manners, Onan!"

"Manners?" Onan looks over at Cozbi, lowering her hand, "isn't that rich, coming from Ms. Banana Lover!"

Cozbi blushes, "W-well you know what? If you keep acting like this, I'm going to tell him about… all your naughty, lightning-related fantasies!"

A baffled "what?" slips out of my mouth.

Onan turns red, glancing at me, "C-Cozbi?! Y-you were the one who kept babbling on about him biting you!"

Cozbi now looks like an attractive tomato, "I-I was… I just…"

“Why don’t we calm down, eh?” My face is on fire and my pulse is hammering, “Go ahead and sit, Cozbi.”

It takes me a moment to realize what I just permitted. This is still okay though, probably. I can just take off my PASTIM if I need to. I got this! I’ll… just let it go on for a little longer, then put a stop to it. Onan has slid next to me by the time I realize the bed is shifting.

I glance over to see her sitting centimeters away, legs stretched out next to mine, her feet only a little past my knees. Before I can gather the willpower to object, she puts a hand on top of mine. I naturally go to shy away but she tugs it towards her, giving me a little smirk and raising her eyebrows.

Okay, I should definitely do something now. But… isn’t it too late? I already did all the succubus no-no’s; giving them my name and letting them touch me and whatnot. Filled with hesitance, I idiotically continue to sit here like a loaf of bread.

The other bed creaks as Cozbi stands up again, “Please scoot over Griffin so I can make sure Onan doesn’t keep bullying you.”

Onan pouts, her grip loosening, “Aww, but I was having fuuun.”

Cozbi starts shuffling towards the bed with determination. It looks like she’ll literally sit on me if I don’t move. Automatic chivalry makes me scoot over, but Onan won’t give me enough room, so Cozbi arrives while I’m still trying to move and ends up sitting on my hand. It feels like my entire body just turned red.

“Come on, Cozbi!” Onan scolds, leaning on me to look over at her, "Can't you see his little puritan face? He's all worried now!"

"S-sorry… I just, felt a little left out." Cozbi giggles quietly, still sitting on my right hand.

"Uh, haha, yeah. Well… uh, also Cozbi, uh, you're kinda si–"

Onan's other hand, the one that isn't holding mine, is suddenly in my lap. I stop talking.

"Sorry, did I distract you? Don't mind me, I'm just getting comfortable." Onan teases.

Without warning, something like a wet paintbrush slides up along the outside of my ear. Did Cozbi just *lick* me?! I recoil, bumping into Onan, as the curly-haired girl giggles and blushes.

"You seem tense, Griffin. There's nothing to be afraid of~!"

"I… w-well–"

Onan takes my hand and pins it on Cozbi's bare leg, pressing up against me to do so. The olive-skinned girl lets out a soft yelp.

"There. That didn't hurt one bit, did it?" Onan's voice is soothing in my ear, her body still half-laid on mine, "I see you're starting to get it now. Nothing bad, just some fun. Right, Cozbi?"

"Y-yeah. We only want you to feel good, that's all."

Over the sound of my pounding heart, I hear voices at the front door. Voices that sound a lot like Kay, Ivan, and Wade.

My body goes into autopilot. In one great spin, I throw the succubi off of me, rip my PASTIM from around my wrist, toss it, and slam back down on the now vacant bed, stomach first.

Agh, what do I do now?! I can't pretend to watch TV because I can't find the remote! I can't pretend to be on my phone because I left it in Toronto! Panicking, I just barely manage to cross my arms and put my head down before the door opens.

"What're you doing in here, you old geezer?!" Wade calls playfully from the doorway.

"J-just taking a nap." I reply, trying to look up as innocent and clueless as I can. My heart is still pounding from everything that just happened in the past ten seconds.

She walks in and tosses a plastic bag at me. I reach out and catch it, hoping that my smile looks sleepy and not guilty.

"We just got you a chicken parm sub and some fries," she says, flopping down on the other bed.

"It's actually pretty good. Also, great choice of music, Griffin." Ivan comments, using his feet to take his shoes off.

"Don't worry about paying me back," Kay says as she sits in the exact same spot and manner as Onan, "it wasn't much."

I nod, uncomfortable, and begin to open my dinner.

"Why is the remote on the floor… and your PASTIM? Hey, yours actually looks pretty cool!" Wade comments.

I turn, my whole body freezing over, and watch helplessly as she picks it up. She scans the room with a dramatic 'oooh' as if she's never used a PASTIM before. Cozbi and Onan must have left.

"Leave his stuff alone." Ivan says, tossing some of his belongings onto the TV stand.

But Wade is silent now, curious. The sweet rush of relief sours into dread. Kay asks the question we're all wondering, "What's wrong?"

"There's an envelope near the TV." Wade reports as she approaches the invisible package.

Oh goodness that's right... didn't Cozbi say she was delivering a package?!

Wade picks up the invisible rectangle and tears it open with her thumb. She then gestures to take out a slip of paper and folds it open with her fingers. Without a PASTIM, it looks like she's doing a really good job at miming. Her face screws up in confusion and I feel my insides twist.

"It's just a winky face... signed 'Torie'?"

Rage and horror mix in my chest. Ashtoreth. This is what she wanted. I know my face is flushing, so I rip open my sub and hide behind the fanning wrapper, pretending to take a bite.

"Torie? Didn't Nisroch mention a Torie?" Ivan asks, checking his phone with apathy.

Come on Ivan! Wade and Kay look at one another, not seeming nearly as apathetic.

"Do you remember, Griffin?" Kay asks, glancing down at me.

"Mmmm, vaguely." I lie, trying to act as natural and unconcerned as Ivan.

"I feel like he said something to you about it." Wade offers, looking at me.

Shut up Wade I just want to kill Ashtoreth and then die is what I would've said if I didn't shrug and say, "Could've, I wasn't really paying him much mind."

My feverishly angry and terrified mental voice comes back again: *'Much mind'? It's 'any mind' you idiot!*

The girls give one another a look. Wade shrugs it off and changes the channel from jazz to some comedy show.

But Kay looks absorbed in thought.

Chapter 13

Maid to Keep Secrets

~ Matthew ~

The middle-aged woman takes a deep breath, staring off into space as if she had just been forced to watch the most horrific internet video of all time. She cocks her head to the side and blinks a little. The wrinkles under her eyes stand out against her pale face.

"Let me get this straight," she starts, her veil of gold coins clacking as she moves, "you saw a giant alien man fall out of the sky last night, and he was somehow still alive–"

"Because he is robot!" Eunseo exclaims.

"Because he… *is robot*," the woman repeats, "and then you said your maid here got up and started reading the symbols on his chest… without ever seeing the language before because it's from outer space…"

"Correct." Soumya says, calm.

The woman studies her, "and so you think she's hypnotized."

"Yes." Ross mutters, clearly displeased with being considered crazy by this woman.

The lady stays silent, then she sighs, "And you are *positive* you didn't have any mind-altering substances before this event? Lack of sleep can lead to hallucinations as well–"

"Look," Ross stops, breathes, and then starts again, still sounding angry, "I didn't come here to get accused of drug use. I came here to figure out why that girl," he points at Soumya with all five fingers, dangerously close to backhanding me, "can speak to giant robot aliens like they're old pals."

"Listen, *kid*," the woman snaps, "I'm a psychic, okay? I tell fortunes, I talk to spirits, yeah, I hypnotize too. And yeah, I get it, my line of work is weird. Wacky, zany, whatever you want to call it. But aliens is where I draw the line!"

"Where you draw the line?!" Ross shouts, "What, are you not–"

He notices as he waves his hands that they are leaving trails of black smoke in the already incense-filled air. Frustrated, he stands up from his heavily cushioned chair and walks out the door.

"What was… what was that on his hands just now?" The woman asks, sounding a little startled.

"Don't worry about it," Marie says, standing as well, "we were just leaving. We'll seek council from a *real* psychic."

The woman looks offended and embarrassed at the same time, her pale face turning pink, mouth widening in outrage, eyes filled with almost theatric amounts of hurt.

"Me? The great Amerythia Clairene, High Medium of the North, Converser of Spirits, Seer of the Great Beyond? You're calling me a fraud?"

The spiritual sister, still with her blindfold on, surveys the trinket, idol, candle, and cushion-crammed room with an unimpressed expression.

"I don't even need vision to see that you're full of hot air," Marie replies coolly, and Amerythia begins to swell with anger, "You cannot see spirits, your title is fabricated, and even your name is fake."

I glance over at the psychic to see her red-faced and with an angry smile. Her elaborate silk robes are heaving as if she just ran a marathon.

"Of course a bigoted *nun*," Marie winces in annoyance, "such as yourself would be close-minded when it comes to things of this nature. How could I ever expect those blinded by *religion* to understand the true spiritual nature of the universe... If I'm a fraud, dear girl, then tell me, what is my 'real' name?"

"Give me a list of names and I'll tell you."

"*Amerythia*," she gestures wildly, trying to further imply that this is the right answer, "mmmm, Leslie, Joann, and Carolyn."

"And?" Marie asks.

"W-what do you mean 'and'? My real name is one of the four." Amerythia snaps.

"No it isn't." Marie responds, composed.

The psychic heaves a great huff of hot air, then continues, "Okay then... *Victoria Diana Susan Grace Elizabeth Andrea Kri–* "

"Andrea." Marie interrupts.

Amerythia stares at the spiritual sister, trying to hide surprise,

"Y-you don't know that!"

Marie nods, and the amount of control she has over the situation is almost embarrassing, "Well, what I do know is that we should have found a psychic in Canada. Just because the States are closer doesn't mean they are of the same quality… we and our $300 will remember that for next time."

The psychic's face flushes at the amount of money. Marie gives her no mercy, nodding once more before standing from her chair.

"Matt, Soumya, Eunseo, let's go."

"Wait!" Andrea says, "Why, you cannot leave! I have seen a vision… if you leave now, you will surely perish!"

The spiritual sister turns back to face us, composed, pretending to be stunned, "Is this so? What are we to do, sit around and wait?"

"No," Andrea replies, swallowing her pride, "I must free your friend from hypnosis. Only then will you all depart safely."

"The spirits told you this, I presume?" Marie smirks.

"Please sit so we can begin." Andrea hisses back.

Ross comes in at that very moment, looking resolved.

"Marie, you were right, we–"

"Are about to see Soumya get unhypnotized. Yes, come and watch." The spiritual sister invites.

Ross is immobile and expressionless, then shrugs and walks over to the table. Once he and Marie are seated, Andrea gets up, clinks over to the main door, draws curtains over the windows, and then clatters her way back to her seat.

She not-so-gracefully clears the lace tablecloth of its crystal ball and tarot cards. From her robes, she produces a dazzling emerald and gold locket.

"Whose mind are we delving into first?" She asks, raising a thin eyebrow.

"Oooh! I can go first!" Eunseo exclaims.

"No Eunseo," Ross says in a fatherly tone, "we have to get Soumya done."

The ninja's smile falls into a pout.

"Very well… you," she points at my maid, "are Soumya, yes?"

"Yes." My maid replies, eyebrows raised but otherwise unconcerned. The psychic throws a triumphant look at Marie before she continues.

"Exactly as the spirits said. Well, my dear Soumya, relax your mind and prepare to go on a journey into your deepest consciousness. Do you feel ready?"

"I suppose."

Andrea flicks open the locket to reveal a black and white spiral, swirling down infinitely to a point in the middle. As she sways it back and forth, the spiral begins to spin.

"Look deep into the spiral. Follow it with your eyes, your soul."

My maid obliges, watching it sway.

"Now close your eyes and lean back."

Soumya does so. Andrea quickly reaches into her robes, waves her hand under Soumya's nose, and then sits back down again. My maid winces.

"I will count to five, and when I snap, you will fall under my spell."

"Okay."

"One… two… threeeee… fooooouuur…"

She surveys the room dramatically before whispering, "Five."

She snaps, loud enough to make me jump a little. Soumya's head lulls back, and then nothing happens for a moment.

"Soumya?" Andrea calls theatrically.

"Yes?" My maid mumbles.

"What do you see?" The psychic casts an arrogant look at Marie.

Soumya is silent. To my surprise, it looks like she's asleep.

"I see…" she starts drowsily, "a room. My quarters."

The skepticism in the room quickly shifts to surprise. Andrea looks as though she's about to accept a Nobel Peace Prize.

"Very good! These quarters are back home in… Pakistan?"

"India," Soumya corrects, "but no, these are my quarters in the Blue House. In Alabama."

I lean forward, intrigued.

"Y-yes," Andrea recovers, "a blue house. Can you exit this house? Don't actually do so, or you may be lost in the astral plane forever… simply try to find the front door and describe it to me."

"I can't." Soumya mumbles.

"You can't?" The psychic asks excitedly, "is there someone blocking your path? Be prepared to return at the sound of a second snap!"

"No, there is no person. There is a metal door with a payphone on it and some initials above it. It would lead to the rest of the house, but it is locked."

"Don't touch the telephone just yet!" Andrea practically squeals, "What do the initials say?"

Soumya is quiet, seeming fully asleep for a moment, then, "D… D… H."

Ross lets out a sigh and Marie tilts her face towards him, nodding.

"You know what that stands for?" Andrea asks, "Is it… dream… drop…"

"Department of Directives and Hypnosis." Ross says.

Andrea shoots him a harsh look, then raises an eyebrow, "Would *you* like to guide Soumya through her mindscape, then?"

"Yeah sure," Ross says, then he turns to my maid, "Soumya, pick up the phone, put it on speaker, and dial 123-456-7890."

The psychic looks as if her Nobel Peace Prize was yanked from her hands. She glances between Soumya and Ross, wanting both to object and let it happen. Soumya lets out a few beeps followed by purring noises.

"Hello, this is Ben Sweezy with the Department of Directives and Hypnosis," Soumya mumbles, a bit louder, "how can I help you?"

"Ben?" Andrea asks, feverishly looking around, "Ben Sweezy? Are you with us in the room now?"

"Uh… no?" Soumya says.

“Someone must be astrally projecting into her mindscape…” Andrea mutters to herself, looking concerned.

“Hey Ben,” Ross calls, “I’m Ross Voltaire in Team Spiral Thunder. Is there any way we can unhypnotize this girl?”

Soumya makes a few ticking noises with her mouth, interrupting herself, “I’m tick tick looking up your file now tick tick tick… this is alias name Soumya Dhumne?”

‘Alias name’? That isn’t her real name? What is going on?! I scan the room for help. Soumya is slumped next to me, Ross and Marie look unsurprised, and Andrea is gazing wildly at my maid. Eunseo is the only other person who looks as confused and surprised as I am.

“Well, it looks like the person who authorized this hypnosis isn’t in your team, so there isn’t anything I can do at the moment.”

Ross looks across the table at Marie, frustrated. The spiritual sister senses his glare and starts speaking.

“Ben? Did you hear about the tip-off for the France invasions?” Marie tries.

“Tip-off? Which one?” Soumya chuckles, “Everyone and their mom has been talking about it.”

“The one with the alien man from outer space.”

Andrea whispers, harsh, “*Girl, this is no time for–*”

“Yeah, what of it?” Soumya asks, intrigued.

Andrea stops talking.

“She was the one who spoke to the alien.” Marie announces.

Everyone is silent, and then Soumya says, "One moment please."

She begins to 'dooooo duh-doo-duh dooooo' a jazz song. Eunseo giggles. I want to giggle too, since watching Soumya make jazz noises in her sleep is adorable, but I'm still stunned that we are talking to a man over the phone *through* my false maid's subconscious.

"She's being possessed by the Othersiders…" Andrea gasps.

"We're on hold." Ross clarifies.

A few more 'doo's, then I go to break the silence. I'm too confused to let this time pass without some answers.

"So… what's this about invasions and stuff?"

"Ah, right," Marie's face turns to Ross', "this is a little bit of a tricky area, seeing that you and Andrea aren't in IPSHA."

"IPSHA?" The psychic asks, "I've been a member of the International Psychic Sisterhood for twenty plus years!"

"No we said IPSHA not…" Ross pinches the bridge of his nose, "never mind. We'll get to that later. So Matt," he turns to me, and the way he repositions himself tells me he's about to explain a lot.

"You remember the show Journey of Shrines?" He asks.

I briefly recall the Japanese live action TV series that aired nonstop on the news. I remember the camera quality was awful and there was no sound so I didn't watch for long. I was impressed by how everything was one continuous shot and how the choreography was super realistic, but I could almost literally count the pixels on the screen, so I dropped the show pretty quick. I think

I had a dream about it recently, too.

“Yeah, what about it?” I respond.

“That wasn’t a show. Oshiro Daiki was sent to a planet called Iesias by Shajiku Sun, his grandfather’s corporation. There, he fought a bunch of actual murderous spirits, not actresses with good special effects, in order to get back home.”

He pauses and looks at Andrea, expecting her to say something. She doesn’t, simply looking back at him without an expression. For some reason, what he’s saying doesn’t feel too farfetched. I glance at Marie, thinking about the prophecy. That guy had a sword... and I feel like someone told me he might be a part of it.

“You remember the military display in Egypt?” Ross asks next.

That was all over the news as well, and in a similar fashion to Journey of Shrines, it was surrounded by frantic confusion. The newscasters were more flustered than they’d ever been covering those reports; the internet exploded with jokes and quotes about it later on.

The whole thing turned out to be one big mistake; a large, anti-missile balloon had malfunctioned and began to inflate, and so they had to send military in from multiple countries to go pop it (seeing as it was anti-missile and whatnot). I now have a sneaking suspicion that that isn’t true.

“Was it not a military mistake?”

“Nope,” Ross says with a smirk, “it was an attack from the Bukanarions from the planet, well, Bukan, which is apparently the one place in the galaxy with the strongest military force."

"Do you hear yourself?" Andrea asks, screwing up her face.

Ross puts a hand on his forehead, "A few months ago I didn't even know aliens existed. Well, I 'knew', but I didn't really believe it. Now we got galactic armies and teleporting samurai fighting hot magical alien ghosts... trust me, it sounds just as stupid on this end."

Andrea shakes her head before staring off at the table again.

"So they are attacking us, and no one really knows why, because they just sorta gave us an ultimatum and then sent down a drill to extract all the energy from the core of the planet *would you just shut up Andrea*."

"I haven't even said anything yet!" The psychic exclaims.

"It was in advance." Ross replies.

The two of them glare at each other as I digest the information. Why did he tell me about the Japanese broadcast and then the Bukanarion Drill?

"How is that drill related to Journey of Shrines?" I ask.

"Well, that's what we're trying to figure out. We thought maybe the planets had some sort of peace treaty, and Oshiro running around hacking up ghosts was a provocation of war. But that doesn't seem right, because during their ultimatum, the Bukanarions kept mentioning–"

Soumya's whining imitation of a saxophone stops abruptly: "Hey, so I did a bit of file searching and things are looking odd. It looks like she's not a part of IPSHA and someone else put her under the hypnosis."

"You see?" Andrea whispers, "the Othersiders are rejecting her due to the power of true love, which is–"

"Can we see who?" Ross asks loudly.

"I'm afraid not," Soumya says in a head-scratching tone, "looks like whomever it was got their name and contact info wiped. Either this person's got some high-up connections or some guy at the registrations desk isn't doing his job right…"

"Can you turn it off?" Eunseo tries, looking at me for some reason. I realize my listening stare is aimed at her eye tattoo and quickly look down at the tablecloth.

"Let me do a little more searching around. The hypnosis could be covering up something very dangerous, so we wanna be careful. I'll also have to run it past my supervisor. Just a sec."

More jazz 'doo'ing.

"Foolish boy," Andrea starts, "if you continue to play with spirits like they're toys, we'll all be doomed! You, and then your aliens, and now this?!"

"I'm about this close to…" he stops and breathes, "just wait."

"Matthew," Marie says suddenly, and I look over at her, "before we get off of hold, I was wondering something. Last night, what happened with the archer? It sounded like she gave you something, what was it?"

I reach down in my pocket and feel the smooth wooden pebble, but before I can answer, Ross does so for me.

“Some weird oval-shaped wood thing.”

“And she claimed you were special…” Marie pauses, “not that you aren’t, but do you know of any reasons why she might say that?”

I think hard. Not that it isn’t flattering, but I wouldn’t necessarily consider myself special. Outside of Arret, which was mostly just everyone else doing stuff and me following them around, I think my whole life has been pretty average.

“She probably meant it due to some things that happened to me…” I pause, weighing what sort of complications might come from mentioning Arret, “last year.”

“Yes, of course…” Andrea tries, “it was actually last year where you first crossed paths with the archer… and you are destined to marry her! The moons of Saturn have–”

“Last year? Can you say more?” Eunseo interrupts.

“He saved the world,” Ross replies, “that blue shockwave thing we all saw was apparently the world getting sucked up, and Matt went with his sister and some friends and got it back.”

My eyebrows raise. How did he know all that?

“News travels fast in IPSHA,” Ross answers after seeing my face, “and, no hard feelings but… so you saved the world. Not really the biggest deal; loads of people save the world in this organization. Eunseo technically saved the world when she got her powers during her training trip in Japan.”

The ninja smiles in a self-satisfactory way.

"So… do you think there was anything *else* that inspired our bow-loving buddy to give you that thing?" Ross asks.

"She must be a Stargazer…" Andrea suggests, "as I said earlier, she was marking this boy has her astral groom."

"Not true, she tries to kill him!" Eunseo says, growing upset, "She does not even let us talk! Ugh, she is very *stupid* person!"

I am touched by the ninja's defensiveness but also a little concerned at her anger, so I add, "Well, maybe it's because I'm the Crescent of Darkness?"

"That you are!" Andrea prophesies, "Son of the Almighty Gibbous of Darkness! I'm surprised; at your age, I would have assumed your father already let you know about his mystical history. Has he been acting strange lately?"

"…my dad died four years ago."

Out of the stunned silence creeps a sadness that I haven't felt in a long time. It's always been there, hovering just below the surface of my mind. Now it's emerging once again.

Ross puts a hand on my shoulder, "I lost my biological dad too. He was a villain and… ended up getting killed in a big standoff. Nothing is the same after stuff like that. I'm sorry, Matt."

I nod.

"We can talk more about this if you want, but let's not do it in front of *her*," Ross shoots a glare at Andrea, who is busying herself with tarot cards, "So, if you don't mind, what is this Crescent of

Darkness stuff all about?"

I give them a quick debrief on Yatniv's prophetic dream about me defeating him. I also tell them about the weird sword that I got and all the magic stuff I could do with it. By the time I'm finished, the sadness has receded.

"But that was with my vira, which is a cool necklace thing, and I haven't been able to find that since I got back to Earth."

No one speaks, save for Soumya and her vocal jazz. She pauses, which makes us all look at her, but then enters into another song.

"Well, I guess that does make you pretty special," Ross says, "Are you going to plant that thing like she said?"

I look at my pocket, "Maybe."

More acapella, then Marie starts, "Matthew, to finish off what Ross was saying earlier; the Bukanarions kept mentioning us destroying some sort of interplanetary conference area, though, according to upper management, no one from Earth was even in attendance this past year due to some weird timing mistakes."

The more words Marie says, the more uncomfortable I become. I am indeed from Earth, I was indeed in attendance this past year, and I did indeed take part in destroying some sort of interplanetary conference area. A heavy dread falls over my body like a weighted blanket and my mouth suddenly feels super dry.

"Matthew? Are you okay? You look sick…" Eunseo asks.

I smile and nod nervously, then Soumya's 'doo'ing ends.

"Alright, the mind scan came back positive. As long as she gives consent, I can go ahead and unlock her real memories. Soumya, is this something that you want on your own free will?"

The room is quiet, and then Soumya speaks again, "Yes."

"Sounds good. I'll go ahead and remove the wall and close out the request. You all have a nice day."

Soumya doesn't say anything, then she begins shouting like she was suddenly thrust on a rollercoaster ride. Her head lulls around, her eyebrows furrow, her arms sway and jerk.

"W-what's happening?" Andrea asks, cowering away.

"I don't know, you're the psychic!" Ross says.

Soumya looks like she's about to fall, so I reach out and grab her. She shifts the other way, falling onto me. Her body is feverishly warm. I begin looking around the room, trying to figure out why nobody is doing anything to help.

"What do I do?!" I ask, feeling like I can't breathe.

"Medicine?!" Eunseo offers, scrambling for her hip pouch.

"Wake her up, Andrea!" Marie commands.

"Wake up!" Andrea casts feebly, snapping again.

Soumya's eyes flick open, pupils rolling back down into view and focusing on me. Her eyes cross, focus, cross, blink, then focus again. Our eyes connect, and there is a familiarity in them different than I am used to.

"Calm down, I am fine."

She sits up and repositions herself on her chair, wiping her mouth with her sleeve and clearing her throat.

"Are you… Ben Sweezy?" Andrea asks.

My maid smirks, "No."

"Soumya?" I try.

"No."

The room is tense. My maid turns to me and raises an eyebrow.

"All that fighting alongside one another and you still don't recognize me? Who else would ever speak as verbosely as I?"

My breath catches in my throat. No way…

"Nima?!"

"Well done, Matthew."

CHAPTER 14

FINAL JUDGEMENT

~ GRIFFIN ~

By the time we reach the quiet suburban street, the sun is midway through setting. The sky is a smooth rose-gold. People sit out on porches, others wash cars. Two kids kick a soccer ball around their side yard. Our car is silent, outside of the softly playing radio. Everyone is exhausted from waking up so early and riding all day.

Ever since we had to give my godmother a call to get her exact address, I've felt dead inside. The jokes and hijinks of the day felt meaningless and small, even the food tasted a bit blander, and there has been some random, ever-present worry hovering just under the surface of my composure since I woke.

Now that the car is rounding a street and pulling into a neat driveway, and my godmother is emerging from her front door dressed in business casual and baring an award-winning smile, now that my journey has finally reached its conclusion, I understand where that fear is coming from.

I'm going to have to admit what happened.

Everything feels numb as I get out of the car and give my godmother a hug.

"Griffin! I haven't seen you in forever! How have you been?"

Despite my awful mood, Godmom's bubbliness is infectious, and I start to feel a little better.

"I'm… I'm at a net good." I struggle.

She chuckles, "Must've been a long drive."

I nod. To my unsurprised horror, Kay gets out of the car too.

"Hello *Paige*," she says Kay's name in the typical mother-meeting-the-crush voice, "good to see you again!"

They share a hug as my skin grows cold. Kay is going to be here for this. I wish I could tell her to go away, to distance herself, but I can't. It's too late; one way or another she is going to find out.

To my *surprised* horror, Wade gets out of the car as well.

"Hello Ms. Carden! I'm Wade, Griffin's friend from back when we were in junior high."

"Nice to meet you, Wade. Please, call me Ellie."

My stomach drops for a second before a calm wave of acceptance washes over me. I just rekindled this friendship, one that used to be one of my strongest, and now it will probably be destroyed, too. Two relationships with one stone, I suppose.

I look at the car, waiting for Ivan to come out too, but he waves his hand, "I'm going to go get us checked in at the hotel. Somebody's gotta do it."

"Are you sure? I've got chocolate chip and snickerdoodle cookies that just came out." Godmom assures.

Ivan does a double take, "Well in that case–"

“Why don’t you run along and reserve that hotel? Ellie just mentioned chocolate chip cookies, which means,” Wade looks dramatically into the afternoon sky, “my time has come.”

Ivan gives Wade a mean glare, “Well, there better be some when I get back.”

With that, he peels off down the road. Godmom nods, makes a silly face at me to cheer me up (I return a smile, but I know it looks weak), and then turns off towards her front porch. Wadc follows excitedly and Kay gives me an encouraging nudge.

I put one foot in front of the other, robotic, walking as though heading to the gallows. The front lawn melts away, the chic porch dissolving into a classy living room. My heartbeat pulses throughout my entire body. My skin feels cold. Even though I know what’s going to happen and I can do nothing to stop it, I still can’t help but feel terrified.

I’m in the kitchen, others are making conversation, the smell of cookies is smothering as opposed to comforting. Then I’m sitting, eyes glued to the back garden. Why did I lie last night? If it weren’t for those lies, I would be fine! *Oh my goodness I’m so stupid!*

Two snickerdoodles and two chocolate chip cookies with a glass of milk are slid in front of me. When I look up, Kay is to my left, Godmom is across from me, and Wade is to my right. Godmom is studying me hard, and as soon as our gazes lock, she speaks.

“Alright Griffin, so you texted me a couple days ago saying you were under a curse. We can get you out of this, but I’m going to need the complete truth on everything you know."

Daggers of terror shoot into my chest. Everything around me feels so distant, so quiet. I can't do this. This can't be happening. I'm about to lose two of my best friendships.

I look at Wade, who looks curious and concerned, leaving one of her cookies half-eaten. I look at Kay, who gives me a supportive smile. That's going to be the last smile I get from her for a long, long time. I look at Godmom, who sees the panic in my eyes but nods solemnly.

"I need you to tell me how you got the curse, all of the parameters that you know, and any symptoms you've been feeling. Again, be as truthful and as detailed as you can, since every bit of info helps me help you."

I can't look up from my cookies. My shame is too heavy. I can feel the three pairs of blue eyes burning into my soul, waiting patiently, focusing on words that I haven't even said yet.

A couple of moments pass, but the room is still silent. The spotlight is still on me. My blue-eyed jury has no more to say until I give my piece. My hands are sweaty. I lift my glass of milk and take a long drink. Despite my obvious stalling, no one says anything. No one laughs or jokes. No one clears their throat.

When I put the milk down, I realize what day today is. *Greed.* I'm greedy for my friendships, greedy for my good reputation, honestly even a little greedy for this curse. *Ashtoreth, today was a bit of a stretch, but I guess you've got a point.*

My confidence falters as I open my mouth. This is still intimidating, regardless of how much I psych myself up.

“I lied.” I blurt, and already my voice is catching, “I’m sorry Kay but I lied.”

She doesn’t respond. No one says anything. It’s as if their bodies are gone; the only things left are their piercing eyes and focused ears.

“I… I was… I…” I sigh, surprised at how fast tears are coming, “Ashtoreth didn’t just wave her hand and put a curse on me… she…” *oh gosh here we go*, “she kissed me.”

It is silent for so long that I feel like maybe no one heard me, but then when Kay speaks next, I wish it would’ve stayed quiet forever, “I don’t understand. Did she force you to kiss her?”

“Well, she pinned me down with magic chains so I couldn’t run away or take off my PASTIM, and…” I pause, stunned at the fact that I’m telling the truth like some sort of idiot, “… then when she leaned down to kiss me I just… I froze.”

“So you let her kiss you?” Wade asks, blunt.

Say it. I hesitate, mouth open and quivering. *Say it now.*

“Yes.”

There it goes. My friendships, my reputation, my chance at getting with my crush. All gone with one simple word.

“What else happened? How do you know you received a curse?” Godmom asks, still neutral.

I look up at her for some sort of support, but her eyes are impartial and professional. I'm not her godson right now; I'm a patient. Kay, over to my left, is staring at the table, wide-eyed, with her hands on her temples. Wade, off to my right, is giving me the most disgusted look I've ever seen, and this is still just my peripherals. Iciness washes over me. They took it just as poorly as I'd dreaded… and now I'm all alone.

"I um, I was backing away towards the church with the priest, and then she looked at me and said–" I can suddenly hear Ashtoreth's voice in my head, as if she is reciting it alongside me, "*With this curse, from this very day until the moment you leave this earthly realm, you will suffer attacks from the seven deadly sins, each sin for each day, each attack stronger than the last.*"

Once it is established that I'm finished, the chair to my right scoots back. Wade passes behind Godmom, her glare absolutely venomous. I try to meet her eyes but I can't. She pauses by Kay, who's chair scoots back as well, and then the two of them head outside.

As soon as the door closes, there is a jerking sensation in my gut, and hot tears begin to roll down my cheeks. There is another jerk, which tries to escape my curled mouth as a sob, but I choke it down. For a while it is just me, sitting there, trembling, my forehead in my hands, tears running down my face.

A pen clicks, and then the chair in front of me wordlessly scoots back. *Even my own godmother hates me*. I almost double over in sobs, sniffling and shaking to stop them from filling the kitchen.

To my surprise, my godmother's footsteps round the table instead of going outside.

"Stand up." Her voice says from beside me.

I do as she commands, not able to meet her eyes. She stands there for a moment, silent, then hugs me. It takes all I have not to break down right here.

"You are a fantastic godson and an incredible young man. Don't let your mistakes tear you down, because that's exactly what the enemy wants."

She releases me and pats my shoulder, appearing as a blurry outline of herself through my tears.

"Take your slip-ups in stride. As you will see, your blunders can be turned into blessings so long as you learn from them and strive to do better."

She smiles, and by now my eyes have cleared a little. I see her take a glance at the front porch.

"The girls are just upset. Apologizing won't be easy but… I think they will forgive you."

Filled with self-hatred, I go to speak, stumbling over my words at first, "I-I don't deserve forgiveness."

My godmom recoils, eyebrows raised, "Whoa now, Griff, no need to get all edgy. I already have one black-haired tattooed child in this family, I don't need another."

We share a laugh. My godbrother is pretty edgy.

"Now then, you eat some cookies and go talk to the girls. I'm going to go grab my thinking pipe and meet you outside."

Before I can object, she shuffles out of the kitchen and up the stairs. For a solid moment, I consider just going out there alongside her, but I know that would be pretty pathetic. I've caused this problem, so I have to face the consequences.

I grab a snickerdoodle, devour the delicious thing in two bites, and then head to the foyer. I can see two figures moving outside of the frosted glass. Here we go. With a sigh, I open the door, and the sight I see makes me recoil.

The entire front yard is covered in a thick blanket of snow. The blizzard blast stretches all the way into the yard of the neighbors across the street. Kids are playing in the road, throwing snowballs and laughing under the supervision of their confused parents.

Wade notices me instantly, but Kay doesn't realize I'm there until I close the door behind me. She quickly looks away from me and off into the street, while the guitarist next to her glares like I just told the world's most offensive and unfunny joke.

I feel more tears coming, creeping back up from deep down, but I push them away.

With a deep breath, I begin, "What I did was unacceptable. You have every right to hate me. Letting Ashtoreth kiss me was the stupidest thing I could have ever done."

Kay refuses to look at me, and Wade is still glaring into the side of my face. I continue and say the unthinkable.

"I guess I'm getting what I deserve. I get it if… if you don't want to talk to me any more after this. Same for you, Wade."

I go to lock eyes with Wade, but she avoids my gaze and looks off towards the kids in the street with Kay. Guilt grips my heart once more, and I have to fight back another growing wallop of dread.

"All I ask is that you forgive me, and know that, despite whether or not we stay friends, I will never kiss a succubus again."

As soon as silence falls, I realize how stupid and childish I sound. Did I really expect forgiveness? I should've just kept my mouth shut. In an explosion of motion, Kay is suddenly marching toward me, eyes flashing, hand raised to slap me senseless…

The open palm swings around and stops before it hits me. Slowly, her trembling hand lowers down in front of my face, morphing into a fist with an extended index finger.

"Do you want to die?" She asks lowly.

"No." And at the moment I would technically consider this a lie.

"Then why would you let a *Supreme Demon kiss you?*" She hisses, lowering her hand but still pointing at me with her eyes.

Before I can answer, Wade chimes in, "Because he's sick in the head. You thought she was hot, didn't you?"

Well that's a bit of a loaded question, she's a succubus, of course the answer is yes. But I only say the very last part of that thought.

"Yes." I look down at the ground again.

The silence is harsh and the children laughing a dozen meters away seems horribly unfitting.

"Of all the years we've known each other and all the times you've done something stupid, this is crossing the line to the furthest level," Kay growls, making my heart sink, "To think that you would do something so *backwards* is just… unbelievable…"

Here it is. She's going to end the friendship. It's down the drain.

"And if you *ever* do anything like this again–"

My heart slams into the top of my head. What?! She's actually forgiving me?!

"–I'm not giving you a third chance."

Ah, that dampened my mood a bit.

"Thank you, Kay." I say with a slight bow.

She grunts and sits on the porch bench. Now with my feeling of mild excitement, I turn to Wade. As soon as we lock eyes, I realize I just pulled the pin on a grenade.

"You're freakin' *weird*, bro," she says, "like, do you even think? I leave for two years and you become a *sicko*? If that's the case, we're going to need to do something to fix you up, buddy."

The fact that she says 'buddy' at the end, specifically the way she says it, sends a second gush of relief through my chest. She certainly isn't happy, but I think she has forgiven me too, in a sense. It takes all I can to keep myself from smiling.

"Thank y–"

"Yeah sure whatever." Wade interrupts, turning away.

Cool; mood dampened again. Now it is silent in a thoughtful, slightly dangerous way. *My my where is my godmother?*

"Sorry for the wait." The person in question says.

I turn to the doorway to see her standing there with more cookies, her platinum blond hair a bit ruffled, her wide nose a little flared. A classy pipe rests in her pressed lips.

"Thing was hidden well… not where I remembered putting it."

She shrugs and walks out onto the porch, footing the door closed behind her. Kay scoots over, curious, as Godmom sits next to her. Wade drifts over towards the cookies, one of which Godmom hands her.

"What's the pipe for?" Wade asks, stuffing the entire cookie into her mouth afterward.

"Helps me think. I don't smoke, though. It's just for aesthetics."

Wade nods and chews in nearly the same motion. Even though her mouth is full, she reaches for another cookie.

"Okay so, let's see… seven sins, seven days, just keeps getting worse. We'll set those to the side for now. What was the time constraint she set on the curse?" My godmother asks, absently insisting that Kay take another snickerdoodle.

"Until 'the moment I leave this earthly realm'." I recite.

Godmom hands me a chocolate chip-snickerdoodle sandwich and chuckles to herself, "Is that all? If so, the answer is laughably obvious."

My heartbeat quickens, and it's not due to the sugary goodness I'm chewing on right now, "Really?"

"Yeah," Godmom says, "Just leave this earthly realm."

I practically feel myself deflate and my godmother notices this.

"No, think about it. Realm means a kingdom, or… a specific area of interest. Earthly can mean temporal, but it can also mean something relating to Earth. Now, if Ashtoreth specified a bit more, using words like 'physical' or 'final', then we'd have a real problem on our hands. But as of now, all you have to do is… well, you tell me." She says the last part with a victorious raise of her eyebrows.

"I have to… leave the planet?" I try.

"Yep," Godmom says, replacing her pipe with a chocolate chip cookie, "Go off to wherever Oshiro went, go to the moon… really, you could just leave the atmosphere and come back."

"It's that easy?" Kay asks.

Godmom shrugs, smirking and removing her pipe, "Yes. A simple case of amorphous connotative malediction, which is the most common issue with chronic type-3 curses like these, especially if they're verbally induced."

"R-right," Wade says, "that's what I'd thought, too."

I look up. Two birds glide high in the big, blank, orange sky. Outer space? Out there in the infinite abyss with the stars and planets… yikes. If I talk to people in IPSHA, I can definitely make it up there but… what will it be like? The thought of being that celestial is unnerving… and what if it doesn't work?

I go to look back down and speak, but then those birds bank in the air and sunlight gleams off of them. Those… aren't birds. One is white with huge wings. The other is blue-gray and streaks through the sky in a very mechanical fashion. Neither of them flap their wings. Those are the flying vehicles from the base… and they are descending.

The others notice it too and get up to give it a good look. For a moment, I just gaze, surprised that my team is here. All at once, I realize that I'm going to have to re-admit my slip-up to the entire team. *Faaantastic*.

Wade hums an exclamation through her cookie-filled cheeks and points down the street. Ivan is rolling back up with his car, driving impatiently behind a few lackadaisical cyclists.

****

The two crafts land in the middle of the street, stopping in the now abandoned lake of watery slush. As soon as the glider comes to a stop, the canopy flies open. Ross climbs out, having an aura of false calmness. Eunseo emerges from behind him.

"Ominous!" Ross calls as he splats down into the melting snow.

I give Kay a glance. She is conveniently not looking at me.

"Had a feeling you'd be here," Ross continues, pretending not to be angry, "It's the only place in Vancouver you'd know about. Still, I'm surprised Eunseo spotted you from that far up."

I look at the vehicles as Ross and Eunseo march up the driveway to see who will get out of the flying car. Is it going to be Alia? It'd be just my luck. She's going to be cranky from the flight, too. I can imagine her now; angry eyes, grating voice, and an unfittingly nice hijab to match.

The doors open. A brown-skinned girl I've never seen before comes out of the passenger's seat, and… agh, *Marie* gets out of the back seat. I expect to see Homero and Alia rounding the corner next; that would only make sense. But if it were just Homero, that would be the absolute best…

A short boy with wispy brown hair and blue eyes rounds the side, alone. What? He wasn't *flying*, was he?

"Hey Ross, how are you?" Godmom asks from the porch, rising and bringing the half-eaten tray of cookies to greet the party.

"Pretty alright, how about you Ms. Carden?"

"Oh, I'm your godmother too for crying out loud! But I'm doing fine. Want some cookies?"

"Don't get too excited," Ivan calls from beside me, "Wade ate all the chocolate chip ones."

Wade looks a bit too full to retaliate.

"I love cookies!" Eunseo yells, hastening her step.

Once they all make it to the porch, grab a cookie, and find a seat against the railing or in one of the extra chairs Godmom and I fetched, the group settles into an expectant silence.

"So… how was the trip?" I ask Ross.

"Well, I taught a 13-year-old how to fly a car, we talked to a giant hivemind robot from the planet Tillayf, and then some magic indigenous chick with a super-powered longbow almost shot all of us to death, so I'd have to say it was pretty chill."

"Indigenous?" The brown-haired boy asks softly, "Like, she was a Native American?"

"Yeah," Ross replies, "have you never met a Native person before?"

The boy shakes his head.

"Hey, way to go, kid. Expanding your horizons." Ivan takes a swallow of milk, "Sounds like one heck of a trip."

"You down for something like that?" Wade asks him excitedly.

"Of course." The drummer replies as if the answer was obvious.

"And you, Griffin?" Marie asks in a not-so-casual tone, "You bolted off, telling your family you had 'business to take care of', and then turn up on the other side of the country eating cookies. Care to explain?"

I want to tell her to stop being such an un-fun nun, but I'm quite sure that would not result in the kindest of outcomes.

"Yeah," Kay mutters, "tell them about how *someone* used their PASTIM inside of the US."

"Oh right," Wade jeers threateningly, "and tell them about how *someone* kissed a certain *someone* while you're at it."

Kay begins blushing, no doubt becoming angry again, and I raise my hands to try and get a handle on the situation. Before I can speak, Ross' eyes light up. I put two and two together and figure he must think I kissed Kay. Sure enough:

"Ayyy!" he bellows, looking at me with a proud grin, "After all these years you finally…"

He notices my wide eyes and subtle head shaking.

"… lost your mind! Taking out your PASTIM in the US?! What were you thinking?!" He corrects.

He and I share a small nod before Marie chimes in, "And what is this about kissing? Surely it was only done as a greeting in the name of our Lord?"

"Not necessarily…" *well that's an understatement*, "it was, an illusion from a succubus, and then she pinned me down and…" I brace myself, "she went in for the kiss and I let it happen."

The others are silent. Ross shrugs.

"Don't succubi kiss people all the time?" He asks.

I have to say it now, "It was Supreme Demon Ashtoreth."

Marie recoils as if Ivan just spat milk on her (and it appears as though he almost did). Eunseo lets out a high-pitched gasp, and I would say it was a bit dramatic, but given the context, it was probably appropriate. Ross is somewhere between a disbelieving smile and a horrified grimace. He soon realizes there are no camera crews coming out, no 'gotchas' or bursts of laughter, and his face falls. I'm suddenly filled with childish panic at the sight of his expression.

"Please don't tell Mom and Dad!" I beg.

"Of course I'm not telling them, but that isn't the biggest of your worries!" Ross exclaims.

"My Lord my King," Marie stammers, looking light-headed, "Griffin kissed a Sister of Doom… I think I'm going to faint."

Ivan is coughing in the background, and Eunseo looks like she's about to cry. This is going both better and worse than I expected.

"Okay everyone, let's calm down," Godmom says, stuffing her empty pipe into her pocket, "we've resolved the issue and identified some next steps. I can assure you," she smiles at me, "Griffin will be just fine."

The confidence in her voice seems to smooth out the panic in the air. Everyone begins nodding blankly and sitting back.

"Yeah," Ross mutters, "yeah okay. If you've got it figured out, we're good."

There is more silence, and then my godmother speaks to Ross again, "Since it's such a nice night out and I've got way too much cookie dough, why don't I put on some more cookies, we relax a little, and you introduce me to our two guests?"

She gestures to the brown girl and the short boy.

"Sure," Ross says, "and I'll grab my deck from the car so we can play spades!"

"Spades?" Godmom asks, interested, "After this long journey of yours, you really want to come here just to *lose*?"

Ross throws his head back with an amused laugh, "See, it confuses me as to why everyone keeps thinking they're going to win around a literal *king*. When I'm playing the game, there is *zero* positivity."

"But Soumya is better. Not Soumya, Nima." Eunseo informs.

"All I know is, Soumya or Nima or whomever," Ivan sits up and puts his empty glass on a side table, "none of you children are beating me in spades."

"What's spades?" Wade interrupts.

The whole porch, including me, is alive with jumbled explanations and laughter. I notice Kay absently pull out her phone. Then Eunseo. Then Ivan. Soon, everyone but my godmother and the mysterious pair have their phones out.

And no one is smiling.

Chapter Finale

Griffin's Fate

~ Matthew ~

Everyone is absorbed in their phones aside from Nima, the cookie woman, and the boy who I assume to be Griffin. Griffin, tall, blond, with brown eyes and spikey hair, shrugs at me. I shrug back, not so much caught up in the weirdness of the cell phones but rather how unfitting this guy's name is. Griffin Voltaire sounds like some young aristocrat, not a stereotypical surfer dude.

"Yikes," the college-aged Asian guy says, scrolling down his phone, "a combat summons. This looks pretty urgent, too…"

"It is in Paris! Big robot man is right!" Eunseo exclaims.

Wade's head snaps up with a similar curiosity to Griffin, while Ms. Carden, the silver-haired girl, and the Asian guy look over with a confused slowness. Ross' eyes flick towards Nima, then me, then the Asian guy, who is closest to him.

"Azimuth was this…" Ross shakes his head, "no time, looks like we need to get moving ASAP. Ms. Car… I mean Godmom, do you have a gem we can use to get to North-Main HQ in Paris?"

"I'll be back in a second." She gets up with a tray of crumbs and dashes off inside.

"Alright everybody, go grab your PASTIMs and weapons from

the car. We don't know what to expect but we want to be prepared for a long haul." Ross commands.

"That's a good idea." The Asian guy compliments, descending the porch steps.

Wade gets up with a bit of difficulty and heads into the house as if to follow Ms. Carden. The silver-haired girl does the same, collecting the empty milk glasses and crumby napkins along the way. Griffin, after a moment of hesitation, trails in behind her. Eunseo and Marie begin to make their way down to the flying vehicles, but Ross stops them.

"Hey, on second thought, we'll just take the car and the glider with us. Better have it and not need it than the other way around, right?" Ross concludes.

The others nod in agreement, but then I start to get a little leery. Phrases like 'urgent combat summons', 'long haul', and 'take the flying car to France' are starting to make me think that I'm not going home any time soon. Things seem a little hectic and I don't want to intrude, so I look over at Nima. She simply looks back at me, seeming indifferent about everything. Oh boy, Sam is going to have a field day.

Ms. Carden emerges from the foyer with a large sapphire in her hand. Wade is behind her, donning what looks like a double-necked guitar. Griffin and the silver-haired girl are shouldering on bookbags in the background. I have to say something…

"Hey," I quietly force out, and I'm surprised Ross actually heard me, “um… I’m not impatient or anything but… what about getting home to my mom?”

Ross freezes, a look of shock on his face, “We were supposed to do that about now, weren’t we…”

“Where do you live?” Ms. Carden offers, “I didn’t get the summons, so I could always drive you.”

“Madison, Alabama.” I grit weakly.

She returns a grit and bows her head a bit, “Mmmmaybe we can explore some other options.”

“How about…” Ross snaps to himself, trying to think as people move about in a flurry of motion, “we… we’ll go to France, sort that out, fly the car to Portugal, and then we can book you a flight straight to Alabama. I know we’ve got more than enough in the team budget to cover that.”

“He looks a little young to be going into an active combat zone!” Ms. Carden exclaims, clutching the sapphire towards her chest.

Ross looks around. Everyone is strapped with their gear and ready to go. He sighs and puts one hand on my shoulder and the other on Nima’s.

“We’ll be fine, they’ve got it mostly under control.” Ross reassures, steering Nima and I toward the crafts.

Ms. Carden, looking displeased, follows us. Wade and the Asian guy get into a car and drive closer to the other vehicles. Nima, Marie, and I reenter the flying car, followed closely by Eunseo. I watch as Griffin and the silver-haired girl get into the glider with

Ross.

Perhaps Griffin looks a little too thoughtful. Perhaps he is biting his nails or furrowing his brow. Perhaps he needs time to rest, time to think, time to recover from whatever kissing Ashtoreth means. But I don't notice it, if that is the case.

"Alright, buckle up. We don't know what we could be dropping down into." Ross warns through the walkie-talkie.

I do as he says, sliding the seatbelt across my chest, and I can hear the others doing so around me. I was actually looking forward to a night of cookies and Spades with the others, and it takes all I have not to show my exhaustion, disappointment, and nervousness.

Ms. Carden apprehensively walks up to the melted snow and raises the sapphire.

"Stay safe and visit more often! And *please* stay safe!"

She hesitates longer, staring at me, and then puts her hand down.

"Get out of the car." Her muffled shout is directed at me this time.

Stunned, I glance at Marie and Eunseo. They seem about as clueless as I do. Nima's shrug gives me a similar impression. I look back at Ms. Carden, who is beckoning reluctantly.

"Go on Matt, get out," Ross' voice comes from the walkie-talkie, annoyed, "we might as well comply because we can't afford to waste any more time."

"Eh," I peep, opening my door with guilty relief, "who's going to fly the car?"

"We'll figure that out when we get there. Thanks for your help buddy." He says.

I look at Nima, who has a surprised frown on her face. As instructed, I put down the walkie talkie and we get out of the car. Marie and Eunseo say goodbye. Once Nima and I march through the thin slush and stamp our feet on the asphalt next to Ms. Carden, the woman sighs, windmills her arm, and beams the sapphire as hard as she can at the ground.

It splats into the slush, and instead of shattering, the slush begins turning purple. Suddenly, the slush, both cars and the glider are engulfed in a sparking, flickering sinkhole, identical to the one that brought us to Canada a few days ago and Arret last year.

Once everything is swallowed up, the street closes finitely. There is no trace of anything, not even the sapphire.

"I'm going to have to order another." Ms. Carden mutters, looking around to make sure no one saw.

After a halfhearted scan of the neighborhood, she gestures for us to follow her back to the porch. I do so without delay, Nima at my side.

When we get to the porch, Ms. Carden finally speaks again, "I'll pay for your flight home. I just," she sighs, "I didn't really want *any* of you to go over there, but the others were made to. Since you aren't required, I thought I'd spare you the trouble."

"Thank you." I reply, realizing just how tense my shoulders were.

"How's this," she says, smiling kindly, "I'll go make you some dinner, and bright and early tomorrow, I'll take the two of you to the airport."

"That sounds great." Nima says, and I nod in agreement.

Ms. Carden gives us a thumbs up and then ducks into her front door. I go to follow, but Nima heads over to one of the porch seats, plopping down as if she is as tired as I am. I glance at the door, then glance at Nima, who is patting the seat next to her. I decide to sit with her.

For a moment we just relax, watching the sky doze off into a lavender sleep, the remaining slush melt into the lawn's grass, and the neighborhood's lights begin to turn on.

"So," she says finally, "I've been your maid this entire time."

"Yeah." I reply, awkward.

More silence.

"Was I a satisfactory maid?" She asks, amused.

"Er… yes." I admit.

She chuckles, "Fantastic. I'll make sure to keep up the front upon our arrival home."

"Yeah…" I say, and a nagging question begins to bubble up, "hey, um, can I ask you a question… even though you might not know the answer?"

"I am certainly interested now." Nima says, sounding relaxed.

"Are you… are you really Nima?" I ask.

She grins and nods, "Astonishingly, yes."

"But then aren't you supposed to be…"

"Democ?" Nima fills in, and even though I was going to say

‘purple’, I nod along, figuring that this was less offensive.

“Well, I’ve been giving that a deep amount of thought during our flight and I think I’ve come to a suitable conclusion. After we defeated Yatniv at the Celestial Conference,” a jolt of fear rushes through me as I remember that this was technically the cause of the current war, “everyone retreated through the portal. Moreover, though I have not seen the others, I believe they have also retained their human and woodish forms.

“However, I was not in my democ form while at the conference or going through the portal. I was under the influence of the Mask Potion, which was powerful enough to transform me into a woodish for a brief period of time.

“Perhaps the combination of the potion and the portal’s properties made me shift once again, but this time into a human. Woodish and humans are incredibly similar, after all.”

I nod, lost. That makes no sense and a lot of sense, like a majority of Arret stuff, so I’ll just drop it.

“Well… what do you think of Earth?” I ask her.

“I’ve been here before, remember?” She objects, and I vaguely recall that she lived in a treehouse or something in the woods once.

“Ah, right, right. Well then like…”

“How am I enjoying the rest of it?” Nima fills in, and I nod, “It is somewhat rudimentary yet quite amiable and undoubtedly prepossessing. I would say overall, rather… *bucolic*.”

“Fair enough.” I say, never having heard half of those words before in my entire life.

More silence.

"W-what about being a human?" I test.

Nima thinks, "Rather liberating. I feel taller and more energetic, and everything feels crisper. My sense of smell is sharper, too. I can jump higher and run faster, my emotions are much more palpable, and it seems refreshingly easy to breathe. But," she frowns, looking at the ground.

"I could certainly do without all the hair. The various, unfortunate forms of mucus are also unsavory… and this ear design seems only minimally useful. The cramps and headaches, while occasional, are still more frequent than democs. Plus, the emotions can sometimes be palpable to the point of discomfort. Perhaps I am at a cumulative neutral."

"Fair enough." I repeat.

Silence again. It's gotten pretty dark, but not to the point where we want to go inside.

"Matthew," Nima asks suddenly, "do you know of whatever happened to the rest of our team?"

"Outside of Sam, Yoseph, and now you, no. I can't even find my vira," I pause, "I was hoping you would have some insight."

"I do not," she responds softly, "I hope everyone is safe."

A car coasts by.

"Hey Nima, do you by chance know who hypnotized you?"

"No," she replies, "after I was rendered unconscious due to the effects from the long-distance teleportation, I simply awoke as Soumya Dhumne. Perhaps reading that Kraues, the language of the Democs, helped uncover some important brain pathways."

"I see."

The door opens and Ms. Carden peeks out, "Dinner's ready!"

****

The pan-cooked chicken with alfredo sauce and asparagus is really good. The three of us eat in silence, Ms. Carden with a smaller helping and eating much more slowly. Suddenly, her phone buzzes.

She picks it up, scrolling through the notification as her eyebrows raise higher and higher.

"Alien threat neutralized!" She exclaims at last, smiling.

I look at Nima, who looks supportively happy.

"Found a few new materials… research says that the foot soldiers in Egypt are the Bukan equivalent to monkeys, with the soldiers in France being the real Bukanarions… peace negotiations now have leverage and seem to be going better…"

She trails off, continuing to read and absently mopping up some alfredo sauce with a piece of chicken. All at once, she puts down her phone and chuckles to herself.

"Sorry, I'd usually be telling my own kids to put their phones down at the table, and now look at me."

She shakes her head and takes a bite.

"Oh, we don't mind." I say, covering my mouth.

Nima nods in agreement, but Ms. Carden waves her hand.

"Please, you're my guests, I need to do better," she takes a sip of ginger ale, "so, how is everything?"

"Delicious!" I admit, shoveling more of the spiced asparagus into my mouth.

"Truly," Nima adds on, "from the seasonings alone, it seems as though you have a very extensive culinary background."

"Oh, I just looked this up online," Ms. Carden blushes, "Anyway, how was the trip here? I think I heard something about a 'giant hivemind robot'?"

Before Nima and I can reply, Ms. Carden's phone begins to buzz. She glances down at it, annoyed, picking it up as if she's about to silence it, but then her face lights up.

"It's Ross!"

He is on speaker phone in a moment.

"Hey Ross!" she announces, "You all won! I was starting to get worried because it was about an hour and a half since you–"

"Godmom," his voice fills the room, quivering and urgent, "what was Griffin's curse about?"

Ms. Carden looks up at us, confused, "… um… that he would continue to experience increasing sin until he left the world, but we figured he could just leave the atmosphere for a little–"

Ross lets out a strained cry, somewhere between anguish and

frustration. I can almost see him, red-faced, teeth gritted.

Our hostess looks up at us, concerned, "Ross? What's going on?"

"Everyone with super speed who got the combat summons was flown up to the starship to scout it out and look for the main engine," Ross sounds like he's on the verge of a breakdown, "they were gonna put an electronic target on it, and then the US was going to launch a nuclear missile at the target. The whole time, they weren't seeing a lot of action because all the enemies were out fighting the jets.

"Once they found the engine, they marked it and left. Every scout," his voice cracks, "*every scout* that went up there had a position tracker on to make sure that they got off the ship before the nuke was launched. Everyone was accounted for and the starship started to retreat at the same time they did.

"But when they got back, I followed the tracker to find Griffin and instead found some," he sounds like he's waving his arms angrily, "*Ker-ry Sti-vers* dude and he's looking at me like he doesn't know anything, and I ask him where Griffin is, and he says last time he saw him they were headed to the exit but Griffin doubled back and went to get something!"

"Wh… what?!" Ms. Carden looks like someone just gut-punched her, "That doesn't make any–"

"EXACTLY!" Ross bellows, "WHY DIDN'T HE WAIT FOR GRIFFIN TO COME BACK?! WHY DIDN'T THAT *STU*–"

The phone suddenly roars with wind like it's been thrown, and then there is a loud crack and the call drops. Ms. Carden stares down at her plate, eyes and mouth wide, still stunned from an invisible blow. Nima and I have stopped eating, sitting in respectful and dumbfound silence. Just a few hours ago, I saw the guy joking and eating cookies. And now…

There is a twinge inside as I realize I never even got to introduce myself.

EPILOGUE

~ ~ ~

"*Vinculum*!" I scream, "*Vinculum vinculum vinculum*!"

A barrage of green curves stream through the air, past the ducking soldiers, politicians, and reporters, and into the giant, floating, cloth-arms connected to this man's turban. Loud ripping fills the great hall as shreds of fabric flick from two of the hovering arms, but the other three arc out of range.

One of them swings down, clipping my Secretary of Finances across the arm, and rushes forward, flat fingers outstretched. I can't think of a spell fast enough so I simply brace myself, hold on to my crown, and raise my guard. It phases right through my magic projectile shield, snatching me so violently off of my feet that my flamberge goes twirling out of my hand, narrowly missing the Ambassador of Nyjjia.

Suddenly, I am moving forward. The walls fly past me faster and faster, confused and terrified faces flashing by. The open doors of my throne room swell at an alarming speed… the cloth prison I'm in melts away and I'm hurtling through the room, headed straight for the large window that overlooks the capital. Oh! I'm about to fly out the window!

"*Ameliorate*!" I shout, my arms flailing.

I stop right where I am without a single bit of whiplash. All the momentum leaves my body at the utterance of the spell, blasting the rest of the room instead. Wind jostles the aesthetic rivers out of their troughs and sends my throne spinning viciously.

I float down until my shoes meet the polished wood atop the conference table. I wheel around in just enough time to see the throne room doors slam shut. The lock clicks, and then the man turns to me, smirking.

"Can I get you something to drink?" I ask, briefly lifting my crown to readjust my hair.

He chuckles, "I'm fine, thank you."

Standoffish silence. The five cloth-arms worm around him, wriggling gently.

"Look buddy," I start, a little annoyed, "you're the ninth assassin that's tried to get at me since the whole thing came out about tricking the Bukanarions and whatnot. I know, I know, and I probably did something horrible to your family some time ago but, well, I'm sorry."

The man doesn't reply, he just smiles.

"Soooo… if you'll excuse me, I've got to get back to explaining myself to IPSHA *and* a bunch of angry neighboring nations *and* a few hundred citizens getting ready to try an insurrection."

"I will do that in your stead." He assures in a deep voice.

"Well, Assassin 2, 3, 4, and 6 already suggested abdicating, and I told them no too, so yeah, please get out." I reply.

The guy straightens his tie (yes, he wore a full suit to confront me, and a very nice one at that) then his smile fades.

"I am capable of things the other assassins aren't."

"Like?"

A wrinkle on his forehead opens, revealing a third, purple-iris eye. Before I can recoil in disgust, there is a magnetic force, and I am thrown onto my butt. So he has a magic turban *and* he's a kupua… looks like he might be a bit–

"*Ecclesia.*" He says.

To my total surprise, I begin to slide forward on the table. This… can't be possible! How can he have magic *and* kupua powers?! He begins to laugh as I slow to a stop at the edge of the smooth wood, my face twisted in surprise.

"You will relinquish your crown to me. I will claim the throne from you and keep you as my lead advisor."

I go to speak but he interrupts.

"Spare me the prattling. My third eye allows me to see into your mind," he adjusts his cufflinks, "You are scared, figuring the heated debates and meetings will come to a head when the Bukanarions arrive. Once you give me the crown, this will not be a problem."

I can only stare, dumbfound. I mean, that wasn't *verbatim* what I was thinking at this exact moment, but–

"Once you give me the *crown*, this will not be a *problem*." He repeats, his neutral frown turning into an annoyed one.

For a moment I am intimidated, but then I realize what game this guy is playing and stand up, "You think I'm going to abdicate to a stranger with three eyes that I've known for five minutes?"

In the same moment, he draws a magic circle in the air and widens his third eye.

"*Deleterious*."

"*C–*" but suddenly, I can't talk or move.

I watch as the red and black dart of magic sinks into my chest. Roaring pain slashes through my heart. Unable to writhe or scream, for a second I think, or maybe hope, that I'm about to die. Then the magnetic force from this guy disappears and I fall back onto the table, gasping and clutching my chest.

The man walks forward, one foot in front of the other, shoulders back, face unamused. His shoes click with every step. Although this is an odd thought, I've got to admit, the suit fits him.

"I am not a stranger; I am Zashul Omarr… the Trifecta. I do not *think* you are going to abdicate to me, I *know* you will." he chuckles a little and smiles, "Also, thank you. I got this suit tailor-made."

He is now right in front of me, one of his cloth-hands outstretched, presumably for me to put my crown in. I can only glare. Zashul widens his third eye and I feel the crown come off and plop down on my lap. After a second… I toss it to him.

Perhaps I can make this work in my favor…

End Credits

Thanks God once again for allowing me to make it this far; may this book help build Your Kingdom.

Thank you (possessing this book) for buying and reading it; I can't believe you actually did this whole process *twice*!

Thanks Mom for taking me to the bookstore so often as a kid and showing me reading is fun; hopefully this series can be enjoyed between mother and son as well.

Thanks Dad, Courtney, and the rest of my family for keeping up the support; I love you guys forever.

Thanks Ris and the beta readers for your edits; without you all this book would have been literally unreadable.

Arigatou Umberger-san and Chowen-san for your translations; you really helped make the book even more awesome to write.

Thanks Kelly, Leila, Blake, Jacob, Colton, Jennifer, Stephanie, Caleb, Ben, Alla, Sophia, Kolger, and Wu; writing about you all is fun :p

BONUS:

OPERATION PRAGMA

THE TALE OF YERA

Between the adventures of Daiki, Matt, and Griffin, a group of familiar faces from Arret must navigate a new, unfamiliar world.

TABLE OF CONTENTS

CHAPTER 1

NOTE BY THE DOOR

~ INVITATION ~

Deep, slow music floats through the hotel room as I dry my hair. This used to be a terrifying place, but I have lived here for so long that it's become as familiar as my body. I've explored every piece of carpet, wallpaper, and glass in this room so many times that I could recite its dimensions.

I pass some of my other artwork; my earlier pieces were abstract and filled with darkness, but now they are landscape paintings of what I think the land below looks like. There is my chair, sitting at the end of a walkway of art supplies. The easel is dark against the morning sun. My unfinished painting of Paris in the Spring is covered in shadow.

I sit down at the easel and pick up a brush, not even bothering to change out of my towel. There is no point, seeing that I'm too many floors up for anyone on the ground to see me. And there certainly won't be anyone coming through the door.

At 0930, I'll eat breakfast. My three daily meals, along with snacks, always just *appear* in my mini fridge each morning, so I could eat whenever I wanted. But my training with the Empress has made me crave a schedule. After breakfast, I'll paint until lunch, then do a bit of studying, look at some news, clean up, and check off my gym card.

On second thought, I might try a movie instead. There was an odd show back in the winter called *Journey of Shrines* that aired on the worldwide news, telling a silent story about a Japanese boy fighting magic spirits. It was all in first-person and all one, continuous shot. This impressed me and kept me hooked.

The show ended after he returned back to Japan, and the news channel has been relatively political since then. It got a little more interesting when they began talking about some unidentified objects flying around in the Middle East, but then the channel started getting spotty for some reason, and the constant technical errors make it impossible to watch.

Meticulously, I add a dark brown line to the edge of the Eiffel Tower, slashing across the blue sky. Even though the music is easy to nod to, I make sure to keep everything as still and gentle as possible. I don't know why. No one is going to see these.

Either way, I stare out past the window and the balcony at the Parisian dawn.

****

Enough paint has covered me in these past few hours that I ought to take another shower! I probably even got some paint in my breakfast… well, whatever. I get up from my chair and head to the restroom sink to wash off my hands. As I'm walking to the bathroom, I notice a small white card and a pack of chamomile tea sitting on top, just in front of the main door.

Huh, the gym card is pretty early today. Every day since I got here, the card and tea have arrived right at sunset. The first week or so I would write back and ask why I was being locked away and swear revenge on them and whatnot.

After I found out how to work the smartphone on the nightstand and saw that I could call people (only the same five people, but people nonetheless), I discovered that if I drink the tea, it puts me to sleep. If I check the box next to the big "*Gym today?*", I will wake up in a large training room, normally inhabited by various weights, mats, and at least one of the five people I can call. More time passed and I began doodling on the backs of these cards, and one day I just woke up with art supplies.

I wash my hands like I meant to, dry them, and then come back around and pick up the card and tea. Does this mean gym time will be before sunset? Should I take my shower now? I look in the mirror at my wild red hair and paint-freckled face. I guess my schedule will be a bit different today.

Maybe I should call one of my buddies and see if they got their card early. I round the second bed, sit down, and get ready to dial. Out of routine, I flip the card over to read it.

I am prepared ☐

I pause, looking at the card in shock. This is the first time anything like this has happened before. Did they make an error? They are always extremely precise. What does "I am prepared" mean? Prepared for what?

At once, the chime of my phone slices through the soft music. I jump and snatch it up.

"Yera?" a familiar voice asks.

"Ellia?" I reply.

"Did you get it too?" They ask, sounding excited.

My phone lights up with another call from Kabel.

"Hold on, I'm going to make this a conference call."

I press and hold the notification, and then Kabel's name appears under Ellia's.

"You there, Kabel?" I ask.

"Hey, Kabel!" Ellia says.

"How you doin', Ellia? Ey, did you getta weird new card unda ya door just now?" His deep voice booms through the phone speaker.

Ellia pauses, so I start speaking, "Yeah, the 'I am prepared one'?"

"That's the –" before Kabel can finish, another voice interrupts.

"Hey, did you guys get the weird card?!" Bacoj shouts.

"Listen here buddy just 'cause we're over the phone don't mean you can start interruptin' me."

My phone lights up again: Virrel. I add him to the line.

“Hey everyone, I just added Virrel.” I report.

A chorus of choppy voices greets him.

“Good to hear you all. I’m going to bring Nale into the call and that should be everyone.”

There is a pause, and then Virrel asks, “Nale?”

“Hey.” Nale peeps.

“That’s everyone, right?” I ask, knowing the answer.

Jumbled agreements come tumbling through the phone, then there is expectant silence.

“Okay,” I say, realizing how quiet the others are, “so it looks like everyone else got a different card outside of the normal gym one today, right?”

I can hear Nale’s confused “no?” among the excited yeses.

“Wait wait wait. Nale, did you say you *didn’t* get one?” I ask.

There is silence, then, “Oh yeah I see it now.”

If it were anyone else, we would laugh. But Nale is the quiet, softer type, so no one does.

“Alright,” I say, crossing my legs, “it looks like we’ve got some planning to do. Anyone got any suggestions?”

“I wanna see what happens if we check it!” Ellia blurts out.

“Hey, not so fast Ellia,” Virrel says, “we’re going to need to consider our options first.”

I can’t help but smile at how casual Virrel’s voice is. When we first got here after the Celestial Conference, he and I were still going through the motions of Empress Rigm’s orders. But time has worn away the formalness and now we've all become friends.

"What other options do we have? I don't see a 'no' option." Kabel remarks. I can hear him flipping the card in the background.

"It ain't even a question. It's just a statement."

"So what do we do? Make the tea and drink it?" Bacoj asks.

"Yes! And make sure to check the box!" Ellia shouts.

"I'm down for it." Kabel says.

"I don't know," Nale mumbles, almost too quiet to hear, "what if we aren't prepared?"

Silence.

"Well, we been trainin' every day for like seven months straight. I don't think there's too much we ain't prepared for." Kabel says.

"I may have skipped a few of those days, but yes Kabel, my thoughts exactly!" Ellia adds.

"Okay." Nale says.

They have a point. Everyone (except Virrel; he's a ghost so he can't fall asleep) has been in the gym rather consistently. We're all much leaner and stronger than we were when we got here.

"I know it's smart to be cautious…" I trail off a little, thinking more, "Well, the card is from the same people who have been feeding us healthy and housing us *and* letting us get in shape. I don't think they're going to turn around and hurt us."

"What if that's what they want us to think, though?" Bacoj asks, "What if they're just fattening us up so they can eat us alive?!"

"Even though they let us go toda gym *every day*. Sure, that's a possibility." Kabel mocks.

"I don't think they're going to eat us, Bacoj. But I do have an idea," Virrel says, "What if you all drink it at the same time?"

"That ain't too bad of an idea." Kabel admits.

"Yeah, that sounds pretty cool!" Bacoj says.

"Let's do it. What time?" Ellia asks.

No one speaks up. For some reason, I feel like I should say something. I look at the clock on the nightstand. 1048.

"How about 1400?" I ask.

After a pause, Kabel says, "Just set my alarm."

The others agree and I can hear clicking in the background.

"So that's it then?" Virrel asks, "See you all at 1400? Or, well, you know, whenever you wake up?"

"Yep! Everyone should wear something pirate-y, too." Ellia says.

There is a pause of confusion.

"Because we're the Earth Pirates!" They clarify.

Everyone lets out scoffs and laughs before leaving the call.

****

I took another shower, ate lunch, and got dressed. Even though I am in sports attire, I tie a pillowcase around my head like a bandana, just to appease Ellia. Right now, I sit on the bed, reading over the *A Guide to Earth* manual one more time. It is more for reassurance than studying; I've read it so many times in English that I started reading the French version for practice.

All of my books and paintings are arranged neatly by the wall. The checked “I am prepared” card is on the TV stand. My painting supplies are tucked away. The TV and the lights are off. I let the sunlight stream through the thin, white curtains.

I glance at the clock. 1350. I fill the electric kettle and turn it on. It feels like it takes years to boil but it is only a couple of minutes. I prepare the tea with honey and sugar, then pour the boiling water and stir. A quick look at the clock shows 1354.

I let the teabag float until 1357. I take it out and blow on the tea. Another quick look at the clock. Still 1357. It stays on 1357 for what feels like five minutes. I grip and re-grip the mug. It doesn’t burn my hand anymore. Another look around the tidy room and then another glance at the clock. 1358.

I can’t wait any longer. I down the tea and finish the last drop right as the clock hits 1400. Whoa, this one is strong! I always forget how strong these teas are.

It seems like they can make everything make me sleepy. This, the shower water in the gym, dessert, I wouldn’t be surprised if they could make the air make me sleepy. I lay my head on the pillow, feeling heavy. Wow, it hasn’t even been a minute yet. This one is really fast acting…

Darkness consumes me at once.

CHAPTER 2

FOUR STRANGERS

~ INTRODUCTION ~

I **wake up in a dark room with my hands tied behind my chair.** My training with the Empress has taught me to wake but not show it, so I try to keep my breathing slow and my eyes squinted. I can hear footsteps pacing behind me, but I can't see very much.

"Uh, Juni? You're *positive* that was Heavy Dreams tea?" A friendly male voice whispers.

"Yes!" a casual female voice replies, "this is like the fifth time you've asked!"

I've gotten the pattern of the steps. As they move away, I feel out the restraints around my hand. It's just one cloth, and the tie is quite loose. I relax my hands right before the pair of footsteps turns around.

"Just making sure! Man, I'm surprised they can sell these in stores. These guys have been out for about an hour now." The original voice says.

"Aren't we not supposed to care?" A higher feminine voice asks with a bitter tone.

There is awkward silence. The footsteps approaching behind me continue but respectfully softer.

“Now Star,” the original voice starts, “let’s not be so hard on Rosenburg. I’m sure she’s just as unhappy with–”

The footsteps suddenly stop behind my chair.

“What?” asks the chipper voice, “You think that one’s awake?”

I feel warmth from a face coming down in front of mine. Although I can’t make out any details, I know it is someone close. They know I’m awake, too.

I open my eyes and slam my forehead into their face. The perfect, Roman-statue-like face of a tan man squints with pain, and I see him stumble to the side. I remove my cloth with one smooth tug, then spin down and foot sweep him.

He is very tall, well over 200 centimeters, and almost all muscle, but he falls just the same. I know there are three others left: Juni, Star, and the happy-voiced guy. In a split second, several things happen at once.

Since I am outnumbered, weaponless, and the large man is likely to get up soon, I decide that running is the best option. But as I turn my head to do so, I notice two slumped figures tied to chairs to my left. One has short, kaleidoscope hair, and the other has blue skin. Ellia and Nale! I can’t leave without them!

I reach out and grab my chair, ready to throw it in the direction of the three voices from earlier, but then there is a harp noise and my arms are pinned to my sides by… glowing rainbows? Oh great, they have magic! I try to run but the rainbows have locked me in place in the air. I watch as the giant man gets up, grinning and cracking his knuckles. My stomach drops.

He walks in close and I get ready to take a hit. Instead of throwing a punch or covering my mouth, he gently takes me by the shoulders and turns me in the air so that I face where the voices came from.

There is a spotlight shining down on three people, spilling shadows down their bodies. One of the three is a pale girl with very short, black hair, black eyes, and a black-clad outfit. She sits on top of a coffin tilted sideways, glaring at me.

Another is a short, blond woman with brown eyes wearing a pink romper. She still manages to look intimidating. In the middle is a tall, thin man dressed as a cowboy. His wide-brimmed hat is tilted down so that I can't see his eyes, but he certainly doesn't look as friendly as his voice sounds.

"Go ahead. Wake your friends. It's about time to get started anyway." He says, sounding both jolly and threatening.

The giant man lets out a malicious chuckle. This can't be good.

"Guys," I say into the heavy air, "hey everyone, wake up."

The others stir.

"Hey guys, it's serious!" I try again, much louder.

The others jump awake. It takes them a moment to realize our situation.

"Ey," Kabel says, as the giant man walks over to him, "what do you think ya–"

To everyone's surprise, the man unties Kabel.

He goes down the line until everyone is untied, then the rainbows around me disappear. The man goes over and stands by the glaring trio. He and the two women reach into their pockets. I get ready to dive roll.

"Welcome to…" the cowboy raises his fingers and snaps.

Light floods the room at once, filling the darkness with bright balloons, dangling streamers, and a large projection board.

"*Orientation!*" The cowboy says, and the others pull party horns out of their pockets and blow them.

There is stunned silence, and then the four strangers start laughing.

"What the *glud* is going on here?" Ellia asks.

I recoil; I don't know much Shwedo, an Arretian foreign language, but I do know that they just used quite an explicit word.

"Well, orientation, silly! You all can't be IPSHA agents without going through a training period!" The blond one, Star from her voice, says.

The others all respond with varying degrees of swears and confusion, but I sit back in my chair. I remember IPSHA from my time with the Empress. They were always the ones to come when there was a magic-related problem. It was usually just Enzo, my homeland's only wizard, up to his tricks again, but they somehow got him to stop every time. He was always eerily silent after one of their visits.

"The last time we heard about IPSHA, it was from a crazy lady with water powers trying to kill us!" Bacoj shouts.

“Really? I don’t remember none of that happenin’.” Kabel says.

“Yeah, I feel like that’s something we would remember…” Ellia pauses, “…not unless you mean that stupid hog–”

“Whoa, language!” Clayton interrupts.

“…not unless you mean that stupid *hag* we fought on the lansit in Koppia.” Ellia finishes, then they look at Clayton.

“Maybe you could’ve been a bit nicer.” He mutters.

“Yeah, that’s her. She used to be a pain in our side before the rest of you joined,” Bacoj says, waving his silver arm, “nothing I couldn’t handle… I’m the reason she joined us later anyway.”

“Not to steal ya thunder buddy but I doubt it.” Kabel admits.

“Right, Edihi Amini is her name.” The cowboy says.

“Yeah, that was it!” Bacoj pauses, “Wait… how did you know?”

“Well, you remember those reports you guys worked on when you first got here?” The cowboy asks.

I remember them all too well. I was scared and confused, and there were giant, red-and-white posters covering the hotel room walls, telling me in all caps to write down what I saw or I wouldn’t be fed. I lasted a day before the wireless TV turned on by itself and wouldn’t stop showing the cooking channel on max volume.

“Yeah. So that was you guys who wanted all that info on Yatniv?” Kabel asks, rolling his shoulders, “I wasn’t too fond of ya interrogation techniques.”

“Yeah, sorry about that. Our boss Captain Rosenburg is a bit on the intense side…” the cowboy says, embarrassed, “But hey, that info is helping us out with a major investigation, so thanks a lot!"

Star mutters, "Yeah, she really *is* intense."

The blonde is glowering so viciously that the other two orientation leaders shrink away. The cowboy just lets out a nervous laugh and waves his hand.

"Enough about our boss! Why don't we get right into introductions? We already know your names, so how about you all share a fun fact and then us orientation folks will also share a bit about ourselves. Any questions before we get started?"

All of us sitting in chairs look at each other. I now notice that each person did, in fact, wear something pirate-y. There is Nale sitting on the outside left with a pillowcase bandana like me, Ellia is between us with their signature eye-patch, me, Bacoj to my right with a hook hand made from a Styrofoam cup and some folded sticky notes, Kabel on the far right with a bed robe done up like a swashbuckler's coat…

"Where's Virrel?" I ask.

"Oh, is he the ghost?" The chipper guy asks, "He'll be here any moment now. Don't worry, he won't miss anything."

There is a small moment of awkward silence.

"So, let's get started over here on the right. Kabel?"

The big guy nods and stands. His deep voice booms out in the room as he introduces himself.

"Ey, I'm Kabel Tatmer, 16, from Edge over in Aplestric… I guess back on Arret. Ah… fun fact… I got this cool bionic arm from ah… an incident on a hayride a while back. But it helps me push like ten times my body weight so… tradeoffs I guess."

He nods and sits down. Next, Bacoj stands.

"I'm Bacoj, I'm 13, from Quepo… from Arret too. I also have a bionic arm that I got from the same hayride but much more recently. I really like making modifications and stuff, like how I made the TV remote into a stink bomb."

"Wait, what was that last part?" The cowboy asks.

"Nothing!" Bacoj sits down.

Here we go. I myself stand up, "Hello, I am Yera Lermint. I am 17 years old, a former resident of Peritari in the Mirthoaten Islands… also from Arret, and my favorite hobby is painting."

The girl in pink smiles and nods at me as I take my seat. Ellia stands next, and the way they do, I can tell they're about to do something sassy.

"You already know our names, right?" They ask.

"Correct." The cowboy says with a polite nod.

They cross their arms, "Well then fun fact… after almost starving us, keeping us locked in the same room for months, and drugging us to get us here, I don't think I want to join your weird club."

"Fair enough," the cowboy says, "I'll see what I can do to get you back to Arret as soon as possible. Granted, I don't think the IPSHA over there is going to want you anywhere outside of prison regardless of whether or not your stories about Yatniv are true, but I'll start the paperwork after the presentation anyway."

"O-on second thought," Ellia stammers, "my fun fact is that I'm half human and half woodish."

They sit down, red with either embarrassment or anger. Nale, realizing it's his turn, bows his head shyly.

"I'm Nale," he mumbles, raising his hand a little instead of standing up, "I think archery is pretty cool."

There is a pause as the staff members nod in approval.

"Sounds good to me. We'll introduce ourselves so that the air is clear and everything, then I'll go ahead and start the presentation!" The cowboy says.

He pushes back his hat a little more so the light catches his blue eyes. With a big smile and a short wave, he starts, "My name is Clayton Loge, and my superhero name is Dead Draw. I kind of wanted something friendlier but the naming program was a bit dark that year. So, my power is that I am the fastest draw in the world, which means that I can pull my gun out of my holster super fast."

The room is silent. Though I suppose that is kind of neat, it's not really the first thing that comes to mind when I think of superpowers.

"That sounds pretty stupid." Ellia spits.

"Well," Clayton says, his shoulders sagging, "everyone is entitled to their opinion…"

"Hold on now, give the man a chance! How fast we talkin', buddy?" Kabel asks, leaning forward in his chair.

"Oh, pretty dang fast. Wanna see?" Clayton asks.

I nod, and I notice the others doing so too.

The cowboy points to a silver gun on his hip (I've gotten used to seeing weird Earth weapons through TV; I think that is called a revolver) and then puts his hand above his head. Suddenly, the gun is just… in his hand?! I didn't even see his arm move!

"That's incredible!" Kabel exclaims.

"… crap, I guess that *was* kinda cool." Ellia admits, frowning.

Clayton blushes, "Aw, thanks guys. I don't want to brag any longer than I have to, but my fun fact is that I beat every game in a certain series, that I can't say the title of for legal reasons, 100% on Proud mode."

No one reacts, so he clarifies, "It's a pretty big deal, trust me. Anyway, let's keep going to our left. Juni?"

"Sure thing," the girl says with a shrug, then she turns to us and… smiles? I mean, of course she should be able to smile, but with the black lipstick and black hair and black clothes I would have figured she would be a brooding type.

"I'm Juniper Webbre but you can call me Juni, and my superhero name is Marimbona. It would take too long to explain, but just know that if I ever were to crack open this coffin here," she gives it a light knock and there are reedy, clinking sounds, "stuff is gonna get real spooky real quick."

"Oh," Ellia says, sitting up, "I love a good spook."

Juni points finger guns at Ellia and winks, yet another strangely cheery gesture for her dreary outfit, "I'll keep that in mind! Hmm, let's see, fun fact… I got my bachelor's in music technology?"

I don't think the others took the time to read about the education system on this planet, because I'm the only one to react with an impressed nod. The room grows silent as everyone looks at the tall, chiseled man. He gives an embarrassed smile and slumps a little. His clothes: a red vest, a button up, jeans, and boots, all seem a little small on him.

"Oh, right," Clayton says, "so, ah, how do I explain this… well, a few months ago, we had two thaumaturgists, or magic scientists, who were researching the Fusion-Caliber Relativity Theory. They could probably tell you more about it, but a quick summary is…"

He looks over at the tall man and raises an eyebrow, "People with superpowers are strong individually, but when their powers both combine into one source, they can… make new powers? Or like… make their current powers stronger maybe?"

The giant winces and does a "so-so" gesture with one of his hands. Clayton waves it off.

"Ah, I've never been one of those magic science types. Anyway, so there was a medical expert Samir Amit and a world-renowned physicist Davis Skioki that worked closely together…"

The cowboy and the large man share an awkward grin.

"They were the first to make a breakthrough on the theory because, well, they fused! And, here they are. Um, 'Davisamir' can't really talk either, because he lost most of his ability to speak through the fusion. His powers are explosion jumps from Davis, fazing through objects at will from Samir, and since they are both one person, he's super strong and fast, too."

Davisamir gives a humble nod. The blonde in the pink romper steps forward.

"Hey everyone, I'm Starli Ebbre, but you can call me Star! The whole last name thing with Juni is just a coincidence, trust me. Hmm, since I'm a wizard I never had to register for a super name, but if I had one it would be something cool like Unicorn Storm or Rainbows of Destruction!"

The other staff members chuckle at Star's excitement.

"Huh, let's see, fuuuun faaaact… I really like wine and musicals?"

"At the same time?" Juni jokes.

"No!" Star pauses, "… maybe."

Everyone laughs, then Clayton pulls a remote from his pocket.

"Alrighty, let's get started. We'll try and speed through this presentation here, then we'll sort out some equipment for you guys, then…" his tone slightly drops as he smiles over at the other leaders, "we'll go have lunch."

CHAPTER 3

HEROES AND VILLAINS

~ ORIENTATION ~

Clayton clicks to the first slide. It is bright red with bold, black letters spanning the screen. There are exclamation marks and hazard signs around the body of text in the middle, which reads:

‘I.P.S.H.A. HANDLES HIGHLY SENSITIVE AND CLASSIFIED INFORMATION, MUCH OF WHICH IS PRESENT IN THIS PRESENTATION. SHARING ANY PART OF THIS PRESENTATION WILL RESULT IN SEVERE PENALTY AS OUTLINED BY THE DIVISION OF DOCUMENTS A.A.R.M. POLICY 101.16.33.”

“Ah, right,” Clayton says, “we usually give this warning out because people might try to post about this presentation on social media, but you guys don’t have any accounts since we disabled that on your smartphones, so we don’t have to worry about this. Just keep in mind when you’re out in public that IPSHA is a secret organization, so try not to be waving around weapons and classified documents and whatnot.”

“Wait… why?” Ellia asks, “Magic was pretty common on Arret.”

“Yeah, I don’t see what the big deal is. The IPSHA back at our place ain't too chatty but they ain't secretive or anything." Kabel adds with a shrug.

Clayton nods and smiles, "Well, Earth is a *little* different from Arret. For starters, you've got the density of your NHAs, or bogeys as I like to call them, which generally operate on a sub-perceptive level, then you've got the Social Proportionality Dilemma, Wilkerson's Hyper-Capitalism Theory–"

"Clayton!" Juni interjects.

"Huh? Oh right, you guys probably don't know what any of that means," he gives an embarrassed smile, "Juni, why don't you go ahead and explain it?"

"Sure. So, there are three big reasons we like to stay secret here on Earth. The first thing, about Non-Human Adversaries, is something we'll get into later."

Just the title of that sends a shiver up my spine.

"The main reasons are societal. Politics get really heated and inefficient here on Earth. Standard people have a hard-enough time treating one another fairly as is, so adding a bunch of super-powered people and wizards to the mix would cause way too much political ruckus. People would start arguing the limits and additions to rights, freedoms, morality, and yeah, it'd get messy."

Juni goes to speak again but then stops, "Um, that was the Social Proportionality Dilemma..." she looks at Clayton, "I can't remember that hyper-thing."

Davisamir raises a hand in the back to speak, then catches himself and lowers it.

“Oh, I had to write a paper on this once,” Star rolls her eyes, “Wilkerson states that everything unique will one day be monetized and become mundane. So, if we were to blow our cover, in a few decades we’d all be working for energy companies or manufacturing plants or something, helping them get an even easier buck.”

Clayton nods, “Spot on you two! Just to recap, we don’t go public because society couldn’t handle it and magic would be exploited by corporate entities. Does that answer your question?”

Ellia nods, “Yeah, but what about those non-human bogeys you were talking about at the beginning?”

“Ah,” Clayton says with a smile, “one of my favorite topics. But we’ll get there in a bit. For now…”

He clicks to the next slide. It reads: ‘New Hire Orientation’.

“New hire orientation!” Clayton says excitedly.

He clicks to the next slide. On it are portraits of eight people. ‘Shuvo Chimaladinne’ is near the middle, a brown man with a broad smile and heavy eyes. Next to him is ‘Ana Aistis’, an unsmiling redhead wearing a large pair of circular glasses.

Below them are three other portraits: the kindly ‘Michael S.’, the timid ‘Rebecca B.’, and the brooding ‘Henry N.’. There are another three above the pair in the middle: a beaming ‘Tolu A.’, a wizened ‘Brock M.’, and a sporty ‘Curtis B.’.

Across the bottom of the slide is a short cursive message that reads, “Welcome and thank you for joining! We look forward to celebrating your victories and supporting your development. Together we win!”

“Ah yes!” Clayton beams, “These are the leaders of IPSHA! Shuvo on the left is the Supreme Premier, and Ana on the right is the Vice Premier. The three on the bottom are the Head Secretaries of the Past, Present, and Future. The three on the top are the Nephilim, Wizard, and Bearing Chancellors.”

I raise an eyebrow; I’ve never heard of a ‘nephilim’ before.

“And what are those positions, Clayton?” Juni reminds.

“Oh, right! Well, each of the secretaries are the heads over… like, time stuff. Past deals with records and artifacts, Present deals with missions and PR, and Future deals with plans and prophecies. The three chancellors are the leaders for the three types of heroes.”

No one says anything. If he doesn’t bring up the nephilim thing again, I might say something.

He nods and clicks to the next slide. It is titled ‘What is IPSHA?’ and has a small timeline and a picture of a large, mechanical turtle underwater. A light blue rectangle with a simplified, golden icon of a turtle rests in the top right corner. White silhouettes of this planet’s continents are on its back.

“So, what is IPSHA? Well, on November 3rd, 1872, a band of wizards and nephilim–”

I perk up. There it is again…

“– led by the legendary Ben Castor created the Worldwide Circle of Magicians, or WCM. After a few hundred years, and finally discovering other planets like you all at Arret, we became the Inter-Planetary Supernatural Helper Association in 1959. Then, just a few years back, we had another name change to what it is now: the International and Planetary Syndicate of Heroes and Associates."

Clayton points his clicker at the presentation board, and a small green dot appears on the screen. He uses it to circle around the robot turtle picture.

"This is SEFASOH, the Submarine Executive Facility, Arcane Storage, and Operational Headquarters. This is where all of our administrative offices are, and we keep a bunch of magic items and stuff in there, too. It's where we get our super cool flag logo from. Also, we'll be going there for your official induction if you pass your test."

The air grows tense. So, there is a test. I lean forward in my chair and focus on Clayton. He clicks to the next slide. 'Terminology'. There is a picture of three models hanging out in odd outfits and smiling. Titles and small descriptions for each of them sit in colorful boxes above them.

"So, there is a lot of terminology associated with this line of work, and I'll explain some of it now. There are three variations of supernaturally powered people: bearers, nephilim, and wizards."

I listen close as he goes through the definitions of them. Bearers are normal people that use magic items, wizards are special people that manipulate magic itself, and nephilim…

Oh? Oh. 'Nephilim' is pretty much the Earthling word for 'kupua', which are just people with superpowers. I feel my shoulders relax a bit.

Since my entire team (except Virrel) is made of bearers, they spend most of their time explaining the differences between wizards and nephilim. I've dealt with both before, so I tune most of this out. It essentially boils down to magic use.

Kupua, or I guess *nephilim*, have a set list of powers that get stronger with training. Use of these powers drains them physically, and extreme overuse can exhaust them to the point of unconsciousness or death. Despite this, their capacity for growth is intimidatingly high, so older or more experienced nephilim can manage some pretty incredible feats.

Wizards are even more impressive, as they can theoretically learn an infinite amount of spells. Their spells drain their magic stamina, which is basically a measure of precision. This isn't linked to physical stamina in any way, so overuse simply results in weaker spells and terrible casting accuracy. There are three different types of wizards, but… well, I wasn't really listening to that part.

Clayton's voice snaps me back to reality, "Good point Star. Any questions before we move forward?"

I think hard. He'd mentioned a test earlier, so I should try to be as knowledgeable as possible for that. Maybe I'll ask if they can go over the three wizard types again.

"How can I become a nephilim or a wizard? That sounds so

cool!" Bacoj asks, excited.

Clayton pushes back his hat and scratches his head.

"Well, buddy… there aren't too many options. You could kind of become a nephilim if you get a magic tattoo, but if that patch of skin comes off, you're back to normal."

"He could always get superpowers cursed on him." Juni suggests.

"I don't think he'd wanna do that," Clayton says with a little laugh, "and the whole wizard thing… sorry but that's a dead end. Being a nephilim is a recessive genetic thing, and wizards just… are wizards. There's no real pattern to who is and who isn't, but if you aren't, you aren't."

Bacoj's shoulders sag, "Oh."

"Yeah," Clayton pauses, "…welp, anything else?"

The cowboy scans the room one last time. Letting him move on without asking something feels wrong, but I'm too embarrassed to try for a recap on the wizard types. I think for a moment before a good one comes to me.

"Yes," I say, "is it possible to have an individual of two types at once? Like being both a nephilim and a wizard?"

"Good question!" Clayton says, "the answer is yes but very rarely. Of course, you can have wizards that are also bearers and the same with nephilim. The only nephilim-wizard is the Trifecta, a person who is a nephilim, a wizard, and presumably also a bearer. But that's like a once-every-one-hundred-years kind of deal."

"Lemme guess, he's the leader?" Kabel asks.

"Oh, no. We've only had one Trifecta as a Supreme Premier before, Emilios Jette. It isn't 'once every hundred years per planet' but more like 'once every hundred years in the universe'. No need to focus on that too much though, the likelihood of ever even finding this generation's Trifecta is suuuuper slim. Anything else?" Clayton asks.

The room is silent.

"Alright! Now it's time to talk about my favorite subject!"

He clicks to the next slide. 'Dangers'. On the left of the slide, there are three men in strange outfits. On the right, there is a woman in silk, a snake made out of fire, a large bear, and a blob of glass with tentacles coming out of it.

"The baddies and bogeys! So you've got two types of bad guys you'll be fighting: people and NHAs. People should be pretty self-explanatory so I'll just run through that real quick."

Clayton clears his throat, straightens up, and says, "Villains."

No one responds.

"Super!" he rushes, "Now we can move on to my favorite part!"

"Uh… you gonna explain 'villains' a little more?" Juni asks.

Clayton waves her off, "Oh, they're smart kids, they know what villains are."

"Really?" Star asks with a smirk, then she looks directly at me, making me recoil a little in surprise.

"Yera. Name a villain for me, please."

"I…" I push my brain as more and more eyes fall on me, "uh, I guess… K-Kyndule Yatniv?"

My teammates shrug and nod in halfhearted agreement.

Star smiles over at Clayton, "Why don't you give them some examples of *Earth* villains?"

"Okay well, let's see… you've got renegades, mercenaries, warlocks, mad scientists, some might say certain political figures, plus I'm pretty sure we still have sea pirates but I'd consider them more of a chaotic neutral–"

"Names, Clayton. She means names." Juni chuckles.

"Oooooh okay, that's easy!" There's–" Clayton pauses, stumped.

"Can't think of any?" Star teases.

"Look Star, I just want to talk about NHAs." Clayton admits.

"If we're talking villains, what about Capital Black?" Juni offers.

The cowboy leans back, "Oh yeah. He's a classic. Most infamous warlock on the planet. Some people say he's responsible for almost half the NHAs running around right now."

"And La Corsage?" Star asks.

Clayton sucks his teeth, and so does Davisamir.

"Oh right, yikes. We definitely don't want to run into her. She's crazy powerful and *despises* all men."

"That don't sound too nice." Kabel mutters.

The cowboy nods, "She lives here in France, too, so let's hope we don't run into her."

"Oh, and Face of the Revolution!" Juni exclaims, snapping.

"True!" Clayton points at her then turns to us, "He's this scary wizard dude with a dragon mask that does all sorts of extreme political stuff. He actually has pretty positive intentions but his execution? Eh… a bit too much on the destructive side."

"Oooooh, what about Birch Brightwood?!" Star asks, excited.

The cowboy frowns, "Mmmm… I know he's not in IPSHA, and he's the strongest wizard alive, but I'm pretty sure he isn't a villain either. Again, more of a chaotic neutral than anything else."

Star deflates, "Oh."

"H-hey, no need to feel down!" Clayton puts a hand on her shoulder, "Those were some good examples earlier!"

She nods, not looking satisfied.

"Well… um…" Clayton readjusts his hat, "so when you guys are fighting villains, be extra careful. Here at IPSHA, taking someone out for good is an absolute last resort. At least with *human* enemies, you might have to pull some of your punches. Cool?"

Everyone in the room nods to Clayton, and he continues, "Good! Now, before we continue to the NHAs, let me preface this by saying: here at IPSHA, we support religious freedom. This being said, the NHAs on Earth happen to have heavy ties with Abrahamic elements. Why? We don't know. Regardless, it is our duty to stop them. Does that work for everyone?"

I nod and look around the room. Everyone else is shrugging and nodding.

"Excellent!" Clayton says with a startling clap, "so the NHAs on Earth work differently than on Arret. Arret has what we call 'monsters', *fleshy* beings with special powers that can live for thousands of years until they are killed *once and for all*.

"Earth also has monsters, but those are really rare. We mostly have 'demons', *spiritual* beings with special powers that can *only* be interacted with using magic and *come back to life* sometime after they are killed.

"These guys are typically invisible, but once you see them, they can come in many different forms depending on their type and level of power. I really like talking about these guys so bear with me!"

Unfortunately, I end up tuning out everything Clayton says for the next hour and a half.

CHAPTER 4

TELEPORTING ITALIAN CHEF

~ CONFLICT ~

My head is buzzing as I stare down at the test. The first part was easy, but everything past Question 4 seems impossible. I glance over at the clock to see how much of my 10 minutes is left. My stomach drops, I only have about 90 seconds to finish the rest of this exam.

I take a subtle glance to my left. Nale, who must have been looking in my direction, quickly looks down at his paper. He doesn't pick up his pencil, though, since he finished his test about a minute after we started.

Ellia is glancing around the room at the orientation leaders and craning their neck to see Nale's answers. A glance to my left reveals Bacoj in a similar situation as I am, viciously erasing something and shaking his head.

Kabel is twirling his pencil around his thumb, frowning down at his exam. From here it looks like he has the opposite problem that I have; the first four questions aren't touched while the last five are completed with confidence.

I bite my lip and look back down at my paper.

1. IPSHA is a secret organization.

A. True
B. False

2. Select the names of the two Premiers of IPSHA.

A. Brock Mainardi
B. Shuvo Chimaladinne
C. Ana Aistis
D. Gina Rosenburg

3. Which of these relies on physical stamina for their magic powers?

A. Bearer
B. Gothic Wizard
C. Tomic Wizard
D. Nephilim

4. Where is the SEFASOH Base located?

A. Underwater
B. United States
C. France
D. Outer Space

5. Which one of these demons are uncommon?

A. Pique (wrath)
B. Pleonex (greed)
C. Languor (sloth)
D. Gremlin (worry)

6. Why do you need a PASTIM?

A. For protection from NHAs
B. For IPSHA identification
C. To interact with NHAs
D. To boost your abilities

7. What is the appropriate response to a succubus encounter?

A. Corner it and aim for the base
B. Use assertive body language
C. Maintain high impetus
D. Run away immediately

8. Which is the highest rank for a demon?

A. King/Queen
B. Lesser
C. General
D. Potentate

Bonus. Who is the best orientation coordinator?

A. Starli Ebbre
B. Clayton Loge
C. Juniper Webbre
D. Davisamir Amit-Skioki

“About 30 seconds left, start wrapping it up.” Clayton calls, looking at his cell phone.

Panicking, I try harder to remember. What was a PASTIM for again? It’s got something to do with those monster things, so I know not B or D… What’s the answer to number 7? I could have sworn he mentioned each of those techniques on each of the NHAs, but which one works on a… *seskoobis*?

Clayton begins counting down from 10. My mind is filled with regret as I mark C for the rest of my answers. If only I had paid more attention! Clayton was enthusiastic and entertaining during that last part but… it was just too much information!

The time is up and everyone but Nale passes in their tests with an air of apprehension.

“So,” Bacoj starts nervously, “was that… our final test?”

Clayton chuckles as he evens out our papers, “Don’t worry about it. We’ll get you your results a little later. For now, let’s get you all your equipment. None of you need any firearms and none of you are old enough for holy water grenades, so it’ll only be PASTIMs and all your old equipment for now.”

Davisamir and Juni round the projection screen and begin dragging out large boxes. I am surprised we get equipment before our tests are graded. Perhaps they might take it away if it turns out we failed.

“After this, we’ll decide who the team leader is and head out to lunch.” Clayton announces.

No one moves.

“So yeah, just come on up and get your stuff and we’ll head into the next part.” Clayton encourages.

While the others make their way over to Juni, I am still thinking about what Clayton said. Team leaders and field equipment seem pretty important, and all that information we received sounded like it was crucial as well. Why hasn’t Virrel gotten here yet? Shouldn’t he be taught all of this?

Cautiously, I approach Clayton, who is taking a drink. The others are talking to Juni and Star. Out of the corner of my eye, I can see Kabel react with glee as Davisamir pulls a giant black scabbard out of his box. Clayton notices me and lowers his bottle.

“Hello, I just had a quick question.”

“Go for it.” He replies with a nod.

“All the information we received seemed very important; is Virrel going to get a condensed version whenever he gets here?”

Clayton smiles, “Oh, no need to worry about Virrel. A lot of this you and he already know, right?”

“No sir.” I respond.

“Oh really,” he says with a short, blank frown, “well, we’ll make sure he’s accommodated for. Why don’t you go ahead and grab your equipment?”

“I will. Thank you.” I reply with a nod, then turn and head over to Juni and Star.

I feel like something suspicious is going on here.

“Hey, Yera, right?” Juni asks.

I nod.

"Take your pick! The design won't affect its abilities, and you can change it at any time, so don't feel pressured. Mine is a custom one my friend made me with a bunch of thyme on it and I tie it around my wrist, so take that as a show of how serious this is."

I peer into the white box. Inside is a heap of what looks like silk cloth squares. They all have a bunch of different logos and patterns on them. A few have the gold and white turtle. Some have feathers, some have flames… I dig around to try to find something cool. Twisting dragons? Not my style. The French flag? Too generic. Mystic eye with gold and purple flowers? Hmm… sure!

I pick it up and show it to Juni. She gives an impressed smile.

"I like it! Head over to Davisamir to pick up your weird wrist thing and your circles."

The zecno! My RCBPs! Excited, I walk around Ellia (who is still digging through the box Star has, no doubt looking for the weirdest design) and head over to Davisamir, stuffing the cloth in my pocket. Kabel is off to the left, hugging his huge, sheathed sword like it's a distant lover. Bacoj is juggling a few green fireballs with a look of awe on his face. Nale gently pulls and eases up on the string of his bow.

I look to the towering, chiseled man standing behind the almost empty table. On it are a pair of red gloves with white crosshairs on them, a black-grey wristwatch with two barrels on the side, a pair of thick, black gloves with hardened palms, and a pair of large metal rings with bladed edges.

I pick up the zecno, which is the name for that black-grey wristwatch, and put it around my wrist. This is an accurate equivalent to a pistol on Arret, as it is fairly lightweight and shoots laser rounds that can be lethal but are recoverable from. Having the weapon back in my possession, especially in a setting like this, feels weird.

I then put on the magnetic gloves and pick up my RCBPs, or Returning Circular Bladed Projectiles. My name is still etched into the sides. With a smirk, I toy with one of the rings, tossing it slightly and letting it slide in my hands. The weight, the durability, it all feels so old yet so familiar.

I magnetize the rings to the back of my gloves so that I don't end up throwing them.

Suddenly, a door in the back slides open. Everybody looks towards it, confused, and then a moment later, Virrel walks through, wearing grey, belted pajamas, and a washcloth over his eye like a rough imitation of Ellia's eyepatch. A puzzled frown is spread across his lips. I begin to walk over to him as he heads towards me.

"Hey, Virrel, wh–"

"I thought it was supposed to be cloudy today." He interrupts, sounding unsure of himself.

"Um… okay?" I reply.

He raises his eyebrows, and then I suddenly know what he's

talking about. Back when we worked for the empress, the guards made up codes to alert one another about threats we couldn't openly discuss. The 'cloudy day' one means there's something going on that Virrel isn't supposed to tell me about and I should prepare.

I slow down, detach an RCBP, and begin slightly tossing it again.

"I see. Is that why you were so late?" I ask, trying to play along.

"Yes, and it's strange because–"

"Sweet! Virrel is here, now we can get started!" Clayton yells from across the room.

We all look over to him and he begins to turn red. He does a quick glance at Star, who is absorbed in her phone.

"Ahem, I was just *excited* that we could get *started.*" He clarifies.

Suddenly, purple sparks spray down from thin air a few meters away. A glowing, twisting circle of color opens up, and a moment later, a man in a chef's outfit pops out. The air closes above him and he lands roughly, almost falling over.

He has on a tall, puffy hat, green trousers, a red dress shirt, a single purple glove, and a white apron that looks burnt in some places. He stumbles a bit, brushing himself off. Something gold falls out of his back pocket and clatters loudly to the floor. He snatches it up, muttering swears, and hides it behind his back. Everyone else in the room looks at one another with confusion before looking at the chef again.

He seems to notice that there are other people in the room,

straightens his back, raises an eyebrow, and smooths out one of the handlebar-looking tufts of hair on his large, black moustache.

"*Ciao*! I ama Vittorio Punnicci, the best pizza maker ina the land. I put the freshest ingredients ina mya pizza every day, but I've always felt mya dishes have lacked… *soul*."

The chef raises the golden thing he dropped, which looks like an odd-shaped teapot. I watch his face fall as no one reacts to what was probably supposed to be dramatic.

"So I thought, why not give a ghost pizza a try? Now, where would I find a ghost, I asked myself. Well, asa the French say, *voilà*!"

He points the strange teapot at Virrel and rubs the side.

"Let's see ifa this genie lamp will work with capturing your ghost friend here!"

Nothing happens for a moment. The whole room just stares, in utter bewilderment, as this random, middle-aged man dressed as a pizza chef rubs the side of a teapot.

Without warning, a branch of lightning leaps out of the spout of the pot and strikes Virrel right in the middle of his stomach. In a flash, he is thrown into the air, and then he begins to float as if gravity has lost its effect on him.

Spinning smoke twists up from the nozzle, engulfing Virrel and bizarrely twisting his body into what I can only describe as a spun-together line of noodles. The pasta-Virrel swirls into the spout of the teapot, and then the smoke and wind stop.

"*Perfetto*! Ina just a few hours, I will have the first, best, and most delicious ghost pizza the world has ever seen! Good luck trying to stop me, *miei amici*!"

He pulls a leaflet out of his apron, throws it at my stunned face, and sinks back into the floor with a snap of his gloved hand and another billow of smoke.

The leaflet didn't really make it that far and just flutters to the ground. The room is silent; stunned and confused, watching as the smoke breaks apart in the air.

"Uh…" Clayton says, "w-well, that was weird! Looks like we should stop that bad guy before Virrel becomes lunch!"

CHAPTER 5

BLUEPRINTS OVER LUNCH

~ TRANSITION ~

I pick up the leaflet as the others fly into a confusion of questions.

"Who the *glud* was that?!"

"Can you stop saying glud? It sounds offensive."

"Where'd he go? Is he still in here?"

"D-did that guy just kill Virrel?!"

My team continues to berate the orientation staff as I read the leaflet. It is all in a different language, somewhat similar to French but not exactly. I look through the long list of what seem to be meal options, and at the bottom is a phone number with… a clear and plain address right below? Does he want to be found? Or perhaps this is a set-up…

"Alright everybody!" Clayton yells, quieting the room, "It's getting a little hectic so let's regroup and figure something out."

Everyone obliges, and we're soon back in our chairs. Well, all except Ellia, who's standing next to theirs.

"Okay, so…" Clayton sees Ellia, "could you please take a seat?"

"I just want to be ready in case a *second* fat pizza chef comes in here with some weird teapot." Ellia explains.

The cowboy frowns, “Fair point. Well then…”

He looks around the room and clasps his hands together, “I guess this is your first run in with a real villain. How do you feel?”

“Confused.” Kabel blurts out.

“Does random stuff like this happen all the time?” Bacoj asks.

“And seriously where the *glud*–” Ellia looks at Clayton, “where the *sheiffy* did that guy come from?”

From my knowledge, their substitution swear isn’t much better than the original.

Clayton frowns again at Ellia, then looks over at me, “Didn’t he leave something?”

I nod and raise it, “It seems like a menu of sorts. His address might be on it too, but I’m not entirely sure because the whole thing is in a different language.”

“Star, Juni, why don’t you give it a look?”

The two women walk up to me and I show them the menu. They stare at it for a moment.

“Looks like Italian to me.” Juni says.

“Yeah, I’d have to agree.” Star adds.

“Oh, lemme see! A coworker taught me a little Italian back in college!” The cowboy rushes up and excitedly takes the leaflet.

There is silence as he squints at it.

“Um…” he furrows his brow, still re-reading, then points to the bottom left, “I know that says ‘telephone’!”

Juni snatches the menu from him, “Duh, anybody could’ve

guessed that! I took some Spanish so maybe–" suddenly her eyes widen and she pulls her smartphone out of her pocket.

"Lunch is here. Star, see if you can figure out what this says. Kabel and Davisamir, come help me with the food."

She gives the leaflet to Star, nods towards the giant near the tables, and heads to a pair of double doors off to the side of the room. Kabel cracks his neck and stands.

"I dunno what's goin' on but if there's food I'm helpin'."

Bacoj gets up from his chair, "Can I give that thing a look too?"

Ellia scoffs, "I'm sure this is the first time you've even heard the word Italian."

"Oh shut it, you dumb cow!" He insults.

They both squint at one another, then grow matching smirks.

"You're up on your farm animals too, huh? Those ones pack a punch." Ellia compliments.

"So, I don't really know any Italian, but from a bit of the Spanish I know, I think this is definitely his restaurant… something to do with a kitchen."

"And maybe *costa* means 'cost', so it's probably an upscale place!" Clayton suggests with confidence.

Star gives a sympathetic smile, leaning close to Clayton and speaking low, "*Costa* actually means 'coast'."

"Oh," he says, his face turning red, "well, I'm just gonna go set up the tables."

****

The room is silent as everyone chews on sandwiches and chips. It's kind of awkward.

"We were gonna get you guys a classic French lunch with salad and meats and cheese and stuff," Clayton peels back a corner of paper from his sub, "but the budget board reallocated some of our funds last minute so this is the best we could do."

"Ey, food is food." Kabel says before taking another huge bite of his sandwich.

More silence and chewing. I want to ask about the test results but it's probably better not to.

"Oh, team leaders," Clayton remembers, "does anyone wanna be it? Any suggestions for one or…"

"I'll be the leader!" Bacoj suggests.

"Too young. Anyone else?" Clayton continues.

Bacoj looks crestfallen.

"Well then I–"

"Absolutely not." Clayton interrupts before Ellia can even finish their sentence, "So that just leaves Nale, Kabel, and Yera."

Ellia mutters something very profane under their breath.

"No need to consider me." Nale mumbles.

"Oh," Clayton replies, "Okay. So just Yera or Kabel."

"Yera for sure." Juni blurts.

"Agreed." Star adds.

"One-hundred and ten percent." Ellia tacks on.

I feel my face grow warm as I fight back a smile. That was a huge confidence boost.

Kabel recoils, "Ey, what's the big idea? I'm sittin' right here!"

"Yeah, come on guys, I think Kabel's pretty cool." Clayton admits.

"Me too!" Bacoj defends, "What about you, Nale? Let's teach the girls a lesson!"

All eyes are now on the woodish boy. His face begins to turn purple (their form of blushing) and he bows his head so that his hair sweeps down in front of his eyes. Even still, it looks like he just glanced at me.

"Oh, um… Kabel is cool but… I think Yera should be the leader." He then takes a nervous bite of sandwich.

"Why?" Bacoj asks, "How could you betray the Council of Men?!"

"Council of Men? You're thirteen years old!" Juni interjects.

"Yeah, leave him alone!" Ellia says before throwing Nale a mischievous smirk, "He has his reasons."

Nale's eyes widen and he turns his head so that I can't see his face, gazing at the blank wall off to the right and taking another bite of sandwich before he even finished chewing the first. There is a little something in me that is curious.

"So ah… what's you guys' plan to get Virrel back? I don't know about you all but I think that Vittorio guy wasn't playing around."

Clayton says, rattling his soda cup and taking another sip.

"You guys don't do that for us?" Ellia asks in between crunching their chips.

"Mmm, no? Why would you think that?" Clayton asks.

"I thought this was all part of the orientation." They reply.

The staff members all look at one another, then Clayton smirks, "Well… I mean…"

"That's absurd!" Star says, and it sort of seems like she's trying to hold back a smile, "We could never plan something like this! Isn't that right, Juni?"

"Yep." The black-clad woman says before stuffing more of her sandwich into her mouth.

The room is suspicious and quiet, then Clayton starts again, "Aaanyway, what's the plan? You've got the menu leaflet, your phones, and us as resources."

"We go in, we hit 'em a bunch of times, he gives us Virrel back. Maybe even grab a slice and a little cash on the way out. No sweat, we'll be done in two minutes tops." Kabel says while unwrapping his cookie. Wait, he *already* finished his sandwich?

"Okay well, one, what you just described is known as 'mugging', which is illegal, and two… where is he?" Clayton asks.

"At the address on the thing!" Kabel chuckles, shaking his head and taking a bite.

The cowboy is silent, and then Juni starts, "I think Clayton's trying to get at the fact that we don't know where that address is."

Since I am the leader, I decide to speak up, “Can’t we search for some directions? We could use that map app on our phones.”

“Good suggestion Yera!” Clayton congratulates, “Go for it!”

I pull my phone out and go to the app, then type in the address. The overhead street view goes from crossroads in any direction to a zoomed-out picture of the entire country. A blue line stretches from the speck of a building that we’re in all the way to a town called Sperlonga in a region named Lazio.

The estimated travel time is 15 and a half hours.

“It’s… about a day’s travel by car.” I report.

Everyone in the room, even the staff members, recoil with genuine surprise.

“A day?!” Kabel asks, “that’s pretty dang far!”

“Are you sure you typed in the right address?” Clayton asks, wiping his hands on his pants.

I hand him the phone and the menu leaflet. He and the other leaders read and re-read, and then they hand me back my belongings, stunned.

“That’s a lot further than we… er, imagined.” Clayton says.

“What is going through that guy’s head?” Star mutters.

“My fist when we catch up to him,” Kabel says, sipping from his straw, “‘specially if we get there and Virrel’s already a pizza.”

“I think we should leave now,” I say, trying to lead, “if the journey is 15 hours, we have no time to lose.”

“We’ll leave now, but I know a faster way to get there. We’ll be right at Vittorio's door in maybe ten minutes." Star says.

"Now ya talkin'!" Kabel cheers.

"Really? How, teleportation?" Clayton asks.

"Yep. I can't do it, but remember, Pengun lives like three blocks from here."

"Oh true, he *did* move here after the thousand bulls thing in Germany. Great thinking, Star!" Clayton gives her a thumbs up.

She smiles and gives one back, "Once we finish lunch, I'll get his address and we can head over!"

CHAPTER 6

EXECUTIONER OF MEN

~ SURPRISE ~

S**ounds of traffic come from the end of the alleyway.** We finally pass our one-thousandth moped and emerge onto the main road. Instead of grey-white buildings looming in on us from either side, I can now see the clear summer sky.

Trees and windows line the car-crammed road. People walk down the streets, conversing in French. A few bicyclists whizz by. The flowers, potted in balconies or springing from road medians, seem to pop with color. Signs for shops, local stores, and banks stretch out from the bases of buildings, glowing with sunlight.

We take the crosswalk to the other side of the main road and walk down the tan pavement, gazing at the storefronts and cars. Although I don't see that tower that I saw from my hotel, this place is still beautiful. Just being able to walk around outside is… so jarring. And it feels great, too!

"I know this sounds stupid but this sun is nice." Ellia says.

"Yeah, I never thought I'd miss the smelluva tree." Kabel admits.

"Jeez, the way you're talking, you'd think we…" Clayton pauses with realization and decides not to continue his sentence.

I try to keep my guard up, looking around to take in any

information I can, but the outside world here is so nice that I can't help but get absorbed in it. This place reminds me of New Earth back on Arret… I guess that makes sense!

We take another crosswalk, and in the distance, I can see what looks like a public park. We're headed in that direction and I'm excited to check it out, but just then, Star stops. She is leading us, so we all stop too. She looks at her phone, turns, and then begins to walk into yet another alleyway. I frown inwardly and follow her.

My team and I walk with the orientation leaders in the shade of the looming apartments. The sounds of the main road are at our backs. This alleyway is lined with cars on either side, similar to the last. It feels oddly empty even though it's the middle of the day.

We pass a downward ramp and a lot full of shrubs. The emptiness of the alleyway makes me want to throw one of my bladed rings and call it back, just for old times' sake. I stifle my urges, reassuring myself that I'll probably get a chance to use them.

Bacoj, Ellia, and Kabel are all in the front behind Star, and I can overhear some of their conversation.

"Who taught you those Shwedo swear words?" Kabel asks.

"I bet you'd like to know you *sheiffing sheiffity sheiffer sheiff*!"

Everyone starts laughing, and I let out a few chuckles too.

"Is this some language from Arret?" Star asks.

"Yeah, Nale taught me." Ellia boasts, "He's the best."

"Why did he teach you but not me?" Bacoj questions.

"Because I threatened to blackmail him."

Kabel, Bacoj, and Star let out low 'oooooooh's.

"Blackmail him for what?" Bacoj prods.

"Obviously I'm not going to tell you, *glud*-face."

"C'maaan Ellia, you and I go way back." Kabel pleads.

Ellia glances over their shoulder right at me, smirks, and then turns to face forward again, "You'll find out eventually."

Now somewhat interested, I turn to look for where Nale is. Perhaps he overheard as well and might have an interesting reaction. He and Davisamir are walking quietly next to one another, out of earshot.

I also spot Juni checking her phone not too far away, using her other hand to roll that coffin she was sitting on earlier (an extendable handle comes out one end and wheels come out the other, like a travel bag). When she's finished, I think I'll probe her with some questions to see how we can catch this villain faster.

Almost as soon as I think that, she turns off her phone and looks over at me.

"What's up, Yera?" She asks.

"Oh, I was just wondering if I could ask you some questions about our mission."

Juni smiles, "I know pretty much all that you know, but sure."

I think in silence. We pass another courtyard, this one filled with cobblestone and a floral scent. Hmm, perhaps I should ask her how exactly we should go about confronting the villain. I open my mouth but another voice speaks from behind me.

"*Zut alors!* Zat would have been so heroic, too!"

The only other person behind us is Clayton, but this is a feminine voice, mature and with a heavy French accent

I turn to see a perfect painting scene: a woman covered in flowers, reaching over the small courtyard gate and holding hands with Clayton. She wears a long skirt, a boa, and a tiara, all made completely of flora. Her brown-blond hair flows down past her shoulders, and her grey eyes shine with malicious excitement. The monotony of the alleyway contrasts well with her colorful and bizarre outfit. The frozen look of mischief on her face and the opposing mixture of pain and horror on Clayton's are all framed nicely, with the gate acting as a centerline for the piece.

I look down to see that this flower woman is holding Clayton's hand… and he is holding one of his revolvers?!

Juni turns too and lets out a loud swear. The others get the cue, and in a moment, we are all facing the colorful woman.

"No… oh no… no you have to be kidding…" Star cries.

Clayton's face is drained of color as he continues to stare at his gun. Davisamir begins backing away, putting a hand in front of Nale.

"Ey, who do you–"

"Kabel, stop!" Star shouts from behind us.

"Davisamir, take the boys and head back to the base port. Forget Pengun for right now." Juni demands.

The giant nods and scoops up Nale. He disappears behind me,

and a moment later, he has Bacoj tucked under his other arm, thundering back down the street the way we came.

"Is she a threat?" I ask Juni lowly, unable to read the severity of the situation.

"Oh, not to you, love," says the woman, then her tone drops as she jolts Clayton, "but to dirty *pigs* like zis, I am… what is it… zee *nightmare*."

"Megan Menzel, also known as La Corsage. She can glide on wind and she has the combined peak strength of everyone who has ever worn a corsage," Juni pauses, "and she hates men."

I don't know what a corsage is, but this doesn't seem like the time to ask.

"Ah, love," La Corsage says, "hatred is not a strong enough word. Zee men are… how do you say… *vile*. *Disgusting*. Zis world would be better if zey never existed."

"Watch it, toots." Kabel mutters.

La Corsage's head snaps towards him and her angry smile turns into an enraged frown.

"What did you say?" She asks.

"Kabel, please shut up." Star hisses.

"*Non non non!*" La Corsage insists, her angry smile returning and her grip on Clayton's hand tightening, "Please, let zee little piggy squeal before it is slaughtered!"

"I dunno what kinda guys you been hangin' around," Kabel starts, grabbing the hilt of his massive sword, "but this one don't like bein' called a little piggy."

"Kabel oh my goodness saying that is the worst thing you could have ever done." Juni hisses, turning pale.

La Corsage's hand tenses up around Clayton's even more, causing him to arch his back. The woman has a pressed smile on her face. With a terrifying amount of ease, she peels back the metal gate in front of her as if it were thin film.

The villainess steps out of the courtyard and everyone except Kabel backs up a little. Star rushes up and tries to pull him away, but he doesn't budge. Suddenly, a pink wand appears in Star's hand and she smacks Kabel in the back of the head with it.

"Ouch! What was that for?"

"This lady is about to kill you but you won't let your ego drop enough to run away like a smart person!" The woman cries, and she is quite literally crying.

"*Zis* is why I hate zee men! Zey are stupid and full of pride and all zey do is hurt and kill and steal! Look! Look, you are making her cry!" La Corsage is red-faced by now.

Clayton is on his knees, gritting and softly crying as he holds his wrist. His hand and his gun are somehow being crushed in La Corsage's grip. How is she so strong?

"Okay dat's it!" Kabel says, slinging his large blade out of its scabbard, "either you let go of Clayton or you lose ya arm."

"Kabel please…" Star sobs.

"It's her you should be worried about. I know we ain't 'sposed to hurt the villains or whateva, but I ain't about to let her break my boy Clayton."

Juni silently and angrily rushes up to Star, helps her stand, and walks her away from Kabel.

"You see… you see…" La Corsage looks enraged beyond words, "Zis is what I am talking about! Zey are stupid! Zey cannot reason! Garbage, all men are *garbage*!"

Sickening pops are coming from Clayton's hand as the cowboy writhes in agony, his eyes wide and ragged gasps leaping from his mouth. Without another word, Kabel raises his sword and brings it down in a split second.

My heart leaps in my throat as I brace for a horrific burst of blood, but La Corsage lifts her free hand and… catches the blade? Instead of cutting through her hand like it ought to, her palm just turns a little pink.

Stunned, Kabel goes to flick a switch on his sword, but the woman twists her wrist and the blade snaps with an echoing pop. We all stare in astonishment as she squeezes her end of the broken blade hard enough to press the metal into a thin rod. The hardened temeotire, one of the stronger metals from Arret, molds in her hand like butter, leaving little more than a glistening, shallow cut.

She drops the squished metal and snatches the rest of the sword out of Kabel's surprised hands. With a graceful twirl, she angles it to the ground, and in one stab, drives the blade halfway into the sidewalk, filling the alleyway with a loud crunch.

“H-how– EUGH!” Kabel can’t finish his sentence before La Corsage has a death grip on his throat.

My heart sinks into my chest as she lifts him into the air. He grabs at her hand, but of course, he can’t pry it open.

“Black-haired love told you,” her smirk returns, “I have zee power of everyone who has worn zee corsage. Ah, how flowers on zee wrist can do so much good. Every year I get stronger from zee millions of young women going to zeir promenade dances and debutante balls. *Girl power*, as zee Americans call it. You know, I am being very gentle, like holding a butterfly. It is as if I am not holding you at all! One real squeeze and you would be like zee *crème anglaise*!”

She giggles to herself as she tightens and loosens her grip around Kabel’s neck, flashing his face between red and pale. She then smiles down at Clayton and squeezes his hand more, making disheartening crunches. The cowboy rasps a weak scream.

I can do nothing but watch as the two boys wheeze and struggle. La Corsage smiles.

“Ah, a beautiful sound, is it not?” She asks the rest of us.

Star raises her wand with both hands. Juni pulls the coffin she’s been rolling a bit closer. I take my bladed rings off of the back of my hands, and I see Ellia raise their machine gun gloves. They’ve been so quiet, I almost forgot they were there.

“L-let them go. I know you think men are the worst but these guys aren’t bad.” Star pleads.

"Is zat so?" La Corsage shakes her head, "It sounds like zey have… how do you say… *brainwashed* you."

"No, they haven't! Please, just stop hurting them!" Star begs.

La Corsage thinks for a while as the two boys quietly try to get any relief they can. I look around the alleyway, but even after all that noise, not a single person is around. No one looking out of their window, no lone moped or jogger coming down the street, nothing.

"Very well. If zese *pigs* have not… brainwashed you, tell me why I should not kill zem. If you make sense, I will let zem go." La Corsage offers.

I look over at Star and Juni. They look pretty worried. Ellia looks like they are trying their best not to look scared.

"We will start down zee line. Each one of you has one chance to talk me into letting one of your friends go. We will start on zis smart pig here," she raises her and Clayton's hand, "and end on… *Kabel*." She squeezes my teammate's neck more, causing him to turn blue and thrash helplessly.

La Corsage giggles with genuine amusement, then eases up and turns back to us, "Blond love, you go first."

"Clayton is a fantastic guy and a wonderful leader! He's always so kind and respectful, and he gives everyone the chance to grow and succeed! He helped me research and practice all my spells, and he attended every single one of Juni's music recitals and concerts. He loves and honors his girlfriend, and I think he's the best example of a stand-up guy I've ever seen!"

Star begins to cry, "Please don't kill him… please…"

La Corsage frowns thoughtfully, then looks at Clayton and asks, "What is your girlfriend's name?"

"Allie. Allie Baneer." He wheezes.

"Have you cheated on Allie? Hit her? Put her down?" La Corsage asks, yanking the cowboy closer to her.

"No! I would never!" He cries.

La Corsage squints at him, "You were zee smart one; you tried to shoot your foot when you first saw me so I would have surprise and all of your friends could run away… and you have been quiet zis whole time…"

She looks at Juni, "Black-haired love, tell me why I should not kill zis… *Kabel.*"

Juni hesitates. Kabel, eyes red, looks over at her, and she glares back at him.

"I know lying to you is a bad idea, so I'll keep it straight: I don't know very much about Kabel, but I know he could have a promising future if you let him go. A few dumb mistakes shouldn't cost someone their life, right?"

La Corsage smirks, "Very sorry, my love, but I will need more zan zat to let him go. Zee future of a man can only be filled with violence; zis is zeir nature. Red-haired love," I jump as she looks at me, "tell me why his future will not be violent."

In my training with the empress, I was taught never to freeze in a situation of high stress. Doing a particular motion, even if it has nothing to do with the situation, is better than freezing. My default reaction is to squat down, and although all eyes are on me, I do so.

I think as far back as I can about Kabel. I did not know him much during the brief times we spent together on Arret, but here in France, I have gotten to know him very well. He can seem brash at times, but he has mostly been a nice and helpful guy. I stand up and decide to start with that.

"Kabel can be cocky sometimes, but he has a good heart. He was there for me during the weeks when we first arrived here…" I decide not to add 'on this planet', "sharing tips with me about the information he'd gotten. Also, he was helpful and supportive during all of our gym times together, reassuring me and pushing me to do my best. You should not kill a man like this one."

La Corsage smirks again and my stomach drops, "Gym times and telling information is not good enough. It seems to me like you all are… what do zee Americans say… grabbing at your straws? Rainbow-haired love, how is zis man not a normal hater of women?"

"I'm not a woman." Ellia says.

La Corsage's face darkens, "So you are a man?"

"I'm neither, you ugly clown-*sheiffer*." Ellia responds.

My skin turns to ice. Did Ellia just insult her?!

"Clown… *chauffeur*?" La Corsage asks, smiling with interest, "Explain."

"I wouldn't explain feces to you if you thought it was chocolate,"

Ellia replies, "now put Kabel and the other guy down or I'm going to make you look like Swiss cheese."

The rest of us are too stunned to speak. With this, I know for sure that Clayton and Kabel are doomed. La Corsage grins and takes a step toward Ellia, still holding Kabel in the air and Clayton by the hand. We all shuffle back again.

"You are scared of me?" La Corsage taunts.

"Why would I be scared of some fat donkey with a bunch of flowers glued to her?" Ellia spits.

La Corsage… laughs?

"You are certainly a woman; you are too brave and… what is it… *creative*. Now, before I crush zee neck of zis little piggy, tell me whatever you want about him."

Ellia pauses, lowering their gun gloves. They stare at Kabel, who is now beginning to tear up. I begin tearing up too, because I truly think he is about to die.

"We went to all the same schools together, starting all the way up to preparation. I can't remember starting school all that well because I was like 6, but we didn't talk much. I remember one time some of his friends were harassing me because I didn't have a dad, and he was there but… he didn't do or say anything.

"In median school I got picked on a lot. Being half woodish and half human meant that everyone hated me. The woodish kids thought I was a freak, and the human kids thought I was some trashy woodish snob like all the others. I'd get called names and pushed around, people would break my stuff and ruin my clothes… and whenever Kabel was there he would just look at them from a distance but never say anything.

"I got my eye taken out by Yatniv the fall break between median and preparation school. I remember the few friends I'd made, my mom, and a bunch of random adults were there afterwards to take me to the hospital. And Kabel was there too. I could see he wanted to step in but he was afraid.

"Preparation school was weird. For some reason, Kabel and I were in every class and every group project. As I spent more time with him, I began to realize he was actually a cool guy. He is pretty annoying, sure, and I know I annoy him, but he is honest and wholesome and wants nothing more than to be the strongest guy in the room… just in case he needs to protect someone."

Ellia gives a little chuckle, "That idiot you're strangling to death sucks, but if you kill him, you're gonna have a bad time."

La Corsage stares at Kabel for a long while. Her face is blank, then annoyed, then vaguely unhappy. My heart leaps with joy as she releases Clayton… but she doesn't release Kabel?!

"All men are evil, and zis man is simply zee exception. However, zis… *Kabel*, is still like zee rest of zem; scared, weak, how do you say, *miserable*. I am going…" she trails off as footsteps approach from down the alleyway.

We all turn to see a man in shorts and a striped polo sprinting towards us. His sandals clack loudly as he runs, echoing off of the alley walls. I turn to see La Corsage's reaction to another man approaching. Rage, just as I'd figured.

She goes to yell something, but he interrupts with a wave of his hand and a "*Torpor!*"

Dandelion-like fuzzballs rush up from his palm, swirling forward in a silent gust of wind and drifting around La Corsage's head. She recoils and annoyedly waves the fuzz away from her.

"What is zis stupidness! What did…" her eyes flutter and then she shakes her head, "What?!"

The man begins to slow his pace. La Corsage's eyes dim for a bit as her head leans forward, then she snaps back to attention. The hand suspending Kabel begins to lower until he can touch the sidewalk with the tips of his shoes. The woman teeters and tries to lift him again, but her arm begins to shake.

She plops him down on his feet and her eyes flutter again. La Corsage then stumbles backwards, pulling Kabel with her, until she bumps into a car. Her head begins to lull around as she fights to keep her eyes open, confused and sleepy. In a last-ditch effort, she slings her arm around Kabel's neck. Then she goes limp, slides off him, and falls onto the hood of the car.

Kabel, terrified and confused, rushes away from the hood. We all stare down at the woman, who is now sound asleep.

"She'll be out for a while, but we still shouldn't stick around for too long." The guy in sandals says.

"Right," Clayton says, his voice cracking, "let's get moving."

I notice he is holding… oh my! His right hand now looks like a crumpled red ball. Metal shards stick out of it, and blood seems to be oozing from everywhere.

“Clayton, your hand!” Star screams.

The cowboy looks down at it with a casual laugh, “Yeah, looks pretty bad, doesn’t it? We should probably get to the hospital. Yera, what’s the move?”

“What do you mean? Go to the hospital!” I reply, confused as to why he is asking me what to do.

“Well, yeah, but you’re the team leader, right? Experiential learning – you gotta decide what everyone does.” The cowboy says, “And, no rush or anything, but this is by far the most pain I’ve ever experienced in my entire life… so, you know, take that as you will.”

I wince in sympathy, then look at Juni and Star for guidance. They look worried. I expect them to offer some advice, but they just look back at me, waiting. With a sigh, I squat down to think.

Okay, first things first, safety.

“Are we still required to finish the mission?” I ask, not looking at anyone in particular.

If not, we’ll all head to the hospital.

“Yes. At least one of you has to confront Vittorio… not unless you want Virrel to get turned into a pizza, haha.” Clayton says.

Okay, that complicates things a bit. We definitely need to get Clayton to the hospital. Kabel looks fine outside of a bruised neck, but I want him to see a medic too. I'm fine to continue on, but everyone else looks too emotionally shaken to consider…

"Star, do you still think you can take us to Pengun's apartment?"

"Well, I'm Pengun, so there's no need for that." The guy in sandals says.

"How did you know we were out here?" Juni asks.

"Davisamir texted me." Pengun replies.

Hmm, I wish I could just ask people how emotionally stable they think they are, but people don't work that way. Star is shivering and teary, whimpering apologetically while Clayton tries to reassure her. Juni just looks concerned, and Ellia seems a bit pale. I decide to stand up.

"Ellia, are you okay?" I ask.

"I almost just peed myself, but outside of that, yeah." They reply.

I think I'll have them come with me. The only problems are Star and Juni. One of them is going to have to escort the boys to the hospital, while the other helps Ellia and me out. But Star is in no state to do either. Which task is the least important? I'm going to go with… Vittorio. I would much rather fight Vittorio on my own than risk Star breaking down on the way to the hospital.

"Star, do you think you could go with Ellia and me to Italy?"

She is quiet for a bit, sniffling and on the verge of crying again, then shakes her head. Juni sighs. My stomach drops. That's going to mess up my plan. I want to push her to say yes, but the only assertive tactic that might work is using logic, and I can't just straight up tell her she's a liability. Looks like I'll have to compromise and hope for the best.

"Okay… do you think you could escort Clayton and Kabel to the hospital?" I ask with reluctance.

She nods and seems to gather herself, "I'll look up where it is."

I glance over at Kabel, surprised he didn't protest. He's gently touching his neck, staring at the pieces of his broken sword. He gives the hilt a bit of a tug, but it is as if the sword is a part of the ground now.

"Kabel?" I ask.

He quickly wipes his eyes and turns to me, raising an eyebrow.

"What's up, boss?" His voice is hoarse and it sounds like it hurts to talk.

"Go with Clayton and Star to the hospital. Make sure nothing bad happens to them."

"I'll try." He responds, tame.

I fight back my worry and return to my leadership role, "Juni, are you fit to go with Ellia and me to Italy?" I ask.

"Sure," she replies, "I'll let Davisamir know we're okay and have the boys meet Star at the hospital."

Her calmness is relieving.

"I'm sorry Juni!" Star blurts, "It would've been easier if we could all go but then La Corsage and you know how I feel about this and I just hate Rosenburg for–"

"Hey hey hey," Juni says, rubbing the blonde's back, "You're fine. There's no reason to apologize, Star. Let's all just do our tasks and make sure everyone gets out of this one safely."

Clayton shifts uncomfortably, probably out of pain. Juni closes her eyes for a bit, then looks at me and nods. I return a nod.

"Alright, let's move out."

Chapter 7

Pengun's Portal

~ Transportation ~

The room has a sharp fragrance about it. The pause screen of a first-person shooter game rests on the TV screen. There is a box with two-thirds of a pizza in it and a half bag of powdered donuts. Empty energy drink cans litter the floor, along with clothes and papers. Outside of this, the rest of the apartment seems organized.

"Sorry, I was… in the middle of tidying up." The wizard says, scratching his short, brown hair.

"Don't worry about it," Juni says, "do you still think you can get us to Italy?"

"Well duh," Pengun brags, "I mean, I beat *La Corsage* after all… teleporting you to Italy is nothing."

"Oh, big guy in town, huh?" Juni mocks.

"You can just call me King Weed Wacker, you know, since I *literally beat La Corsage*. Just King works too." Pengun replies.

"Just get us to Italy already." Juni demands, rolling her eyes.

"Ugh, fine." Pengun replies, mimicking Juni.

The wizard ducks into a back room and begins shuffling through some papers. Juni, Ellia, and I stand awkwardly in his living room.

I watch the barrel of the gun on the screen move up and down as if the character were breathing.

"So, Juniper, right?" Pengun asks from down the hallway, still shuffling papers and clothes about.

"Yep." Juni calls back.

"Are the other two new team members?"

"No, we're training them. They were supposed to be doing a quick grab-and-go mission because…" she clears her throat, "*because*, but then the villain decided to have his base in Italy and we ran into La Corsage."

"Oh… grab-and-go mission…" Pengun stops rummaging around, "I'm sorry."

Juni laughs, "What's there to be sorry about, weirdo?"

Pengun keeps rummaging, "Right… right yeah that was weird of me. I was just…"

He emerges from his hallway with a wooden box. His mouth is scrunched up to one side, as if he'd just read something disheartening.

"Um…" he seems a lot less enthusiastic now, "so, you want me to teach them about teleportation?"

"Yeah sure, that would work… 'King Wack'." Juni says.

Pengun gives a humorless chuckle, then opens the wooden box. Inside are a few different gems and pearls. On the other side of a divide is a large wad of business cards, all of different colors and styles. He takes out a small, baby blue pearl and hands it to me to inspect. I roll the smooth ball in my fingers as he starts.

"I don't know how much magic knowledge you two have, but usually things are pretty free range in terms of spell rules. Outside of having to pay attention to your magic stamina, you can pretty much do whatever you want if you put your mind to it. The only real rules are like no permanently altering the laws of physics or space-time and… yeah. But magic subdivisions are where all the rules start coming in."

I hand the pearl to Ellia. They toss it and use their palm to continue batting it in the air.

"Teleportation isn't any different. Some magic styles look cooler than others, some have different conditions for teleporting, and some don't even have teleportation at all. Since we're using a magic item… and the nuances get a little tricky… let's just say it operates on its own system too. It's going to teleport you in a different way than… say, a gothic wizard. Items take you through a wormhole, while gothic wizards do this weird, loud, spinning thingy and just sorta… yeah."

"Can't you teleport us?" Ellia asks, handing the pearl to Juni who hands it right back to them.

"No. I mean technically yes, if I knew how to summon something that could do it or… maybe if you all grabbed on to me and I cast *Transference*… but let's be honest," he gestures to his lean frame, wrapped in casual summer clothes, "does it look like I know spells that crazy? No, in situations like these, you've got to rely on enchanted gems or enchanted paper. Or potions… something to do with chemical bonds I think."

"How does it work?" Ellia asks, distracting themselves by flicking the pearl up in the air and catching it.

"Pressure mostly. Magic timers or sensors and stuff also work, but you could just throw it on the ground really hard too."

Ellia catches the pearl and raises it, "Can I try?"

"No," Pengun says, putting out his hand, "That will send you to the East-Main Operational Headquarters in China."

Ellia reluctantly hands the pearl back. Pengun puts it with the other gems and begins thumbing through business cards.

"Gems are for super long range or important places, while business cards are what all the normal people use. Where in Italy do you need to go?"

"Sperlogna." Juni says.

"Oh, that's perfect! My boy Ben lives down there. You know, Ben Sweezy, funny mustache, beard, likes that weird game with the keys in it?"

"Ah…" Juni smiles, furrowing her brow, "right, Ben."

Pengun pauses and smirks, "You have no idea who I'm talking about."

"Nope." Juni's shoulders sag.

"That's okay, Ben's cool. He can get you wherever…" the wizard is quiet for a moment as he thumbs through more business cards, then, "Phew, still got a couple left."

He pulls a white and purple card out of the large row, then hands it to me. I take it, giving it a quick glance. It looks like a normal business card. Hopefully this works and this Sweezy person lives near Vittorio.

"Huddle together and rip that bad boy in half, and you'll be at Ben's in no time." Pengun says, returning the box to where it was.

Awkwardly, Juni and Ellia shuffle closer to me.

"Alright, get out of here. I gotta change my gamer tag to 'WeedWhacker' because I just wacked *La Corsage herself.* Or should it be 'xX_WeedWhacker_Xx'? Maybe I could put a–"

Juni snatches the card from me and rips it in half. Bright purple sparks leap from the paper, skidding across the ground and making a circle around the three of us. I'm terrified that the carpet might catch on fire, but Pengun looks more mockingly offended than concerned.

"Oh, well *bye* then!" He snaps.

The carpet under my feet grows softer, then sags as if there was no flooring beneath it, then it disappears and the three of us fall into darkness. Pulsing neon shapes spin up from everywhere. Invisible textures press against me from all sides. A twisting waterfall of pink dots showers around us, swirling down into an abstract infinity.

There is a bright flash, and then a circle opens up underneath us. All three of us violently crash onto a couch in a sunlit apartment, surrounded by ethereal smoke. Juni's coffin makes an extra loud bang as it smashes into the carpeted floor. The impact was more jarring than painful, and it seems like that was the case for Juni and Ellia, too. Granted, Ellia is swearing loudly, but I think it is mostly from habit.

This apartment is much neater, with a coffee color scheme and a fresh, sea scent. There is a kitchen bar to our left and a large TV to our right. The window is open in the kitchen, letting in a warm breeze, and the radio on the countertop plays calming guitar jazz. A young man with shaggy hair, a large moustache, and a well-groomed beard, stares wide-eyed at us from behind his book and coffee mug. If only I had my sketchpad right now…

"Um, can I help you?" He asks.

"Ben Sweezy?" Juni asks, picking herself up.

"Yep." He replies.

"Juniper Webbre. Pengun lent us a business card so we could resolve a job."

"Is that so?" Ben inquires, folding the book closed over his thumb, "Any way I can be of assistance?"

"Well, since this is a training… actually, sure, what are your powers?" Juni asks.

"Um… I'm actually just an office guy." Ben offers with a shrug.

Juni squints, "Zero field work?"

"Zero." He admits, taking a sip from his mug.

"In that case, could you take a look at this leaflet? We're looking for a man named Vittorio Punnicci."

“Vittorio?” Ben asks, putting his mug down, “Like the pizza chef down at *Cucina sulla Costa*?”

“That’s him! Is he nearby?” Juni asks.

“Yeah, he’s right down the street. Once you leave the apartment, head down the street to the coast, then take a right at the last road and he’s the third building down.”

“Awesome, thank you!” Juni says, spotting and heading towards the front door.

Ellia follows her, but I stick behind, feeling like I need to do something leader-like. Ben notices me and doesn’t go back to reading.

“Everything alright?”

“Yes, I was just wondering if you knew of any ways we could return to Paris after we are finished with our mission.”

“Hmmm, I don’t have any business cards for Pengun, but the nearby post office has a hero substation that might have some. I’ll drive you all there if you come back after.”

“Thank you.” I say, and then leave with a nod.

****

The sun is beaming down from the clear skies above. The roads here, paved with black and red asphalt, are lined with cobblestone sidewalks. Smells of sea salt float in the midday breeze. We pass white-walled shops and rustic stone, with summer greenery seeming to burst from everywhere.

Colorful signs stand tall against the sides of the road, covered in what must be Italian. The sound of AC units rattle in the air. We pass some homey apartments and a few beat-up buildings, then finally emerge at a wide cobblestone roundabout.

The royal blue sea stretches out to meet the warm sky behind some palm trees in front of us. To our left are white, blocky buildings, rising up on top of one another as if they were built on a large hill. To our right are terraced restaurants. People sit under large white umbrellas or red overhangs, eating colored ice dishes and conversing in Italian. I've never wanted to paint a scene so much in my entire life.

We walk down the storefront, taking in the sea and the comfortable architecture. Soon, the three of us are staring up at the sign on the overhang above a crowded restaurant terrace: *Cocina sulla Costa*. Juni's coffin is getting a few looks from passersby and restaurant patrons.

"This is the place." Juni says, taking note of the well-trimmed shrubs encircling the patio.

I detach my RCBPs and spin one around my finger. It catches the sunlight as well as the attention of a few more patrons.

"Maybe we shouldn't *start off* throwing the giant bladed rings." Juni offers.

"Right." I say, reattaching the rings in shame.

There is awkward silence, then Juni starts again, "Well, you're the leader, what do we do next?"

I want to squat and think, but too many people are watching.

"Hmmm, there are probably a lot of civilians inside. My RCBPs and your coffin are sure to make us noticeable…"

"Who cares? I say we go in, kick the crap out of the pizza dude, get Virrel, keep kicking the pizza guy–"

Juni stops Ellia by raising her hand, "Yeah that's a no from me."

I'm suddenly struck with a plan, "Ellia, would you feel comfortable sitting outside and keeping watch?"

They look at me and raise an eyebrow, "What, so you and Juni can get all the glory for yourselves?"

"No, so that you can take care of any back-up that may arrive."

I doubt there will be reinforcements, but Ellia reacts just the way I expected them to.

"*That* I can do." They grin.

"Good. Juni, if it's alright with you, I'll have you leave the coffin out here for Ellia to sit on. I'm also going to leave my RCBPs out here. We will have to go stealth above all else, but if there is physical conflict, bystanders are too close to try anything outside of hand-to-hand. How is that?"

Juni smirks, "I'm impressed! Let's do it."

I detach my bladed rings, trying not to let Juni's compliment get to my head, and then set them next to Ellia and the coffin.

"Hey Ellia," Juni says, "make *absolutely certain* not to open this coffin, regardless of what it whispers to you, okay?"

Ellia turns pale, “Wait, what?”

“Sweet,” Juni says, “let’s go.”

She strides into the shade of the restaurant and I follow. I am hit with the smell of zesty sauce and warm bread. It is dim inside, lit by orange lamps and festive string lights. Fire light flickers from what must be the kitchen. Many of the seats are full of people, eating and talking and joking. Clinking of utensils and frequent hearty laughter fill the air. A flicker of gold catches my attention, but something is a bit more pressing.

Vittorio is standing right by the cashier, looking directly at us.

CHAPTER 8

DANCING OF THE BLADES

~ SHOWDOWN ~

I **ready my zecno, prepared to fire some warning shots if need be.** Juni tenses up, expecting a fight as well.

"Ah, you came so soon! I must say, I did not see such a pleasant surprise coming!" Vittorio greets.

"How did you know we arrived?" Juni asks.

"Three girls standing outside mya restaurant, one with rainbow-hair, another with a coffin, the third with big sharp rings. You don't think that would catch attention?"

Juni and I are silent. So much for stealth.

"Come come! I have a table for two, just for you!"

The chef sidles deeper into the restaurant. I trade a glance with Juni and follow. Vittorio leads us to a small table with a white tablecloth, a candle, glasses, and silverware. He pulls out a chair, and since I'm first, I uncomfortably accept it. Juni takes her own seat before he can show her chivalry.

"*Un momento*, your food iza coming right upa!" Then the chef hurries off to the kitchen.

"Weirdo didn't even give us a menu," Juni mutters, "Yera, tell me if you spot Virrel's lamp anywhere. It's probably in the kitchen, but knowing this nutcase, he might have it lying out in the open."

I look to where I saw the flicker of gold earlier. Sure enough, there is a window in a brick wall separating the kitchen and oven fire from the eating area, and the lamp is sitting right on the mantle.

"Found it." I reply with a nod.

Juni follows my gaze and lets out a chuckle, "You've got to be kidding me."

Suddenly, Vittorio and a waiter rush out of the kitchen towards us. Juni and I watch as they approach.

The waiter reaches us first, filling our glasses with water, and then Vittorio slides two plates of classic pizza in front of Juni and me. I am shocked, because I assumed pizza here was cut into triangles like movies have implied. But these slices are cut in squares, just like back on Arret.

Gooey cheese, tomato paste, and warm bread fill my nose with a delicious aroma. Slices of tomato, mushrooms, and spinach leaves lie on top of the pizzas, somewhat sunken into the cheese.

"*Bon appétit*, asa the French say!" Vittorio boasts.

I want to start eating, partially because the food looks and smells so good, partially due to politeness. But Vittorio hasn't left the tableside and Juni hasn't reached for her utensils, so I don't move either.

"What's the matter?" Vittorio asks, "Never had Italian pizza before? It iza made fresh and served hot, so please use your fork and knife!"

“Thanks.” Juni replies.

Another awkward pause, filled with the sounds of the restaurant around us.

“Are you just gonna keep standing there?” Juni asks.

“Why ofa course! It, eh, iza Italian tradition for the chef to see his patrons’ first bite!”

“Oh really?” Juni is absolutely unconvinced.

“*Sì sì*!”

Juni responds in an octave that makes it clear she’s lying, “Well, that’s too bad. I just got my wisdom teeth removed so I can’t have anything hot or scratchy like this!”

“Right,” I say, playing along despite being unfamiliar with whatever wisdom teeth are, “and I have already eaten, so while we appreciate the meal, it would greatly discomfort us both to eat it.”

“Iza that so,” Vittorio says, looking crestfallen, “not even one bite?”

“Nope.” Juni snaps back.

The chef is silent for a while, then smirks, “What a shame… mya plan was going so well!”

“What *was* your plan, by the way?” Juni asks, scooting her chair back and crossing her legs.

I catch that she’s getting ready to act, so I put my hand on the table, the hand with the zecno around the wrist.

“Ah yes, ofa course! I ama an enchanter, you see. My pizzas are so good not only because ofa the great skill passed down through mya family, but also due to a pinch ofa magic. This one would have put you to sleep, you see. So when you came to me and asked–"

"Ah dah dah!" Juni interjects, "Y-you can skip that part! Start with Virrel."

"Oh… kay then, eh, ever since I was a young boy, I always wanted to be the leader ofa this beautiful country. But mya only skill was pizza making! Upa until Virrel, I thought that pizza was all mya destiny held. But when I heard about him, I figured I could use him, the essence ofa a soul, to cook the greatest magic pizza ina the world!"

Vittorio dramatically raises his fist and looks into the air with triumph. Juni and I are silent. I am unsure about her, but I cannot seem to follow this man's logic.

"Okay… so then what would you do after you made your… soul pizza?" Juni asks.

Vittorio looks down at us, surprised, "Oh, it iza not obvious? I will feed the pizza to the Mafia, they will love ita so much that they will give me their loyalty, and then I will take over Italy and rule forever!" He dramatically raises his fist again.

There is a high-pitched rush of air from Juni's mouth as she chokes back a laugh. The chef and the orientation leader look at one another, and then she lets out a few more laughs.

"Are you… *what*?" She is overcome by giggles.

Vittorio looks genuinely confused, "I… what iza wrong?"

"Are you serious?"

“Yes. Is ita not a great plan? The greatest ofa all plans?”

Juni puts a fist over her grin and looks off into the distance with watery eyes, trying to regain composure.

“I… I have several questions.”

“Please ask!”

“How,” Juni takes a deep breath, “how are you going to get *the literal Mafia* to come try this pizza?”

“Oh, I just asked.”

“And… the Mafia… the most infamous crime organization *in the world*, is going to show up to your restaurant after *one phone call*?”

“Well, look for yourself!” Vittorio gestures to the entrance of the restaurant with excitement.

Juni and I turn. Sunlight makes everything beyond the entrance look like it’s glowing. I can see the backs of a few patrons’ heads and chairs, the corner of Juni’s coffin with Ellia sitting on it, and a large group of men in business casual attire.

The one that seems to be the leader is short and middle-aged, with a black suit on and sunglasses to match. His gray hair is slicked back and his expression is a mix between curious and amused.

Juni’s eyes widen, “You’ve got to be joking.”

“Not ata all, *miei amici*! That iza Frank Martini, also known asa… Cheese?” Vittorio tests, delighted.

Juni stands and whips her head back to Vittorio, seeming a lot more serious and panicked than before, “*Cheese*?! How did you get one of the biggest crime bosses in Europe to…”

She takes another look at the patiently waiting group of men.

"Yera, take care of Vittorio and figure out how to free Virrel. I've got to handle this, it's pretty bad. Oooh man, this is *really* bad."

Without another word, she begins sliding past tables and towards the entrance. I turn to Vittorio and stand, worried about Juni and whatever the Mafia and Cheese are. Since this seems like an overwhelming situation for her, I'll see how quickly I can free Virrel so the two of us can offer assistance.

"Vittorio," I say, trying to sound threatening, "release Virrel and call off Cheese before anyone gets hurt."

A smirk comes across the pizza chef's face as he backs away from the table. From his apron pocket, he produces a green glove. Wordlessly, he fits it on his hand, grinning a mustached grin at me all the while. I raise a half-guard, unsure of what he will do and ready to provide return fire if necessary.

With a snap, an accordion appears in front of him, first all white, then filled with greys and greens and browns. The only reason I know what this instrument is called is because Ellia was oddly amused by them when they'd first discovered them.

Vittorio plays a harmony of notes and presses the accordion inward. As the note grows louder and longer, a small force begins to grow larger against me. It's like one moment I am standing normally, and then suddenly, I'm being pushed harder and harder away from the chef.

The force grows to the point where I almost fall over. I push against it but end up sliding backwards as opposed to standing my ground. Tables and chairs, still with food and patrons occupying them, begin to slide away as well. A surprised murmur raises up from everyone as they hurry out of their seats and to the edges of the eatery.

Vittorio stops the note and the force disappears. I stand still in the commotion, surprised and intimidated. With such a weapon, I don't think I will stand a chance empty-handed. I've got my zecno and my RCBPs are outside, but there is a host of problems with using both.

While a laser firearm is much more precise than an Earthling one, there is a small chance that the accordion could have a perfect light manipulator on it, such as a diamond, and the beams could end up splitting and hitting civilians.

I could resort to my RCBPs, but they may be out of magnetic range and I wouldn't want to disturb Juni. In addition, they are very sharp, so if I hit Vittorio, he would be gravely injured. Even worse, if I were to throw one and miss, it could severely damage one of the civilians standing on the wall.

Hand-to-hand seems like the best option, for I believe I would have no problem overpowering Vittorio despite his gender and size. But since he is armed with that magic accordion, approaching is going to be tricky.

"Very well, strange girl! You will earn back your Virrel only through the Dancing ofa the Blades! Defeat me in a fight, ora in a dance. To the tune ofa *Tico Tico!*"

I brace myself as he begins to play. He starts off with a few warmup notes, getting the beat down, then does a fluttery rift and looks up at me with a smirk. Here we go.

Suddenly, his fingers begin flying on both sides of the accordion, pecking dozens of buttons and keys as he gently presses the instrument together. Everyone's heads begin to bob, even mine, as an energetic, festive tune fills the restaurant. For a moment, I have a twinge of regret for not learning how to dance.

I start to notice the forks and knives that were once lying on tables begin dancing as well, bouncing for a little before floating up in the air, traveling towards Vittorio in jerks. Soon, the accordion reaches its pressed maximum, and the chef begins to pull it apart.

I only have a second to duck before a fork shoots past me and into the far wall. I dive roll behind a table as a steak knife twirls forward and bounces off of the floor right where I was. His attacks are in sync with the beat!

"Are you hungry? Come, have a *slice*!" He taunts, yelling over his music.

I lean the table over to act as a shield, and right on cue, I hear a plate crash on the other side. The tips of three chef's knives appear through my end of the table, each thudding to the song's half-beats.

I back away from the table a little, and there is a shower of shards as a wine glass shatters against its surface. As more plates and silverware batter my table shield, I look at the walls to see if the patrons have gotten to safety.

They stand there, in awe and… entertained?!

Suddenly, the barrage on my cover stops. I notice the forks and knives that were deflected beginning to dance upward. It sounds like we've reached a bridge in the song. I take a quick peek over the edge of the table to spot Vittorio compressing the accordion again. Cutlery, vases, and dinnerware circle his hat like space rocks around a moon, bouncing every so often to the festive beat.

"Now would be a good time to strike! Don't you want a *pizza* me?" Vittorio shouts, then he begins to dance along to his own beat by hopping on one foot.

All at once, the objects floating around him burst into flames. He begins chanting, "Hey! Hey! Hey!" as he dances and plays, spinning while hopping on one foot. Patrons clap and chant as well. I notice that the accordion is pretty compressed and hurry over to a different table, flipping that one for cover.

I have never been in a situation like this before, and a lot is happening, but I am not panicking. Perhaps it is the customers clapping or the festive music. Despite the barrage of flying knives and flaming plates that are sure to come my way, I feel rather cheerful. Like I said, I would dance if I knew how to.

Either way, I need to retaliate. The front entrance to the shop is relatively clear. I don't see Juni's coffin, and many of the terrace patrons are looking off to the left. I think I hear music, but I'm not sure over Vittorio's accordion. The song shifts into the bouncy part again and the thudding and crashing begins to sound on the other end of my cover, now accompanied with the whoosh of flame.

If Vittorio's dancing is cyclical, which it appears to be, he will be standing in front of the kitchen window once he returns to the chorus. No one is standing there, so I could use my RCBPs and not risk injuring patrons. I will aim for his accordion to see if I can render it ineffective, then subdue him.

I stretch my arms out to the entrance of the shop, but nothing happens. The battering of the table is much more violent now, with knives and glasses smashing against the surface on every quarter beat, like a machine gun.

Hot glass showers down around me, then a few shards of ceramic bounce off of some nearby objects and spray me on the sides. I pull in my legs and duck my head but keep my arms and fingers outstretched. I thought I was in magnetic returning range for my weapons… did I miscalculate?

To my relief, the two bladed rings slide around the corner and begin scraping across the ground towards me. As soon as they enter the eatery, they overcome gravity and fly up into my hands. I can't help but let a grin spread on my face.

The song switches again and the battering stops. Immediately, I peek around my cover. Vittorio is standing right where I'd figured, spinning around on his other leg now. I stand fully, take aim, and throw the sharp disk as hard as I can. Vittorio notices and arches his body in a way I didn't think he was capable of. The RCBP zips past him, missing by a few centimeters, darting into the kitchen, and proceeding to make expensive crashing sounds.

To the beat of his song, I launch the other. He brushes his fingers down all the accordion keys and a chair shoots up from beside him. The projectiles meet in the air, mine sinks into his, and the clashing momentum sends the two of them spiraling down into a table.

"Iza this your best? You have *mushroom* for improvement…" Vittorio mocks, rolling his shoulders.

I notice his accordion is close to being fully pressed. I have three options: seek cover again, recall my RCBPs, or open fire with my zecno. I know I do not have the time nor coordination to do multiple. He can outspeed my rings and it is entirely possible that he could use them in his next attack, which will easily slice through one of these tables given the force.

Without another thought, I raise my wrist. The trigger flips up from the bottom of my weapon and I grab it, pointing at the thicker part of the instrument where the keys meet the base. As soon as the green dot from the trainer laser appears, I open fire.

The restaurant is filled with heat and red light as thin beams of energy stream from my wrist and into Vittorio's instrument. There is no recoil, so the weapon buzzes around my wrist with each shot to help me keep pace.

The first hit burns a hole straight through, so I widen my shot group to do as much damage as possible. Luckily, there is no light manipulation, and Vittorio is pressing the instrument with controlled slowness, so the only thing damaged is the accordion.

I stop firing as everything around Vittorio's head is extinguished and falls to the ground. The side of the accordion where I shot is full of melting holes and small, flickering flames. The instrument's beautiful music is replaced with screeching off-notes and wheezing from gaps of air.

"Noooo! Mya accordion!" He looks down at the instrument, then back at me with an angry smile, "Now the true fight begins!"

He takes off his green glove and throws it on the ground. As soon as the glove is off of him, the accordion disappears. There is a perfect opening for a shot, but I do not have orders to kill this man and doing so in front of a packed restaurant seems unwise.

Should I approach? Should I take defense? He reaches into his pocket and pulls out a brown glove. As he's fitting it on, I figure that having a weapon isn't a bad idea. I stretch out a hand to recall one of my RCBPs, but he already has the glove on now, so I grab the nearest chair.

He snaps, and then a large, wooden paddle with a long handle appears in his hand.

"You *feta* get ready!" He shouts as he charges towards me.

Ah, good, close range combat. I drop the chair and leap over my cover table to meet him in the middle of the eatery. He rears back and swings the paddle, thin side first. I see it coming easily and duck, then rise and hit him with a backfist.

The conflict management protocol for being a guard of Empress

Rigm is to try non-violent solutions for as far as possible and use aggression as an absolute final resort. This aggression is to be fully exhausted, used until the subject is rendered unconscious or unable to retaliate due to severe damage. Any amounts of apologizing and pleading are to be ignored. So this is what I do.

With the same hand, I grab Vittorio by the back of the head, slam his face into my elbow, then into my knee. I allow him to stumble back, dodge a downward swing, then send a side kick into his stomach followed by a spinning back kick to the head. He falls onto his butt, dazed and bleeding from both nose and mouth.

"*Mamma mia*! I never *sausage* a violent–"

I pick up a chair and break it over Vittorio before he can finish his sentence. The chef crumples down on the floor and doesn't move. I check his vitals to make sure he is still alive (he is) and walk over to grab the lamp off of the mantle.

Waiters begin rushing out from the kitchen, some armed with brooms and dustpans. I prepare to fight again, pushing down a surge of intimidation, but they intentionally run around me. Two of them pick up Vittorio and carry him to the kitchen. Many begin sweeping up the shards and utensils on the floor or putting the tables and chairs back into place.

One of them shouts a long sequence of Italian and begins clapping, and then the rest of the restaurant claps and cheers before taking their seats again.

The one who made the announcement turns to me and explains,

“I said it was a movie. We will get you what you need now.”

I watch as a waiter pries my RCBP out of a chair, and then he disappears into the kitchen. A second later, he and another waiter approach me with shaking hands, one presenting my weapons and the other presenting Virrel’s lamp.

I take them, feeling bad for making the rest of the civilians afraid, and then the announcement waiter pops up out of nowhere. He begins ushering me towards the exit, and I can hear his voice trembling.

“Rub the lamp and your friend comes out, okay? Have a good day. Sorry for the mess. Call if you have questions or want pizza. But do not come back, okay? All the pizza you want, all free. But only delivery, no eating here, okay? Goodbye!”

I am weakly pushed out into the shaded terrace, then the door slams behind me.

CHAPTER 9

DECEIT

~ END OF TRAINING ~

There is a lot of laughing going on outside the restaurant. Juni is shutting and locking her coffin, laughing a very artificial laugh. Ellia is smiling and nodding behind her, looking out of their element. The genuine cheering and chuckling around them is settling back into normal talk.

"Thanks again very much for that, Juniper," the leader in the suit, Cheese, says, "My daughter loved it. Like I said, anything you want, just call me. You're part of the family now."

His voice is thick with the drawl of a gangster. It's easy to hear how he's talked his way through illegal deals and coolly sentenced people to death in his past.

"Thanks Mr. Martini! I'm glad Rosella liked it. I'll be sure to call!" Juni says with an unnatural amount of youthful formality.

A very fancy black car pulls up and the mobster gets in without even paying attention, "Please, just Cheese from now on."

Someone closes the door for him and the vehicle speeds off.

The rest of the henchmen begin dispersing, heading to random stores or off to the beachfront, melting into the civilians. The three of us stand in front of the terrace, awkwardly silent.

“Ah,” I say, trying to take the lead, “I got Virrel.”

The other two look at me, both interested and distracted.

“Sweet, do you know how to get him out?” Juni asks.

I raise the lamp with a shrug and rub the side with my palm. Nothing happens. I do it some more, pressing harder, and then a spiraling blue cloud of smoke rises out of the lamp. A heavy breeze begins to swirl around the cloud, forming it into a large ball, then the ball explodes and Virrel pops out with an excited roar.

He no longer wears his grey pajamas. Instead, he’s draped in baggy, exotic silks and gold jewelry, carrying a spiced, perfume smell. A tear-drop-shaped hat rests on his head, and he now has a goatee which is tied long. Feathers rain down around him as the clouds dissolve in the air. He also looks older, like in his late thirties as opposed to his early twenties.

“That was amazing! It was like a prison, but everything was exotic pillows and the music was…” he looks concerned, “Why does everyone look so startled?”

“Well, Ellia and I just became part of the Mafia and I’m pretty sure Yera killed that pizza chef so I think we’re all technically villains at this point.” Juni offers.

“Also you’re like 50 years old now? And look like some circus man or something?” Ellia notes.

“I thought he looked more like a genie.” Juni mumbles.

“Ah, right,” he remarks, looking down at his clothes, “I think I have an explanation for that. Do you all have an explanation for your… changes of heart?"

"Yep!" Ellia replies before I have a chance to clear things up.

"Sweet, you guys go first." He gestures in front of him.

"We'll have to walk and talk," Juni says, "I got the directions from Ben, so we'll need to head over to the post office ASAP."

"What's the rush? We've got Virrel back!" Ellia prods.

"We gotta…" Juni pauses, and she seems rather sad for a moment, "head back to the hospital and meet up with the others."

Juni looks down at her phone and begins following its directions, rolling her coffin behind her. The three of us tag along as well, silent and a little concerned.

"So…" Ellia says, "Why are you old and dressed all weird, Virrel? Your beard looks kind of dumb, by the way."

"Hey, that wasn't very nice! I'm not too sure about the new clothes, but I think I'm older because my soul was being extracted. When I got shot out, I guess I got all of my strength back but kept the look. Personally, I don't think the beard is *that* bad…"

"How did you know what was happening to you?" I ask, wincing, "Could you… feel your soul weakening?"

"No, I just heard it all when Vittorio explained it. There was music but I could still hear everything going on outside the lamp! You youngsters are something else. Speaking of that," he looks at Ellia, "what is the Mafia?"

"Business crime lords that almost shot Juni and I because of pizza!" Virrel recoils in surprise, but Ellia continues.

“And Juni was like ‘hEy ThErE iS nO nEeD To Do ThAt’,” Juni’s reserved demeanor is broken with a smile as Ellia’s impersonation of her comes out high-pitched and off-key.

“And Cheese was like, ‘wussin it fah us?’” Juni and I recoil in surprise as Ellia is almost spot on with the gangster’s heavy, hoarse voice

“And then Juni told him about her powers and Cheese said if she made some skeletons dance and he showed a live video to his daughter because she loved stuff like that then he’d let us off the hook. And that’s what happened!”

“Sounds like you enjoyed yourself,” Virrel remarks before turning to Juni and asking, “How did you make skeletons dance?”

“I’ve got a marimba, among other things, inside this coffin,” she raises the handle a bit, then continues to roll it like normal, “when I play it, I can summon specters and skeletons and whatnot to do my bidding. It’s pretty much like I have an entire Halloween department store under my control, if that makes any sense to you guys.”

I vaguely remember Halloween, that odd time shortly after my arrival where pumpkins and scary themes seemed to take over the TV in my hotel room. I’m not quite sure what a marimba is, but nonetheless, I start making connections in my head.

“Juni, you have an enchanted instrument?” I ask.

She shrugs, “Yeah, you could call it that.”

“Vittorio had one as well. His was an accordion that controlled all of the cutlery and ceramics in his eatery; he made them fly after me during our battle."

"That sounds awesome!" Ellia exclaims.

"It was," I admit, "I really wish I knew how to dance. I would have danced along and earned Virrel back that way instead of beating up the poor guy."

"I mean," Juni pauses, "we can help you learn how to dance."

"Really?" I ask, interested.

"Yeah, we can go to the magic tattoo parlor after…" the woman seems to realize something and sinks back into quiet.

I look at Virrel and Ellia. Virrel looks concerned and confused again, searching for words to approach with, but Ellia shakes their head and stops walking. I stop too, then Virrel, then Juni.

"Come on guys, we gotta get moving." She drones.

"Nope, you're gonna have to explain yourself first." Ellia says, crossing their arms.

"What do you mean?" Juni asks, but I'm also starting to get the feeling that she's hiding something.

"You were really cool and stuff until we saved Virrel. Now you're all edgy. What's the deal?" Ellia asks.

Juni stares at Ellia for a moment, then lets out an exasperated sigh, "Yera, tell your teammate to fall in line."

She said it in a dismissive, casual way, but it still felt very unnatural. All eyes are on me. Even Juni, who is staring at the ground impatiently, glares at me with her peripherals. While I understand that Juni is entitled to her emotions and she probably outranks me in whatever hierarchy this organization uses, I start to feel as though maybe she *is* acting a bit strange and maybe it *is* best to get some answers.

"Ellia…" I hesitate, apprehensive about actually disobeying Juni. I feel my teammates' stares intensifying.

"… continue."

Juni looks up with an unreadable expression.

"You got it!" Ellia replies, grinning, "So, as I was saying, why are you acting strange?"

"You'll need to be more specific. As far as I know I'm acting perfectly normal." Juni responds.

"Your tone!" Ellia says.

"What about it, Mom?" Juni mocks.

Ellia opens their mouth to retaliate and probably insult, but I hold out a hand. I think I know how to address this one.

"Juni, you have been very secretive about our mission. I recall specifically when we confronted Vittorio about his plan, he was beginning to make a statement that implied you all had prior contact. Why was that?"

Juni looks at me with a solemn, confused face, but it seems as though there is a hint of a smile that she is fighting back very well.

"Yeah, and when we first talked about Vittorio at lunch, the guy with the funny hat and that blond chick were acting all weird about me saying this was part of the act. We're on to you, *glud*-face."

Ellia jabs.

Juni looks down and lets a laugh slip out of her mouth. For a moment, I relax, glad it was all just a ruse, but then I notice tears welling up in Juni's eyes as her smile quivers.

"I… I frickin' hate that you guys have so much personality…" She admits, laughing.

I'm unsure how to feel now. I think Ellia is at a loss for words, too. Just by how well she handled the La Corsage situation, Juni is probably the last person I'd ever expect to see crying. Granted, I've only known her for an hour or so, but still.

"Why do you say that?" Virrel coaxes.

Juni composes herself, nodding as she pushes her glasses up and wipes her eyes. Without warning, she lets the handle to the coffin go. It slams onto the ground with a lot of clinking and clattering inside. Pink with exasperation, Juni stomps over and sits down on top of it.

"You know what? Screw it! Fine! Ask me whatever you want, and if you guess far enough, I'll tell you. I don't care about Rosenburg's orders anymore."

The three of us are apprehensive.

"But…" Ellia starts, timid, "but didn't we already–"

"Oh come on Ellia, that's obvious! Of course this whole thing was supposed to be an act! We always hire people to come in and give the trainees a little first mission; Vittorio just turned out to be an actual villain! I want you to figure out the real big picture! Come on, I know you're smart enough!"

She leans forward, resting her elbows on her knees. I look at the others, and they look as confused as I feel. It seems like this is another leader issue. With a sigh, I squat down.

Big picture… I want to point out obvious things but they just trace back to Vittorio… I'm going to need to analyze small things and work my way up. I've got it: Virrel. We know how to work off of one another, and he's also had the least amount of exposure to the mission-related business with Vittorio, so he may be able to pick out the smaller, choicer hints.

"Virrel, are you thinking what I'm thinking?" I ask.

"Probably," he says, stroking his tied goatee for a moment, "Juni… you all didn't know Vittorio was a real villain?"

"Nope." Juni admits again.

"But you always hire people for new trainees?" I repeat.

"Yep." Juni says.

The interrogation protocol for Empress Rigm's guard group is to always interrogate in groups of two and make it appear as though someone and their partner are in sync. This gives off an intimidating air, as if the truth were so easy to find that two people thought of it at the same time. I don't really know what Virrel is thinking, and at the moment I'm just saying what has already been said, but I have to keep up the façade.

"Is there not an approval process of sorts to make sure something like this doesn't happen?" The ghost probes.

“There is…” Juni nods, eyebrows raised.

That must have been a good point.

“But ours must’ve been skipped… no, bureaucracy doesn’t work that way. More like –”

Ellia interrupts me, “Rushed.”

I look at Virrel, but he is equally as surprised.

“Why would we rush the screening?” Juni asks, holding back a grin by squinting off towards the shore.

“I don’t know, but I remember you’d said it was a ‘grab-n-go’ mission back at Pengun’s and then he started acting all weird. I know that phrase means ‘quick food’ or whatever because I wanted to make an insult out of it after I heard it in a movie.”

The phrase ‘quick food’ triggers a memory of earlier today, “Another indicator that this was rushed is lunch. I remember Clayton mentioned having something upscale prepared but resorting to subs due to ‘last-minute budget cuts’.”

“That’s strange,” Virrel says, “it seems like an established trainee program would have an established budget…”

“Exactly, it’s being rushed.” Ellia says.

“Are you sure?” I challenge, thinking hard, “They had ample time to get ready. We were in those hotel rooms for a little over a half a year…”

The other two are silent. For a moment, I fear that I’ve put a jam in our momentum, and when they don’t have an answer after a while, I throw a little something else into the air to get our speed back.

"Perhaps they were stalling for something and waited a bit too long." I try with a neutral tone.

"Nonsense," Juni says, but I can tell in her voice that she is trying some sort of trick, "you were just in the hotel rooms because we had to process all of your paperwork."

I want to challenge her, but that argument seems like an endless loop. I've dealt with paperwork in the past; it can definitely take a while. But perhaps attacking this system's overhead is a good way to make progress.

"Fair point," I add, thinking hard, "I bet… Rosenburg was having a hard time handling that much work."

Whatever friendliness Juni had leaves in an instant. I glance at Virrel. We've struck something.

"And Rosenburg is the coordinator of this program," Virrel concludes, "She's the one who made you swear secrecy."

"Kinda." Juni spits.

"She must be pretty bad at her job, since if I was in her place, I wouldn't lock a bunch of people in hotel rooms for seven months," Ellia complains, "I hope we get to meet her so I can… give a little feedback."

"I don't think she would meet with us…" I start.

Back when I first woke up, I remember that the orientation staff was talking about her and Star made a comment about not caring.

"I don't think she cares about us, and she doesn't want any of you to, either. Isn't that right?" I ask Juni.

She glares back at me.

"That would explain the budget, Vittorio's screening, and why we were stuck in the hotel rooms for so long." Virrel adds.

"I could care less what some dumb clown-*sheiffer* thinks of me," Ellia says, "I just want to know why this all matters."

Juni relaxes a bit. It seems like we might be getting off track. Luckily, Virrel notices this and ties it all back together.

"I think the fact that Rosenburg doesn't care matters a lot. Why would the coordinator of a well-established program not care about a specific session? And why would the organization allow that?"

The three of us think as Juni observes us anxiously. I know we are close, and it is hard to think over the excitement.

"Maybe they don't like us 'cause we're aliens?" Ellia guesses.

"IPSHA is an open-minded community which doesn't discriminate based on any status, condition, or non-base affiliation." Juni recites in a mockingly grating voice.

"Well then, maybe we aren't as important as the other sessions?" Ellia says with a shrug.

"Not true," I say, "If we weren't important, they wouldn't have spent *any* money on us."

We're all silent, then Virrel says simply, "We're disposable."

"Bingo." Juni replies, pointing at Virrel.

"What?" Ellia asks, "I never learned that word."

"It means we're going to be discarded after we're used," I start putting pieces together, "that's why no one was supposed to care about us. That's why the funding and the background checks were not done correctly. That's why…"

Something that had been nagging me for a while now suddenly makes sense.

"That's why Pengun was so remorseful after Juni said it was going to be a quick mission. He knew she was wasting her time."

"Wait… so La Corsage was planned, too?" Ellia asks, snapping their head to Juni.

"Absolutely not!" Juni says, eyes growing wide and hands coming up, "She came out of nowhere; that definitely wasn't supposed to happen."

"But then how did Pengun know about us… getting bingo'd or whatever this is?" Ellia asks, circling their arms around.

"It must be well known…" I conclude, even though that doesn't make sense. Why would a hodgepodge training program for some expendable trainees be well known?

"Yera or Ellia, did your news channels start acting funny after a while?" Virrel asks suddenly.

"Now that I think about it, it did." I admit.

"You *know* I never watched the news." Ellia says.

"Fair enough. Hear me out: whatever we're going to be disposed on is something pretty big. Probably a suicide mission of sorts with some big implications. IPSHA is a secret organization, but whatever it is, it's big enough to make it into normal news. That would explain why our news was acting up, and why this Pengun person, who I'm assuming is somebody with an employee perspective, understood what our training was leading up to."

"So he was remorseful for Juni because…" I remember what Juni said earlier, about hating us because of our personality, "because he knew you'd get attached to us. And our likelihood of surviving this big mission is slim."

"Seems like we're on the right track?" Virrel asks, shooting Juni a glance.

"I'm baffled at how well you put some of that together." She admits.

"Well, that's what 80+ years of life experience and two smart partners does to you," Virrel says with a grin, "The only thing I can't seem to put together is what the suicide mission is, exactly."

Juni is quiet for a long time, nodding. My heart thumps with anticipation. Finally, the black-clad woman looks up and opens her mouth.

"Operation Pragma."

"Pragma?" I ask.

"Short for pragmatic, I'm guessing." Virrel offers.

"You're on a roll." Juni says.

"Wait, what does pragmatic mean?" Ellia asks.

"You know, like, utilitarian." Juni replies.

"I've never heard that word before in my entire life."

"Practical."

"I… I feel like I should know that one but I don't."

"Good in the numbers, not good when you start factoring in morals and emotions and stuff."

"*Ooooooh* okay. So what's the mission?"

Juni sighs and begins, "We are currently under alien attack by these guys called the Bukanarions due to some weird space politics that we're still trying to figure out. They've given us two options; become enslaved to them or they'll steal the energy from the core of our planet. Pretty extreme, but obviously we aren't going to do either, so they just set up a base in Egypt and started digging.

"Since you can only drill but for so far on Earth, and I'm taking it most places, they have this laser pulse drill thing that's been helping them get pretty far. Whenever we send in troops to slow them down or fight, the alien soldiers and the big drill just wipe them out.

"The UN… which is like IPSHA for normal people, had discussions with us and we came to the conclusion that it would be best to send in an IPSHA team. Shuvo, the leader of IPSHA, passed it down through the bureaucracy, and someone somewhere crunched some numbers and decided it'd be best to send you all."

She looks at the ground for the next part.

"You all are disposable, yes. Many of you have had prior combat and training experiences. None of you have family here, nor do you have friends since we kept you locked away. You really don't have any tenure, or experiences, or connections to this planet at all outside of what you've seen on TV or the things we've done today."

I find myself, to my surprise, becoming angry.

"So you're just going to, what, sacrifice us to this drill thing? We don't even get the chance to check out this place and you're gonna kill us to save your own damn skin?" Ellia asks, flushed.

"Not to mention the fact that my team is made of teenagers!" I add, feeling more anger and disbelief building, "Even with our prior experience, wouldn't it be better to get someone else to do this?"

Juni bows her head lower, "IPSHA… usually isn't like this. For the four years I've worked here, they've been an upright and pretty noble organization. But now… you gotta understand… the higher ups are scared. They're panicking and honestly desperate. It's cruel and unfair but… it's what we've got to work with."

"*It* being the excuse they use to send children to war?" Virrel concludes, his voice even and calm.

I can tell he is as livid as I am.

Juni is red with shame, "…the mission isn't guaranteed death, but the chances of survival are low. You all are going to be escorted by troops to the drill site, and while they draw away fire, you are to run and put a light manipulation blanket over the hole. Then you return to the convoy and get the heck out of dodge."

Anger rushes in my ears, but now I am also a bit relieved. That doesn't really seem too hard.

“What makes this a suicide mission?” Virrel asks.

Juni sighs, stands up, and grabs the handle of her coffin.

“Trust me, this will be far more intense and dangerous than anything you’ve faced in training. Come on, I’ll tell you the rest at the hospital.”

CHAPTER 10

FINAL TEAM

~ DEBRIEFING ~

The steady beep from Clayton's monitor fills the hospital room. We all sit in silence, waiting for the other team to talk. Davisamir seems additionally uncomfortable, with his giant frame hunched into a small chair next to Juni and Virrel, who are sharing the coffin (getting that in here was pretty funny).

Bacoj and Nale take the two remaining seats, Ellia sits on the small arm table, and Kabel and I stand. Star is sitting on the edge of Clayton's bed. After a few more beeps, the cowboy clears his throat.

"So Juni," his voice is less chipper and much more straightforward, "how did the encounter with Vittorio go?"

"Great," she says, skipping over the magic accordion and the encounter with the Mafia, "how will your hand be?"

"Fully recovered in a week," Clayton says with a satisfied nod, "All the sewing stuff will be nice and bound later today and I've already set up an appointment with healers over at the base port."

The beeping goes back to its normal dominance before Juni blurts out, "I told them."

"About Pragma?" Clayton asks, neutral.

"Yeah."

"Don't worry, we told them too."

Juni looks up at Clayton, surprised.

"Yeah, I was trying to hold it but then when Star saw the boys again, she just broke down and said everything." The cowboy informs.

"No I didn't!" Star says, turning in a bounce towards him, "You ended up talking about it while you were under anesthesia, so we had to reveal the whole story!"

"Yeah sure," Clayton replies, "like *I* was the one all in tears when we faced La Corsage."

"But you were." Juni says.

Clayton is silent for a moment, then, "Aaanyway, it's good that you all already know the background. Since you beat Vittorio and got Virrel back, we can register you all as Emergency-Tier Conscripts, so congratulations and welcome to IPSHA!"

The orientation leaders let out a short round of applause. Clayton pats his thigh instead of clapping.

"Will we get our tests back?" Nale asks, and everyone else on the team is hit with a sudden look of embarrassment. I totally forgot about those… and I was hoping the orientation leaders did too…

Juni chuckles, making Nale blush, "Nah, you guys were gonna get hired no matter what."

"Besides," Clayton smirks, "the answers were just A-B-C-D over and over again."

The room is silent and relieved, so the cowboy continues.

"We would usually decide team names, assign field aliases, and crush the paperwork now, but we can do that…" Clayton pauses, "after the mission. Speaking of that, I might as well explain what it is, exactly."

He shifts up in his bed, "We're going to fly you out to Egypt tomorrow. The Bukanarions set up their drill in the fourth lowest place on the planet, the Qattara Depression, because the lowest three were near bodies of water, which I guess might mess with some structural things for the base they've set up nearby.

"We've created a special, lightweight, ultra-strong material that reflects lasers perfectly and won't be detected by their drill sensors. We need four of you to go out, spread it across the drilling hole, then let it fall in. Armed forces from multiple nations will draw away the attention of the drill and surrounding troops for you."

"You can't use planes?" Virrel asks.

"On top of them always getting shot down, they can't deploy the tarp precisely enough."

"What about a really fast car?" Bacoj asks.

"I mean… that's essentially what you all are doing." Clayton says.

"How do we get inside the base?" I ask, my anger from earlier now turned into a bitter formality. If they see us as just a bunch of numbers, then I will see them as just a list of orders.

"It's a temporary base, because they have to be able to move in case the ground falters. We'll just drive you through it." Clayton replies.

"*We*?" I ask and, realizing how harsh my voice sounds, I add, "You're not going anywhere with a hand like that."

"Oh, yeah, Juni volunteered to drive the Humvee for you guys," the black-clad woman blushes as we look over at her, "she and Star have been adamant about helping you on your mission."

"I don't see what the big deal is," Kabel croaks, "we go in, put a blanket over a hole, and leave. What's so dangerous about that?"

"Well, for starters, the Bukanarion foot soldiers have advanced weaponry. The turrets they have shoot red lasers, which cut and burn things, plus the soldiers have guns with acid bullets. Also, there are a few cannons that shoot blue lasers, which blow things up. *Also* the drill has a massive pulse laser that disintegrates anything it hits."

"But the other guys are gonna be distractin' em, so what's the problem?" Kabel asks.

"Not all of them will take the bait. You might also have to end up dodging friendly fire. Plus, there will be a very big aerial fleet coming in to distract the drill, and some of their missiles might get a little close." Clayton explains.

"Eh," Kabel rasps, waving his silver hand and looking away, "lemme do it and I'll finish in thirty minutes or less. Badda bing badda boom, don't think twice, so clean you could eat off it."

Clayton grins, "I like your optimism, buddy, but you're not going out there."

Kabel quickly turns towards him, "What?!"

"You're an official member of IPSHA, which means you must follow protocol, which means you've got to take a mandatory three-day recovery time for injuries."

"Ain't we doin' this next week?" Kabel asks.

"They're drilling to the center of our planet, Kabel," Star snaps, "we should've been out there yesterday."

"No need to get all huffy." Kabel mutters.

"I have every right to get huffy!" Star shouts, standing, "If you hadn't tried to be a macho man out there you could go, but you were a big dumb idiot, so you can't."

Kabel cowers away from her until 'big dumb idiot', "Ey, let's not start with the name calling, toots."

"What are you gonna do about it?" Star spits.

"What am I gonna do about it here I'll tell you *I'muna smack you across ya stupid lil–*"

"Kabel, Star, that's enough," Clayton interrupts.

Kabel goes back to looking out into the hospital hallway. Star plops down on the bed again and looks away from him. The cowboy sighs and looks up at me.

"Yera, we're shipping you out to Cairo in a few hours. Tonight, you'll get some armor and a bit more debriefing with your regiment. Juni and Star are coming with you, and you've got to choose three others to lay down the tarp with you. Not me, not

Kabel, and not Bacoj, so I suppose you already–"

"WHAT DO YOU MEAN NOT BACOJ?!" Bacoj explodes.

"You're 13. We're not letting you go into the middle of a war zone." Clayton replies, annoyed.

"But you're putting everyone else in the warzone and they're underaged!"

Clayton's annoyance is broken with discomfort, "W-well yes, but that's because the statistic guys… they're like…" the cowboy pauses, choosing his words, "What I meant to say was, this whole deal is way new and awful for everybody, and while *some* IPSHA operatives have approved kinda questionable things because of this, *I'm* not about to be one of them."

"What about Ellia?! They're 14 but you didn't mention them!"

"Ellia also helped save Kabel and I from La Corsage, beat Vittorio, and has machine gun gloves, which go further and do more damage than your fireballs. I hate to say it like this but… they just have a better chance overall."

"Hmm…" Ellia smirks to themselves, "I too think Ellia is better."

"That's not fair! Yera, say something!" Bacoj retaliates.

I look at Bacoj, then survey the room. Based off of what Clayton told me, it seems as though I only have Nale, Virrel, Ellia, and Davisamir to choose from. Virrel is a given, but I will need to be strategic with the other three. I don't feel comfortable bringing Ellia, since they're a little too young, but Clayton did make a great point about the gloves.

I am about to address the room, but then I remember Bacoj. His eyes are glistening; he probably feels doubly betrayed. I recall that mindset from not too many years ago, feeling as though everyone thought I was too young and weak to handle the real world. This stuff is way too delicate for me, so I try and play neutral.

"I'm sorry, Bacoj," I say with a frown, "I can't change the rules."

"So that's it then?" Bacoj asks angrily, "I do all this training and both times I get to fight I'm not allowed… just because?"

"You will get the chance, Bacoj," Star says, "just not this time."

"Fine." Bacoj growls, then he gets up and walks out of the door.

I wish I could console him, but as the leader, I need to make a decision. I'm probably going to have to go with Virrel, Nale, and Davisamir. Even though Davisamir might be a liability due to his muteness, Ellia is just too young.

I know Nale is the same age as me (or maybe older? or younger but equivalent? I can't remember how woodish age), and of course the others are above age. This would only be fair to Bacoj, too.

"Nale," I ask absently, "did they ever give you back that hovering armor you were telling me about?"

Back during one of our gym times together, Nale told me how his mother's lab developed an anti-gravity vest that he swiped after their research was destroyed. That could be useful here.

"Ah," he blushes, "n-no. They gave me the bow back instead."

"Yeah, our researchers wanted to look into that tech a bit more. Sorry about that." Clayton apologizes.

"No worries," I say, "I've made my decision."

The room falls silent and all eyes are on me.

"Virrel–" he nods knowingly, "Nale–" he recoils at his name, "and Davisamir." the giant puts a hand up in acknowledgement.

"Screw you." Ellia says, crossing their arms.

"Look Ellia," they actually look at me, and I'm taken aback because they look genuinely hurt.

"I know you've got what it takes to help us. I remember back on Arret on the hayrides in Drax Forest; you've experienced combat, you've seen…" I shudder as some of the events from that night threaten to resurface in my memory, "you've seen people die in ways they shouldn't. You could hold your own against monsters and skeletons and whatever else Yatniv threw at you. You even stood up to La Corsage and those Mafia crime lords."

"Wait what?" Clayton asks.

"But this is different," I continue, "This is war. These are ranged weapons the Bukanarions are using. Acid, lasers, advanced tech, hardened battle strategy. These are things you've never experienced before. Although you've proven yourself in the past and I know you can adapt to a climate like this… I don't want this time to be your first time."

I decide to lean in and whisper something extra, "And if I don't make it, I'm going to need someone to keep the boys in check."

"Gotta say, I was really looking forward to arguing with you… and I really *really* wanted to shoot up some bad guys... but I guess you just said no to both so…" Ellia takes Bacoj's seat, shrugging and crossing their legs.

I know they aren't happy, but the fact that they understand is good enough.

"I'll do my best, Yera." Virrel reports, his hearty smile and cheesy thumbs up serving to reassure me.

Davisamir gives a nod, and the restrained smirk on his face makes me think he is happy that I chose him.

"Yeah," Nale mumbles, looking at the floor, "me too."

"She's only taking you because she knows you like her." Ellia says, voice low but clearly audible.

Nale looks like he is about to faint, and once the words register in my head, the room is immediately filled with awkward heat.

CHAPTER FINALE

ANUBIS DRILL

~ MISSION REPORT ~

Canned laughter fills the hospital room as the bickering French couple on the TV screen take a comedic pause. The TV is huge, seeming to take up the entire far wall, as if stretching out to grab my attention. The machines I'm connected to beep softly. Weak, lavender light seeps in through the window.

I could only sleep for a little bit before it all came rushing back. The explosions and the gunfire. My face still tingles from the acid. It was so loud… I've never seen so much swirling dust in my entire life. There were so many explosions it felt like an earthquake. I can still feel the panic, the hot Egyptian sun, the grit… and the door…

Someone enters my room, inviting in fluorescent light from the rest of the hospital. My heart leaps as I look over, hoping to see Ellia or Kabel or maybe even Clayton coming in to check on me and see if I'm okay.

The woman who walks in is one I've never seen before. She has a hooked nose, short hair, dark eyes, and despite the shadows around her face, it looks like she's never smiled in her entire life. She wears military formal wear and is holding a bright pink box.

She comes in, glancing over at me without enthusiasm before

grabbing the remote and turning off the TV. She then takes the seat nearest my bed. I watch as she puts the box on the table next to me, pulls a small book out of a pocket within her uniform's coat, and starts scribbling down notes.

I say nothing and continue to observe her. The medals along her chest and arms catch a few hints of light from the sunrise. Her face is calm and soft in the morning's darkness. I squint my hardest to try and read any text I can. The writing on the side of the pink box reads *Dani's Donuts*. I can smell the sugar from here. Further away is her name pin, and it reads…

G. Rosenburg.

For a moment I continue to squint, trying to figure out where I've heard that name before. I even consider drawing her later on. Then it all hits me at once: this is the woman who sent me out into a warzone to die. She was the coordinator of my program, the one who considered my team 'disposable', she's the reason why… *why they're gone…*

She takes a peek up at me, looking a little concerned. I only now realize that my heart monitor is beeping much more quickly. We meet eyes and she sits back in her chair, confusion melting into formal apathy.

"I did not realize you were awake. I am Commander Gina Rosenburg, Branch Chief of IPSHA North France. This means that I am the Administrative Officer to Captain Loge's team and now yours as well, Captain Lermint. Good to see that you are doing well."

She says that last part with indifference; she doesn't care how I'm doing.

"The reason for me coming here is to gather information on the Anubis Drill blitz. You may be relieved to know that all of Loge's teammates that were with you survived. However, we have little information on the whereabouts of your own teammates. Do you have any information that could help us find them?"

We coast through the temporary base, passing trotting soldiers, parked vehicles, and sun-bleached tents. Wispy, formless clouds drift in the distant sky. There are none near the large, black machine we are riding towards.

Another wall and group of waving soldiers pass us by, and then we are met once again with lonely desert roads. The ground outside, once sandy and yellow, is now hardening into a burnt brown. I peer out to see other Humvees coasting alongside us in the distance, headed toward the giant block.

"I don't know." I lie, rushing to pull myself into the present.

I would rather think about anything else.

"Please try your best. I'm here for you." Rosenburg says as if she's been instructed to do so. She doesn't even look up from her notes.

The rumbling from the road is joined by something else. It isn't the distant thundering of fighter jets. Nor is it the clanking from the trailer attached to our rear bumper, which holds the giant light manipulation tarp. It's a deep, vibrating pulse that reverberates through the ground and sky. The approaching, crusted cliffs pull back, revealing the lower half of this object we've been driving towards, and my heart leaps in my throat.

A massive, solid black pyramid floats upside-down in the air, spinning slowly in the desert sun. Rhythmically, a bright, purplish white laser streams out of its peak, disappearing inside of a wide hole in the desert floor a second later. I've never seen a laser of this color before.

The alien stronghold is set up around it. White barricades make a spotty wall, the gaps filled with gleaming metal turrets. Foot soldiers, small with camouflaging armor and bulb-like heads, patrol the perimeter, armed with their special gray and black rifles. They are much higher in number than I'd hoped.

"I'm sorry… I can't." I reply, and I can hear my voice shaking.

"Okay," Rosenburg says, poorly hiding her impatience, "why don't you just tell me what all happened and we can work from there?"

Outside the vehicle, chaos spreads across the shadowy, arid land. Bullets and lasers flash through the air. My ears are filled with relentless explosions, the slap of Earthling guns, the whine of Bukanarion acid rifles.

A crimson javelin streaks through the front windshield and flickers past my neck, melting through the back door. We all cover our heads as more lasers beam through the windshield. A turret appears right in front of us and we ram into it at full speed. I slam into the backs of seats as windshield glass sprays into the inside of the vehicle.

"Captain Lermint," Rosenburg interrupts, sounding irritated, "please give at least some attempt of recounting the events to me or I may have to take administrative action."

Her cold words and tone draw up a well of emotions inside me. Lying in this silent room with no one but her to talk to… I don't want to be here. I want to be back in my hotel room, blissfully trapped, watching TV and painting. I want my friends.

The room begins to blur as tears prickle under my eyelids. A tissue appears and I take it, blinking and wiping my vision clear. My arms feel stiff and sore. Rosenburg puts down the tissue box and sits back in her chair, watching me as if it were vomit I was wiping from my face.

"We… conducted the blitz as planned." I report, feeling my heart turn cold.

Rosenburg gives a short smile and starts to write. I feel disgusted, both at myself for crying in front of this woman and at her for being so uncaring. The more I think about her apathy, the more rage begins to build in my heart. I continue.

"We passed the alien base and entered the structural red zone, then continued to the drill site's edge. The drill reacted to the incoming aerial diversion, stopping its pulse and allowing us to get into formation…"

Fearful, I leap out onto the trailer. The tarp is slipping open and the strap I'm supposed to grab is flapping in the wind. I snatch it up and jump off the side of the trailer before I can hesitate. The ground hits me harder and faster than I was anticipating.

I roll to a crouching position, a little stunned at how solid the ground is. The strap begins tugging in my hand. Right! I get to work and have the strap secured in a few seconds.

A flash of heat from above makes me look up, another successful airstrike. The drill retaliates, swiveling silently in the air. A sweeping column of white-purple rushes out and erases four entire formations of jets from existence. I look at the massive hole next to me. Only a few meters and then it's a drop into nothingness.

"After we spread the light reflection tarp and released it, we were noticed by an outcrop from the enemy encampment. I…"

An acid bullet explodes in the dirt next to me, spraying up scorched rock and clear liquid. Another whistles past my head. I dive to the right and raise my zecno. Three alien troops take aim at me. I fire wildly, sending a volley of red light towards them. To my surprise, I get one near the chest. They take cover and I lower my arm, but one of the unphased aliens from the trio gets back up and trains its rifle on me. The Humvee with Virrel in the trailer roars up to me from the left. I get up and run.

"… the origin of my injuries… or rather I…"

I'm running in slow motion, stake and hammer in one hand, zecno trigger in the other, blindly returning fire. The ground is trembling beneath me. The Humvee seems so far away, bullets are whistling past me, and then there is a crack in my right ear.

"I'm sorry; once we were, I mean the encampment, no…"

I'm knocked to the ground, dizzy, with loud sizzling coming from my head. There is no pain? I reach up to feel the side of my face but then realize I have a helmet on. That must be what it hit. Another shot whistles past me and I crawl forward.

A hail of acid bullets hit the ground around me, there is a brilliant fan of liquid, and something like boiling water splatters in my face. I turn away, horrified and senses alive with pain. There is another crack to the head, this time in the back as I cower away. It blows my already damaged helmet off, so I curl into a ball.

"The enemy fire–"

"Was anyone killed or left behind during this firefight?" Rosenburg blurts.

The interruption sends my thoughts tumbling. No one got tagged, right? I remember Davisamir got acid on his arm… everyone else was fine because they…

"No, everyone survived that encounter and escaped on the vehicle." I report, my voice shaking.

"Then let's skip over that part. What happened after you escaped?"

I am so enraged all I can do is stare. A part of me remembers that this is my new boss and that I need to remain professional.

"Did they get you?!" Virrel asks, lying next to me in the trailer.

"No," I pant, my heart pounding, "they just got my gear and a little splashed on my face. Is it bad?"

He looks at me for a moment, then, "I'd still be happy with my grandson dating you."

That makes me laugh.

"Listen Yera," Virrel starts, "the Bukanarions are onto us. I'm going to have to draw away attention while you–"

"No!" I scream, grabbing his arm tight, "no, you're not."

"Yera, just listen–"

"Stop!" I scream again, my emotions swelling, "Virrel, you're not. Stay in the trailer. I won't... you're not dying today."

"That's the thing, Yera. I'm already dead."

I start to feel tears well up in my eyes, "Stop it."

"No, seriously. I am currently deceased. I'm not being figurative. I'm a ghost, remember? Ten bad things, a thousand good things?"

He points to the faint halo above his helmet. I start to recall Virrel's situation and feel embarrassed, letting go of his arm, "... right, sorry."

"No worries," he says, "I just thought I'd let you know ahead of time. You youngsters are always getting emotional. I remember back in my day–"

"Oh would you shut it!"

I don't smile like I did then.

"We had too much enemy attention to escape properly, so during the retreat, Virrel Nothron decided to dismount the vehicle and provide a distraction. We continued on without him."

"This was the ghost, correct?"

He was much more than that but, "Yes."

"Interesting…" Rosenburg mutters, writing for a moment in silence, "then?"

Why is she treating this like it's nothing? The heart monitor is beeping very fast; I'm surprised Rosenburg doesn't notice.

"The full-scale retreat started, and as the ally forces retreated…"

Davisamir points to the Humvee and makes a looping motion, then gets up and leaps directly at the back of it. I expect him to slam into the hole-riddled door, but he uses his powers and fazes right through it.

"J-just undo the trailer and hop in the back?" Nale asks.

"Yes," I reply awkwardly, "that's the plan."

I swallow the urge to cry. Not to sob and wail, just cry. It would be a soft cry, filled with confusion and dismay. But it won't happen, not in front of this woman.

"… as the units retreated, the drill returned to its original position. Davisamir," I pause, trying to remember if I ever learned his last name – it was probably in the orientation presentation but I can't remember, "was able to enter the vehicle while…"

We both take a cautionary peek over the edge of the trailer. All forces begin to retreat as the Anubis Drill revolves in the air, turning back to its hole. The aliens at the base are now dealing with what I assume to be Virrel's telekinesis. The turrets are still firing at us, and one misses Nale's head as we duck back down.

"…while N-Nale Walalec and I remained in the trailer, suppressed by sparse enemy fire. Then…"

The Humvee slows to a stop and the side door closest to me opens. A red laser darts past it. The two of us peer over the trailer again to see the Anubis Drill back in its normal position. My skin turns cold as I look at Nale.

"We got out of the trailer…"

Nale and I both hop out of the trailer as fast as we can. The drill fires the pulse, and the next second, there is a monumental flash of light, like a second sun was just created. I leap into the Humvee and hear someone slam the door right behind me.

"and the drill exploded and Nale didn't have enough time to get in so he closed the door behind me."

Silence. Rosenburg writes while I stare forward. I can still feel the door pushing me as I got in. It was firm yet gentle, more like a swift suggestion as opposed to some sort of panicked command. There wasn't enough time for Nale to get in; he knew it. The moment the door closed, we were flying. Then everything went black.

"Thank you for sharing." Rosenburg says, closing her notebook and standing, "For future reference, please try to refer to all parties as first initial last name, and do not be that hesitant to reveal information to your superiors, because in situations like these, you can come off as suspicious."

For a moment, I'm frozen, stunned. Am I being graded on my recounting of the story? When I haven't even gotten time to process it all? She doesn't seem to notice anything wrong, tucking away her notebook and turning to me.

"Those donuts are for you; a friend of mine runs a bakery and thought she would send over a gift after she heard about the events. Well done Captain Lermint, and I look forward to working with you. Any questions?"

I reach up with my plastic-feeling arm and flip the donut box open. I grab one of the thick, glazed pastries and hold it up to my face. Like with the tissue and the box lid, its texture is static-like and distant. A pleasant sweetness curls up through my rage and I find the words to speak.

"How did you manage that?" I ask, my face throbbing.

"Manage what, the donuts?" Rosenburg asks.

Heat gushes through every part of my body, "No, a friend."

There is a stunned, disapproving silence, then Rosenburg asks gravely, "I'm sorry?"

"Yes," it comes out sharp, just like I wanted, "yes you are sorry. You are the sorriest excuse for a human being I've ever met."

Rosenburg looks like I punched her, staring at me with surprise and deep offence.

"Might I remind you that I am your superior officer?" She asks.

"I know."

"And that I can very easily employ disciplinary actions against you or your team if I think they're necessary?" Now it's her turn to be sharp.

Compliance and remorse start to spread over me. That was stupid; I shouldn't have said any of it. But I can't bring myself to apologize, either. So I just put the donut back.

"Don't speak to me that way ever again. I assign missions, designate housing, and manage promotions for the entirety of Belgium, Luxembourg, and Northern France, so I highly suggest that you show me some respect."

The fury that was reluctantly receding shoots back up with so much force that I think it might launch out of me.

"You want me to respect you?" Is all I can manage.

"Yes, Captain Lermint. Perhaps they should check your hearing as well." Rosenburg jabs.

"Listen to me," I start, and the look of offence on her face doesn't scare me at all, "I am a 17-year-old girl. I have been on this planet for all of 7 months. And despite all of this, you put me and my team in an active warzone, willingly accepting the fact that we might die?"

Rosenburg says nothing.

"*Exactly!*" I shout, "Exactly! How am I supposed to treat you with respect? *Huh?* I want to hear your excuse!"

"… you may disapprove of my actions," Rosenburg mutters, "but coming from your perspective, I don't expect you to understand the importance of the mission."

All I want to do is scream.

"Your lives were put on the line for the greater good. Your actions saved millions, possibly even the entire planet. Virrel Nothron and Nale Walalec sacrificed themselves for this cause. You should be grateful of them for their heroism and for us, frankly, for honing your skills, sustaining you for free for multiple months, and allowing you such an honorable privilege. As the–"

"THEN NEXT TIME, WHY DON'T YOU GO OUT THERE?" I scream, unable to take this any longer, "WHY DON'T YOU WATCH PEOPLE DIE? I BET YOU'D LOVE THAT, HUH?"

"Be considerate of other patients." Rosenburg interrupts.

Total rage threatens to engulf me. I lean forward, needles and tubes trying to tug me back. The heart monitor is going wild.

"Why don't you get one of *them* to go out there? Go ahead, kill *their* friends! Let *them* get shot at and watch acid eat people's limbs and make *them* the hero! *Or do it yourself!*"

My lungs are filled with steam. I wish I were Ellia right now – I wish I could hurl every insult in existence at her. To shatter that poised figure standing silently in the dark of the morning.

"Yeah!" I can feel myself about to scream again, "Yeah, you have *nothing* to say! *Because you're sick!* YOU'RE A SICK, PATHETIC PERSON!"

Rosenburg is still, nearly frozen.

"*LEAVE!* HOW CAN YOU STAND THERE AFTER WHAT YOU'VE DONE?! YOU MURDERER! *GET OUT!*"

Her shoulders bounce as if she was struck by a sudden cough, but then I notice her eyes glistening.

“I see that this arrangement won’t work. I will have your team moved to East Spain’s jurisdiction.”

Gina Rosenburg then turns on a heel and races out of the room. Steam is still swirling madly in my lungs and now tingling in my eyes. I snatch a donut from the box on the table and stuff it into my mouth.

Tears stream down my face as I eat a stranger’s gift.

Find more info about the author and Tales of Vagary at

www.bladesoftrinity.com

www.ingramcontent.com/pod-product-compliance
Lightning Source LLC
Chambersburg PA
CBHW020616310726
48979CB00008B/1515/J

* 9 7 8 1 7 3 2 6 5 4 8 8 4 *